GENIUS DE MILO

A TALE OF COSMIC LUNACY BY RUSS COLCHAMIRO

There are worse things to lose than your mind...

CRAZY 8 PRESS

Jason's smile dropped away, replaced with a silent, open-mouthed slug of resignation, that whatever was happening was authentic, and unfolding in real time.

In a shared-brain moment Jason and Theo slowly panned in Jamie's direction until finally she felt their accusatorial eyes lock on her. And though neither of them spoke, the imputation of blame came through with perfect enunciation: *What did you do? What's coming?*

But what could she say? Which cluster of words could encapsulate both the scope and nuance of their predicament? Jamie could offer a pretty good guess as to *why* their immediate surroundings morphed before their very eyes—it had to be Brigsby-related, didn't it?—but when it came to the *what*, she was equally mystified.

So all she could do was stand there. She blinked a few times. Then a few times more. The night went bracingly still, as if every fractal of sound had been drained from the Universe. The three of them held in place, petrified, as if the incredible forces converging upon them were seemingly just to be unleashed. Which, of course, they were.

Acknowledgements

Thanks to everyone who read early drafts of *Genius de Milo*, and offered feedback and encouragement, particularly fellow scribes Michael Wolfe and Don Philbrick, who ceaselessly called b.s. on me whenever needed, which was more often than I'd care to admit. And thanks again to my trusted copy editor extraordinaire Barney O'Neill, who catches all the little things I inevitably miss.

Also, thanks to my pals at Crazy 8 Press, especially Aaron Rosenberg, who brought me into the fold and once again did a great job laying out this book. And big thanks to Roy Mauritsen, who created the brilliant cover you are holding in your hands.

Of course, a very special thanks to my wife, Liz, who puts up with my late nights and weekends clacking way at these pages, and ever more to my children, whose own wackiness, humor, and wisdom inform me as a writer, and more important, as a dad.

And thanks to all the returning and future fans who keep on reading, and whose enthusiasm for my crazy ideas give me the fuel to power through when I'd much rather lay back on a comet, mindlessly take in the Universe, and wonder what life would be like if I were really just a man trapped in a dog's body. Or vice versa.

Finally, to my partner in all things cosmically loony . . . Karl . . . two down, one to go, mate! I'm coming for you!

Dedicated to the memory of Murray Rolfe

PART I
WANDERING SPIRITS

Chapter 1
Fill My Snifter

Brigsby
Eternity

It began with a flicker.

Eternity, yes, of course, because that's where all of Creation originates, where even just a single idea, a notion—a tickle in the back of the brain—alerts you to the possibility that something is brewing. Something delicious. Strange. Alluring.

You're not quite sure what that glimmer might be—that flicker, that tickle—but whatever shape and form it takes, whatever it eventually becomes, well, you know you're onto *something*.

But this was a different kind of flicker.

As the Minder of the Universe—the presence overseeing the Cosmos—it was Brigsby's job to notice these kinds of things.

Yet as the host of *Breakfast with Brigsby*, the top-rated talk show in Eternity, Brigsby was an entertainer to the masses, hidden in plain sight. He needed to interact with Eternitarians at least enough so that he could gauge their response to his grander endeavors, but even the good folks of Eternity weren't ready to know just who and what he really was.

So talking to them through their TV sets about food, fashion, and relationships made it a heckuva lot easier to conceal the fact that he was also responsible for the creation of the Universe and everything in it.

"Larry! The TV's fritzing again. I thought you took care of it."

"Yes, yes, keep your shirt on. And it's not fritzing. It's just a flicker." Larry swiveled the massive flat screen and looked in back. "Here. See. The plug is loose. Here we go . . ."

"Oh, my dear, Lawrence. You always have the lugubrious tonic that soothes my achy temperament. You'd think I would've had my fill of *LOST* by now, but I just love that Sawyer. A bit of a temper on that one. But he's feisty. I like that."

"*LOST* made me crazy. Too many dead ends. And don't get

me started on that ending . . ."

When entertaining guests, Brigsby drank blue martinis, always a blue martini. But when he needed to unwind, nothing did the trick like sitting on his couch, in a silk bathrobe, with a snifter of chocolate milk. His slippered feet rested on the coffee table.

"Now-now, Lawrence. Don't be such a Whiny McWhinerson. It was twisty and fun and set on a crazy tropical island with beautiful people in compromising positions. Sometimes that's enough. And how could you not love Hurley? He's the best. So funny!"

"My apologies, sir."

"And don't call me, sir! You know I hate that!"

Brigsby may have had power and influence beyond the scope of comprehension, but his appearance was that of a frail, wrinkled, middle-aged man who could be easily floored by the flap of a butterfly's fart. He shuffled in his seat so that his chocolate milk sloshed within the snifter, peaking over the lip, spilling into his lap. "Oh, will you look at that . . ."

Lawrence let out a wry smile. Not only did he serve as Executive Manager of the CBM Warehouse—the storage facility securing Cosmic Building Material, the Universe's liquid DNA, the building blocks of all Creation—he was also Brigsby's personal attaché.

As such, he gave Brigsby the business now and then just to keep him honest, Minder of the Universe or not.

Brigsby wiped his robe clean. "Ha . . . ha. You are quite the jokester tonight, aren't you? I think you've done enough. Now let me get back to my show. It's the one where Desmond keeps flashing back and forth through time to find Penny. So romantic. Tell me you didn't just *love* that one!"

"Yes, of course. That was pretty good. But before I go . . ."

Brigsby offered an exasperated sigh. "What now?"

"Have you seen the flicker?"

"Lawrence. Really. I just want to watch my show. Yes. You fixed it. You're a peach. What would I ever do without your keen ability to jiggle the wire in—"

"No. Not the TV. Out there. Earth. It's . . ." Lawrence stepped up to the window so that his reflection mirrored back at him. The distant sky was black, peppered with stars too numerous to count. The magenta pinwheel of the Andromeda galaxy swirled in the distance. Nearby was the permanent nothing of Milo's Smear. ". . . Flickering, B. It's twitching, it's . . ."

"Fluxing?"

"Yes. Fluxing. Exactly. It's fluxing."

Brigsby sighed again. "I know, Lawrence. I know."

"Oh. Well . . . should we look into it?"

Brigsby lifted the remote, paused the episode. He swirled his snifter and took a healthy swig. "First thing tomorrow. I just don't have the strength right now. I decommissioned thirty-four star systems today. Breaks my heart sometimes . . ."

There was a look on Brigsby's face—it wasn't the good look. Lawrence turned to the fluxing Earth, and then back at Brigsby. "Might I ask . . . ? How bad?"

"It's that fakakta jar again."

"What . . . you mean . . . the Jason Medley jar? The Theo Barnes jar?"

"That's the one."

"I thought the boys took care of that. Ira. Howard. They said not to worry. That we were all set."

Brigsby sipped his chocolate milk. "Yes," he said. "They did. They used to be a lot more reliable . . ."

Lawrence stared into the great expanse. Of the countless celestial bodies in the Universe, Brigsby had taken a special liking to Earth. When he commissioned the planet's creation, he had it written into the design blueprints that the inhabitants be fashioned with the innate ability to evolve into beings far greater than their consciousness would allow them to initially perceive. If they were to ever reach their true potential, the inhabitants of Earth would need to survive their own self-destructive impulses long enough to strip away their ego and realize that their very existence was only the first step toward a much grander design.

"The flicker," Lawrence said. "The flux. I admit, I hadn't noticed. How long has it been like that?"

"A while now. It hasn't resolved. So like this damned TV, it's going to need a manual adjustment. A loose wire, I suppose."

"How much time do they have?"

On the surface Lawrence had asked a seemingly straightforward question. But as applied to the standards of Eternity, time was not a simple conceit. The passage of time could speed up or slow down. It could leap ahead or jump back. It could travel in loops. It could bend (but not break). It could twist, flatten, knot and gyrate, as well as oscillate, pendulate, undulate and rotate. It could also whirl, purl, revolve, slant, spin, expand and retract, and—when it really got going—whiz, shimmy, shake, buckle, tangle, tremble, tread, roll, flip (although not flop) and even completely reconfigure. And it could all happen simultaneously or in any combination.

Brigsby clarified to the degree that was possible. "The flux is . . . sporadic, but the pace is picking up. If they don't get to it soon . . ."—rare for Brigsby, he looked genuinely sad—". . . Earth will flux right out of existence."

"I'm sorry, B. I know how much you like that little planet."

"Yes, well . . . I am rather fond of it. But that's not my biggest problem."

When Brigsby said he had a *problem*, Lawrence never knew quite what that meant, given the countless cosmic issues that arose on a rolling basis. But in this case, he understood this to be a *Problem*, with a capital P. "B? What is it? What's out there? What else?"

Brigsby finally got up, and in his pink bunny slippers, shuffled to the window. "Milo," he said. "He's back."

"Oh, not that miscreant. I thought we had more time. How did he reconstitute so quickly? That's way too fast."

Though the fate of Existence was summarily at his whim, Milo was one irritant Brigsby could, at best, contain, and then only for short durations. Even Brigsby didn't know how or why he himself was the Minder of the Universe, where that power ultimately came from, or what fibrous tissue ran through the grand Consciousness. He had always *been* and, as far as he knew, would always be. Until his time was up. And until that occasion presented itself, Milo would remain his eternal foil. The Jester to his ultimate court.

"No idea. But he's out there mucking up my Universe. And I'm not having it." Brigsby slurped down the remainder of his chocolate milk. "If Milo's back this soon it means he's up to something. And I've spent way too much time and gone to way too much trouble to let him ruin Earth for me now. There's no telling how much damage he'll cause or what else he has in mind."

Brigsby refastened his robe tie and stared out into the Universe. He motioned with his snifter. "Hit me again, Larry. It's going to be a long night."

Chapter 2
Simon Is Like a Diamond in the Ruff, Ruff, Ruff

Jason Medley
Brooklyn, New York
September 2008

His hands were shaking.

Jason Medley would have chalked it up to getting his first cover story assignment with *SportsNewsWeekly*, a 1,600-word article about the New York Yankees striving to complete one of the wildest seasons in baseball history, including their quest for another World Series victory. The article was to include interviews with Derek Jeter, Bernie Williams, Jorge Posada, Paul O'Neil, Mariano Rivera, Joe Torre, and the owner, The Boss himself, George Steinbrenner.

Jason had made his way from unpaid intern to staff writer and was now being groomed to possibly take over the recently vacated Senior Writer slot. But that wasn't it.

There was also the recurring dream he'd been having of late, with him zooming along the tracks of a massive rollercoaster before being tossed off the side. Not that either.

Jason's biggest worry was that at 27 years old, he was still massively in debt thanks to his student loans. And he was dead broke. As in cash poor. As in he was eating store-brand rice puffs for dinner three times a week. As in his bank account balance was $46.71.

Because earlier that day he had left his Manhattan office cubicle on the 7th floor, walked four blocks to his financial institution, and drained his savings account, such that it was.

Even though New York City's daily resident, worker, and tourist population exceeded 8.5 million, consumed with their own personal dramas, Jason was convinced that each and every one of them were money zombies. That via their undead radar they had sniffed out and were consumed with the $3,250 in cash he had folded over in his left front jeans pocket. And that by any zombie means necessary, they were going to eat his money brains. And possibly his actual brains.

Heart pounding, Jason cabbed it to West 47th Street between Fifth Avenue and Avenue of the Americas, otherwise known as the Diamond District. There he met his pal Stephan, who had introduced him to Avi the Jeweler. As arranged, Jason handed over his life savings, and in return received a sparkling diamond engagement ring, in a black box.

And now—having successfully averted any and all zombie attacks—he was in the living room, in his one-bedroom apartment in Park Slope, Brooklyn, standing in front of Anna, who had no idea that he was about to propose. They'd talked about the *idea* of getting married . . . eventually, someday . . . but they hadn't discussed it in months, and not once did she pressure him to make a decision.

Jason made this one on his own. From the first time they met at a party in a tiny hostel in Barcelona, she was *the one*. More than a gut feeling—it came from somewhere deep inside, like a glow stick that alights when reunited with its source—he knew that Anna was destined to be his wife. And he didn't care if it sounded clichéd, stupid, or downright goofy.

Because what really freaked him out, what made his hands tremble and his head go all oogly, was that marriage also meant he was destined to be her husband. And that meant *he* had to become this other person, to assume this new mantle of responsibility. Forever.

Wife was about Anna. *Her* role. *Her* persona. What *she* would become. But *husband*, well . . . that was all *him*. And that made it real.

Anna kissed him. "Hi, Baby. What's shakin'?"

"Um . . ." His throat went dry. "I, uh . . ."

Anna picked up their tabby, Simon, who purred loudly. "I taught him the song. Check it out." With each syllable, Anna motioned the cat's paw in Jason's direction. And despite their pet's feline DNA, she sang a doggie version of the song, because it made her laugh: "My name is Sigh-muuuhn, like a dia-muuuhnd, in the ruff-ruff-ruff." Anna snorted, gave Simon a snuggle kiss, then tossed the cat on the couch. "I'm hungry. Let's get a burrito."

Hand in pocket, Jason squeezed the black box. Tight. The ring was inside. "Food," he finally mumbled, staring blankly, and managed a meek swallow. "Okay."

"Should I get your usual? Lettuce, extra cheese, and sour cream, no pico?"

Conceptually speaking, Jason understood the value of letting this particular life-changing event unfold as it would, without adding any pressure to the moment. The strategy sounded quite good—when he stopped to think about it calmly. But he struggled to fully embrace it.

Instead he concocted all sorts of wow-level romantic scenarios about how, when, and where he would propose. His fantasy was to do so late on a sunny Saturday afternoon, along the middle of the Brooklyn Bridge. But he was terrified that as he faced Anna, with a shaky hand he would accidentally drop the ring and watch it plummet between the wooden slats, lost forever to the East River. So that was out.

There was also a delusion about burying the ring box in Brooklyn's Prospect Park, in the flower garden by Military Plaza, and then leading Anna on a scavenger hunt, where she would pluck a rose and pull up a string, with the ring box at the other end. The list went on and on.

But now that Jason was standing before her, in their living room, he felt a different kind of panic, one that comes immediately prior to knowing that you are on the verge of a profound change, that you are the initiator of that change, and that you are indeed going to absorb and experience it, one molecule at a time.

All he could focus on were the last items he thought he would ever see, ever: an orphaned pen cap on the book shelf; the frayed back of the computer chair; Simon's slightly torn catnip sock on the floor; a sign Anna bought at the 17th Street flea market and hung above the kitchen archway: *Leave the Crazy Outside*

Feeling far similar to an inebriated sock puppet than a

grown man in control of his faculties, Jason was keenly aware that he was occupying a distinct point along the Cartesian plane of his existence, in which the life he had known up until that moment in time and space was about to end, and his new life—where he would be engaged, a *fiancé*—was about to begin. And he didn't have a plan.

The phrase *will you marry me?* was surely tucked away in his brain, and he was at least moderately confident that he had the functioning facial muscles and mental acuity to enunciate those words. He'd said them aloud numerous times individually and as part of other phrases, but never in that particular sequence with its specific, unambiguous intent. Yet the only sound he was able to fashion as Anna read off other Mexican menu items was "uhhmm . . . uhhh . . ."

Jason had an inkling then to take her hand and go for it, when suddenly—in a scenario he hadn't experienced, since he first met Anna—there was a blast of white light. There were streaks of screaming fluorescent color. There was the sensation of being sucked through a tornado. And there were throw pillows on the couch. Lots and lots of throw pillows.

Jason gave a slight shake of the head, and refocused. Anna had the cordless phone in one hand, a *Joey's Italian* take-out menu in the other. Simon was perched on the windowsill, staring at a squirrel that darted across a phone line, looking out onto Bell Boulevard in Bayside, Queens.

Jason and Anna had lived there together for almost a year, and he had been in line for a promotion to Senior Writer at *The NY Real Estate Gazette*.

Although for the briefest of moments, he looked about his fourth-floor apartment like he was seeing it for the very first time. And in a way, he was. That his place in the world seemed odd and distant, as if he had suddenly and without warning been transported into someone else's life, yet one that also felt comfortable and familiar. A life he knew as his very own.

I gotta stop daydreaming, he thought. *I need to focus.*

"So whaddaya think, Baby? Plain? Broccoli? Hawaiian?"

"Uh . . . huh?"

"Pizza. You know? Thin crust? Sauce? Cheese? Your favorite."

"Just, um . . . you pick. Whatever you want."

"I'm thinking pepperoni tonight. Ooh. And a beer. Yeah. That's it." Anna announced their dinner items with her best Italian accent. "Peh-per-OH-ni and a Per-OH-ni. Mmmm. Gonna be a good night."

Jason thumbed the ring box in his pocket, reminding himself of what he had planned to do. What it all meant. *Am I ready for this? Am I sure?*

As Anna placed her order with the pizza dude, Jason was engulfed with another blast of white light. There were streaks of screaming fluorescent color. There was the sensation of being sucked through a tornado. And there were origami swans. Lots and lots of origami.

Jason took a quick look around. Anna was sitting on the couch with a menu from *Dave's*, a burger joint on DeKalb Avenue in Fort Greene, Brooklyn. They had just moved into their spacious, two-bedroom apartment and were experimenting with local cuisine. Simon, who had taken to the place quite nicely, was sprawled across the computer desk, leg behind his ear, and licking his belly. His attention was drawn to the Japanese paper folds dangling from the ceiling. They rustled from a light breeze that crept in through the window. Jason had already told Anna about the possible cutbacks at *Modern Pharmacist News & Report*, where he was a staff reporter, but that his job seemed safe.

Anna offered her suggestion. "Burger and fries?"

"O-kaaay," Jason said, as if he was supposed to have known exactly what she was talking about. And then he remembered that he *did* know what she was talking about. Dinner. They had finally unpacked the last box of books and were ordering food, and before she would have time to even guess what he had in his pocket, he was going to propose and . . .

Jason's Spidey sense started to tingle. He had a strange feeling just then that he needed to speak with his pal Theo Barnes. They hadn't seen each other in three years, but of all the people Jason knew, there was no one likely to appreciate those odd and mysterious feelings moreso than Theo.

"So," Anna said. "Whaddaya think? Burgers okay? But I could do Thai food, if you want."

Two pens dropped to the floor. Simon leapt down from the desk, tail up, and rubbed his side against Jason's leg. The cat wasn't shy about asking for attention.

Jason smiled. *Take it easy, dude. She's the one. Just relax.*

"Sure," he said. "Burgers sound good. Order mine with Swiss, and fries extra crispy. I'm in that kind of a mood. Just remind me when we're done. I need to make a call."

Chapter 3
Nothing Like a Good Chainsaw

Theo Barnes
Auckland, New Zealand

Theo Barnes would never be confused with a workaholic.

He didn't see himself that way, and had no desire to become as such. Yet his *Barnes & Co.* landscaping and greenhouse business was, for a daydreamer of his modest wants, a reasonable success. He had one van and one flatbed truck, an expanding customer base, and enough revenue to support one full-time helper and two part-timers. His girlfriend, Lea, who was also the mother of his twin girls, kept the books and made the appointments, as Theo couldn't be bothered with details and paperwork. Too much hassle.

Theo was also slightly less than diligent about collecting fees. He could submit all the bills he wanted, but getting some of those wankers to actually hand over the money for services rendered was something else entirely, and yet another frustration he hated to deal with.

But today was going to be a choice day. A damn choice day. Theo was excited to test out his new Power Rip 3000 chainsaw. Old Freddie Berman's *Kawaka* tree had finally died, so he called Theo to come over and slice that sucker into pieces, down to the stump. Other jobs paid far better, but Theo didn't care. Any chance to slap on the work gloves and hold that mechanical thunder was a job worth taking.

Before heading off, Theo stood in his driveway and powered up the saw. Test run. *Rum-rum. Rummmm, rum-rum.* He gave it another go. *Rum-rum-rummmmm.* Birds scattered from the bushes. Dogs howled. Theo admired the humming machine. "Hoo-heh! Sweet."

The screen door to the house's side entrance snapped open. Hope. Rascal number one. "G'day, Dad. Are you gonna cut the twees, yeh?"

"Where's Tess? She with yer mum?"

"Noooo," Hope said in that playful sing-song way she had, as if she was up to some sort of mischief or another, and maybe wanted you to try and figure out what it was. "She's out front, pwaying with Dexter."

"Leave the cat alone."

"It's not me, Dad. It's Dazzle. It's Tess."

Theo didn't worry about Hope. Every day she was becoming more like Lea, a good egg with a handle on things. Tess, however, was another matter. Rascal number two. She was more like him. Always up to something, off in her own world, planning to be somewhere else. And in her mind, she was already there.

Theo shut off the saw, raised his goggles, and placed the power tool in the back of his truck. His tool box sat atop a handful of postcards he agreed to hand out as a favor to his friend George, who owned a nightclub, and performed as Angelique.

Set against a black background, the phrase *GenderBender* stretched across the top of the postcard. Beneath it was the image of an Asian drag queen, in a red, sequined dress, high heels, and a black wig with long curls. Also in the background were a peppering of stars and the magenta swirl of the Andromeda galaxy.

Theo shook his head and chuckled just looking at the postcard, when Tess popped up from beneath a tarp inside the flatbed. She scared the bejesus out of him.

"G'day, Dad."

"Ahh!" Theo put a hand to his chest. "Tess. Don't do that, yeh?"

Tess giggled. "Got ya', Dad."

"Yeh," Theo said in his New Zealand lilt. "Great. You got me."

Theo admired Tess's creativity and adventurous spirit—she was her daddy's little girl for sure—yet he also wanted to conceal his daughter in head-to-toe bubble wrap so she couldn't do any real damage to herself or anyone else.

With each passing day he had a deeper, richer appreciation of the grief he must have caused his own parents during his youth. And now that Theo was on the receiving end, they loved every minute of it. They often told him as much.

"Come on, sweetheart. No Razzle Dazzle near the tools.

You're gonna hurt someone."

Tess giggled again.

"I ohways tell her," Hope said. "Not by the toows."

"I know you do." Theo pulled off his gloves. "Razzle. Dazzle. Sit here." He leaned against the edge of the truck, and scooped up his daughters, one on each thigh, an arm around their backs. He motioned to the yard, leading to his greenhouse. "You see that path, the one with the stones? When I get back from Freddie's, I'm gonna widen the path, and you're gonna help me, yeh?"

Theo's Uncle Pete had moved to Brisbane the year before when he eloped with his new Aussie wife, and gifted the house to him. It wasn't much, just a small, three-bedroom ranch with an enclosed deck in back, a fifteen-minute drive from downtown Auckland. Theo's greenhouse took up half the yard, but there was still plenty of room for the girls to play, and a slight hill on the far side of the house overlooking the rest of the neighborhood.

The bush-lined landscaping also afforded them a bit of privacy, which was growing more and more important, given the ability of his girls to teleport short distances.

The Razzle Dazzle.

Lea stuck her head out the back door. "You gonna talk to them, yeh? The Rascals. They're at it again."

When they first met, Theo and Lea were exploration guides in the Waitomo Caves, down in Rotorua, just messing about, having a good time. There had never been so much as a single discussion about whether they would have children, live together, or even keep the relationship going. And though Theo had long expected that he would visit every corner of the globe before settling down—the idea of him being a *family man* would have been a laughable suggestion just a few years back—he took comfort in that old saying that life's what happens when you're busy planning something else.

As it turned out, being that very family man suited him far better than he ever would have thought. And his bond with Lea was far more satisfying than he imagined being available to him. They weren't married, but that time would surely come.

With two kids, where was he going?

Theo nodded to Lea, and then addressed his girls. His rascals. "We had a deal, yeh? No Razzle Dazzle on your own. Only when I'm around. Or mum."

"But you *are* around," Tess said.

She had him there. He was technically *in the vicinity*. "That's not what I meant. I mean . . ."—Theo sighed, fighting off his exasperation—"only when we're all together, and when I know where you're going, and when you're going to do it. Okay?"

Theo knew it was only a matter of time before Hope and Tess really got the hang of the Razzle Dazzle—the teleportation—and ended up as juvenile delinquents. Or bank robbers. Or secret government operatives. Or worse.

But maybe if he could establish some rules for them now, if he planted the idea that they were better off with his supervision, that plan would take hold. Theo wasn't exactly the model of discipline himself, but what choice did he have?

I'm totally screwed, he thought. *I. Am. Screwed.*

The jar he found that one time deep in the Waitomo Caves was now long gone, dumped into the South Pacific Ocean off Cathedral Cove. But the effects lingered.

The first time Tess disappeared, she was only four months old. Not even crawling yet, she was in her baby swing one minute, gone the next. Lea found her out front, like in those old stories about infants being left on the doorstep. Theo and Lea had no idea how it happened, and after they got over their initial panic—they absolutely *lost . . . their . . . shit*—they chalked it up as one of those crazy moments in a baby's life, and let it be.

But when a week later Hope wasn't in her crib where they left her—she turned up in the laundry basket in the basement—and then a few days after that they found her on the roof of the house with Dexter curled in her little lap, they knew something was up. Tess also got a kick out of suddenly appearing in the bathroom just as Theo was dropping a deuce, so even his morning twosy had become a team sport. Moreso when Hope joined in for group giggles.

There were only so many logical probabilities as to how and why his children could do the Razzle Dazzle, and when they had all been ruled out, only the illogical remained. Theo didn't want to face it, but it had to be the jar. What else could it have been?

Charting back the timeline, Lea figured conception must have occurred in Theo's second-floor apartment in Waitomo, above the parking lot, the day she found him alone in the caves.

Theo had only just come into contact with the jar that day, and their lovemaking had been so intense, so otherworldly, that he felt himself commune with the very fabric of Creation. He initially thought he'd dropped acid and then forgot about it—he sure as hell wished that had been the case—but ultimately he knew it was the jar.

The jar that caused him to hallucinate.

The jar that sent him trekking across Europe.

The jar that introduced him to Jason Medley, split them apart, and then, finally, brought them back together.

The jar that put him on the run from a bunch of kooks from this world and the other.

The jar that brought a biker gang and an armed gunman to his living room and scared his mum, and inspired his dad to fire up the helicopter.

The jar that sent Roger off to Rotorua.

The jar with the Universe's liquid DNA.

That jar.

And now that his twin girls firmly understood their ability to teleport short distances—the Razzle Dazzle—he constantly had to remind them that there were rules, and that the rules were in place for a reason. This coming from a young man who defied rules as often and thoroughly as he could get away with.

You think potty-training toddlers is tough? Try getting them to rein in their teleportation. Theo didn't even want to think about what daycare would be like.

Composed again, he offered a stern smile. "Remember what we said, yeh? What's rule number . . . ?"

Theo trailed off, sensing a distant but familiar tingle. There was a blast of white light. There were streaks of screaming fluorescent color. There was the sensation of being sucked through a tornado. And then he was in the living room.

Their house, the one they bought on the cheap at auction, still had the new paint smell. Next up was an expanded greenhouse. Theo couldn't run his business without one. He looked around, and regained his train of thought. Lea was playing with the twins.

"So . . . ," he said, semi-confused. "What was I saying?"

Lea clarified. "Turtle Bay. Said you were heading out there this weekend."

Theo thought that might have sounded right, but wasn't quite sure. "I did?"

"Turtle Bay," Hope said.

"Yeh-yeh," Tess said. "Turtle *Bay*."

"Oh, yeh-yeh. Right. Okay. I need to go to Turtle Bay. Good conditions out there. I'll hike a bit. Guess I'll head off on Friday." Turtle Bay was 104 kilometers to the east, about two hours' drive to the Waipoua Forest. Theo needed to fill the petrol tank, and pack some supplies. He picked up Tess, and then rubbed her nose to nose. It wasn't that he didn't believe his girls, but he felt the need to confirm with them that he was in fact planning the trip they said he was.

Simply taking their word for it was a risk unto itself. And with the Razzle Dazzle twins, it was a risk loaded with the potential for teleportation-type consequences.

Tess nodded. Lea did the same, which satisfied him.

"Okay, then. Turtle Bay it is." Theo just had one more question about his trip, for anyone who had the answer. "Um . . . *why am I going, exactly?*"

Chapter 4
Beware the H-Bomb

Jason Medley
Manhattan

Writing was a funny business.

Jason had all sorts of ideas about what it would mean to be a journalist, about how he might emerge in the field, about the clacking of keys, of delivering clever lines. Because his plan all through college was to become a high school English teacher—a plan he scrapped months after graduating and receiving his state teaching license.

Only trouble was that he hadn't taken a single journalism course, nor had he written for the school newspaper. So when it came to being a reporter, he knew, essentially, zero. Unless his paper route when he was twelve counted as *experience*.

But through sheer tenacity—and a recommendation from his pal Hank—Jason had first landed an internship with a mom-and-pop B2B magazine publisher in Westchester, New York. There he learned the basics, writing and reporting about equipment for persons with disabilities, including wheelchairs, crutches, and, more often than he anticipated, colostomy bags.

Yet when asked what he did for a living, he liked to tell people that he was a *journalist*. Even though he had been told repeatedly that the heyday of the newsroom was long gone, that thanks to the quality-draining influence of the Internet, he was getting into the action too late, to Jason, the word still conveyed a sense of loftiness, as if he was doing something vaguely important. As if what he did mattered. And as a healthcare journalist, he really did feel that way. He was delivering practical information to doctors and various other practitioners, updates that would be used to better treat their patients. His mom. His sister. His grandmother. Real people in the real world.

Healthcare journalist. Yeah. I like that.

Jason then landed his first full-time job, at Intelacorp, as a staff reporter for *Modern Pharmacist News & Report*. It was a truly useful entrée into the field of healthcare reporting, as pharmacists dispense medications for every type of ailment, including head lice, the subject of his very first feature assignment.

But now that he had been promoted to Senior Reporter, the powers that be switched his beat, moving him to *Gastroenterology Today*. The publication covered medical specialists who take long, thin, rubber tubes with a tiny camera on the end, and feed them up the booty or down the gullet, and poke around inside.

Hank found the assignment amusing. His grey hair was extra spiky that day, his way of trying to feel *in* with the hipsters.

"Whaddaya say, Kid? How you liking *Ass-a-Thon News & World Report*? See any good hemorrhoids today? Some anal polyps?"

"Har-har-HAR-dee-har-har. I still don't get how you even work here."

"I told you, Kid. You gotta get out there and meet people. Network. Rub elbows. Have drinks. You know . . . live a little. You gotta work it."

Jason still couldn't get used to seeing Hank in a suit. Intelacorp's CEO, Andrew McCann, was a buddy back from his executive days, before Hank's ten-year hiatus as a wandering, pot-smoking, acid-dropping vagabond, including a stint as a waiter at *Funzie's*, where Jason and Hank first met. But Hank was back and, in a position to help Jason's career along. Plus, Hank said, now that Jason had at least begun the process of extracting his head from his bunghole, and was moving up in the world, he missed having him around.

"Yeah, yeah," Jason said. "I'm living just fine."

The new Intelacorp offices were located in Manhattan at the corner of Ninth Street and Broadway, in the old Wanamaker's department store building, a short walk from Cooper Union art school and St. Marks Place, where Jason liked to buy comic books and used CDs.

The editorial team was housed on a large, open floor with massive columns, thanks to the old department store layout. Jason's station was a cubicle, among rows of cubicles. His fellow reporters and editors, assigned to various beats in healthcare, finance, business, travel, and real estate, were milling about on various deadlines.

Hank polished his black-rimmed glasses. "Still haven't proposed, huh? It'll come."

"Shush! Yikes. Not so loud."

"Ooh-hoo. Look at Mister Sensitive over here."

Gene Gilligan was on the other side of Jason's shared wall, in a cubicle, crunching away on Belgian pretzel nuggets.

Jason spun around in his chair. He motioned for Hank to come inside the cubicle. It was the only way to get even a semblance of privacy. "Look, it's . . . I wanted to do it. I had the ring in my pocket. I just . . ."

"Couldn't get it up? Yeah, I knew you had performance issues."

Jason ignored the wisecrack. Too easy, even for Hank. "No. I wanted to. I was going to. I was excited to."

"Nervous?"

"Of course I was! But that's not the point. It was something else." Jason looked around to make sure no one was eavesdropping. "You ever feel . . . I don't know . . . ," he was searching for the right word, ". . . off? Like, something's not quite right? I've been having the rollercoaster dream again. Almost every night."

"Kid. Have we met? I like me some good wake n' bake. And waffles. You should come over tomorrow. I've got real maple syrup. Better than your Aunt Joe Momma."

"Jemima. Hank. . . . Come on. Will you just listen, please? I'm serious."

"I am serious, Kid. I'm listening."

Jason seemed unconvinced.

Hank leaned against the desk. "Okay-okay-okay. You have my sincere and undivided attention. Shoot."

"I'm not quite sure how to describe it. It's like . . . I wake up every day, and there's Anna, and there's the cat, and there's my stuff, and I take a shower and get dressed, and then I head out and buy my newspaper on the way to the subway, and . . ."

"You can't tell if it's really your life?"

"Yes! Right! That's *exactly* how I feel. It's like I'm me, but not me either. Like, I'm a version of myself, on a dial, in between settings. . . . You know what I mean?"

"Listen, Kid. Everybody you know . . ."—Hank gestured to the cubes of co-workers— ". . . they all feel like an imposter. They're just pretending. They're playing a part. And between the hours of 8:30 a.m. and 6 p.m., it's the role of *employee*. And then they go, well . . . wherever the hell they go, and they try to be *that* guy, *that* girl. Husband, wife, boyfriend, girlfriend, party dude, rock climber, blogger, junkie, asswipe . . . whatever. As for you . . . you're about to get en*gaged*. Of *course* you're fucked up. Your life is about to change! Drastically. You're making a decision. You're taking a chance. It's kinda nice to see. Glad you got it in you."

Jason would never say it out loud, but despite the accompanying snark he wanted Hank's approval moreso than from anyone else. On paper, Hank wasn't the ideal mentor, but for Jason, he was. Hank's off-kilter mojo often hit the right notes. "Thanks, but that's not what I'm talking about. It's . . . remember when I went overseas? With Theo?"

"How could I forget! That's when you finally unbunched your panties."

"Thanks," Jason said, trying very much to forget the Jason Medley he had been even just a few short years earlier, ". . . remember how I told you about the . . . you know?" He ducked down, whispered again. "The . . ."

"Oh . . . you mean the jar!"

"Sush-sush-sush. *Ssshhh*! Yes. The *jar*."

"Yeah. You said it made things . . . trippy."

"Yeah, well . . . I'm starting to feel that way again. Like everything around me's just not . . . quite . . . right."

"I don't know what to tell you, Kid. I'm sure it's just cold feet. Although in your case,"—Hank made sure to raise his voice— "more like icy balls. Oh, hey. H-Bomb's coming. Gotta go."

H-Bomb was Glenn Hauman, the healthcare division's Managing Editor. Hauman was an oddly large man, over six foot five, with a giant head, as if meant for someone at least a foot taller, and topped with a poof of gray, thinning hair. His voice held a deep, aristocratic timber, but his attitude was often somewhat less sophisticated than his dialect would imply. He also had small eyes, sunk back into hollow sockets, as if a bomb were about to explode.

As a bully tactic he used to great effect, especially with the junior staff, Hauman liked to approach his reporters while on deadline, stare as they frantically clacked away to get their copy in on time, and then grumble their names, to entice a sense of diminutive stature in his presence.

H-Bomb produced a sheet of white printer paper, littered with red marks. "Mr. Medley," he said, his words long and drawn out. "I received your latest . . . article, if you insist upon calling it that . . . on gastroenteritis in the prison population."

There was little chance H-Bomb was pleased with the quality of his reporting.

"Uh . . . okay . . . ?"

"Hardly. I realize that you are still attempting to become an actual reporter, and that you are coming from a position of significant disadvantage, given your obvious lack of talent, skill, instincts, experience, professionalism, common sense, and the ability to distinguish hypertension from hypotension. Yes, you made that mistake once again." H-Bomb slid the severely marked-up paper across Jason's desk. "Nevertheless, if you have any hope of maintaining your position here I might suggest that, to begin, you remain awake for at least a small portion of the time you spend conducting interviews and pretending to fact check. Unless, of course, you need me to write this all out for you at a level even you can understand? In crayon, perhaps? Or a nice pop-up book?"

H-Bomb squinted, rolled his eyes, and then returned from whence he came.

Hank reappeared. "You're really winning the guy over. Niiice."

Jason offered a mock smile.

"Hey," Hank said. "Why so glum? You should be happy."

In his earlier newsroom days, Jason would have felt very much like running out of the office, quitting his job, and then falling into a weeks-long journey of depression and existential self-examination. Now he only felt like a steaming pile of ostrich dung, determined to improve the very document he had been

accused of desecrating. And it may have been just as well—
H-Bomb wasn't one to offer constructive edits, but at least he
knew a well-written story from a bad one.

As for his *being happy*, Jason was unconvinced. "Yeah? How's
that?"

Hank ran a joint under his nose, and inhaled its aroma, as
if it were a Cuban cigar. "Now you know exactly *why* you feel
so fucked. So let's go smoke this bad boy, then grab a couple of
slices. My treat. I want to ask you about your trip to Baltimore
this weekend."

"Sorry, Hank. Trip's canceled. Can't make it. Couldn't get a
car."

"Nevertheless. Let's get outta here. This place is has bad joo
joo. And I feel like smiling."

Chapter 5
Lord of the Forest

Theo Barnes
Waipoua Forest, New Zealand

Turtle Bay wasn't technically a bay, but Theo didn't care.

Located deep in the Waipoua Forest, Turtle Bay was nestled within the Hokianga region, surrounding the Hokianga Harbor, a long river valley on the upper west coast of New Zealand's North Island. A two-hour drive north from Auckland, Turtle Bay was named far less so for its primary inhabitants—turtles, although a few could be found—but rather for its shape.

From a distance, a small hill leading into the forest looked very much like a turtle's shell, with the smaller, bulbous-type hill to the northeast much like its head, and the longer, reedier pathways extending from its body, like its arms and legs.

To Theo, the Waipoua Forest was a real-life fantasy, a subtropical preserve protected by a forest canopy. Beneath it existed an abundance of rare fauna and flora, including *taraie, kohekohe,* and *kowhai* trees. Yet further below were shrub layers, and then beneath the many trees were tall, dense strands of *gahnia* and *kauri* grass.

Within this wondrous ecosystem lived several endangered species, including the largest remaining population of North Island brown *kiwi*, as well as other birds such as the *fantail, grey warbler, shining bronze cuckoo, kingfisher*, and the New Zealand pigeon, called *kākupa*, a clever little bird that spreads the seeds of many plants—sowing, as Theo liked to joke, the seeds of love.

But Theo came for the mighty *Kauri*, ancient trees dating back 190 million years, with smooth bark and small, narrow leaves. As young plants the Kauri grows straight upwards, with branches sprouting along the length of the trunk. But as Kauris grow taller, the lowest branches shed, making the tree all but impossible to climb.

And finally, by full maturity, the top branches form a crown, as if ruling over the other, subservient trees throughout the forest.

From the road, Theo could already see several Kauris, but once he made his way deeper inside the forest—reachable only by foot, beneath that canopy—he ventured upon one of New Zealand's oldest, *Tāne Mahuta*, the Lord of the Forest. Estimated to be at least 2,300 years old, *Tāne Mahuta* was 47 meters high, with a trunk five meters wide.

A giant among giants.

Theo smiled, dwarfed within its shade, wondering, perhaps, if the ancient tree—a living God—had any advice *he* was willing to share.

Maybe you know what to do, mate. I sure don't.

In awe of the mighty tree, Theo thought then of the Maori legend of Creation. It was said that the eternal love of *Ranginui*— the Sky Father—and *Papatuanuku*—the Earth Mother, was so strong that these two Kauri trees could not bear to be apart. Yet because of their immovable embrace, their children were imprisoned within it, blocked from the light.

And then one day *Ranginui* shifted, allowing a beam of light to shine through a crevice in *Papatuanuku*'s armpit and onto her six children, who yearned to emerge from eternal darkness— to enter the world of light. Emboldened by this radiance, they struggled mightily to break from their parents' embrace. Yet they couldn't get free. Their parents' love was too strong.

But just when all felt hopeless, the colossal *Tāne Mahuta*— the Lord of the Forest—lay on his back and dug his shoulders deep into his mother's body beneath him. Meanwhile, with his legs, *Tāne Mahuta* pushed against his father, and with all his strength, attempted to let light into the world. He ignored his mother's cries to stop, pushing even harder, until the embrace between his parents began to loosen.

With his every last bit of his strength, *Tāne Mahuta* extended his powerful legs, forcing his father to the heavens and flooding the world with bright light.

Legend has it that today, when *Ranginui*'s tears fall from the sky as rain onto his beloved *Papatuanuku*, it is a reminder of his grief and longing for her. *Papatuanuku*'s pain is visible in the red ochre clays of the earth, still stained by the blood drawn during the separation.

It is also said that among his legacy, *Tāne Mahuta*, the Lord of the Forest, stands victorious in Waipoua Forest, with his shoulders still pushed hard against his Earth Mother and his feet stretched high toward the heavens of his Sky Father.

Theo had no idea if the legend of *Tāne Mahuta* was true. And while it had resonated with him since childhood—an ancient tree, a God, holding up the sky on its shoulders—the legend took on an entirely new meaning for him as an adult. Or, more to the point, as a father.

Standing now before the Lord of the Forest, Theo was never more aware that he himself wouldn't live forever, which made him pity and snicker at the rest of the world. If his children were vanishing and reappearing now, as three-year-olds, what would they be like as grown women, for others to contend with?

Good luck, mates. You'll need it.

And as had become almost a daily occurrence, thinking of his children drew Theo to his own father. The conversation hadn't yet occurred, but even Theo knew it was only a matter of time. Oskar Barnes was of ill health, whatever the cause, and unless there was a medical intervention, he was likely to draw his final breath sooner rather than later. Theo wasn't ready for that.

It was only over the past years, when the Barnes clan awoke from a long, hazy slumber, that Theo had finally felt like he'd had a real father, and that he was becoming a real son. Even so, there was still so much they hadn't shared with one another, and it was becoming clear that time might be running out on them just as they were getting started.

Although he did not often seek out his father for parenting advice, nor did Oskar offer it unsolicited, Theo was comforted simply by his father's presence. His father just *being alive*—his very existence—helped establish perspective for him, supplied balance. Theo knew he was leaning on his father, abdicating at least some portion of his responsibility by not thinking about what to do—or how to be—if his father were actually to die, leaving Theo as the most senior of the Barnes men.

It was not a role he felt even remotely equipped to handle.

And if his attitude was deemed immature, then that burden would be his to carry. Theo just wasn't ready to handle more. Which is why he suspected—he feared—that *more*, in fact, was coming his way, whatever *more* would turn out to be.

Gazing up again at *Tāne Mahuta*—Lord of the Forest, the enabler of light—Theo felt like a sooky bubba in comparison.

How do you do it, mate? How do you shoulder that load? Haven't you done your share? Don't you ever want to let go?

Theo was overcome then with the need to speak to his father. It didn't matter what they talked about, just so long as they spoke.

Unsure if he could get a signal, Theo dialed his mobile phone. It rang four times before it clicked. His heart began to flutter. He wasn't sure why. His mother spoke through the phone.

"Alright, Theo. No, sorry luv. Your dad can't chat now. He's off for a nap, yeh? But are you okay? How're my darlings?"

Not a nap, he thought. *I know it's worse.*

"The same. You just saw them yesterday."

"I know. But you're all my everything."

"I know, Mum. But how's Dad? I just want to—"

"Oh, someone's at the door. I'll ring you later, Theo. Love you. Bye."

You're running away from me again. I'm worried, Mum. I'm scared.

Theo's failure to connect with his father now was emblematic of their relationship. Like inviting someone to a party when you already know they can't come, Theo once again waited to reach out to his father until he was in a location that made their connection all but impossible. And yet as Theo feared for his father's life—as Oskar Barnes had begun to crumble—Theo still couldn't break the habit.

So when he surveyed for the turtles he knew he would never find—the ones Hope and Tess insisted were there—he looked up at *Tāne Mahuta* one last time, to say goodbye. And then his phone vibrated again. Surely his mother calling back.

Theo fumbled for the phone, eager to hear his father's voice yet terrified at what it might sound like. What it might reveal.

Only the flip screen showcased a 011 international code. America.

Who do I even know from. . . ?

"Jason. . . ?" he said into the device.

"*Theo! Buddy!*" The signal was surprisingly clear. "*I finally got you. I can never find a good time. The time difference. It's crazy. It's like three a.m. here.*"

Theo wore a smile rich with depth and meaning. "Yeh-yeh. Um . . ."

"*So, listen,*" Jason began, "*can I ask you something?*"

Theo knew that when Jason started a conversation as such, they weren't going to do the usual chit-chat. He had something on his mind. He wanted to *talk.* That's how Jason was. He couldn't let things be. When he got a hold of an idea, he needed to think about it. Dissect it. Internalize it. It was how he figured things out.

"Yeh-yeh."

"*Okay. Here goes. Have you . . . do you think . . . oh, screw it. . . . Are you feeling kinda . . . weird lately? And I mean weird weird, not regular weird. Like . . . you-and-me weird.*"

Unlike anyone else he knew, Theo could always count on Jason to *get* him, even if Theo barely got himself. Surrounded by the dense forest, he responded with greater enthusiasm than he intended. "Yeh! I do!"

"*You have. I knew it! I guess I shouldn't be so excited about that, but . . . I'm glad it's not just me. I thought I was losing it. Okay, so . . . I know it's not easy for you to get away, what with the twins and the business, but . . . I had a dream last night. One of those crazy dreams I have. You know the ones? Only this one was about rollercoasters and hot dogs. I'm not totally sure why, but I kinda feel like you're supposed to come to New York. I think we need to go to—*"

"Coney Island?"

"*. . . Y-y-yeah. How did you know that. . . ?*"

"Because last night, yeh . . . ?" Theo looked once more upon *Tāne Mahuta,* that living god, and offered the only answer he could. "I had the same dream, too."

Chapter 6
Is That a Blotter on Your Desk or Are You Just Happy To See Me?

Emma and Lex
San Francisco

The Starlight Connect had become one of the most recognizable Internet café chains in Arizona.

Emma and Lex opened their first location in Yuma, expanded with two more in Tucson, and after a little political wrangling—including a duffle bag filled with cash—they had finally made their way into Phoenix with another three cafés. Two more locations were on the way.

The business model had been simple enough. Each café had a celestial theme, the walls and ceiling decorated with all manner of shooting stars, nebulas, and swirling galaxies. The music—what Emma called hipster douche rock, or HDR—played with a constant, low buzz, loud enough to keep heads mildly bopping but not so loud as to annoy anyone, especially Emma.

The company logo was, of course, a crescent moon, only this iteration included a smiley face wink, with the moon sporting a wireless headset. Emma was also committed to top-flight infrastructure, so she paid for the highest-quality bandwidth available at the time, and upgraded those capabilities whenever possible.

Activity picked up another notch when she added a bakery, although power bars sold just as well as scones, while heavily sweetened energy drinks like *Zort, Blast-o!,* and *Yowsa* easily outsold coffee and espresso (those classic beverages were so cost-effective, however, that Emma spent the extra money on a high-end, stainless steel dispensary).

In any case, caffeine plus snacks plus 24/7 access to online gaming and the local nerd community had adopted *The Starlight Connect* as their unofficial homes away from home.

The success of *Starlight* might have also had just a little something to do with the IT staff. Because, you know, they had boobs.

Although illegal under state and federal statutes, Emma's unofficial hiring guidelines were that each Startie (*Starlight* tech hottie) had to be, in her words, *totally fuckable*. With a red pen Emma would write the letters *TF* with a circle around them on the upper right-hand corner, call the applicant back for closer inspection, or else toss the form. When questioned, Emma would say that *TF* stood for *tech fulfillment*, which seemed to satisfy anyone who asked.

Starlight uniforms included ripped jeans, loose-fitting overalls, or a denim skirt, as well as a Pearl Jam t-shirt (or its HDR equivalent), and at least one obvious facial piercing, although Emma herself had none. She didn't get the whole jabbing-my-flesh-with-a-metal-object thing, but she got that the nerds got it, and that was enough for her.

Thongs were strongly encouraged (although not technically required), and if the Starties also sported a tramp stamp—especially one that was easily visible when the girls bent forward or stretched; with dragons, snakes, and tongues disappearing toward their nether regions in front, back, or both—then all the better.

If the Starties also had actual, useful IT skills . . . bonus. And some of them did. Emma was often surprised at just how many young women could install a motherboard, serve coffee, and tolerate what was often the spillover from the nearby comic book shops. At one point she even considered buying *Eddie's Comics*, but the highly caffeinated beverages and books combo proved to be a bad mix.

Emma initially assumed that *Starlight* clientele would skew far more heavily toward a sausage party, but the girls showed up in droves, diversifying mainly among lesbians, freaks, and cherds (chick nerds). The nerdosphere wasn't Emma's world by instinct, but it sure as heck paid the bills, and then some.

And yet . . . Emma really had to hand it to Lex.

The newest *Starlight* location—on Valencia, near 19th Street, in San Francisco's Mission District—was the model for all future stores, and their new home base. Relocated into the Bay Area, Emma was thrilled to be out of the desert's godforsaken heat. San Francisco was more her style.

Partners in all things *Starlight*, Emma and Lex stood beside the counter, admiring their customers and Starties. And now also proud of their newest endeavor—*The Starlight Café*—Emma scratched Lex behind the ears. His ID and rabies tag jangled. Her former assistant—and sex partner—in Eternity, Lex was now her companion on Earth. And a brown Labrador. And her best friend.

"You know," she said, "I never would have come up with this. Medical marijuana. What a racket. Good call."

Lex was not only a favorite among the patrons and Starties alike—receiving all manner of scratches, pets, kisses, and close-breasted snuggles. He had also become a connoisseur of the establishment's herbal menu items. As they often were, his eyes were glossy, bloodshot, and barely open. His long pink tongue dangled, in need of refreshment. "It's bong-tastic," he said, then chopped his jaw.

Besides two dozen varieties of bud, *The Starlight Café* dispensed THC-infused cookies, brownies, truffles, toffee, peanut brittle, dinner rolls, lemon meringue and key lime pie, crispy rice and granola bars, hard candy, and their newest and most popular item, THC lollipops.

Despite the numerous scammers looking for government approved weed—or what Emma called her core customers—*The Starlight Café* did have numerous legitimate patrons afflicted with all manner of ailments, including HIV/AIDS, cancer, multiple sclerosis, migraines, hepatitis C, post-traumatic stress disorder, inflammatory bowel disease, glaucoma, Huntington's disease, Parkinson's disease, sickle cell anemia, anorexia nervosa, and many others.

Regardless, an approved doctor's note for *cannabis* merchandise was about as difficult to obtain as one of Lex's room-clearing farts.

Emma offered a contented smile. "Stoners on one side, gamers on the other. Nice, my friend. Very nice."

"Hey," Lex began, then stared at the wall, at one of Emma's custom designs. Within a single frame were seven galaxies. Four made an outer circle, with another two within, and then one more in the center. Their striated curls gave the appearance of galaxies swirling in opposite directions. Lex was starting to swirl himself, as if being hypnotized.

While Emma's banishment to Earth came with her transformation from svelte vixen to oversized malcontent, Lex left Eternity a slender, athletic young man and woke up on Earth as a four-legged creature—a dog. A bona fide canine.

The shift had also wonked his memory, which vacillated between lucid, analytical, and downright hazy. Details about his life in Eternity were clear and easy to recall one moment, illusive the next.

Just then Lex thought of his sister—at least he had a vague sense that it might possibly be his sister, assuming he actually had one—and that her birthday was coming up. It was all just a distant, undefined reflection. But then all he could think about was that he had the munchies something fierce.

"Did we get those, uh . . . you know . . . pizza hot pocket thingies. . . ." He was now full-on obsessed. Another effect of his canine form. Once he got a hold of a smell, game over. "Pizza. Mmm. Could go for some. But, uh . . ." He snapped out of it. "I need water. Where's my dish?"

The marijuana dispensary had quadrupled profits in just the first six months, with Emma expecting them to possibly double again within a year. She planned to replicate the model in two more Bay Area locations, and then expand as opportunities presented themselves.

Running a successful Internet café chain—now with the dual function as a dispensary for government-approved, top-of-the-line cannabis—wasn't quite as thrilling as being the grand designer of galaxies.

Her former profession, in Eternity.

Before her banishment.

Before her exile from the realm responsible for all creation in the Universe.

But all in all, her life on Earth wasn't half bad. The mobile phone in her pocket started to vibrate. "Hey, skank. What's up?" Emma nodded. "Yeah, probably. Hold on." She held the phone aside. "You want an eggroll? It's Nina. She's ordering take-out."

Lex lifted his face out of his dish. *"Chen Palace or Dumpling Dragon?"*

"Lemme check." She inquired, nodded. *"Chen Palace."*

"Yeah. Eggroll and wonton soup. And pork lo mein."

Emma relayed the order to Nina, their upstairs neighbor. "And brown rice for me. And steamed vegetables. And make sure there's no oil. They always fuck that up. You have to insist. Tell Ming Li. . . . No, not Jane. Ming Li. She'll get it right."

Emma listened. Nina was generous about complimenting her appearance, partly because Emma gave her a break on the rent in exchange for some odd jobs, partly because Emma was generous herself when it came to weed doggie bags, and partly because Emma was slowly but surely reclaiming her former sex kitten status, and fed off the encouragement, genuine or not. And if she was allowing herself to be manipulated, well, she could live with it. Even Emma was susceptible now and then.

"Yeah, I know. I feel good. Thanks. You're sweet. But I've still got about ninety pounds to go. And you don't get to be a size two by scarfing down pints of chicken fried rice. Although it is tasty."

Since she accepted her plight—destined to live out her days on the very planet of her design—Emma committed herself to shedding the über pounds saddled upon her by the Minder of the Universe, also known as the Big M.O.U., as part of her banishment. In Eternity, Emma was a foxy, raven-haired babe who aroused all manner of erections (dongs and nipples). Yet on Earth, she had been sentenced to a flesh-and-blood prison, one that maxed out at 337 pounds, which, on a good day, left her about nine inches too short to support such girth. And with greasy blonde hair.

But after three years of rigorous training, exercise, and portion control—and a fabulous makeover—she was down to a more manageable 204 pounds.

At one point she considered gastric bypass, but that wasn't

her way. Emma knew that a short cut would deny her the satisfaction of having earned—and bragging about—her ideal body,
and that if she cheated her way to reclaimed hotness, it would
undermine her in all other ways. She would have the option of
telling people whatever she wanted, but deep down, she would
know. She was not above lying to herself if need be—but not
about this.

Nope. Her goal was to get down to a wicked hot and slinky
113, and unless someone—or some*thing*—intentionally prevented her from doing so, she was damned sure going to reach
that goal, on her terms, in her way. And once she did, she was
never going to allow those pounds back on. Let the Big M.O.U.
suck on that.

The red light above the front door flashed three times.
Another customer. Working the front counter, Annabelle
pressed the little white button. *Starlight* had become significantly more popular, and profitable, and therefore also a target
for junkies and criminals looking to rip the place off. Which is
why Emma invested in a state-of-the-art security system that
instantly communicated with the local police station. Sergeant
Ortiz was a personal friend and one of her latest fuck buddies.
Yet security cameras, steel gates, three guns, and silent alarms
weren't enough.

Emma hired Aaron and Mack as on-site security to discour-
age idiotic decisions. The seasoned nightclub bouncers—who
doubled their earnings thanks to Emma—were beefy, quiet, and
ridiculously strong, and had dispensed many beat downs over
the years. The frequency decreased as their reputations grew,
but then, there was no accounting for the stupidity of others.

Aaron and Mack were also royal queens. Not with each
other, but queens for sure. Emma insisted upon it, to remove
any and all temptation for employer/employee hanky panky.
Been there done that. Aaron had a shaved head and five small
hoops in each ear, while Mack sported a black and gray ZZ Top-
style beard and a tattoo on his left arm depicting the cast of *Les
Miserables*, vampire style.

Emma scratched the underside of Lex's chin. "I'm going in
back. Need to check the receipts." She slipped into her office,

closed the door behind her, locked it. Inside the file cabinet were a series of folders. She set the Tuesday order forms on the desk blotter. But underneath the blotter itself, in a thin tie-string envelope, was a sheet of paper.

On that sheet was an image, one she had drawn over and over. She stared at it. Because as much as Emma had made a new life for herself on Earth, if ever the chance arose to get her hands on that jar—the one those pinheads Jason Medley and Theo Barnes so royally bungled up for her—she would finally . . . *finally* . . . get herself off this crap-ass planet and back home, to Eternity, where she most definitely belonged.

And if that day ever came, she was going to reclaim all that was hers. And never let go.

Chapter 7
The Chuck and Dooly

Jamie
Eternity

There was still no answer.

Jamie had called Lex every day since the Emma incident, and though it had only been a few weeks, in Eternity, that was practically a lifetime.

They all saw what happened. During the media event to unveil Emma's career-defining project—the Milky Way—she violated the most sacrosanct rule of galaxy design. She named a planet after herself. Within seconds of doing so, out on the Great Lawn, Emma vanished. Gone.

The Minder of the Universe saw to it, and immediately had the planet named—not re-renamed, but properly named—as he had originally decreed: *Earth*.

It was generally understood that Emma had been banished, because—even in Eternity—few alternatives seemed plausible under the circumstances. Where she ended up, in what form, or the severity of the predicament was unknown, but her disappearance was in all the papers.

But when it came to the media-gazing public, Emma's second in command—Lex—had been a nonstarter. It was all Emma all the time. As far as Lex was concerned, no one seemed to notice, or care. No one but Jamie.

She was hoping to stop by Lex's apartment, to see if her brother had finally turned up, but *The Rubicon Hotel* was doing great business. She couldn't get away from running the check-in desk. The night shift was always hectic.

"Hello, Mr. Abladeujé. Very nice to see you again. The usual suite?"

"Yes, please," the dapper gentleman replied. "It has quite a view."

Jacques Abladeujé, the President of Renolo Enterprises,

was one of the most influential executives in the galaxy design industry. Jacques was also a strategic business associate of the *Rubicon*'s primary owner, Brigsby, the famous talk-show host who had recently expanded his empire to include a magazine, restaurants, three clothing lines, cologne, and now, a hotel.

The *Rubicon* had a rainforest theme. The lobby was practically its own ecosystem, with multiple waterfalls, live trees, exotic flowers, and a cadre of birds flourishing among the various support beams, couches, chairs, and archways.

Though the daily room rate, by design, was inflated to keep out the riff-raff, Brigsby alone drew all manner of executives, celebrities, and their groupies. Brigsby, among all else, wanted the illusion that the *Rubicon* was a paradise for all—as long as you could find your way in.

A red-tailed parrot, with a blue streak on its forehead, flew overhead, and perched on the edge of the front desk.

"Here you are, Mr. Abladeujé." Jamie handed him a small device that acted as a keycard, and also operated all of the room's amenities, including lights, window shades, TV, sound system, and video phone. "Your room is—"

"Jacques." His voice was soft, calm. "I insist."

Jamie blushed. She had a weakness for sophisticated, older men, and Jacques Abladeujé was a temptation difficult to resist. Just two short years earlier she would have melted in his presence. But having greeted thousands of guests since then, she had become skilled at handling the various flirts, come-ons, and invitations from men and women alike, and could give as good as she got.

"Now, now, Mr. Abladeujé. You know I can't do that. But I'll tell you what." She leaned forward, slightly, so that her neckline—exposed thanks to her top two unfastened buttons—was just a bit more evident. Jamie was average height, with brown, wavy hair, green eyes, and a small nose. And what she may have lacked in breast size she more than made up for with a lithe, athletic figure, and an unconscious habit of gently puckering her lips, which kept them moist. "You enjoy a complimentary bottle of bubbly—which I'm having sent up to your room—and promise to think of me when your lips touch the glass. It'll be our little moment."

Jacques offered her the kind of smile that can only come from a man secure with himself. "You are quite a young woman, Jamie. My thanks. Perhaps we will have the opportunity some evening to enjoy one another's company in a more . . . familiar arrangement."

Behind the counter Jamie dug the point of her left shoe heel into her big right toe—and pressed hard—to smother her instinctive subjugation to his charming persistency. "Here you go, Mr. Abladeujé. Enjoy your stay."

Jamie's personal phone buzzed in her side pocket before she even had time to exhale. She didn't recognize the number. "Hello . . . ?" No response. "Hello. Who is—?"

"*Yeah.*" A nasally, growling voice. "*It's Chuck. The doorman.*"

"Uh . . . where? Here?"

"*Lady. Where's here? I'm at The Dooly. Downtown. By the pier.*"

"The Dooly . . . ? What's the . . . oh! Lex's building! Yes. Hi. Have you—?"

"*Yeah, listen, dollface. I got a package here for Lex, in 4K. He ain't been around, ya' know, and I can't hold this thing forever. I open doors and greet the guests. Like real classy. But I ain't nobody's personal thing-keeping guy, and he left your name on the list. You know, the . . .*" Jamie could hear him fumbling for the words—"*. . . the whatchmacallit? The emergency contact. Yeah. That's it. So, yeah. You gonna come get this thing or what?*"

"Uh . . ." Jamie took a quick survey of the lobby, hoping for a lull in the action. It was hectic for a Tuesday night. Rafi, her relief, was supposed to have been on the desk a half hour ago, but he got called upstairs to handle some private party on sixteen. "S-ssshhh . . . ure. I could come by—"

"*After midnight. Or tomorrow after eleven. I gotta lock this thing up. Can't be leavin' things sittin' out for whenever you feel like gettin' your butt over here. I got responsibilities, ya' know! Gets lost or stolen, management blames me. And that ain't happening.*"

"All right. I'll pick it up after midnight. About . . . twelve-thirty?"

"*Yeah. That'll do. And, hey. Dollface . . . ?*"

Jamie didn't like the direction of this exchange. ". . . Yes?"

"I seen your picture, ya' know, at Lex's place. You fix up pretty good. Whaddaya say . . . come on over, pick up this thing here, then I buy us a drink? Around the corner. At Oscar's. Got great clams. If you're inn'erested."

Overlooking the river, *The Dooly* was one of the newest luxury apartment towers downtown.

The rents were outrageous but the views were truly stupendous, especially at night. The lights reflected off the water shimmering in the darkness. Jamie had to hand it to Lex.

Her brother had a blind spot for gorgeous, sexually domineering women, and often ended up disappointed, used, or, as it was now beginning to appear, banished to somewhere in the Universe. But he knew how to pick an apartment.

Jamie only had an hour for dinner, and it took almost twenty minutes to get there, so she had to make it quick. Chuck the doorman was wiping down the front window.

"Heyyy. Will you look. At. That." He eyed her up and down. "You made it."

"Yeah," Jamie said. "I made it."

Like a boxer who had lost many fights—short and punchy with a crooked nose—Chuck retrieved the package from behind the counter. It was about the size of a shoe box, concealed in silver wrapping paper. He held out the package, but pulled it back before Jamie could take it. "So." He raised his eyebrows, grinned. "You think about my offer? Clams? Vino? Sparkling comma'sation? Eh? Eh . . . ?"

"Uh-huh . . . uh . . . huh . . . uh, you know, I'd love to"—Jamie looked at the nametag fastened on the breast pocket of his uniform—"Chuck. But I have to get back for the rest of my shift. I'm working a double."

"Oh, yeah, sure, a' course. Welcome to my world." Chuck handed over the package, but didn't let go, so that they both had a grip on it, extending the dialogue. "But you ain't gonna be workin' a double every night. Maybe t'morrow? Or the day after?"

Jamie needed to get the package and back to work. "Say . . .

Chuck." She encroached, pushing him back a step. "I meant to
ask . . . my boyfriend is just *dying* for an apartment in the building. He's filming a movie with Clyde Baxter and Yvette Simmons,
and needs a place for six months. Maybe a duplex with a wrap-
around balcony? You know any for rent? Anybody moving out?"

Chuck released the package like it was a leaky diaper. His smirk
disappeared. "Wouldn't know. Filled up. Long wait for newbies."

"Oh, well. Never hurts to ask." Jamie produced an extra set
of keys to Lex's apartment. "You mind if I head upstair—?"

A disco beat pulsed in Chuck's jacket pocket. He retrieved
the phone. "What?! . . . Ma. I know. Ma. Ma! . . . MA!" He
turned away, spoke with gritted teeth. "Not. Now. I'll call you
back. I'll call you back. I'll . . ."

Jamie jangled the keys. "Lex's place. Mind if I—?"

"Yeah, yeah. Just go. . . . No. Not you, Ma. Some annoying
broad with a stick up her . . ."

The first of two elevators opened just then. Jamie took full
advantage, pressed the button for Lex's floor. Once in the apartment, she set the box on the couch, and looked out the window. The moonlight bounced off the water. Sailboats and yachts
lined the marina.

She did a walkthrough. Kitchen, bedroom, bathroom. Her
brother's place was tidy and well furnished. But it was also
unmistakably quiet, as if Lex hadn't been there in weeks. A
home without an occupant.

On the glass coffee table was a framed picture. In it, Lex and
Jamie were standing side by side, wearing large, round wicker
hats, each making the peace sign in one hand, holding up a
giant glass of mango margarita in the other. Her birthday.

Jamie smiled, sat beside the box. She tore off the wrapping,
broke open the seal. Packing peanuts spilled out. Inside she discovered a small, cream-colored envelope, and a picture frame,
encased in bubble wrap. With a fingernail she sliced open the
envelope. A hand-written card. It read:

Dear Lex,
I have enjoyed our talks. I hope we get to do it again soon. You are an
interesting young man. I apologize for your long walk home. I thought

*you might want the time alone. Time to gaze into the night sky. I know
you have questions. Let's see what we can do about finding you some
answers. The future is just a dream. But is the dream really your future?*

Pop up for a drink. Room service is nice.

Toodles.

B-

In the picture, Lex was standing next to a man Jamie rec-
ognized immediately. Brigsby. The talk-show host. There was a
lipstick kiss mark on the glass.

My brother knows Brigsby? How does he know Brigsby?

But as Jamie thought about that relationship, maybe it wasn't
so surprising. Lex had that affable quality, adaptable to any social
situation, unbothered by crowds, lines, or velvet ropes. He didn't
see them as impediments. He simply ignored them.

Jamie held the envelope by its corner, flexed it open. *What
the . . . ?* A keycard fell out. She eased against the back of the
couch, breathed deeply, and thought of the note:

The future is just a dream. But is the dream really your future?

"Good question. Good . . ." Jamie sat up. Attentive. She
tapped the keycard on the arm of the couch.

*Lex would do it, wouldn't he? He would go right up there and just
take his chances. Yeah. I bet he would.*

Jamie liked to hang around the action—the thrill of proximity. But she wasn't much for jumping in the middle. Life gets
messy that way. After two years at the *Rubicon*, Jamie was still
a desk clerk instead of an assistant manager—for a reason. You
start taking on too much responsibility and others start expecting more of you.

But maybe I need my life to get messy. I damn well need something.

"Oh, hell. So Brigsby's one of the most powerful men in
Eternity. And he's the owner. I'll just let myself into his private
suite . . . unannounced . . . ask how he knows my brother, and
if he happens to know if Lex was also banished with Emma."
Jamie stood up, smoothed the wrinkles out of her blouse, and
nodded. "Sounds good, Jamie. An excellent plan. . . . What
could possibly go wrong?"

Chapter 8
Brother, Where Art Thou?

Jamie
Eternity

The elevator doors opened into Brigsby's penthouse suite.

Consisting of the *Rubicon's* entire top floor, and an extended balcony, no one except a private concierge team had access. Even for a luxury hotel, Jamie was impressed. But not for its extravagance.

She entered slowly, with delicate movements, as if the floor were a thin layer of ice that could easily crack, dropping her into frozen waters below. Into the abyss.

Across the main foyer, Brigsby was sipping a blue martini. Dressed in a red and white paisley motif, he sat on one of only two black leather couches. The furniture arrangement, such as it was, also included a coffee table, rolling bar, and flat screen TV. Otherwise, the living room was empty.

A taller gentleman in a light brown suit and holding a glass of Scotch stood by the wrap-around ceiling-to-floor window. The lights were dim against the dark of night. "Brigsby," he said. "She's here."

"Ah, yes. What a nice surprise."

Jamie ducked instinctively, despite the high ceiling. "It . . . it is?"

"Of course," Brigsby said. "Lex spoke of you often."

Starstruck, it took a moment for Jamie to accept exactly where she was—and why. "He was? He did? Oh, I . . . didn't know you even knew. . ."

"Ah. My manners. Jamie . . . Lawrence. Lawrence . . . Jamie. Lawrence is one of my . . . advisors, but mostly he just likes to boss me around. *Tch.* You're such a meanie." Lawrence gave a slight eye roll. "Oh, just a little teasing, Lawrence. Don't be such a Fussy McFusserson. And please . . . offer our guest a refreshment. Something cold."

Lawrence poured a blue martini. Jamie accepted the cocktail, still afraid that she might plummet through the ice. Gate crashers at the *Rubicon* were not treated well.

Through the large window, Jamie glimpsed the distant, elaborate swirl of the Andromeda galaxy. Swirling. Swirling. Purple around the outer edges, the inner swirls faded into magenta, finally spiraling into its black center—a funnel into the Universe. There was also a low, distant rumble, like a dragon waking from its long slumber. Some thought it to be the language of Eternity—the hum of all that ever was, is, or would be.

So Jamie drank. The tinge of alcohol hit her lips, setting off an inner alarm. *What am I doing here?! What am I doing? What am I . . . ?* She closed her eyes then, breathed in, gulped down the remainder of her drink in one throw. If she was *in*, she was going all in. *Lex would do it. He definitely would.* She exhaled deeply, and then wiped her mouth with her forearm. She sat opposite Brigsby.

Her host offered an impressed nod. "Might I ask? How did you even know to come here? How did you get in? I certainly don't make it easy. One must keep an air of mystery, don't you know? I have no intention of sounding like an elitist snob, but . . . I am rather fabulous." Brigsby flipped his wrist in mock jest. "Don't want to sully the experience by sharing it too often."

"I read the note to Lex," Jamie said. "With the picture you sent."

Brigsby looked to Lawrence. "And what picture might that be?"

"Of you. And Lex."

Silence. "We never took a picture. I rarely do."

Jamie shrugged. "Maybe. But I saw it."

"Oh, I'm sure you saw a photograph, my dear. Perhaps you saw twenty. I really don't know. But I can assure you, I've never been in a photograph with your—"

Jamie produced the photograph.

Lawrence intercepted it. He stared at the image, looked to Brigsby, and then back again at the photograph. "Where did you get this?"

Okay, Jamie thought. *I'm getting somewhere. Stay cool, stay cool.* "Chuck," she said.

"Chuck?" Lawrence handed the photograph to Brigsby. "Chuck who?"

"The doorman."

Lawrence and Brigsby were both at a loss.

"From *The Dooly*? Lex's building. Downtown. By the marina. There was a package for Lex. Chuck called me to get it."

Lawrence nodded suspiciously. "And you said something about a note. Do you have—"

Jamie held it out.

"Yes," Brigsby said. "I guess you do. May I?" He studied the note, and then handed it to Lawrence, who did the same. "What did he look like? This . . . Chuck?"

"Shortish, stocky. Broken nose. Kinda scrappy. Momma's boy."

Brigsby and Lawrence looked at each other, and sighed. They spoke in unison. "Milo."

Brigsby went to the window. He stared at the magnificent pinwheel, the magenta swirl of the Andromeda galaxy, and next to it, that permanent nothing.

Lawrence refilled his drink. "I think he's serious this time. We'll have to speed things up."

Jamie was almost afraid to ask. "Who's Milo?"

Brigsby pointed through the window. "I'm sure you're familiar with Milo's Smear?"

"You mean," Jamie began, stood up, and gestured toward the great distance, toward the most famous nothing in all of the Cosmos. "Milo? As in . . . disintegrated Milo? Got drunk on a work site and spilled his CBM jar into the Universe Milo? Wiped out an entire quadrant Milo?. . . *Milo* Milo?" The story of Milo was legendary.

"Yes," Brigsby said. "The same. He's been having a little fun at my expense. Causing all sorts of mayhem. He likes to send me messages. And in this case . . . you, my dear Jamie, are the messenger."

There was a rush to the head. Jamie's fear center began to howl, overcome with a sudden, intense compulsion to get the holy heck out of there—immediately—lest she never leave again. Busting in on Brigsby was one thing. But the return of Milo? Cosmic shenanigans? Uhh . . . no, thanks. She was just a hotel desk clerk, and despite any fleeting desire otherwise, she oh so very much wanted to keep it that way.

Jamie dashed to the elevator. The doors opened. But as she stepped across the threshold, to escape back into an inconsequential existence, she inexplicably found herself back in the foyer she had just left. The laws of physics as she knew them, even in Eternity, were not holding up with her life experience. "No, this doesn't . . ." She reached for the hall closet, opened the door. One step through and it again led to the foyer. Back to where she started.

Increasingly confounded, Jamie ran from room to room, door to door, each again leading her back to the very same place in time and space—the right here and right now, in front of Brigsby—that she was desperately trying to escape.

"Sit, dear. Relax." Brigsby handed her a drink. "You know what they say." He sipped his own. "No matter where you go . . . there you are. So why don't you take a load off? It'll be much easier on you. And, quite frankly, on me, too. You're making me dizzy."

Jamie dragged her feet across the floor, and took her seat beside Brigsby, who she now realized was a person with far more gravitas than she ever would have suspected. She squinted, looked at the talk show host, turned away, and then focused on him more completely. The grand creator.

"You're . . . him, right? You're the . . ." She choked on her words. They weren't easy to think, much less speak aloud. *I can't really say this . . . can I?* "The . . . B-b-b . . . Big M.O.U.? The Minder of the Universe?"

Brigsby nodded, offered a closed-mouth smile. "You're taking it quite well. Better than Lex."

"He vomited," Lawrence said. "Twice, if I recall."

"Yes. You know . . . I think you're right. But that could have also been the martinis . . ."

Brigsby offered his hand. Despite the remarkable power it possessed, his clasp was slight, fragile. He led Jamie to the window. "Do you see that flickering? Right there?"

Jamie squinted. She did see it. "Y-y-yes."

"Hmm. Interesting." Brigsby turned to Lawrence, then offered a troubled, curious nod Jamie couldn't decipher. "You are here for Lex, correct? You want to know if he's been banished, too. And if it was because of Emma."

She nodded.

"Well . . . he is, and it was. Although, technically, he volunteered. . . . Don't ask me why. It still baffles me, and as you might imagine, I do not baffle easily."

"Do you know . . . *where* they are?" Before Brigsby could answer, Jamie already knew. "Earth. That's it, isn't it? It's Earth. You sent them to Earth."

"Very good. Indeed, I did. But that flicker you see? That flux? That's our pal, Milo. That's his doing."

Jamie half shrugged. She accepted the premise, but couldn't grasp the significance.

"You know about the CBM jars, correct? And how they work?"

Jamie nodded again. All Eternitarians knew what they were and how they were used, but much like with the Minder of the Universe, they had no idea how, when, or from where CBM—Cosmic Building Material—originated. Nor did they want to know. Their blissful ignorance.

"Good. The CBM jar for Earth, well . . . for the entire galaxy, is down there on the planet. The actual jar, that is. Don't get me started. That's a whole other mishegoss, and a story for another day. But seeing as how the jar itself is down there, somewhere, it appears that Milo has found a way to open it, a jar that—by design—cannot be opened by anyone, in any way. Not without this." Brigsby offered a silver harmonic key which produced a sequence of high-frequency notes specific only to that one jar. "Nonetheless, now that the jar has leaked undiluted CBM, the Earth is fluxing in and out of its natural state."

Surprising herself and even a little bit impressed that she was able to comport herself with a minimal amount of calm, Jamie called upon her hotel training. *Don't be overwhelmed by your guests. Dignitaries, celebrities, or ordinary citizens. See them as equals. And equal to you.* "Okay. So? What's this all mean?"

"Yes! I thought you'd never ask! It means, my dear Jamie Jamie Bo Bamie, Banana Fama Fo Famie, that I need you to go down there for me—to Earth, that is—put a lid back on that pesky thing, and, in doing so, save my little planet. I know it's not much in the grand scheme of the Cosmos—the Universe *is* rather large—but I kinda like Earth. It has sentimental value."

"Wait. You want me to do what?"

Brigsby tapped the harmonic key in her hand. "Take some time off. And don't worry. I'll work it out with your boss." He winked. "All you need to do is track down the jar, blow into this key, and all will be well. And while you're down there, feel free to check in on Lex. You do that for me, and you'll be back here in no time. And when you return . . . my guess is that your station in life will be vastly elevated. You will have greeted your last guest."

"O-okay," Jamie mumbled, not really sure what else to say. ". . . I . . . guess . . . I . . ."

"Splendid! You might want to see a young fellow by the name of Theo Barnes. He seems to have a knack for this sort of thing. Anyway. Enjoy your trip."

"Wait! Theo who? What are you talking about?! How am I going to find—?"

There was a blast of white light. There were streaks of screaming fluorescent color. There was the sensation of being sucked through a tornado. And then there was sand. Lots and lots of sand.

Jamie was facing the ocean. There were only a handful of people on the beach, dressed in hats and jackets. The sky was cold and gray. The wind was strong.

Transported to this vast and distant land, she hugged herself, to keep warm, just knowing that she was, genuinely, on Earth, in the Universe, outside the realm of Eternity. Alone. Which meant that if she didn't find a way to help Brigsby, and do it soon, then one thing was for certain.

Finding Lex would be the least of her troubles.

Chapter 9
Little Buddha

Jason Medley
Brooklyn

The small, glass-blown Buddha gave him an odd look.

Jason picked the trinket off the bookcase, gave it some crinkle-eyed consideration. He bought Little Buddha from a street vendor on Canal Street in Chinatown a week before landing his first full-time reporter job, and when on the subway ride home he effectively sidestepped a shrieking catfight between a pair of scrawny teenage girls over which of the two was destined to become the next *American Idol*—um, neither—he took it as a good omen.

Little Buddha was pear green, eyes closed, with a slightly upturned smile. His hands were joined at the waist, palm to palm.

What are you trying to tell me, pal? If you've got something to say, now's the time.

Anna peeked through the living room window overlooking the street. Theo was due any minute. "Are you excited? You must be excited. Oh, my god! *I'm* excited!"

Jason twitched a little. Unable to sleep, he'd been up most of the night engaged in a *Star Trek: The Next Generation* marathon on SpikeTV, and now that morning had finally come he was thinking: *Holy crap he's coming he's coming it's gonna be so freakin' awesome I can't believe it's been three years since I've seen him we're gonna have the best time ever so look out world here we come you can't believe how much fun we're gonna have you have no idea what we've been through already so WOO HOO! HOLY CRAP! YEAH BABY!*

But what he actually said was: "Yeah. You know. . . . It's cool."

Anna smirked. "Uh-huh. Cool. Okay. So . . . do you want to wait for him up here or are you going to hide in the bushes and then tackle him in the street when the cab pulls up?"

That would actually be awesome if I jumped out and surprised him like that, but . . .

"Don't worry. I'm under control. I'm good."

Sensing that he might have misjudged Little Buddha, Jason nodded, and then rubbed the trinket's belly with his thumb.

Okay, okay. Sorry about that. It's possible that I'm a little worked up.

His sight line then drew to a streak of sunshine inching its way across the floor. And as it finally crossed from the living room to the kitchen, the sound of a closing car door sent Jason into a nervous spasm.

He's here!

Anna kissed his cheek. "Show time, tiger. Go get 'em."

Trying not to trip over his feet down the hallway stairs, Jason barreled to the front door of the apartment building. But then he stopped, composed himself. He didn't want to seem eager. That would have been lame. He squeezed Little Buddha. Tight.

Shut up. Don't judge me.

Jason pushed the door open. And as he stepped into the daylight—exiting one reality and entering another—the sun was strong on his face. He tried to hold back a smile, but was beaming nonetheless. "Hey, there, ya' maniac. Great to see you."

Jason hugged his friend, and as he patted Theo's back, he instinctively braced himself for a jolt—a crackle of otherworld electricity—an intense sensation that would somehow reset his karmic coordinates along the space-time continuum. Jason had been having some of those lost moments lately—at least he thought so—and through pure muscle memory intuited that making physical contact with Theo would somehow trigger another one. It didn't happen.

Certain the *BZZT!* was still coming, Jason clenched his eyes, bracing for impact. Which left him hugging Theo longer and harder than he intended, face buried in his friend's shoulder.

But when after a time no psychedelic transmogrification had overtaken them, Jason realized that his embrace was probably getting awkward. "Um, yeah, so . . . I'm gonna let go now." He stepped back, smiled, took Theo's rucksack. "Good flight?"

Theo chuckled. "Yeh-yeh. The usual."

Jason immediately exhaled, comforted by Theo's soft, mumbling cadence, with a tone, rhythm, and inflection that to Jason's untrained ear was a quasi-hybrid of the Australians, Brits, and native Maori.

That's all I needed to hear.

Anna greeted them on the sidewalk. She whispered to Jason, "smooth." Then she hugged Theo. "Oh, my god. So nice to see you again. It's been so long."

Up in the apartment, Jason placed Theo's rucksack on the couch. Simon rubbed against Theo's ankle, and started to purr. Already Jason felt that their home was fuller. Warmer.

"He can't wait for his next trip to New Zealand," Anna said. "He always talks about it."

"Oh, stop. I do not."

"Don't listen to him. He's just being shy. You made quite an impression."

"Yeh-yeh. Lea says the same about him."

"Well, there you go. Are you hungry? Thirsty? Tired? It's such a long trip."

"I could go for a feed."

"*Go for a feed.* I love that! That's so Kiwi of you, although, I really have no idea what that means! Ha. Listen to me. So . . . I'll slow down. Theo. What do you think? Go out? Order in? You're the guest."

"Yeh. I dunno. Wouldn't mind stretching my legs a bit."

"Of course. What am I thinking? Oh! I know. Let's go to the German beer garden. We'll get the Wiener Schnitzel. It's sooo good."

As Theo and Anna chatted amongst themselves, Jason realized why he'd been anxious to see Theo again. He was afraid that he might have romanticized their time together in Europe and New Zealand, and that they would never be able to recapture the magic of their transcendental misadventures. That the legitimate distractions of distance, time zones, and the daily churn of their individual lives away from one another were all that had really kept the mystery alive. That their friendship had been chugging along on the fumes of the past rather than the propulsive fuel of the present and future. That any new shared experiences would fall far short of his memories.

Watching Theo and Anna he could see that wasn't the case. For all of Jason's protests to the contrary, he knew Hank was right. That the root of his anxieties was just good, old-fashioned cold feet. He wanted Theo to see Anna again, spend some time with her, and then tell Jason that he was doing the right thing. Jason had no doubts that he loved Anna and that she was equally devoted to him. But he wanted Theo's stamp of approval. From his partner in all things bizarre and unexplainable, Jason wanted, of all things, a reality check.

That's all it was, Jason thought, and rubbed Little Buddha again. *Yeah. That's all it . . .*

And then, suddenly, there was a blast of white light. There were streaks of screaming fluorescent color. There was the sensation of being sucked through a tornado.

And there were video games. Lots and lots of video games.

Theo

Barcade was pinging and chirping.

Q*bert. Donkey Kong. Donkey Kong Jr., Tetris, Joust. Ms. Pac-Man, Tutankham. The Union Avenue bar in the Williamsburg section of Brooklyn wasn't crowded, but it was only 2 p.m. on a Tuesday, so that wasn't much of a surprise.

Beer in hand, Theo sidled up to an *Asteroids* machine. He hadn't seen one in ages. Jason was next to him, going full tilt on *Galaga*, while Anna was eight machines down, engaged in an epic *Centipede* run. Two guys were shooting pool nearby. The bartender inspected a beer supply order form, secured to a clipboard.

Theo inserted his change, and then *tap-tap-tapped* on the white *Asteroids* button, blasting those space rocks into glowing debris. Before the new screen reset he looked around, studied the menu on the slate wall—dozens of beers written in blue, yellow, and orange chalk—and couldn't remember how he got there. He had just come off the plane at JFK Airport, wondering if he'd be able to get a cab, and then his phone vibrated. A text from Roger, although he couldn't remember the message.

And before Theo could annihilate another electronic space

rock there was a blast of white light. There were streaks of screaming fluorescent color. There was the sensation of being sucked through a tornado. And there were bicycles. Lots and lots of bicycles.

The view from the Brooklyn Bridge was everything Jason said it was. The sun sparkled off the East River. Pedestrians and bicyclists filled the pathways in both directions. To the west was the Lower Manhattan skyline, even grander than Theo had anticipated. And then he paused, gazing between the skyscrapers, at the space where the Twin Towers once stood, where the citizens of the globe awaited the new glass skyscraper to rise at the World Trade Center site, restoring balance and fortitude to a world whose tenor had changed irrevocably.

"This is where I want to do it," Jason said, of his pending marriage proposal. "Right here. Just hand her the ring."

"Oh, yeh? That would be choice. That would be . . ."

There was a blast of white light. There were streaks of screaming fluorescent color. There was the sensation of being sucked through a tornado. And there was traffic. Lots and lots of traffic.

Theo rubbed his eyes. After thirty-four hours of travel in tight quarters he expected to be a little cranky. Over the years he'd been across much of the world, but never to the United States. Never to New York. He couldn't see the famous Manhattan skyline from where he was. Not yet. But the cabbie said to wait. It would be coming soon.

What was I just thinking about? Didn't Roger want to tell me about . . . what was it? Or was I going to tell him? Or was it Jason? Hell. I dunno. Maybe the twins again. I hope they're not driving Lea insane. But better her than me, I guess. Lea's got the touch. Oh . . . who am I kidding? She makes it all work. She's the backbone to our mad little family. Lea and my mum, and Carla, too. But me? Roger? My dad? We do okay . . . kinda. Or do we?

There was another blast of white light. There were streaks of screaming fluorescent color. There was the sensation of being sucked through a tornado. And then there was purring. Lots and lots of purring.

Theo was sitting on the couch, Simon in his lap. Anna was

at the table, finishing off a kebob. Jason cleared the dishes.

Anna wiped her mouth with a napkin. "So . . . how are your little ones? Are they just running around like crazy? Playing *Hide-and-Go-Seek?*"

You don't know the half of it.

"Hope's the mellow one, yeh? But Tess? She's got two speeds. Full throttle and sleeping. If Bart Simpson has a smarter, sister clone somewhere, it's Tess. She's always up to something. Of course, my dad loves it. I was the same way. Not as many brains, but you get what I mean. My dad calls 'em the Rascals."

Jason came back with a dishrag sticking out of his pocket. "Listen to this guy. Goes three years without a trip around the world and makes it seem like he's been in the dungeon. Although I guess for you, maybe you have."

"Hey," Anna said. "Don't get all boo-hoo-hoo on us. You've had quite a few adventures yourself, mister-I-can't-come-back-to-New-York-yet-I'm-actually-heading-to-New-Zealand-for-a-few-weeks-before-I-come-home." She kissed Jason on the cheek. "Speaking of adventures . . . I'm sure you two are up to no good. So I'll clean up and get out of your way. But, Theo . . . before you go . . . you might want to check in with Lea and see how she's holding up with those Rascals of yours. Who knows what kind of mischief they're getting into now."

Chapter 10
Suspicious Minds

Jamie
Piha Beach, New Zealand

Wow, Jamie thought as waves rolled in off the shore. *I am so not ready for this.*

Covered in goose bumps, she had no idea where she was. But accustomed to that hotel eye-in-the-sky surveillance camera watching her every move, she instinctively looked to the heavens, and assumed that someone—Brigsby, in this case, or, as she recently discovered, the Minder of the Universe—was studying her on a monitor somewhere safe and warm and sipping a blue martini, while she was down there, on Earth, freezing her butt off, with no specific path for her to follow. No protocol.

There was an unreality to her experience. Sure, she was on Earth, alone, outside the realm of Eternity. And yes, she was stranded—on the planet of Emma's design, no less—until or unless she successfully recovered Brigsby's missing CBM jar.

A jar filled with a batch of the Universe's liquid DNA, modified specially for the creation of the Milky Way. The very jar causing Earth to short circuit to the point where the planet might just permanently blow its fuse.

And Brigsby didn't want that because, well, he thought Earth was *cute.*

Jamie did not consider herself to be a particularly complicated Eternitarian. Just a young woman with a messy apartment, a middling fear-attraction complex toward older men, and enough self-awareness to know that she wasn't half as ambitious as she probably should have been, and was willing to accept far less than she desired as long as it meant avoiding major confrontations or having to make big decisions and then be responsible for the outcome.

She saw herself as a reliable though unspectacular worker bee, content for her life to continue in that general direction.

And a nice (but also tiny bit naughty), good-looking, well-adjusted, financially secure boyfriend with a firm tush wouldn't have been totally uncalled for.

But the day prior she was working the *Rubicon* check-in desk and now she was running errands for the Minder of the Universe, who, doubling as Eternity's top-rated day-time talk show host, was in the midst of what appeared to be a recurring, petty game of one-upmanship with the infamous Milo. And more than just gossip recounted at parties, Milo also appeared to be Brigsby's eternal foil—a cosmic gremlin whose sole purpose was to muck up the fabric of the Universe at the Big M.O.U.'s expense because, hey, that's what cosmic gremlins do.

Jamie wasn't being intentionally obstinate, but she was having just a wee difficult time accepting her predicament.

Come on. Really? Me? Seriously? Why would the Minder of the Universe waste his time with me? I mean, yeah, sure, my brother got himself mixed up with that selfish wench, Emma, and I suppose there's a tangential connection there if you really look for it. But there has to be an easier way for the Big M.O.U. to get some resolution here, right? Because if I'm really his best option—me, Jamie, queen of the scavenger hunt, and funk parties, competent at much, the best at nothing—then the Minder of the Universe is outta luck. Or lazy. Or drunk. Or delirious. Or mentally ill. Or all of the above. But . . . no! Wait! Forget I said that. Forget I thought that! Can he read my mind? Can he? Can you? . . . Are you listening? Are you there? Are you in my mind right now? Are you . . . ? I mean . . . oh, I so want to be in my bed right now under the covers hugging my stuffed giraffe. I miss my Ralphie. He's always there for me. Hide me, Ralphie. Hide me.

Lex was really gone, though, and Jamie was really on Earth. She just didn't want it to be so. And yet, maybe she did.

A stiff breeze refocused her, and though she wasn't large-breasted, her nipples were, for reasons she never understood, particularly sensitive to the wind. So, naturally, of all moments, they were now poking through her blouse. And between the narrow valley of her chest dangled her harmonic key—her way back to Eternity, when the time came—fastened along a silver chain.

Jamie hugged herself again, to keep warm, and conceal her

possession, when she noticed two small girls—one with pig-tails, one without—running in the sand, giggling. Unlike Jamie, they were both dressed appropriately for the weather: cargo pants, windbreaker, and scarf. Their sneakers flashed with little lights—blue for pigtails, pink for no pigtails. Each girl was hold-ing a small, plastic jar of bubbles and a plastic wand.

"Hi, there," Jamie said, rubbing her arms. "What's your name?"

"I'm Razzle," pigtails said. "Hope."

"I'm Dazzle," no pigtails said. "Tess."

"Ha. Razzle Dazzle. You must be twins. How cute. I'm Jamie." She pointed to the young couple coming their way, also dressed for the weather. "Um . . . who are they?"

"That's Uncle Roger," Hope said.

"Yeh-yeh," Tess said. "And Carla. That's his girlfriend. She's really nice. And smart. Mum says she makes Uncle Roger be less of a dumbass." She giggled again. "But he's nice, too."

Jamie nodded. "I like your sneakers. The lights are so cool."

"Thanks," Hope said. "I picked them out."

"Did not," Tess said.

"Did so!"

"Did not."

"Did so.

"Did. NOT!"

"DID! SO!"

The twins' escalating banter drew the attention of Roger and Carla.

Jamie nodded to them.

"Well, well, well," said Roger, tall, skinny, with short-cropped hair and a thin spike down the center. "Aren't you a babe?"

Carla—shorter, blonde, curvy—shook her head. "Don't mind him. He's just posturing. You know? Boys."

"Yes," Jamie said with a sigh. "Yes, I do. Um. So . . . Razzle and Dazzle are just a couple of peaches, aren't they?" She smiled at the twins, who shrugged coyly. "This might sound like an odd question but . . . I'm looking for someone. Maybe you can help me?"

"Yeh, I dunno," Carla said. "I'll try."

"It's one of those I-know-a-guy-who-knows-a-guy-who-says-he-knows-another-guy kind of things, but I'm hoping to find . . . Theo Barnes . . . ? Is that right? Name sound familiar?"

Roger and Carla both immediately frowned, inched closer together, in solidarity, then offered matching looks of suspicion.

Okay, Jamie thought. *They know something.*

"Why?" Roger said.

"Yeh," Carla said, a lot less friendly than just a moment earlier. "Why?"

"I'm looking for my brother. We got separated a while back. Theo might know where he is. I think so, anyway."

Roger raised an eye. "Who's your brother?"

"Lex. About my age, dark hair, trim. Scruff on his chin. Nice guy, but chases the wrong women."

"Sorry, luv. Doesn't ring a bell."

"Ruff-ruff," Hope said.

"Ruff-ruff," Tess said.

The twins repeated the barking, then again, in one voice. "Ruff-ruff-ruff." Jamie wasn't sure what they meant, but it felt like a sincere response to her plight.

Roger looked to Carla. "Oh, not this again."

Not being of their culture, planet, or even their plane of existence, Jamie wasn't sure how to interpret the exchange. "Not what?"

Carla gave a restrained eye-roll. "He's a good uncle, but not always a patient lot when it comes to supervising the children. I'm still working on him."

"Yeah. Good luck with that. So? Theo? Can you help? I really want to find my brother."

"He went to see the turtles," Hope said.

"Yeh-yeh," Tess said. "Big turtles. Little turtles. Wots and wots 'a turtles."

Jamie looked to Roger and Carla. "Turtles? Any idea what they're talking about?"

Roger shook his head with a look of continued annoyance. "They've been yammering on about Turtle Bay, off by the Waipoua Forest. Theo buzzed out there last week. But he's long gone."

Frustrated, Jamie comported herself. "Where's he now?"

"Not sure. Off to the States, last he said. I dunno. Crazy fucker takes off like this all the time, although not since this lot showed up." He pointed at the twins. "First trip away by himself in ages. Though knowing him, he'll hook up with Jason. The Yank. Sometimes I think those two wanna bugger each other. I bet they're donkey deep in it right now." Roger shrugged. "Eh. But what the fuck are you gonna do about it?"

The States. Okay. I don't know what that means.

Roger pressed the issue. "How do you know Theo? I know all his mates. I never heard of you."

"We never met, actually. But I think my brother knows him."

"Yeh. You said. But how? I never heard Theo say anything about a Lex."

"Yeah." *Think quick, think quick.* "I think . . . they . . . met . . . on . . ." *Travel, travel, Roger said he likes to travel.* ". . . one of his trips? Yeah. I'm pretty sure that's what it was. Lex . . . has . . . the . . . travel bug, too. And he's pretty chatty! He meets all kinds of people."

Jamie waited for a response. She feared she'd said too much, that the more she talked the less convincing she sounded. So she held herself in place, afraid she might disrupt the spell she was trying to cast. She could see Roger mulling her story over in his mind, his eyes drawn close, his forehead ridged.

The twins sidled up to Carla, and hugged her leg, one on each side.

And they all waited. And waited. And waited.

The silence made Jamie nervous, as if another grain of her fragile lie fell to the sand with each passing second, exposing her weakness. Exposing her. She knew that she should hold on, to let the story settle, and wait for Roger to speak. The first one to break . . . loses. But she couldn't take it anymore. She had to fill the space, fill the void. She had to say *something*.

"Any idea where he might be now? I hate to be rude, but I'm kinda freezing here. Forgot my jacket. It's a long story."

Please be okay with it please be okay with it please be okay with it please be . . .

"Fucked if I know," Roger said finally. "He doesn't exactly

keep an online diary. I hardly ever know where he is. He doesn't tell anybody."

Oh, yes, thank you.

With raised eyebrows, Carla gestured to Roger's hand. To his phone.

"Um, right, 'kay. I could text him if you like, yeh? But he never answers the damn thing. Theo's kind of a techno boob. Not sure he can even spell, let alone turn his phone on."

"Yeah. Okay. Maybe." Jamie thought a moment. "Any other way to reach him?"

What's wrong with you boneheads? Why is everything so slow down here? Why is this so hard?

Razzle then tugged on Jamie's shirt. Dazzle offered her a postcard.

"What's this?"

"Look," the twins said simultaneously. "Look."

Set against a black background, the phrase *GenderBender* stretched across the top of the postcard. Beneath it was the image of an Asian drag queen, in a red, sequined dress, high heels, and a black wig with long curls. Also in the background, against the black, were a peppering of stars and the magenta swirl of what appeared to be the Andromeda galaxy.

Hope and Tess started blowing bubbles. For two small children they seemed to produce an extraordinary display, like an entire field of dandelion petals set loose in the breeze.

"Okay. What am I looking at? I don't get . . ." Jamie wasn't immediately sure what was happening, but amidst the bubble barrage the galaxy on the postcard started to swirl. It was slow at first, and then faster, faster, faster-faster-faster until it swallowed all of the stars. Jamie then felt the beach dissolve beneath her feet.

"*Turtlesszz,*" the twins said as they faded before her, disappearing within the bubbles. "*Visit the turtlesszz.*"

"What turtles?" Jamie said. "What tur—"

There was a blast of white light. There were streaks of screaming fluorescent color. There was the sensation of being sucked through a tornado. And there were, she now saw, turtles. Lots and lots of turtles.

Face up against a glass pane, Jamie was barely separated from the shelled reptiles, who where swimming through water, and lounging on rocks. She looked around. A sign above an archway said: *Coney Island Aquarium.*

"Yep," she said. "I totally had that coming."

Chapter 11
You're Not Really Going To Get on That Thing, Are You?

Jason and Theo
Brooklyn

He wanted to ralph.

Two full-length *Nathan's* hot dogs and a full order of french fries down and Jason was in bad shape. Theo, meanwhile, was ready for more. They sat on a bench along the Coney Island boardwalk, in the shadow of the *Cyclone*. The first ride of the day had not yet begun.

Overlooking the Atlantic Ocean, with Staten Island across the way and the beach filling up like a carnival side show, Jason couldn't help but smile. He slurped a soda. The carbonation gave him a jolt. "Remember the first time we did this? Just staring at the water?"

Theo nodded, chomping on the last of his hot dog.

"We were in Venice. We'd only known each other for what, like, an hour? But there we were, watching the bikinis go by, eating gelato. It was so good."

"Yeh-yeh," Theo said in his soft mumbling cadence. "Went back for seconds."

"That's right. We did! I forgot about that." Since returning from his first trip overseas, that time away had increasingly felt for Jason like a happy, elliptical dream. But the experience had been far more significant. Whereas the ends of some journeys can inspire loneliness or depression—*the glory days have already passed me by* syndrome—to Jason, his had very much propelled a new beginning. "Man, we covered a lot of ground back then. Now look at us. You've got kids, and I'm finally writing, and about to propose." Jason shook his head. "What a life, huh? What a life."

Theo wiped mustard off his face. He let out a satisfied sigh.

Four kites fluttered overhead. Nearby, a little girl in a yellow one-piece bathing suit sat in the sand, crying. Jason wasn't sure why. And though the sun was warm, and his belly was full, those toddler tears gave him pause. His possible future. He turned to Theo.

"Can I ask . . . ? I know you didn't plan to have a family so soon. Hell, maybe ever!" Jason elbowed playfully at Theo, to retract himself from his own potential for fatherhood. He squinted at the sun. "I mean, I love your Rascals. They crack me up. But I'm not there, right in the middle of it. I just have no idea what it really means to carry that responsibility every day. The struggle, the pressure. Is it like they say? That raising kids is the best and the hardest thing you'll ever do? I know it must be stressful, but . . . is it *that* difficult?"

Theo turned from the ocean, then shifted uncomfortably. "Yeh, I dunno. It's . . . the twins, yeh? They're wicked smart and give me a hard time. I mean . . . I love 'em to bits. I can't imagine my life without 'em." He looked away, and then back. "I know you're not supposed to say it, but . . . sometimes I just want to run off, ya' know? Take another year. Two years. Just jump back on the trains and go to China. Or South America. Backpack again. Like I used to. I know I can't, yeh? That time is over. I do get away, sometimes. Last year I took the four of us to Fiji and the South Island of New Zealand. But it's not like before, when it was just me, and I could pack up and leave everything behind. But, yeh, it's like you said. The best and the toughest."

Jason nodded. "I keep thinking what it would be like, if I had kids. Anna will be an amazing mom. And it's easy to think about all the fun stuff. Building LEGO towers, taking them to the beach," he said, pointing at the sand. "Tossing the ball around and watching those great animated movies they have now. *The Iron Giant* is like my favorite movie ever. But I see some of my friends with kids . . . and they're *always* exhausted. Always. And totally stressed out. Their bodies ache. They're broke. They all love their kids, of course, but . . . I don't know. I just wonder if I'm cut out for it. I don't want to mess it up. I don't want to be a bad dad."

"You won't."

On some level Jason knew that he was fishing for a compliment, for reassurance, but the immediacy of Theo's response genuinely surprised him. "How do you know?"

Theo grinned. "Some guys are *born* to be dads. And some guys just *become* dads. Me? It just happened. But you? It's who you are, yeh? You should be a dad. Be a shame otherwise."

Jason tried to retract a smile. It didn't work.

"But my twins? They've got this other thing, yeh?" Theo looked about, then rolled his shoulders. "The Razzle Dazzle they do."

"What Razzle Dazzle? Is that a game or something?"

Theo sighed again, mumbled. "Yeh. I dunno."

Jason knew that look. Theo had something important to say. Something mysterious and bizarre that could only come from Theo, and mean something that couldn't possibly be true in the same way for anyone else. He just wasn't ready to say what it was.

But before Theo could elaborate, the Coney Island park operators unleashed the *Cyclone*. Lines formed around the famed rollercoaster.

Pulled from Theo, Jason suddenly became anxious. Staring at the trestles, he thought they looked rickety. As in dangerous and unstable. Screams from the first batch of riders didn't help.

Especially for someone who had a legitimate medical inner ear condition that triggered a vertigo-inducing fear of heights. Jason was, in an intense, tangible fashion, terrified of the 85-year-old rollercoaster, which he assessed as being one clack away from collapsing.

There was a huge sign: *LAST WARNING – REMAIN SEATED AND HOLD HAND BARS AT ALL TIMES.*

Theo gestured to the beast, signifying that he was ready to take his turn.

Jason was less enthused. Having kids was one kind of rollercoaster fear. Riding the *Cyclone* was quite another. "You're not really going to get on that thing, are you?"

Theo stuffed another french fry into his mouth. He nodded. "Oh, yeh. Definitely."

Noticing Jason's hesitancy, one of the ticket takers chimed

in. His name tag said: *Hi, I'm Barney.* "You guys wanna thrill?"

"Uh, not really, no," Jason said. "I'm good."

"Sure, you are. Listen guys. You like rollercoasters, *Cyclone*'s the best. Check it out." Barney went on to explain—as the Coney Island ticket takers had for decades—the legend of Emilio Franco. A coal worker from West Virginia, Emilio was rumored to have been stronger and tougher than his five best friends combined. He had also been mute since childhood. No one knew why. "But he comes to Coney Island in 1948, gets on the *Cyclone*, thinks it'll be a hoot. But then those first few clacks on the track start creeping in—*clack, clack, clack*—and then big tough ole Emilio's gettin' nervous. It's eighty-five feet high up there."

Jason craned his head, to take in the zenith. The peak was not reassuring.

"And then," Barney continued, "once Emilio's at the top, there's this pause, ya' know? The cars sit there. And for just a second—the view really is incredible, he's just watchin' every-body down on the boardwalk—and he's thinking he's totally fine, he's totally safe, it's all good. And then . . . WHAM-O! Cars drop 60 degrees at 60 miles an hour and Emilio's crapping his pants. Rumor has it, when the ride was over, he stumbled off, and for the first time in his whole life . . . a guy who's been mute since birth, never said a word . . . he speaks! Know what he said? He said, 'I feel sick.' " Bill puffed out his chest with *Cyclone* pride. "Now *that*, my friends, is a rollercoaster." He slapped his hands together. "Okay. Who's in?"

Wide-eyed, Theo turned to Jason. "I am. You coming?"

"Oh, hell no." Even after all they'd been through together, Jason never mentioned the car accident, or the psycho/spiritual toll it had taken on him. He lived with it, but wasn't really over it. "You are *never* getting me on that—"

A tingling erupted. He'd felt it before. There was a blast of white light. There were streaks of screaming fluorescent color. There was the sensation of being sucked through a tornado. And then there were clacks. Lots and lots of clacks.

Cyclone. Front car.

Theo grinned with demented rollercoaster glee. But unsure

how he got there, or why, Jason clung to that metal car as if it was exactly what it was—a half-cocoon of safety, and possible implement of doom.

Roaring around the nearly century-old tracks, Jason felt his gut wedge between his lungs and esophagus. His head throttled back and forth at the turn toward the peak incline. Like a carsick dog he was practically drooling on himself.

Certain he was going to plummet to his death—and a grisly death at that—Jason breathed Lamaze-style, to control the panic, when he had a moment of clarity. Even though he and Theo hadn't been together in years—and Jason, generally speaking, kept his shit together now far better than he ever did before—they were already back in their old rhythm.

Theo was again embracing a new experience while Jason resisted one he would never have entertained on his own, instinctively fearful of some undefined boogeyman that lingered in the ether. Although in this case he felt that his terror was well justified, given that three people had actually died in accidents on the *Cyclone.*

Still, roaring at mortality-snubbing speeds Jason decided then and there that it was time—metaphorically speaking—to relinquish his grip. He was incapable of altering the experience until either the car returned to its safe haven at ground level, or the tracks gave way and he went flying onto a pretzel stand below. So while Jason didn't suddenly enjoy being throttled about, he hated it just a little bit less, and given his predicament, he took that internal shift as a personal victory over one of his emotional and psychological trapdoors.

Jason hadn't realized until then just how much Theo enjoyed these kinds of thrills, how anyone could. But maybe, Jason thought, some people—like Theo—were just innately primed to embrace them, and some people—like him—just weren't.

Regardless, Jason was going to look over at Theo, and force out a smile, to prove that he not only could deal with but even welcome the wild and unknown, when the tingling returned. And as he suspected was beginning to occur with regularity, he experienced yet another blast of white light.

There were streaks of screaming fluorescent color. There

was the sensation of being sucked through a tornado. And there were dolphins. Lots and lots of dolphins.

The elegant mammals dove through hoops, rewarded with whole fish. They swam in a synchronized routine. Sitting among the crowd at the Coney Island Aquarium, although with just a vague memory of how he got there, Jason laughed and applauded, covered in water, splashed from the tank. But he could see that Theo wasn't enthusiastic. If anything, he actually looked puzzled.

"Hey. You okay? This is awesome. Those dolphins are great."

"Uh . . . yeh. It's just . . . dolphins. I don't trust them. They're up to no . . ." Theo shook his head. "Never mind."

"Oh, come on, Theo. This is the best part." Just as Jason was about to extend his hand, to reach out toward the dolphins in a gesture of applause, he felt a tap on the shoulder. He turned around. An attractive young woman smiled at him. She wore a light blue t-shirt that said: *I Had a Splash at Coney Island.*

"Sorry," she said. "Did you just call him Theo?"

Jason was sitting in the stands. He knew that. Yet he distinctly remembered meeting Theo at the airport the night before, taking the subway to his apartment, and then eating . . . hot dogs? Or did they come straight to the aquarium? It was all a bit hazy.

Think, bungle brain. Think! Airport, Theo. Airport, Theo. Apartment. . . ? Maybe . . . ? Oh, crud. Why can't I remember? Why can't I . . . ?

And then the young woman tapped Theo's shoulder. "Are you Theo Barnes?"

Theo's eyes popped open, projecting his full attention. "Yeh," he said. "Yeh-yeh."

"Ah. Coolio. Any chance I can get a word with you two?"

Another dolphin splash soaked them all.

Had he just let the moment be, Jason likely would have fallen under her sexy, wet-haired, wet-t-shirted spell. But already he didn't like this girl. Not one bit.

She shook the water off her hands and face. "Well, I'd say we're already in this together, then. I'm Jamie."

"Theo," Theo said, and extended his hand like a toddler

crushing on his teacher. "But . . . you . . . already knew that. Yeh? So . . . uh . . ."

"And you must be Jason."

Jason also wiped tank water from his face. The draw of his hand—quick, precise—had an edge to it. So did his response. "Yeah, I guess I must be. So . . . *Jamie*. How *do* you know his name? How did you find us, exactly?"

"Oh, right. Sorry." She focused on Theo. "Your brother. Roger. He told me you'd be in New York. I ran into him at Piha Beach. It's a long story. My friend flaked out on me, as usual, so I'm flying solo. Anyway, Roger said that you're always game for an adventure, and the two of you were probably up to something—I think he said *a few logs short of a Barbie*—although I'm not really sure what that is."

Theo readily accepted her story—his dopey grin said it all. But Jason wasn't buying it. Something wasn't right. He was about to shift into hardcore reporter mode, to inquire further, but Jamie got ahead of him.

"So whaddaya say, boys? I'm new in town with absolutely no place to be. Who wants to buy me a drink?"

Chapter 12
Be Good or Be Gone!

Jason
Manhattan

Light and dark.

Those were the only two beers on draft. New York City's oldest Irish pub, *McSorley's Old Ale House* opened in 1854, and still held the rustic look from its earliest days, back when it was a men's only joint. Located on East 7th Street near Cooper Square, *McSorley's* was certainly convenient enough, just a few blocks from Jason's office, and the beer was actually pretty good.

But Jason's pal Kevin—who was obsessed with all things New York City—had dragged him there ad nauseam, never passing up a chance to educate anyone and everyone who would listen about the watering hole's significance in the greater context of the city's storied evolution.

And lest Jason protest, Kevin liked to remind him—also ad nauseam—that he shouldn't hold grudges about *McSorley's* just because some girl he chatted up there once left with a taller, more handsome, better-dressed guy who also probably made a lot more money.

Yet Jason had texted Kevin that he was heading into Manhattan for beers, because for all of Kevin's lies and propaganda, he had a great instinct for people, and Jason wanted to get his take on Jamie. Wanted his mistrust validated.

So once again, *McSorley's* it was. As usual, it was crowded.

"Oh, I like this place," Jamie said.

"Yeh-yeh," Theo immediately agreed.

Jason was already annoyed. He wasn't buying Jamie's story—she was up to something—and was particularly surprised that Theo wasn't also suspicious, as he was naturally suspicious of anyone he didn't know. Not to mention that Theo had flown halfway around the world—just to see *him*—exactly because they'd both had even greater suspicions about whether the trouble they'd gotten into once before had resurfaced. And Theo didn't get into *regular* trouble.

Uh, hello. Don't you remember being chased around Europe because of that damn jar of yours? Your house being practically ransacked at gunpoint? Your dad firing up the helicopter? Your brother hunted by a biker gang?

Fair or not, Jason also had a tinge of moral indignation. Theo, a practically married father of twins, was obviously—and shamefully—smitten by this young woman, this stranger who just rolled into their lives, as if she had materialized out of thin air. Which, in fact, she had.

"J-Man! Beer me!"

Kevin burst into *McSorley's*, waved a fifty dollar bill, which then drew the attention of the surly, white-haired bartender, who quickly delivered eight short mugs of ale, four each of light and dark. Already acting as host, Kevin passed around the beers. He pointed above the bar to a long, secured string. On it were wishbones, covered in dust an inch thick.

"They're from World War I. Soldiers hung them before they got shipped out. If the bones are still up there, it means they never came back."

Not intending any disrespect toward the somber subject, Jamie laughed. "I guess you've been here before."

Kevin took her comment in stride. "Once or twice." He raised a mug of dark ale. "Cheers, guys. Welcome to New York." They clanked mugs.

Kevin whispered to Jason through the side of his mouth. "Damn. Who's she? She's hot."

Jason turned his shoulder to shield his comments from Theo and Jamie. "You think? I don't know. Something's up with her. Can't put my finger on it."

"Bah, c'mon! Don't be jealous! Just relax."

"I'm not, you know . . . jealous. That's . . ."

Kevin pointed to the famous, wood-carved sign mounted above the bar: *Be Good or Be Gone.* "Jason. You've been warned. Be good or be . . . *gone!* Now drink up!"

And then another familiar face appeared, further upending Jason.

"Hank! What are you doing here?"

"You called me. Said to meet you here."

Jason himself had arranged this gathering, yet already he felt like the odd man out, awkward, lonely, and sinking farther away. "I did? When?"

"Kid. You just called, like two hours ago. From Coney Island. Said you wanted me to meet your kiwi pal, Theo. Did you pass out on the *Cyclone*?"

"*Cyclone*? In your dreams. Like I'd ever . . ." And then Jason had the strangest sensation that he *had* ridden the *Cyclone*, or maybe thought about it, only . . . he couldn't quite remember. *Did I? I would never do that. But . . .* Images flickered in his mind. *Arch of the tracks. Metallic roar. Theo's delight.*

Kevin corroborated Jason's doubt. "Him? On the *Cyclone*? No way, Hank. Noooo way. You can maybe get him on the bumper cars. With a seatbelt. And kneepads. And football helmet. And duct tape him to the steering wheel. And don't let the big kids in there. But a rollercoaster? Oh, no. Good luck. Been that way forever."

Jason offered a fake, conciliatory nod. "Yeah. Bite me."

"Yeh-yeh," Theo agreed, laughing. "He's not much of a speed demon."

An influx of new patrons forced everyone to shift around the table, with Jamie and Jason now side by side. Jamie gave him a quick nod. "Hi, there."

Jason offered a tense smile. "Hi."

"You know," she said, ". . . you're not exactly Mr. Warm and Fuzzy."

"It's . . . it's not that. It's just. . . I haven't seen Theo in a while and . . ."

"I'm busting in on your good time. I'm sorry. Look. . . . I just really want to find my brother and I really thought Theo could help. . . . That's all."

"But how did you know we were even at Coney Island?"

"Roger texted me."

"Y-yeahhhh. I really don't get that. Why were you in New Zealand to begin with?"

"Lex was supposed to . . . meet me there, but he got a head

start. By the time I made it, he was already gone. A . . . friend of the family, I guess you'd say . . . he told me to look up Theo. I found Roger instead. I've been calling Lex's phone, but he doesn't answer."

Jason was caught in that in-between state of believing her and not. She was telling him a lot of top-line information, yet he didn't know much about *her*. He heard a lot of words—vague, illusive descriptions—but was getting very little substance. But then, he thought, and almost chuckled to himself at the irony of it, who was he, given his own experiences, to reject a story about two travelers—separated across the globe, by circumstance—now trying to reunite?

"Huh," he said finally, accepting that the alcohol might be compromising his capacity to reason with lucidity. "That's weird. Were you on Theo's flight? You could have been sitting two rows apart. You probably didn't notice each other."

Jamie's eyes lit up. "You know. I think we were! How funny is that?!"

Growing more comfortable with Jamie—or had she just outlasted his line of questions as his intoxication swelled?—Jason gestured to the bartender for another round of drinks.

"Check it out." He pointed to Theo and Hank, who, at the other end of the table, clutched their beers, caught in the history lesson they were getting, whether they asked for it or not. "If I had to guess . . . I'd say Kevin's starting in right now about how John Lennon used to drink here. And Woody Guthrie. And Abraham Lincoln. Normally . . . I'd feel bad for those two."

"But now?"

"Yeah. Not so much. Better them than me!"

They shared a moment there, Jason and Jamie, who laughed, clinked mugs, and polished off their beers. The bartender brought yet more refills. And then Jamie jostled him.

"Are you stressed out? About Anna?"

Beer perched at his lips, Jason froze. He hid behind the mug. "Theo told you about that?"

"He mentioned it."

"W-when? Why?"

"Don't be mad. I could tell you didn't really like me . . . so

I asked him about it. He said not to take it personal. You were just tense about proposing."

"He told you that, too! Oh, good grief. He never even talks!"

"Happens a lot. It's my job to listen to people. Plus, we've got beer, so . . ."

"Yeah," Jason said reluctantly. "Okay. I think. But still . . . ."

"So . . . you and Theo. You seem pretty close. Best friends?"

"Uhh . . . kinda. It's weird. We don't really talk that much. He's got kids, we both work, we're on opposite sides of the globe, in different time zones, so just being available at the same time is logistically impossible more often than not. And he's not big with email. But, yeah. We've had some adventures. It's the way we know each other. But we've never just lived our regular lives in the same place at the same time, having regular days and doing regular things. We only seem to do it *big*. And I'm not really a do-things-big kinda guy. Theo is. But me? I'm more . . . I don't know . . . boring."

Jamie grinned.

"What? What's so funny?"

"Look. I know I barely know you, and I have no idea how you spend your time . . . but if I had to describe you . . . *boring* wouldn't do it."

"Um . . . thanks?"

"No, no." Jamie smiled, touched his hand. "It's just that you think about things. Like . . . a lot. Most people I know . . . they just let the minutes, the days, the months go by without giving them much thought at all. Just one after the other, like tiny waves on the ocean that dissolve into foam. But you contemplate things. That's it. That's how I'd describe you. You contemplate."

"Ha. Contemplate. I like that. I'm usually accused of overthinking."

"I was trying to be nice."

"Yeah, yeah. I get this from Hank all the time. I don't need you busting my chops, too."

"So . . . your girlfriend? Anna? I don't want to stick my nose in, but, are you really going to propose? Do you have the ring? That's so exciting!"

Jason was intensely private around people he didn't know, and as a reporter, was used to asking the questions. But now that he was on the other end of the interview, he couldn't seem to stop talking, as much as he knew that he was better off just shutting his yap.

"She's the one. I knew it from the beginning."

"Really? Ohhh. That's so sweet."

Finally seeing Jamie as a real person, and not some mysterious intruder, Jason considered her through a calibrated lens, which only made him want to talk more. To divulge himself.

"We just fit, you know? She gets me, and even if she doesn't *totally* get me, she accepts me. She loves me—I know she does—but what means the most, is that she *likes* me. Maybe that sounds weird, but until Anna I never really appreciated just how important it is to be pals with your girlfriend. You can do the romance thing, and we do—but if you're not pals, too, I'm not sure how it lasts. And with Anna, I *want* to be her pal. We *are* pals. She's really something." He smiled, in quick succession recapping in his mind many of the bad decisions he'd made and losses he'd suffered over the years, across all facets of his life. The car accident. The hospital. And what happened later. "I used to think the gods owed me one. But now . . . I think we're even. I might even owe *them* one."

Jamie offered him a smile in return. "But you still haven't proposed?"

Jason sighed, and took a gulp of beer. "Couple of years ago, Theo and I were traveling in Europe. You know, backpacking, having a good time. It was my first trip anywhere. I had no experience, no plan. Really no idea what I was doing. But early in my trip—my first full day, actually—I met this girl in Rome. An American. She got under my skin. It happened fast." He shook his head at himself. "You ever have those moments when you feel like you've known someone forever, even though you just met?"

Jamie nodded.

"Lilly, that's her name. Lilly . . . she was more than that. It's like . . . we were connected somehow. Not all goo-goo eyed, like with the slow-motion rock video and her hair blowing in the wind—but in some deep, fundamental way. It was surreal. Intense. So—"

"Important?"

"Yes! That's right. Important. Exactly. And the thing is . . . it wasn't physical between us. I'm mean . . . we were drawn to each other, powerfully, but it was like . . . she had no shape. No form. She just had this . . . energy. This way about her. We only spent a few days together. And we never had sex. We never even kissed! How lame is that?" Yet again, he shook his head at himself. "We ended up going to Venice together, but she was so . . . distant, withholding. I tried to ignore it, but then we got off the train and into the main plaza. One minute she was standing right next to me . . . and then she wasn't. No explanation, no goodbye, no nothing. Just gone. *Poof*. Like she disappeared. I never saw her again. And then a week or so later, in Budapest, I thought I spotted her from a distance, like I could just *feel* her presence. Turned out to be nothing. I know it shouldn't matter as much as it did, but I think I was in love with her. And it wasn't pals-in-love. It was that kind of crazy we're-linked-across-time-and-space-and-I'm-going-to-rip-out-my-own-soul-through-my-gullet-unless-I-get-to-kiss-you-at-least-once-and-hold-you-in-my-arms-right-now kinda love."

Jamie laughed.

"Oh, god. Do I sound like an idiot? Am I just another dope?"

"No, actually. You don't. I've never felt that way about anybody. And I don't think anybody's ever felt that way about me." She sipped her beer, and looked around, giving them a moment to collect themselves. "So what happened?"

"It didn't occur to me until after she was gone, but I'm pretty sure I'd dreamt about her long before we met. I know it sounds ridiculous—and I don't know if I even believe in this kind of thing—but I thought maybe it was a past life thing. You know . . . star-crossed lovers or some nonsense. I know. It's stupid."

"No. It's not stupid. I get it."

"You do? For real?"

"Yeah," Jamie said. "I do. Sometimes I feel like my life's just a disguise. Actually . . . that's not even right. More like a distraction, like I've been intentionally misdirected. I work in a nice hotel. I live by myself. I have some fun, I guess. But my life doesn't seem to mean anything. I'm inconsequential. Staying close to the action, on the periphery, trying to keep the crazy from overtaking me. Life just feels . . . safer that way. A fair, lame trade. Nothing extraordinary ever happened to me. And until recently, nothing too awful, either. I thought I was okay with it."

"And now?"

Jamie sipped her beer. "Not so much."

"So?" Jason said, relieved to be out of the spotlight, the one asking the questions. "What are you going to do about it?"

"Good question. It's partly why I need to find Lex. I think maybe I'm also looking for myself. Yikes. What a cliché, right? I need to find myself? Now who's being stupid?" She took another sip. "But what about you? Are you still in love with her? With Lilly?"

Jason bristled, back under investigation. "Nah. Maybe. I don't know." *Oh, my god I'm totally obsessed with her. I'm such a tool. I really am.* "No. I don't think so. But it gnaws at me, sometimes. She's always somewhere in the back of my mind. She lingers."

"Have you looked for her? Can you just call her?"

"I've . . . searched her name on the Web a few times, to . . . you know . . . ?"

"Spy?"

"No. No-no-no. It's . . . I . . . like to think of it as doing, you know . . . light reconnaissance . . . from a safe distance." He offered a lame, hopeful smile, mixed with a half-squint, half-cringe.

"So . . . spying?"

Jason dropped his head, sighed. "Yeahhhh. . . ."

". . . And?"

"I never really got that close. . . . I . . . sorta want to know, I sorta don't. Truth is . . . I don't need answers from her. I don't need to know how she is or what she's doing. We don't need to touch, or even talk. I just need to see her. Once. That's it. Just be in the same room with her at the same time, to prove to myself it wasn't just a dream. Love me, hate me, hug me, ignore me. It doesn't even matter. But I need a face-to-face encounter. I need an intervention. So I can finally let her go."

"Well, then." Jamie raised her mug. "To letting go."

Jason reciprocated. "To finding yourself."

And then above the escalating barroom chatter they heard Kevin let out a mighty roar. "That's it, Hank! Be good or be *gone*! You're *outta* here!"

"Okay," Jason said. "That's our cue. Before we get into any real trouble . . . ? Time to go."

Chapter 13
The Enchilada Man

Lilly
Sausalito, California

Sizzling peppers.

Lilly wasn't going to be anointed the next top chef, but she did make a mean enchilada. Red sauce was the key. She turned down the second burner, so as to not overcook the meat, then poured herself a glass of *Modelo Especial*, her favorite Mexican beer.

One sip, then another. Then one more. She exhaled a satisfied sigh, wiped away her beer-foam mustache, and licked the residue off her finger. Ben was in the bedroom, taking a nap.

"Should I wake him?" Lilly craned her head to look at the white cat clock above the sink. It was a little before 5 p.m. "Nah. Give him a few more minutes. He's had a long day."

A 13-inch flat screen TV was playing on the kitchen counter. Local news. A story about her friends' new restaurant.

"... *Peter and Tanya Sorensen, two Sausalito natives, are about to open* **On the Site**, *what they hope will be the newest eatery to capture our hearts—and taste buds. There's indoor seating for up to forty patrons, but along with a winning combination of California cuisine and good old-fashioned comfort food, it's the thirty-two seat outdoor patio with the harbor view they believe will draw in customers from miles away.*"

Lilly was excited for the opening. Pete and Tanya had been helping her along, made it okay to be on her own, to finally settle in one place.

"*Weather is coming at the top of the hour, and then we'll hear from an emerging group of conspiracy theorists who claim the apocalypse is coming sooner than any of us think. Calling themselves the* **Genius de Milo**—*a take on the ancient Greek sculpture Venus de Milo—they claim that large, unexplainable shadows are washing over the Eastern seaboard, as if they are resetting—or even wiping away—Earth's signature along the Milky Way's galactic plane . . .*"

Lilly muted the TV. She sat at the kitchen counter, and flipped through a photo album she found in the drawer. But even that wasn't true. It was a game she played, another round of *Oh, my goodness, I haven't seen these photos in ages. How funny.*

Third time this month. She felt increasingly compelled to look, to remember. Her one and only trip to Europe hadn't exactly gone the way she planned. Blackmailed, manipulated. Acting as Emma's fixer. Her gopher. All about that stupid jar she thought Theo had. And to what end?

But it had all been for the best, hadn't it? Lilly found her way back to her dad, decided it was time to give up her fantasies of becoming a famous *artiste* and put her reasonable, but not star-making, talent to good use. She only had one semester to go, and then she could take the state board exam to become a certified art therapist. And now she was thirty years old and Ben was asleep in the next room. It wasn't the life she ever thought she'd have, but now that she had it, she wouldn't ever give it up.

Lilly smiled at the notion, and then flipped through the pages. Within a plastic sleeve was a photograph of her standing outside a fireworks distributor in Lexington, Kentucky. Another of her with Ray the mechanic at a roadside diner outside of Indianapolis, and then a page full of photos of her with Theresa and Jini during that one crazy summer in Franconia, New Hampshire. The pages went on and on. Old friends, lovers. Some she remembered fondly. Others . . .

But one way or another they brought me here. One way or another.

And then, in the lower right corner, the last photograph on the page, was Lilly in Yuma, Arizona, kneeling down, scratching Lex beneath the chin. Emma's Lex. Which meant that the very reason she opened the photo album in the first place—as much as she tried to deny it to herself, part of her game, that foolish denial—was just one turn away.

Lilly clutched the corner between her thumb and forefinger, to peel the page, to make the transition. But she stopped. Her heart fluttered. And then she closed the album with her fingers trapped between the pages, holding her place. She needed a minute to prepare, as if she would be magically protected from the images on the other side if she didn't look directly at them, like shielding her eyes from the sun.

Lilly took a deep breath through her nose until her lungs were full. She held it. Then she exhaled. And then another deep breath. She took a gulp of beer.

Okay, she thought. *Okay.*

She exhaled again, turned the page.

There were only three photos. In the first, Lilly was with Jason, the night they met, having dinner at an outdoor café in Rome. She touched the photograph, let her fingertip linger on it. In the second, Jason stood on a stone platform in the Ancient Ruins, posing beneath the midday sun as one of the Roman gods, flexing his biceps, and sticking his tongue out. Lilly smiled at that one.

And in the third, Lilly leaned on the stone railing overlooking the Spanish Steps, looking away from him, avoiding him, as he stared right at her, like she was the only star in the sky. That was the night she abandoned him, at least in how she treated him, because even though they'd only known each other a few days, she felt in every molecule of her being that she wanted to fall right into him, and maybe stay there forever.

And what happened next, well . . . she didn't like to think about that too much. Her final moments being *that* Lilly. The old Lilly. Before she became *this* Lilly. The Lilly she was starting to like. A Lilly she was even starting to respect.

Jason never said the words to her out loud—she left him before he could—but he didn't have to. She knew. And in the years since, time and again she'd closed her eyes and imagined him confronting her at last, if she ever gave him the chance.

"I know why you ran away. You thought I wanted to swallow you whole. To devour you. That I saw you as the savior of my soul. But you know what I really wanted . . . ? I wanted you to hold my hand. I wanted you to sit down on the couch and lie right here," she imagined him saying, pointing to the nook formed by his arm and shoulder. *"I wanted you, to just be there. I wanted your lips on mine. To share that warmth. That moment. I wanted to look into your eyes, and see you looking right back at me, and not wanting to be anywhere else."*

Lilly liked that part. It always made her blush.

"I wasn't planning our whole lives. I wasn't thinking about getting

married or having children or being together forever. I really wasn't. But you and me . . . we have the kind of connection that doesn't develop over time. It can't be bought, manufactured, or conceived. You either have it or you don't. And we do. On the very first day of my very first trip of any real consequence I walked into the very first room I could find, halfway around the world, and of all the people on the Earth I could have possibly met . . . I met you. It wasn't coincidence or random, and it definitely wasn't luck. You and I found each other at that one singular moment because the rhythm of the cosmos led us to each other. I don't know how and I don't know why. And maybe it doesn't matter. I don't even care. But I do know that the Universe drew us together. Who are we to argue with that?"

Lilly smiled despite herself. She imagined Jason stopping there, and pausing, because that's how she remembered him. Running away with passion, then taking a breath to realize what he'd done.

"Okay," she imagined him continuing, in a moment of self-awareness. "I just heard myself say that out loud. Yeah. That does sound pretty epic. But screw it! So what if it's epic?! I wanted the chance to be together. Maybe it would have lasted more than two days and maybe not. Maybe it would have flamed out because some bands of energy just can't be sustained. But you know what? I don't think so. We had legs. We could have shared our lives. We had a chance to make it work. Even if it was just for a little while. And I didn't care about the wheres, the whys, and the hows. I would have figured it out. I would have lived almost any-where just to be with you, and then taken my chances. I loved you in that crazy irrational can't eat, sleep, or drink kind of way that doesn't make any sense but makes the most sense of all. There was something under-neath it, something true and real. And what really breaks my heart, what keeps me up at night even after all these years, is that you know I'm right. You felt exactly the same way. The only difference is that I was willing to go for it . . . and you weren't."

Like so many times before, Lilly's heart pounded. She put her hand to her chest. The pure intensity brought a tear to her eye.

"I wasn't ready," she said aloud, as if Jason was standing before her, in that moment. He was a reporter in New York City. She had Googled him more times than she would ever admit—usually with a few glasses of wine in her. She even read some of his articles. He was out there somewhere, participating. But she also didn't want to learn more. To get too close.

I did feel it, she thought. *I feel it right now.* She touched the photographs again. *But you didn't really want me. Not really. You were on the chase, and I was on the run. How could I have been with you?* She laughed again, nervously, because she didn't know how else to respond. *I didn't want to be with myself.*

Lilly stopped herself just then. It was one of her traps. Punishing herself for the past when she needed to focus on the present. The moment. She let out a long, deep breath.

The sizzling peppers brought her back to the stove. She lowered the flame, then served up dinner. As it cooled on the table, she opened the bedroom door, slowly, leaned over, and kissed Ben on the forehead. She took him in her arms. "Okay, sleepyhead. Time to get up."

"M-mommy. I want my juice."

"You got it, little man. We're gonna have dinner now."

"Encher-rahders?"

"Yep. Enchiladas."

"Mmmm. Yummy." Ben's eyes lit up. "I like encher-rahders."

"I know you do, baby. I know you do."

But if Lilly's cross to bear was that she ran away from Jason without ever telling him the truth, then she would allow that failure to serve as her reminder, to never let the good pass her by, because she was finally eager to accept as much of it as the gods were willing to bestow upon her. Ben was her life now, and if she was finally going to find Jason, she had to be ready to tell him things that maybe he wasn't ready to hear.

Before Jason, though, she had to do one thing first.

Three years earlier she let Emma manipulate her, sent her off on a fool's errand, because that's who Lilly was then. But not anymore. And though she'd broken away from Emma—from her physical girth, from the leverage she once held—Lilly still didn't feel free of her. She needed to stand before Emma, to listen to more of her lies, and still be okay with herself. And even if Lilly couldn't be totally okay, she needed to look Emma in the eyes, and just not completely fall apart.

That's all I need to do. Just keep it together.

"Soon," she said out loud. "Soon."

"Soon what, Mommy? Soon what?"

"Oh, don't worry about that. Mommy's just being a goofa-goofa. Talking to myself again."

Ben giggled. He wore a Spider-Man bib, with a Doctor Octopus pouch in the front. "You do that a wot."

"I know, baby. I know." Lilly tapped his nose. "Now eat your dinner, my little enchilada man. Mommy needs to figure something out."

Chapter 14
Dream Away

Lex
San Francisco

REE-URRN!

Lex craned his neck, eyes starting to swirl. Up in the corner, the TV had him mesmerized.

REE-URRN-URRN-URRN!

The blonde and brunette sponsor girls initially drew him to the telecast of the Saratoga 500 NASCAR qualifying tournament. They wore tight orange spandex short-shorts and white t-shirts (two sizes too small, with a checkered flag logo above the right boob), with the shirt bottoms tied above their pierced navels. Security guards Aaron and Mack ignored the telecast, but Lex couldn't turn away. The cameras panned from the girls, and settled back on the race.

REE-URRN! REE-URRN! URRN-URRN-URRN!

Lex's eyes flickered.

REE-URRN!

Whipping around the track the cars seemed to morph together, stretching like vapor trails. And then Lex heard a girl's voice, melded with the *REE-URRN!*

"*. . . Chase meeeee, Lex. Commmmmme and finnnnnd meeeeee . . .*"

REE-URRN! REE-URRN!

"*. . . Your turnnnn to finnnd me, Lex. I'm running away. I'm runnnnnning . . .*"

REE-URRN! REE-URRN!

The voice was familiar somehow, but distant. Confusing. And yet . . . he knew that voice, felt a connection to his . . . home? His childhood? But . . .

REE-URRN! REE-URRN! URRN-URRN-URRN!

The racecars just kept whizzing around the track. The camera panned up to the crowd, which blurred together, and then back down on the race.

REE-URRN! REE-URRN!

Wait, Lex thought. *Did I have a . . . cousin? A sister? Neighbor? I just can't remember. But I know that voice from . . . somewhere.*

The memories of his former life were scattered, unreliable. His recall was clear, lucid, and specific at times . . . hazy and fragmented at others. And sometimes it was simply gone.

Yet . . . he knew he wasn't crazy. He assumed so, anyway. Lex had no doubt that he had originated from Eternity, the plane of existence responsible for all creation in the Universe. And he also remembered with precision and exactitude that he had been banished to Earth, in the Milky Way, the very planet and galaxy he helped Emma design. And he also knew, with testicle-licking assuredness, that he was now—thanks to the Big M.O.U. himself—a dog. Woof-woof. So who was the crazy one?

Although with little else to occupy his time, Lex was snacking on the new THC edibles pretty much nonstop, and thus wasn't a reliable witness, neither inside nor out of his own noodle.

REE-URRRN! REE-URRN!

But there was the voice again. Louder. More distinct.

"*. . . Come on, Lex. Mom's gonna call us in. One more chase. You can be the planet this time, I'll be the star. No! Wait! Even better! Let's be comets! Yeah! How cool? We'll zoom across the western edge of Eternity and then far into space and everyone will see our streaking tails across the skkkyyyyy . . .*"

REE-URRN!

In his mind's eye Lex saw a face. A girl. *Jenny? Jasmine? Jocelyn? No, no, no, that's not it, but . . .* He couldn't quite get a hold of . . . *wait-wait-wait. Jada? Jemma? Jamie? Is it Jamie? No. I don't . . . Jamie . . . Jamie. Jamie. Yeah. Why do I know that name? I know that name! I . . .*

Lex blinked several times, to break the spell, and then stepped on the remote control. He shut off the TV.

He ambled through the curtain of beads, waited for the *buzz click* of the triple-ply metal security door, and moseyed into the Internet café.

Jamelia was working the counter, while the gamers were doing their thing, clacking on keys, whispering into wireless headsets, lost in their own worlds. A few new faces—and new scents—but mostly the regulars. Lex liked them.

Darla and Jeff in the back were quiet but always said hello, and Charlie, Sibyl, and the two Saras (brunette and redhead) were usually good for scratches under the chin and the occasional belly rub.

Conquest of Alandra's Fire was on tap. The gang was doing battle as the *Pegorians*, or *Pegs*, against the overlords of the *Fular Dreen*. And though the gamers spoke at respectful volumes, to Lex's canine hearing their voices were clear:

Jeff: *The gates aren't far. Take the east hill.*

Charlie: *But watch for trolls. They're nasty.*

Sara redhead: *Yeah, but you like it nasty.*

Sibyl: *So nasty.*

Charlie: *Ha ha. Just because you're a fairy slut bag doesn't make me nasty for trolls.*

Sara redhead: *But you are nasty for trolls. You live for troll stump.*

Sara brunette: *Totally troll stump.*

Sibyl: *Totally.*

All but Darla, who had thus far refrained from the mocking, broke out in a unified chant: *Troll stump! Troll stump! Troll stump! Troll stump!*

Darla finally chimed in with a stern command: *Pegs. Quiet. We're near the gates. Buddy up. Swords out. We've got one shot at Alandra's sister. She's locked in the dungeon. We rescue the sister we have a shot at the fire. But focus on the sister. Get the sister.*

Lex took a mini, full-body shudder. *Sister. Sister. Do I have a . . . ?*

Emma rubbed his back, whispered. "Again with the fire game?" She rolled her eyes. "I swear I don't get it. I so don't. But I'll hand it to those geeks. They pay, they come back, and they bring their friends. So what do I care?" Emma moved onto more mundane topics, such as order forms and delivery times for the dispensary, but between the multi keyboard clacks and quiet calls of online gaming battle, Lex was plenty distracted.

Darla: *Move in, Pegs. There's an opening through the shed.*

In an impressive 360-degree slicing motion, Charlie's avatar decapitated three Fular Dreen soldiers and took the arms off a fourth.

Charlie said: *How's that for troll stump?*

The gamers laughed.

But the celestial bodies Emma had painted on the walls—the planets, the moons, the stars . . . the comets—grabbed Lex's attention. He had seen them countless times, but they now took on a whole new meaning. The distant voice echoed. *Chase me, Lex. Chase me.*

Not so much speaking to Emma as near her, Lex posed a question. "I wonder what that would be like."

"To play the fire game? Who cares?"

"No. Not that." Lex head-gestured to the wall. His tags jangled. *"That."*

"That *what*? I have no idea—"

"You know. Up there."

"Lex. Up there *how?*" Emma was getting snotty, even for her. "I need you to specify, to articulate, to clarify. Like . . . with the words. And have them, you know, make sense. Give it a whirl."

"Before we were down *here*, on Earth, we were up *there*, in Eternity. You with me so far? Am I being clear? Have I articulated myself? Am I ah-NUN-see-yating?" Lex gave Emma an impatient, half-eyed stare, a tactic he found considerably more effective as a four-legged creature than when he strode upright. "While we were up there, you designed galaxies and all the celestial bodies within them. I procured the materials for their construction."

"Yes, that's true. Aaaand . . . ?"

"Now think about a comet."

"A comet?"

"Yeah, a comet."

Emma went to the wall. "A rock going really fast in space. Like this one, here. The one I painted. Okay. A comet."

"No," Lex said. "Don't just point to the comet. *Be* the comet."

"Be the comet?"

"Yeah. *Be* the comet. Embody it. Don't just think of it as a space rock. Think of it as *you*. Think of it as . . . what if your body wasn't the body you have now," Lex said, and with his front left paw, pointed to her, "but you're still you." He heard distant laughter. *This is so much fun, Lex. Chase me. Chase me.* "No arms, no legs, no torso, no face. You're still Emma, but instead of being a person, you're a space rock. A comet. You don't live *in* the comet. You *are* the comet."

"I am the comet? Okay. I'm the comet."

"And you're not just any comet, but a comet that's *ripping through the Universe.* From one galaxy and into another. It would be like painting yourself into one of your designs there on the wall, and then having it come to life. Soaring at speeds that would tear a trolley car to shreds. But up there, it would be totally natural. Like a fish swimming through the ocean. Like a bird across the sky. Only . . . in space. Getting as close as physically possible to the stars and the planets and nebulas without being pulverized. . . . Now *that* would be cool."

"Um, Lex . . . ?"

"Yeah?"

"No more weed for you. It's nap time."

"No, I'm serious."

"I know you are. That's why it's nap time."

Lex knew that Emma would never understand him, and not because she was incapable, but because his words frightened her. She wanted to always and forever remain who she was, only realigned as her idealized self.

"Okay," he said. "Fine. But a guy can dream, you know."

"Dream away, my friend. Dream away. But maybe in your next dream, you're not a lump of rock. You know. Just something to think about."

Lex wasn't going to say any more. And then he did anyway. "I had a sister, didn't I?"

Emma went still, validating his suspicion. Like a freshly baked cinnamon toffee scone dipped in a vanilla late, he could smell it on her. He was a dog, after all.

"Jamie, right? Her name was Jamie? I can't even see her face. . . . I had a sister—maybe I still do, I just don't know—and I have no idea what she looks like. I don't know what she does, where she lives, or what her life is like. I just know that I miss her. It makes me smile to know that there was this other part to me, that there's someone out there who cares about me . . . but there's a hole in my heart, Emma. It took me this long just to remember she even existed. Will I remember her a week from now? Or tomorrow? I'm afraid to fall asleep, because what happens if can't remember her even an hour from now?" Lex surveyed the room of nerds. Playing their game. Together. And in the distance: *Chase me, Lex. Chase me.* "But if I can't remember, I won't even know to miss her. So problem solved, right?"

Emma remained still. Lex had rarely seen her so immobilized.

"But you know what? Even if I can't remember her face, she won't really be gone. She's awake in me now. She's coursing through my veins. I have a sister, Emma. Did you know that? But, of course, you did. I should have known. She wasn't just my sister. She was my friend. And I know that now. I know it."

The gamers were wrapping up. Jamelia came by to reset the terminals.

Lex shuffled toward the dispensary. He left Emma standing there, by the wall, the comet above her head. "Come on," he said. "I need to smoke a bowl. And when I sober up after that, who knows what I'll remember. If I remember anything at all."

Chapter 15
The Alley at Viking Hill

Jamie
Manhattan

They spilled into the moonlight.

It was Jamie's first night in Manhattan. Her first on Earth. She wasn't sure where they were off to next—Jason said something about the West Village—but she didn't really care.

Thanks to Emma's naming stunt during the unveiling of her Milky Way galaxy design—and her instantaneous banishment—the blue and green orb became an endless source of gossip, entertainment, and general sniggering throughout Eternity. The Minder of the Universe also had a well-publicized affinity for Earth, although his reasons were as unknowable as the Big M.O.U. himself. That alone made all things Earth even more salacious.

And while Jamie had no galaxy design, maintenance, or upgrade clearance to speak of, accepting a quest to Earth hadn't really been open to negotiation. She clearly understood that the suggestion—such that it was—in actuality was a mandate cloaked as a *choice*.

When the Minder of the Universe gives you a purpose, pushback isn't a plausible option.

Beyond which Jamie found that her physical presence on Earth was far different than she had anticipated. Life in Eternity was a tactile experience grounded within each moment. Yet her existence there was imbued with an ethereal quality—a rolling, dreamlike mist—one she now appreciated with distinction and specificity, mainly because it was gone.

Earth, however, felt denser somehow, weightier. Much like all celestial bodies, the planet was constructed from a unique formulation of Cosmic Building Material—the Universe's liquid DNA—encoded with the burning embers of Eternity. But since Eternitarians did not experience birth and death as it occurred outside the boundaries of Eternity—in the *Othersphere*—Jamie was terrified and alone. And yet oddly exhilarated.

Her emotional conflict may have also been at least partially alcohol-related, but it was her first time getting inebriated on Earth, so she didn't have a proper frame of reference.

Standing in a street lamp's halo, her vision was slightly blurred. The cascade of city lights glowed and swirled. "Hank. You coming?"

"Nah, you go ahead. I'm getting too old for pub crawls. Besides, the missus will have my head if I'm late again."

Theo laughed. "She's saving you from yourself, yeh?"

"Every day, Theo. You have no idea."

Before anyone could rope Kevin into their next stop, he hopped into a yellow cab, and, slurring his words, failed to hide a drunken smile. "I'm out, too. Early day t'morrow."

Jamie threw Jason and Theo a raised eyebrow. "Booty call . . . right?"

"Ha HA! You cracked the code!" Jason broke out his finger guns, and made the *chk-chk* sound. "That's right boys and girls, big J is on the scene!"

Jamie laughed, then looked about. "Hey. Where's Hank?"

"Yeh-yeh. Where'd he go?"

Jason wiped tears from his eyes. "Who knows? He's a crafty old dog. So . . . you up for round two?"

Despite the fun she was having—the West Village reminded Jamie of Notter Circle in the Eastern Sphere of Eternity—she wasn't sure how, or if, Theo was going to lead her to Lex, but she figured that she might as well enjoy the ride, for however much longer it lasted, seeing as how she was Earthing it and all.

So she followed Jason as he led them across East 9th Street, Broadway, and University Place, then down the tree-lined side streets to the New York University cluster of brownstone buildings around Washington Square Park. There they ambled through the park's massive, stone arches, beyond the fountain, and then zig-zagged to West 4th Street across Sixth Avenue.

On top of the buzz they already had going, they put down a beer each at *The Music Inn*, *The Four-Faced Liar*, *Pink Pussy Cat*, and *The Slaughtered Lamb*, then stumbled down Barrow Street, a narrow alley street with a combination of low-rise, brick-faced apartment buildings and glass-front restaurants.

Jason finally brought them all to *Viking Hill*, a Nordic-themed saloon boasting a sign with, naturally, a brutish looking Viking, holding a chicken leg in one raised hand and a beer stein in the other.

Inside the tavern various crests and sailing ship elements were mounted on the walls. Flat screen TVs showcased the Yankees-Red Sox game, with the Bronx Bombers up 5-2 in the seventh inning. A picture-in-picture box of a newscaster related an item about the *Genius de Milo* tracking a miles-long black streak moving north-bound up from Tallahassee, Florida.

A carnival-style popcorn machine provided free refills in silver boats. Led Zeppelin's *Misty Mountain Hop* roared through the jukebox.

Spread out in a corner booth they were approached by a stout, raven-haired waitress with a hefty bosom hoisted by a tight, leather corset. A black and red spider tattoo inched along the side of her face. She offered up the two-for-one drink special, a *Mind Eraser*—vodka, kahlúa, and tonic—and a beer chaser.

Jamie wasn't a full-on drinker—two fruity cocktails was her usual limit—but before long the three of them found logic morphing into alcohol-propelled delirium.

The gents first entertained her with the tale of how they met in Venice, and in what seemed like an obvious attempt to make Theo blush, Jason started in about a wild party they stumbled upon in a Budapest hostel bar, where Theo was propositioned by an attractive red-headed transvestite, who ended up being fabulous company, and bought several rounds of drinks before disappearing into the night with a large, dopey Austrian rugby player and his diminutive girlfriend. Theo wound up puking through the night and sleeping it off most of the next day.

"Dude! Dude! Charlene was so into you! She got you so hammered! It made your kiwi gibberish sound normal!"

Jason's effusiveness got Jamie laughing so hard she spilled beer down her leg. To wipe it off she reached into her pocket for a tissue—she hadn't had time to pick up even a small travel purse—and in her boozy haze removed a handful of assorted items: a tube of lip balm from Coney Island; a salty popcorn kernel; the crumpled tissue; and a slightly creased postcard.

The noise swirled around them—jukebox music, inebriated chatter, raucous laughter—but Theo went silent. Tense. He reached for the postcard. On the front was an Asian drag queen set against a black background, littered with the moon, stars, and the Andromeda galaxy. Across the top, in sparkly letters, was the phrase *GenderBender*.

Jamie couldn't tell why, but Theo was clearly transfixed. She was about to speak aloud—*What is it? Tell me! Did they send you, too?*—when suddenly his eyes went wide. Jamie also stared at the postcard. The stars twinkled. The galaxy swirled. And the moon, she thought, winked at her.

With urgency and purpose Theo grabbed Jason and Jamie by the wrists and hurried them outside. Centered on Barrow Street, they were mid-block along the alley-like stretch and set way off from the intersections in both directions, with no quick way to reach the corners. They were, in essence, trapped.

Theo pivoted quickly. "Uh, uh . . . which way, Jason? Which way?!"

Jason snorted, then looked to his feet. "Hey. Is it just me . . . or is the street getting a bit . . . oogly?"

In her short time with them, Jamie knew Jason to be the nervous Nellie of the two. So Theo starting to freak out was not reassuring. "Oogly? What do you mean *oogly?*"

"Oogly. You know. Like we're on little boogie boards and the street is turning to water." Jason's smile dropped away, replaced then with a silent, open-mouthed slug of resignation, that whatever was happening was authentic, and unfolding in real time.

In a shared-brain moment Jason and Theo slowly panned in Jamie's direction until finally she felt their accusatorial eyes lock on her. And though neither of them spoke, the imputation of blame came through with perfect enunciation: *What did you do? What's coming?*

But what could she say? Which cluster of words could encapsulate both the scope and nuance of their predicament? Jamie could offer a pretty good guess as to *why* their immediate surroundings morphed before their very eyes—it had to be Brigsby-related, didn't it?—but when it came to the *what*, she was equally mystified.

So all she could do was stand there. She blinked a few times. Then a few times more. The night went bracingly still, as if every fractal of sound had been drained from the Universe. The three of them held in place, petrified, as if the incredible forces converging upon them were seemingly just to be unleashed. Which, of course, they were.

Panicked and depressed over the notion that her quest had already disintegrated, that she had failed miserably, as she suspected—with Lex once again lost to her forever—Jamie was drawn to the triangulation of the alleyway and the street's uneven blacktop. The angles created an optical illusion, such that there were no corners to turn down or doorways to enter. As if they were boxed in. Only Jamie knew that it was no illusion.

And then the ground began to shake.

R U M B L E R U M B L E R U M B L E R U M B L E - RUMBLERUMBLERUMBLE . . .

Until the short-stack buildings around them dissolved. Same with the pavement beneath their feet, and the night sky above.

Jamie reached out belatedly to the person she had been calmly casing. "Theo! I need to tell you that—"

There was a blast of white light. There were streaks of screaming fluorescent color. There was the sensation of being sucked through a tornado. And with a tremendous *WHOOSH* the alley was submerged in water, corkscrewing them all.

Twisted on their sides, Jamie and Jason covered their mouths, to keep the air in. But after finding their footing, deep in the underwater alley, they hopped in place, as if constant motion would somehow ward off their inevitable suffocation.

"Wait," Theo said. "I've done this before, yeh? It's weird, but we're okay. I think we're okay." He sifted air through his pursed lips, like testing hot soup. Then once more. He waited. "Yeh-yeh. All good."

Jason stated what under ordinary circumstances would have been accurate—and obvious. "What do you mean we're okay?

We're gonna drown! We're gonna . . ." Perhaps realizing that he was able to speak and breathe normally—underwater—he paused.

Jamie unclamped her mouth, gently gummed the water. "No. I think he's right. Hmm. Freaky. I think we're okay."

A booming voice—one that came from a blue whale, the size of a jumbo jetliner—set them straight. "Are you sure about that?"

Jamie clutched Jason's arm. Hard. Her heart was doing flip-flops. *Big whale. Biiig big whale. Not good, not good, sooooo not good.*

Ira the bottle-nosed dolphin came along, sniffed her neck. A bit of a close swimmer. Jamie clutched Jason's arm even tighter.

"Heyyy," Ira said. "New girl. Nice."

Theo sighed. "Oh, bollocks. Not you two again. What now?"

Ira swam closer. "How do you like that, Howie? We help the guy out with that kooky jar of his, and this is how he says hello? Sheesh. Good to see you, Theo."

Ira scooped psychotropic plankton between his gums. His eyes instantly went glossy and bloodshot. His grin went droopy.

Jason's eyes, already bulged, re-bulged. "Y-you know him? You've seen him? You . . . ?"

Howard's chuckle—a thunderous, baritone *huh-huh-huh*— knocked him back a few feet. "Indeed, we do, Jason. Indeed we do . . . thanks to this little lady."

Jamie's throat went tight. "What?! No! I don't know them. I don't know, I . . . I . . ."

"I KNEW it!" Jason said. "I knew it. I *knew* there was some-thing up with you. Woo. *God*, that feels good."

"But . . . but . . ." Jamie stammered. "I've never seen them before. I swear!"

Ira chuckled again. "Okay, Howie. You've had your fun."

The whale sniggered. "I love this part."

Ira drifted on his back, stretched his flippers, then leaned against Howard. Ira produced a toothpick. He worked on a hunk of plankton wedged in his teeth and turned to Jamie. "No need to pop an eyeball, sweetheart. I think they know that now. But you and telling the truth . . . ? Not so much."

Jamie had spent the better part of her lifetime believing that the best way to get by was to do just that—get by. *Don't over-reach. Keep it small, keep it simple. Let others have the glory.*

Yet there she was, on a journey outside of Eternity—the very epicenter of Existence—and into a world that had moved to the top of the *ain't gonna be here too much longer* list. And all in concert with the Minder of the Universe.

And still she instinctively recoiled at being called to task with—and then possibly have to acknowledge and accept—her sins of disappointment, and then find a way to negotiate peace, to maintain the social contract. Back to equilibrium. The comfort zone.

Jamie had traveled a distance unquantifiable by any known measurement, and still she hadn't gone far enough to sidestep *the talk*. So talk she did.

Such that by the time she worked her way through her childhood, to Lex, and finally, to Brigsby—the Minder of the Universe—she was simultaneously relieved, exhausted, delighted, exposed, and strangely enough, empowered.

With nothing left to hide, there was no more reason to run. Leaving the boys with stunned looks was an added bonus. She didn't know she had it in her.

"Okaaaaay," Ira said, then mouthed *wow*. He turned to Theo. "I guess that brings us to you. The jar you found and then chucked into the ocean? Actually . . . the one *you* chucked." The dolphin gestured at Jason, who blushed and started to stammer. "Well . . . Howie and I kinda . . . you know . . . opened it."

Jamie, Jason, and Theo responded in unison. *"You opened it?!"*

"Uh-yep."

"Why?!" they uni-shouted.

Ira shrugged. "For funzies."

Jason was particularly riled up. "For funzies?! For funzies?! What the . . . ?"

"Hey," Howard said. "Didn't he used to work at that restaurant? *Funzie's*? Wasn't he a waiter there? *Funzies*? Get it? . . . Good one."

Ira agreed. "But speaking of good ones . . . that jar of yours—now that it's been opened, *whoever* did it—has pretty much gone crazy. You're gonna have to find it, sedate it, and put it back where it belongs. There's probably a shelf of some sort."

"Bollocks," Theo said. "You do it, yeh? *You* opened it.'

The corner of Ira's mouth turned up into a half smile. "Technically . . . I suppose that's true. But had you just left that jar alone—it was buried down in those caves for a reason—we wouldn't be in this mess, now would we? And it's not like it's still open and you need to screw the top back on. Once that baby spilled out, there's no mopping it up."

"Then what are we supposed to do, yeh?"

"I told you. Put it back. For safe keeping."

"Put it back? Where, mate? . . . *How?*"

"Ask Jamie," Ira said. "She has the key."

"Yeahhhhh," Jason said. "That's true. You're supposed to do *what* with it now?"

"Uh . . . Brigsby told me to find the jar and then blow into this harmonic key. Like this." Jamie blew into it. Nothing. "I-I-I . . . I don't know. I swear. I don't."

"Ira," Theo said. "Seriously. What's up with this?"

Ira shrugged again. "Beats me."

"What the fuck? That's piss in a bucket."

"Sorry, pal. Not my department. But now that we're done pointing fingers and flippers . . . this little ball of fun you call a planet is fluxing in and out of existence. And if you hadn't noticed, it's getting worse. You need to intervene or it's going to flux away—permanently. Like buh-bye, for good. So . . . I can say with confidence that you really don't have anything better to do. Because if you don't get that jar back where it belongs—key or no key—if you don't stop it from reaching its final mega flux—and believe me, it's coming—you'll never have anything to do again. Ever."

There was awkward silence among them.

"Sooo," Howard interjected. "Good luck with aaaaaall that."

"Ha," Ira said. "I love that *Seinfeld*."

"Love the Sein," Howard agreed.

"Love the Sein."

From the outset Jamie had known in some tiny nook of her mind that Brigsby hadn't been entirely truthful about what he was recruiting her to do. He had gone to great lengths to promote his public persona, a mask for his true identity. Retrieving the jar and returning it to its rightful place was the price for her *opportunity* to find Lex and, if she could actually locate him, make their way back to Eternity. But Brigsby failed to mention their very existence being erased if she wasn't successful.

Now that the dawn of reality was beginning to rise, she had only one concern. "What about my brother? Where's Lex?"

Ira rubbed his flippers together. "Ah, yes. I think he's really gone to the dogs. Ha-ha. But seriously, he's out west somewhere. Yuma, I believe. Best I can tell you."

"Yuma? Yuma? What the heck is Yuma?"

"It's in Arizona," Jason said. "Southwest part of the state. About ten miles from Mexico. Pretty much a direct route to Tijuana."

"Hey," Howard said. "Look at mister geography over here. Pretty good, kid."

Jamie waved her hand before her just then. She swirled it in the water, then looked right at Ira. Just stared at the bottle-nosed dolphin. Staring. Staring. Staring.

And then seeing herself reflected back in his eyes, she remembered. "Wait." She pointed at Ira. "Brigsby said *Milo* opened the jar. He told me *Milo* did it."

Jason shook his head. "Brigsby, Brigsby . . . ? I know that name. I've heard it before. It's . . . wait. Who the hell is Milo?"

"H-he's . . . ," Jamie waved her finger at the dolphin. "He's the . . . the-the guy, you know. Milo. The trouble maker. The gremlin. The . . ."

"O-kaaay," Ira said to Howard. "Time for us to vamoosevoux."

Jamie reached again for the dolphin. "No! Don't go—"

There was a blast of white light. There were streaks of screaming fluorescent color. There was the sensation of being sucked through a tornado. And then they were back on the street, dry as a whale bone.

Moments passed before anyone spoke. A breeze trickled through the narrow side street. With it, the *GenderBender* postcard fluttered by, and drifted, until it landed at their feet.

"So," Jason finally said.

"Yeh-yeh," Theo said.

"Uh-huh," Jamie said.

And then the three of them stumbled back into Viking Hill, took seats at the bar, and ordered round after round of Mind Erasers, hoping the name of the cocktail, if they consumed enough, would actually come true.

PART II
FROM THE EARTH TO THE MOON

Chapter 16
Fill 'Er Up

Jason
Brooklyn

There are hangovers and there are hangovers. The sensation they all experienced was something else entirely.

Yes, Jason, Theo, and Jamie were suffering from various degrees of dehydration, exhaustion, and nausea. But given the amounts and mixtures of alcohol they had consumed the night before—and their shared back-alley transportation/hallucination—it was nothing short of a minor miracle that they weren't laid up in the emergency room with banana bags pumping clear fluids and electrolytes back into their systems.

Theirs was more a hangover of the cosmos, a pummeling of the soul.

Jason had the car up to 67 miles an hour heading west on the Belt Parkway, through the southern strand of Brooklyn, en route to the Verrazano-Narrows Bridge, one of the longest suspension bridges in the world. With two main towers for massive cables, the bridge's length at 13,700 feet end to end, averaging almost 230 feet above water, supported some 200,000 cars daily.

But just reaching that bridge—connecting Brooklyn and Staten Island and marking the gateway to New York Harbor—was itself an essential checkpoint.

Just get me across, he thought. *Reach the other side. We'll figure the rest out later.*

Jason adjusted his sunglasses as sunshine pierced the windshield of Kevin's car, bearing down with the intensity and focus of a trained sniper following the trio via black ops helicopter, and using a red laser targeting dot to track Jason's skull. His knees ached. His surgically repaired elbow, too. "I feel like the Hulk body slammed me into a battleship."

He accepted a half-empty water bottle and a handful of

aspirin from Jamie, whose head hung low, as she slumped next to him in the front passenger's seat.

"I don't know who the Hulk is, but that sounds about right."

Theo was lying down in the back seat, groaning. He rubbed his eyes. "Should'a flown, yeh? Could'a slept on the plane."

Unable to see Theo through the rearview mirror, Jason gestured to his right. "Yeah, well . . . talk to your girlfriend, here. Maybe the Universe doesn't require photo I.D. for inter-galactic wormhole travel—or whatever that flippy trippy flash phase thing was—but the airlines and rail services are kinda strict about that. No I.D., no ticket. Although . . . at least the air conditioning works. So that's something."

"Speaking of no I.D.," Jamie said, "you said it's what . . . three days to Arizona if we drive in shifts? Kevin loaned you his car for that long? He won't need it?"

"Well . . . *loaned* might be an exaggeration."

"He won't be mad?"

"If Ira's for real—and I'm not saying he is—but if Ira told the truth and life as we know it is literally coming to an end . . . I don't think Kevin will be too worried about his car."

The three of them shared an uncomfortable chuckle just then. Theo sat up, so that Jason could finally see him through the rearview mirror.

"Glad to see you're still back there. Had me worried for a minute."

Jamie sipped an orange juice. "Where'd you think he went? You heard him talking."

"Hey. Gimme a break. I don't mean to be all paranoid, but flux me into an Armageddon-style conversation with the cast of Sea World, and a guy could develop trust issues. Just saying."

"Yeh-yeh. What was that about Milo? Who is that wanker?"

Jamie sighed. "You guys know what a gremlin is?"

"Yeah," Jason said. "It's a mythical creature that intention-ally causes trouble. Mischief. Because it's fun."

"Yes, well . . . what if they aren't mythical, and they do worse than mischief?"

"You mean, like unscrewing a jar filled with magical, cos-mic gobbledygook—some kind of galactic sludge—which has started to disintegrate the Earth?"

"I don't know that I'd call the Universe's DNA *sludge*, per se, but if you mean that the Earth, the Milky Way, and everything on, in, or near it will be wiped out, as if they never even existed, then . . . yeah. I'd say a lot like that."

Jason tapped the steering wheel, slow at first and then in rhythm with the traffic flowing in both directions. *Whidzh whidz whidz whidz. Whidzh-whidz whidz-whidz.* And then his hands shook. He was about to hyperventilate, to just start flipping out because he didn't know what else to do, when he gazed out the window.

With the Verrazano-Narrows Bridge drawing closer, two large tanker ships made their way south between Upper and Lower New York Bay. Fort Wadsworth—a now-closed, concrete military outpost constructed in the 1600s—was across the harbor, at the Staten Island base of the bridge. From there they traversed much of the borough westward on the Staten Island Expressway, taking Route 440 south all the way to the Outerbridge Crossing, over the Raritan Bay and finally into Perth Amboy, New Jersey.

Their drive to Yuma would have been shorter by a hundred miles or so had they started off by cutting through southern Pennsylvania, but Jason got pulled over once along the windy back roads for going just one mile over the speed limit, and with time almost literally hunting them down now, he needed a stretch of highway where he could go as fast as the flow of traffic would allow. So the New Jersey Turnpike it was.

The next hour passed without incident, or conversation, which made sense when Jason saw that Theo and Jamie had both fallen asleep. Given that they still had another 2,400 miles to go—and he was the only one awake—Jason pulled into a rest stop, to recharge.

With Theo and Jamie still out, Jason went inside, first to the community rest room, and then to the food lines, where he grabbed a cheeseburger, fries, and soda, an assortment of snacks, and as many drinks as he could carry in two plastic bags.

Back in the car he drove through the crowded parking lot over to the multi-lane gas pumps. A short, pug-nosed attendant knocked on the window.

"Whaddaya say, pal? Whaddaya need?"

Jason chuckled. "A miracle wouldn't hurt."

"Yeah. Sorry. I'm fresh out. . . . Where you headed?"

"Yuma. Arizona."

"Yuma? Whoa, that's a long-ass trip, pal." The gas attendant looked into the car. "What's with those two?"

"Don't ask. It's . . . we have to find her brother before something else ridiculous happens. And we have to get there like . . . yesterday. The whole thing makes my brain hurt."

"One'a those, huh? Well . . . what can I get ya'?"

"Fill 'er up," Jason said, and handed over his credit card.

"I'll check yer windshield wiper fluid and oil levels while I'm at it. We usually don't do that kinda thing, but . . . you look like you could use a break."

Jason nodded. "Yeah. I really could." He then reached for his cheeseburger, unwrapped the foil. "*Tsch.* Ahh . . . crud."

"What's up, pal? Problem?"

"They forgot the ketchup. I know it's not such a big deal, but I'm really hung over and—"

"Say no more, pal. Sooooo been there." The gas attendant reached into the booth between gas lanes. "Here. I always keep a few packets nearby. Nothing worse than a dry burger."

"Thanks, buddy. I just . . ."

"All good, pal. All good. You dig in and I'll get you squared away."

Jason applied the ketchup, chomped his cheeseburger, then leaned back in the seat. With the end of the world in hot pursuit, even the smallest gesture gave him the juice to head once more into the breach.

"Who knows?" he said, chewing with his eyes closed, envisioning a room full of laughter that had yet to present itself. "Maybe this trip won't be so bad after all."

Despite a steady flow of cars, trucks, motorcycles, vans, buses, and trailers speeding in front, along, and behind them on the

Turnpike, Jason was surrounded by silence.

His thoughts scattered, like random TV channels, with instantaneous leaps of logic. Anna laying on the couch, in her red sweatpants; Simon curled up in the chair; his book shelf; the living room window overlooking the street; parked cars; the accident. The crash. The hospital. Being nine years old; playing stickball; back to the accident; the hospital again; his mother laying with tubes in her nose; his own nose; the movie *The Sting*; Robert Redford; *Butch Cassidy and the Sundance Kid*; jumping off the cliff; mountains; rolling white clouds; and a darkening sky until Jason's thoughts so overwhelmed him that he was unable to think rationally.

"I can't do it. I just can't do it," he said, his foot depressing the gas pedal harder, bringing the car up to almost 88 miles per hour, closing in on the red four-door ahead of him.

With a thundering heart Jason gripped the wheel with such force his hands started to cramp. He weaved through traffic, still increasing speed, up to 90, then 91, 92, and almost 94 miles an hour until finally the car started to shake. He was really in a panic now—his breath forced and labored—terrified he was going to lose control, the car about to flip over and over, recreating his worst moment ever. In his mind's eye, he saw it happen.

And then the left rear hubcap actually popped off. Same again with the front right.

About to put them into a tailspin, Jason forced himself to regain control.

"Slow it down, dude. Slow it down. I gotta stop, gotta go slow. Go slow . . . go slow . . . go . . . slow." About to rear-ended a black SUV, Jason finally eased his foot off the gas, dropping speed down to 87 miles an hour, then 81, then 77, until he put his foot back on the gas pedal, regulating the speed, settling them in at a comfortable 71 miles an hour, safely between cars.

"Okay," Jason said, exhaling long, deep breaths, his heart still thundering away. "Okay. I'm okay. I'm . . ." He peeked through the rearview mirror. Theo was still out. Jamie was curled against the passenger side door up front, also asleep. He rolled his eyes. "You're a big help, guys. Thanks."

It took Jason the better part of an hour and a half for the

adrenaline to wear off, cruising past Cherry Hill and other town-ships in New Jersey, and over the Delaware Memorial Bridge, onto the Delaware Turnpike morphing into the John F. Kennedy Memorial Highway, and across Millard E. Tydings Memorial Bridge in Maryland, headed toward Baltimore.

He eyed a fully loaded car carrier trailer then as it entered the highway from a service road. The rig was purple, with ten cars on its rear platforms, five each on the upper and lower, in piggy-back formation. Theo and Jamie finally stirred. "Hope you had a nice nap. It's been nothing but smooth sailing since . . ."

And in a jolt the massive car carrier swerved in front of them.

"Fuck!" Jason jerked their car to the side, barely avoiding a collision.

"Ahh!" Jamie shouted, throttled against the door.

"Shit!" Theo yelled, tumbled in the back seat.

"I know I know I know I know I know I know I know!"

Jason shimmied the wheel to and fro, desperate to keep them from crashing into any of the cars behind or next to them. Then the car carrier braked, sending the hulking vehicle into a serpentine skid through traffic. Smoke billowed from the screeching tires. The abrupt, violent force jostled the two-tiered carrier platform, slamming the secured cars in place, tipping the entire vehicle so that the five thick wheels on the driver's side were angled on the road—a metallic beast leaning toward the asphalt, about to roll over.

Jason also slammed the brakes, met behind with more screeches, and crashes, resulting in a multi-car pile-up. The shock of the moment prevented Jason from speaking coher-ently, but what he knew—with the tilting car carrier in front about to crush them—was simple and clear:

We. Are. Dead.

He squinted then, clenching, in the shadow of doom. But in doing so he got a good look at the truck driver, who didn't appear to be the least bit afraid. If anything, he seemed to be enjoying himself. And looked awfully familiar.

Jason assumed his mind was playing games with him, facing

death and all—his final cognition—but he was sure that driving the car carrier was the same guy who just hours before pumped his gas.

The pug-nosed driver winked at Jason, offered a big grin. "Look out boys and girls. Big J is on the scene." He unholstered his finger guns, and made the *chk-chk* sound.

And then the driver yanked the steering wheel to the side, and barely, slowly . . . fighting mass, velocity, and gravity . . . just inches at a time, the car carrier started to tilt back to center, until it dropped on its wheels. But the force was so violent that the massive vehicle rolled the other way, toward the passenger side, about to smash a white minivan.

Just before impact, the driver once again yanked the steering wheel, this time in the opposite direction, pulling the carrier back to center once more. The additional cars, within the carrier, slammed against the two-tiered steel ramps to which they were secured.

Although Jason somehow got the car back into gear, to ease it around the debris of stalled vehicles, without further warning the engine seized up, followed by a loud, metallic *rattle* and *clank*. The back axle snapped, dropping to the asphalt, the abrupt halt jostling them once again.

The truck driver opened his door, revealing himself to be a tall, beefy redhead, not the pug-nosed gas attendant from the rest stop. "Holy crap," he said. "You guys okay? I don't know *what* happened."

Hands trembling, Jason pulled on a lever, to clear off the windshield, which was covered in dust. Because even if he couldn't keep them all safe, at least he could clean up this one mess. But rather than blue washer fluid, ketchup and mustard sprayed, the wipers smearing condiments all over the windshield into a thick, brown paste such that he could barely see through the glass ahead.

Jason slammed his hands on the steering wheel. "I can't take this," he said to anyone who would listen. "I can't, I can't, I just can't. I . . ." And then inspiration hit him like a thunderclap. "JebbFest! We gotta go to JebbFest!" Hands still trembling, he pressed 2 on speed dial. It picked up after just one ring.

"Duuuude," said the phone voice in a giggly, whiny sing-song they all could hear. *"I'm gonna spread my gooey butter on your man bagel."*

"Jebb!" Jason fumbled with the device to disengage the speakerphone, which he hadn't realized was on. "Hang on hang on hang on." He glanced at Jamie. "Uh . . . he's just uh . . . ."

Jamie needed clarification. Her voice was soft, jittery. "D-did he just say that he was going to spread his gooey butter . . . on your *man* bagel?"

Thrilled to be distracted from their pile-up, Jason was nonetheless frantic to conjure any phrase that would have been even marginally less embarrassing. He sighed, answered, also in sing-song, watching the road ahead through a small gap in the window smudge. "Y-y-yeaahhh . . . ."

Theo rolled over in the back seat, the release of terror coming out in uproarious laughter.

Jason inserted his earpiece.

Jebb had a question. *"You had me on speaker?"*

"Yes," Jason said with a frazzled sigh. "Yes, I did."

"You didn't mean to do that, did you?"

"No. No, I did not."

"Well . . . blow a monkey's uncle, then. What's up?"

"Dude. I know it's JebbFest, but I need a favor. I need you to come get me. We're close, about half-hour away. Car's wrecked. There was an accident. We're okay, but we need a tow."

"Shit, dude. Sure you're okay? But, wait . . . I thought you couldn't make it. You know . . . popping the question?"

"I am! I will!" Jason shouted, unable to control the adrenaline rush. "I'm going to! Long story. But I can't deal with that now. My car's fucked up! I'm fucked up! . . . WE'RE ALL FUCKED UP! You gotta come get me! I gotta get back on the road! We're headed out west. We have to go now. There's a guy we need to—"

"Easy, dude. Easy. Don't crap a house sideways. I'm texting Low-Jack now. He'll bring the truck. Just tell me where you are."

"Yeah yeah yeah, okay. Thanks. Okay. I-I-I . . . I'll see you soon. Okay."

Despite far more pressing issues, Theo and Jamie nonetheless had the same question. "What's JebbFest?"

Jason shook his head without answering. And as they waited amid the wreckage for his Baltimore friends to arrive, he glanced through the rearview mirror, and thought for just a moment that the corner of the sky—way off in the distance— seemed to be receding somehow, dissolving, leaving emptiness in its wake.

Chapter 17
The Funky Monkey

Theo
Eldersburg, Maryland

Simplicity enabled the deception.

From the outside looking in, Jebb's house seemed perfectly quaint and serene, with beige shutters on the windows, and a white front door with green trim, guarded by a white and brown ceramic dog wearing a red bowtie and a name tag that said *On Duty*. Hardly the scene of a raucous party.

But as Theo stepped inside he immediately felt a whoosh of energy. *Something So Strong* whumped through the speakers, Jason was pulled into a series of high fives, hugs, and hand-shakes, while Jamie excused herself to wash up.

About two dozen JebbFestians were munching on various snacks and drinking beer from red party cups. A busty, bushy-haired brunette in a tight-fitting *Battlestar Galactica* t-shirt with the phrase *Frak yeah, these are real!* across the boobs was arguing with three attentive dudes over which time travel-themed TV show rocked more—*Sliders*, *Voyagers!*, or *Quantum Leap*.

Jebb's wife Trina and four of her girlfriends were in the kitchen laughing over a pitcher of frozen peach margaritas. A co-ed game of strip *Northern Exposure* trivia was under way in the den. And before he could ask where it came from, Theo found a cold *Dos Equis* beer bottle in his hand.

Jebb led Theo out into the backyard, where the keg was being well serviced.

Beneath the starry sky four other JebbFestians lounged in lawn chairs. They drank from more red party cups and passed around a joint. A motion-sensor floodlight, secured above the back door, shone down on the patio. The air was ripe with pine trees lining the yard. Jebb pointed.

"Theo. Check it out. Pizza on the grill. Invented right here at JebbFest."

Curious, Theo leaned over the grill, where he found, as advertised, six large slices of deep-dish pepperoni pizza. He had never been so hungry.

Jebb gestured to the grill master. "Josh. Hook him up."

"Righty-oh. Nice and crispy."

Jebb leaned over the pizza, inhaled deep. "*Man*, that smells good. Jason discovered it a few years ago. I don't like to give him too much credit." He winked at Theo. "But there's no accounting for what a late night of beer, bongs, and the munchies will lead to."

Josh dug the metal spatula beneath the slices. "Takes some real skill. You need to let a regular take-out pizza get cold. Leave it in the fridge at least a few hours. Overnight is even better, so it gets a little thick. Rubbery. Then you slap that bad boy on the grill. Something about that barbeque heat makes all the difference. You want to let the crust get nice and crispy . . . but not black. We usually end up torching a few slices, but what can you do? It's worth it."

Maybe it was nothing but hunger, beer, or just the fun of his first American cookout—or that he had nearly been pulverized beneath a 50,000 kilo car carrier on his way, once again, to avert the galaxy's meltdown. But it was the best damn pizza Theo ever tasted. Then without asking, Jebb took the slice from Theo's hand, chomped himself a mouthful, and handed it back, teeth marks and all.

Much like the snowflake no two countries, cities, or towns were exactly alike, what Theo loved most about his travels—for however much longer circumstance would permit them. He had been across half the globe already and easily adapted to the various cultures, dialects, and rituals. But he was still adjusting to the American ways. They took what they wanted, when they wanted it, and didn't seem to care what you thought about it. Theo stared at the bite mark in his pizza.

"It's okay," said Jebb, short, black, with horn-rimmed glasses. "We're all friends here. Cooties are prescreened."

Theo smiled, and then went back to work on his JebbFestian snack.

"So, Theo. Duuuuuuude. You finally made it, eh? Jason talks

about you constantly." Jebb laughed. "I think he's in love with you."

Theo held in place, mid-bite. A crumble of pizza fell from his lip.

Jebb stared at him. And kept staring. "I'm just fucking with you," he said finally, which got Josh laughing uproariously. "But seriously, dude. Your highway wreck aside, you've worked some crazy-ass voodoo on him."

Theo chuckled sheepishly. "Oh, yeh? I dunno."

"Oh, no, seriously. You didn't know him before. He was in Buffalo with us for like five years. Dude never went *anywhere*. Hardly ever came on road trips, never came to Toronto. It just freaked him out. I'm kinda surprised he even went to Buffalo at all. . . . Josh. Remember?"

"Who? The Adventure King? Oh, yeah. Jason was always a great guy, don't get me wrong. I love him like a brother. He's crazy loyal and there in a pinch, rain or shine, day or night. And if you're down and out he'll sit with you as long as it takes. He listened to me blubber for a week straight when my girl dumped me. But he was always afraid of new places, especially new people. When we first met him . . . he needed to get laid in the *worst* possible way. Wow."

"Yeh," Theo agreed. "He was kinda . . . I dunno . . ."

"Uptight?" Jebb said.

Josh shifted the spatula beneath another crispy pizza slice. "I didn't think he was going to last even one semester."

Jebb gulped his beer. "No joke. I thought for *sure* he was going to drop out and go home. It was really hard for him at first. He didn't trust *anybody*."

Josh kept working the slice. "He was the sweetest guy. But edgy, man. Intense. He was one ear flick away from a total meltdown."

"But now," Jebb said, "dude wants to go *every*where. China, Alaska, South America. I don't know what you did, or what you guys saw, but once he came back from New Zealand . . . that was it. It's like he jumped through a hole in the space-time continuum and came back from another dimension."

You have no idea, Theo thought. *No idea at all.*

Jebb then turned mildly serious. "He told you about the accident, right? Not today. From way back?"

Theo shook his head. ". . . No. What accident?"

"Ohhhhhhh. Dude. No *wonder*. Here. I need another beer." Jebb went to the keg, flipped open the black spout, refilled their cups. Twinkling stars above. Laughter spilled out from inside the house. "Jason was like nine or so, I can't remember. It was his parents, him, and his sister Jill, piled into the car. First family vacation, I think ever. Jason was pretty psyched. They were driving from New York down to Florida, to go to Disney World. It's all going fine, the usual backseat bickering with his sister and whatnot, and then somewhere in South Carolina . . . pow. They blow a tire, car flips over like . . . shit . . . six or eight times. By some miracle, Jason's okay. Just a few scratches. But the rest of 'em . . . oh, man. It was bad." Jebb pulled a slice off the grill. "Dad's a mess. Jill's a mess. His mom was in a coma for a few days. In the end, they all physically recovered. But Jason? It really shook him up."

Theo felt a pit in his stomach. That scene was eerily familiar, one they almost recreated just a few hours earlier. "He never said."

"Yeah, well . . . it's worse. They've only got a small family to begin with, just a handful of relatives here and there, so they're stuck in South Carolina, and nobody to look after Jason. But he's got this cousin, Brian, who was like twenty at the time. He was in the Caribbean working at Club Med or some shit like that. A summer thing. He wasn't even that close to Jason, but without hesitation he leaves his job, flies to South Carolina, then takes him back to New York, and stays with him. When Jason needed somebody, Brian stepped up *big time*. And not that it matters, but Brian was gay, like . . . totally flaming out there gay, at a time when it wasn't always safe to be open about it. But Brian didn't care. He didn't let anyone tell him how to be. Super nice guy. His just being there relieved a lot of Jason's anxiety. But beyond that, I think Jason responded to his strength. Being *out* even fifteen years ago wasn't like it is today."

"I thought you said—"

"Just the calm before the shit storm. About a month later,

after his parents and Jill were okay to travel, Brian went back to the Caribbean for the end of the summer. But when he left, he had a little bit of a cold. Nothing major. Just a low-grade fever."

Theo blinked. His heart pounded. "Wasn't a fever . . . was it?"

Jebb gulped down his beer. "Nope. Turns out he had spinal meningitis. By the time they figured it out, it was too late. He died three weeks later."

Theo sighed, as if Brian, someone he'd never met, was now lost to him as well. "Oh, no."

"Yep. Jason was always a good dude. Lots of opinions, whether you wanted them or not, but a good dude. Never bothered anyone, stayed out of trouble. But between the accident and his cousin . . . it just fucked him all up. His sister was the opposite. She took it as motivation to do everything she could while she could. But Jason kinda . . . hid . . . inside himself. That's the way his sister tells it, anyway. I think the real reason he went to Buffalo, honestly, was to test himself. He could've stayed local, to make it easy, but I think he forced himself to take a long trip, and then be far enough away where he couldn't just run back home if he got scared. I think he knew, deep down, that he needed circumstance to drag him out of his shell. And believe me . . . he needed dragging! *Jeez.* He was like these two guys at the same time. Eighteen going on thirty and eighteen going on twelve. Smart and funny and mature beyond his years in some ways, and in another way a paranoid stress ball stuck in junior high school. You just gotta let him get comfortable. It's when the real *him* comes out."

"Yeh-yeh. Same. It's how he was with me."

"Well I gotta tell ya' . . . he's come a helluva long way since then. Europe, New Zealand. And now he's with Anna. I don't know *what* happened on your trip, exactly, or what you said to him, but whatever it was . . . he's finally becoming the guy I think he wanted to be all along. Just took him a while to get there."

Theo laughed. *You'll never know what he's been through. And he'll never be able to say. Me and him both. How could we?* "Yeh-yeh. He's a good mate."

Jebb winked. "Yeah . . .but, uh . . . let's not tell him. You know."

"No joke," said Josh, who chomped on a crunchy pizza slice, hot off the grill.

"Totally," Theo said. "The wanker. Ha."

"Well," Jebb said, "now that we've all got our pizza on, why don't we mosey on down to the basement and get a little funky."

"Uh . . . okay?"

"Don't worry, Theo. Wet bar's down there. It's where the magic happens. If you think you can handle it."

Theo took one more look at the stars just then, up at that American sky, and then breathed in the pine-tinged air. He knew the Universe was calling his name, to intervene, but even if only for just a short while, he was just where he needed to be. "Yeh-yeh," he said. "I think I'll be okay."

Jamie

Jamie remained on the toilet long after she finished peeing.

Holding that harmonic key as it dangled from her neck, she needed a minute to herself, away from the laughter. The music. The noise. Reminders that she was indeed the strangest kind of stranger in this very strange land.

Sure, she thought, Jason, Theo, and their friends were all nice enough as far as dweebs went, maybe even the kind of friends she would have liked to have had herself . . . if she actually didn't belong back in Eternity, a plane of existence responsible for the very planet they were inhabiting. A planet which had nearly killed her already and whose expiration was fast approaching, and far in advance of what the Big M.O.U. had intended.

And if she didn't find Lex before any of that happened, the life she had known up until that point—the one she had wasted serving others so that they could more thoroughly explore theirs—would have all been for nothing. The way things were going, that very outcome seemed entirely possible, if not likely.

She buttoned up, washed her face, and then stared into

the mirror. At herself. A droplet dangled from the tip of her nose.

Come on, Jamie. Don't get sidetracked. You've waited long enough. Time to take action. There literally may be no tomorrow.

She crossed the hallway, with conviction, and car accident or no, was determined to get Jason and Theo back on the road, one way or another. If her short time away from Eternity had taught her anything thus far, it was that obstacles are only temporary inconveniences. There's always something more important to worry about.

And then a guy walked by. Jamie only saw him from the side, but on his forearm was a starburst tattoo. He strode by an active lava lamp, which illuminated the starburst tips. She instantly thought of the Andromeda galaxy and its incredible pinwheel swirl she loved to gaze upon through the *Rubicon's* glass ceiling. She then reached into her back pocket. From it she removed the postcard Theo's twins gave her. The galaxy. The starburst.

Jamie tapped the postcard, then followed the tattoo. But its owner opened a hallway door, stepped through, and disappeared down a flight of stairs. She rushed down after him as he joined more JebbFestians, gathered around a small, hand-crafted bar, with holiday lights strung across the walls and drop ceiling. The wood-paneled basement was further populated with bookcases of pulp novels, comic books, trade paperbacks, DVD and Blu-ray box sets, and superhero, cartoon, and *Star Wars* figurines. Hanging on the walls were framed movie posters, including *Raiders of the Lost Ark, Jaws, Blade Runner, The Goonies,* and *Back to the Future.*

Behind the bar, Jebb mixed up a banana liqueur concoction, then passed around shots. Jebb's wife Trina kissed Jason's cheek, and whispered in his ear. He wrapped his arm around her waist in a way that only close friends can, smiled, nodded, then pulled Theo over. Others took their drinks. And then Jebb reached up to a string secured along the ceiling, supporting a green, potato-sized, plastic monkey.

Jebb flipped a red switch on the primate's back, which sent the monkey's long green arms in motion, limb over limb, maneuvering across the string. "The Funky Monkey has spoken. L'chaim!"

In one voice everyone repeated *l'chaim*, then downed their shots.

The Power of Love by Huey Lewis and the News came bopping through the speakers as Jamie made her way to Jason. "Hey. Where's the guy with the starburst? The tattoo?"

"Oh, hey. Where'd you go?"

"Starburst," Jamie demanded.

Jason reached for his beer. "Who? You mean Low-Jack? He's over there. By the *Batman* poster."

"Oh. *That's* Low-Jack?" *He towed our car. How did I miss that?* "I didn't notice it before."

"Yeah. It's new. His first tattoo. No idea what it means."

"Oh. Okay. But . . . why do you call him Low-Jack?"

"Ha! Check it out." Jason gestured to Low-Jack, whose back was to them. "Hey! Bob! We need to Low-Jack you tonight? We gotta lock you down?"

Without turning around, Low-Jack raised his starburst arm, extended his middle finger.

And then a new ruckus erupted. Jebb gathered his guests.

"Oh! Dudes! You hear about the *Genius de Milo*? End time's coming. I'm tellin' ya'. Watch out! Last night there was a tsunami in the Great Lakes, Maine had a total blackout, and Rhode Island was overrun by hamsters!"

Grill master Josh was unimpressed. "Oh, for fuck's sake, Jebb. Those guys? They're a bunch of crackpots. First off, it was a few dozen gerbils that got loose in a pet store. But even so. What? The entire Earth is dissolving? Come on . . ."

Jamie grabbed Jason's arm. "Did he say *Genius de Milo*? He said *Milo*?"

Jason shook his head. "Not sure. I—"

"You never know," Jebb said. "Look at those ding-dongs who say global warming isn't real. Now the polar bears need snorkels! Glub-lub-lub."

Josh wasn't having it. "Jebb. Let me get this straight. You're comparing polar ice cap erosion to a planet—this planet—slowly vanishing from space? Really? You want to stick with that story?"

The basement dwellers leaned forward, hanging on his next words. Jamie did the same, because for all she knew, Jebb had more insight and intuition about her predicament than she did.

There was a long pause, until Jebb formulated a response. He raised his beer. "Fuck it," he said. "*Genius de Milo*, dude. *Genius de Milo*."

And then the room broke out into a chant:
VEE-EE-NUS! DEE-MY-LOW! VEE-EE-NUS! DEE-MY-LOW!
And then one side of the room: *VEE-EE-NUS!*
And the other: *DEE-MY-LOW!*
And then back: *VEE-EE-NUS!*
And back again: *DEE-MY-LOW!*
Back and forth they went until finally there was a victor.
DEE-MY-LOW! DEE-MY-LOW! DEE-MY-LOW!

The JebbFestians all broke out into high fives and smiles, chugged their beers, and then slammed down their cups.

Jamie turned to Low-Jack, to find that starburst tattoo. But he was gone. She took off up the stairs and into the kitchen. "Hey," she said to the room. "Have you seen Bob? I mean Low-Jack? You know? With the tattoo. The starburst."

"Check the den," the *Battlestar* brunette said. "Said he wanted in on some strip *Northern Exposure*."

Jamie took the stairs two at a time, then barged in on five players in various states of undress. "Low-Jack?"

"I think he left," one of the mostly naked guys said. "Shoulda Low-Jacked him when you had the chance. I think he took off again. Good luck."

Feeling like the only person on the entire planet who appreciated the actual significance of the *Genius de Milo* and the urgency to get clarity—and get out west—Jamie ran for the front door, out into the night.

The overhead porch light gave off a glare. The ceramic dog was still on duty. Various cars were parked on the suburban street, which curled around the corner, to a slight hill. A half-dozen porch lights were also illuminated.

To her side, a drunken JebbFestian couple pawed each other in the bushes, while the party inside remained in full effect. Jamie wandered toward the street. She looked left, then right. And then, in the darkness, she squinted, and ambled toward a parked car. Their car. Still hoisted on the tow truck, dangling from the rear bumper, looking very much like it had almost been totaled, which, of course, it had. Ketchup and mustard stains were still caked into the windshield.

Low-Jack was slumped over in the tow truck's front seat. Jamie reached for him, rolled up his sleeve. She wasn't sure what the starburst tattoo would tell her, but once she saw it up close, it seemed to have lost its luster.

Or maybe, she thought, *I'm just losing my mind.*

Jamie leaned against the side of the car, angled forward because of the tow hoist, and stared at Jebb's house, knowing that while she was essentially alone in the Universe—for however much longer that swath of reality would last—Jason and Theo were more important to her than ever.

Noticing then that the hood was slightly ajar, she curled her fingers underneath, propped it open. Before her was a disassembled engine, with parts scattered on the curb, and in the street. "That's not good."

And then from within the car, in the dark: "Stop it," Low-Jack mumbled, eyes closed, barely conscious. He pounded the seat. "Stop it!"

Jamie came to his aid. "What? What's wrong? Stop what?"

"Too bright. Make it stop." Eyes still closed, he kept pounding the seat. "Stop it! Nooo!"

"I don't understand. How do I stop it? I don't—"

She looked to his arm, to the starburst tattoo. The edges started to glow, growing brighter, brighter, and brighter still, singeing his skin.

"Nooo! Stop! Stop it! Make it stop! Nooo. Huh-ho!"

Jamie reached for her back pocket, which was scalding hot. "Ow! Shit." She removed the postcard. The starbursts were also aglow. By the corner, she held the postcard up to Low-Jack's arm, starbursts shining brighter as they came together.

"Nooo! Stop! Make it stop! Noooooooo!"

And then without warning the starbursts came to a white-hot glow, and fizzled out. Steam came off his flesh.

"Ahhhh," said Low-Jack, who started to pass out again. "Better."

Unsure of what to do next, Jamie marched right back into the house, grabbed herself a red party cup, and headed out back for the keg. It *was* JebbFest, and if this was to be her final reprieve in all of Existence, she wanted to grab a slice off the grill, before it was all gone.

Heavy-eyed and in need of showers and breakfast, Jamie, Theo, and Jason huddled around their car. What was left of it, anyway.

Low-Jack Bob was already up, trying to reassemble the engine, but couldn't find half of the pieces. The rear axle was still trashed. But if nothing else, he had wiped the windshield clean. "Oh, man. Sorry guys. I'll pay for it."

"Don't worry," Jason said. "I think this car hates us. Besides . . . it's not even mine."

Jamie rubbed her eyes. The morning sun was bright. "This is why you call him Low-Jack, I presume? He always do this?"

"Last year he disassembled the neighbor's motorcycle. About three years ago it was the van up the street. First JebbFest he went for the police cruiser around the corner, but we got to him before he cracked the hood open. Low-Jack starts out okay, but after a few drinks we lose track of him, and then he wanders off. By the time we find him . . . it's too late. This was bound to happen, sooner or later."

"JebbFest," Jamie said.

"Yep," Jason said. "Speaking of which . . . Jebb . . . I could use a ride into town. I need to rent a car. Mine's kinda . . . you know . . . smashed."

Theo, who had been quiet thus far, looked over the dismembered vehicle, at Jamie and Jason, and then up to the morning sky. Off in the distance, a TV helicopter flew by.

"Nah," he said. "Forget the car. I've got an idea."

"What?" Jason said. "You're making me nervous. I've seen that look before."

Theo tousled his hair, stood on his toes, and then stretched up as far as he could reach. "I can get us out west," he said. "But I don't think you're going to like it."

Chapter 18
Flight of the Bumble Bees

Brigsby
Eternity

Brigsby sipped his drink.

There were five sections behind the bar, along the back wall, each with three dark wood shelves and frosted glass paneling, backlit with fluorescent light blue. Stacked on each shelf were various liquor bottles, and glasses. The fluorescent blue reflected on the wood bar, polished to a shine.

Blue martini was his standard casual cocktail. When he just needed to unwind at home, in his slippers, cold chocolate milk. But at the hotel bar, after his show, there was nothing simpler, and more relaxing, than drinking a fresh, cold beer in a frosty pilsner glass.

Chioma the bartender, as bartenders do, wiped down the counter. Up in the corner was a flat-screen TV. Playing was the *Breakfast with Brigsby* segment he had recorded earlier that day: *Picking a Fight Makes It Easier To Break Up*. And as they had done after each show for as long as either of them could remember, Chioma and Brigsby dissected the episode.

Chioma had a broad, flat nose, deep-set eyes, and long braids curled in a bun. Her ebony hue appeared even more so against Brigsby's pasty white skin.

"Breakups are no fun, that's for sure," Chioma said. "I don't like to fight myself, but sometimes . . . ooh . . . it feels like the only way to get through it. The only way to move on. At least until you can get over the sting. Insightful topic today, Mr. B. Good show."

"Really? I can't watch it. I feel wrinkly. Old."

"No. You look good."

"You're sweet. Full of binkle bunk . . . but sweet. Speaking of which . . . you have any of those candy-coated peanuts? I love those."

"Sorry, sugar. On back order. But I have the red pistachios.

You like those."

"Mmmm . . . nah. The red gets all over my fingers, and then I can't help myself and lick it all off, and next thing you know it's a red pistachio orgy and then I'm back in the hot tub with a gaggle of young companions. And between you and me . . . I'm not in the mood."

"How about some pretzels? Simple . . . but a classic."

"Sure. Why not? That'll do."

The video phone rang just then. Like a perfectly choreographed dance, Chioma gracefully eased to the other end of the bar, studying the day's program. She knew when to move away.

Brigsby focused on the call. Lawrence was in full view, from the main CBM Warehouse.

"B," Lawrence said. "I stopped by *The Dooly*, like Jamie said. I spoke to the management company and four of the residents. There's no Chuck on staff. The doorman. There never was. So I reviewed the security tapes from the night Jamie went to see him. There was just a split second—less even—but Chuck sneezed, and slipped in and out of Milo mode. It was crystal clear. It's him. No doubt."

"That's an issue for us, Lawrence. What do we do now?"

"Have you checked on the Milky Way lately? On Earth? The fluxing has intensified. It's worse. I think Milo is actually down there."

"Huh. That *is* new. And . . . what about the warehouse? Or the other jars? Did he tamper with them?"

"Not that I can tell."

"Are you with Donnie?"

"Yes. Danielle, too. You want to talk to them?"

Brigsby sighed. "Not particularly, no, although I suppose I need to. But I *don't* want them coming over today. Make sure of it. Okay . . . let me get this over with. Put them on."

Off screen, Brigsby could hear his friends arguing.

"Let me talk to him, Dear. It's better . . . I know . . . I won't, I . . . sigh . . . yes, Dear. Okay, Dear. Yes. Right. No. No, of course. You're right, you're right. Okay. I love you, too. I—"

An audible *SLAM!* ended the conversation. Donald appeared on screen.

"Donnie, my boy. So how *is* your lovely bride?"

"She's uh . . . fine. Fine. Just a little stressed out."

"Ya' think?"

"Listen, Brigs. I'm kinda busy here."

"You hear that, Lawrence? He's too busy to talk to the boss. Whaddaya know?"

Donald's tone was edgy. "I just debriefed Lawrence on sensitive company business."

"I'm sure you did," Brigsby said. "What's that got to do with the boss?"

"Lawrence *is* my boss."

"For sure. And I'm his. So, technically . . . I'm your boss, too. You know. Assuming that matters."

"Ha! Listen, Brigs. I know you're all mister famous talk show host and now you're also a big-time hotelier and you just generally think that you're the boss of everyone because they can't wait to kiss—as Danny likes to say—your skinny white ass. But I'm really swamped. I don't think you appreciate the magnitude of what I do here, and what I'm dealing with right now. Can you pontificate to me later, over dinner maybe?"

"Now is better."

"Brigs, I really don't have time for this."

"Mmmm . . . I think you do."

Donald expelled a long, breathy sigh. "And why's that?"

"Because I'm on the board of directors of the CBM Warehouse. I'm not *technically* your boss. I'm *actually* your boss. As in . . . I decide who gets hired and fired, who gets what job, and how much they get paid. You know . . . the boss."

Brigsby knew that he shouldn't—he was the Minder of the Universe and in theory above such petty manipulations—but he took some naughty, voyeuristic delight in seeing his friend squirm a little.

Donald looked to Lawrence, who nodded in agreement. A bead of sweat trickled down Donald's bald, white pate. "Since, uh . . . since when?"

"Not sure. Lawrence. How long have I been on the Board?"

"Let me see. Since . . . always."

Donald's eyes popped up. "Always?! What do you mean *always?*"

"Yeah," Brigsby said. "Always. That sounds about right."

Donald's voice dropped, but held a tinge of resentment. "Oh. You never said."

"Well . . . you never asked. So nyeh." Brigsby stuck out his tongue.

Donald stepped out of view from the video screen, and mumbled to himself, although the audio was clear. *"Brigsby's my boss. My boss! What the mother . . . ?! Danny was right. She said he would do this. That he'd find a way to control me, to keep me on his hook. She always tells me not to trust him, but I do it anyway. I never learn."* He took a deep breath, sighed again before stepping back on screen.

Brigsby clarified the status of their joust. "You know I could hear you, right?"

Donald offered a mock smile. "Of course. I was speaking loudly."

Brigsby sipped his cocktail. "Touché. So . . . what's the status of the warehouse? Are any of the jars missing?"

Donald squared his shoulders, held a stare, and then let out a sigh of resigned annoyance. "Not that we can tell. Danny's been surveying Sector Five all week. It's why she's burned out. It's a big job."

"Indeed. I imagine it is. Have any of the jars been tampered with?"

"Not exactly."

"What does that mean? *Not exactly?*"

"A few have been stocked in the wrong slots."

Brigsby needed clarification. "It's a big warehouse. What's *a few?*"

Standard warehouse shelving units extended the equivalent of 4,113 Earth miles in length and 74 Earth miles high.

"Um . . ."

"Come on, now, Donnie-babe. Out with it."

"About a million," Donald said. "Give or take."

"*A million?*"

"Well . . . actually . . . closer to two million."

"Two million?"

"Three million eight hundred forty-seven thousand nine hundred and thirteen."

Brigsby thought a moment. "I see."

Lawrence unfolded his arms. "Just shy of four million? That's *a few?*"

"Actually," Donald said, "by percentage . . . yes. There are more than nine hundred fifty-one trillion jars in this one warehouse alone. There are another sixteen warehouses as big as this one and another dozen just slightly smaller."

"There's actually far more than that," Brigsby said, "but your point is well taken. These four million? Could that just be standard percent error?"

"No. The system is designed for *zero* percent error. Jars cannot be misfiled within the warehouse. It's a physical impossibility. The grid won't allow it. Any jar forced into the wrong shelf space sets off the alarm, and locks out the jar."

"Surely there must be some sort of override? A big, red button? You know? Like in all the movies? *Code Red! Press the button! Code Red!* It's always so exciting."

"There *is* no override. That's the whole point. Each jar of Cosmic Building Material is individually engineered for creating, shaping, and building a specific element in the Universe. No jar has ever been misfiled in the history of Eternity. Ever."

Brigsby affirmed their position. "Until now."

"Correct," Donald said. "Until now."

"Who might have the capacity to override the non-override?"

"You mean . . . other than the Minder of the Universe?"

Brigsby bristled just then. He looked to Lawrence for assurances, communicating without speaking: *Is Donald just asking me the appropriate question, or is there subtext here? He doesn't know who I am . . . does he? Does he?* It might have been the scope of the crisis, or that Milo genuinely unnerved him, but Brigsby needed to think. With few exceptions, no one's opinion had mattered more to him at any point throughout his immeasurable existence, but it was different with Donald. Brigsby truly cared, as foolish as he knew that to be. But he was growing tired of being the Minder of the Universe, and wanted a friend, as much as that was possible.

Yet rather than confessing his true identity, he sipped his drink, purely for effect. He studied Donald, considered him in full. Lawrence, meanwhile, offered a barely perceptible shrug.

Nah. He doesn't know. Nuh-uh. He doesn't know. He doesn't know.

"Yes," Brigsby said finally. "Other than the Minder of the Universe."

"Then, no," Donald said of the CBM Warehouse. "There's no one."

"Alright. We'll look into it. But for the moment . . . what's the worst that could happen? If by accident some Cosmic Building Material from the wrong jar is used on a construction site? What are we talking here?"

Lawrence interjected. "There's no way to envision all the possible scenarios. But just to postulate . . . imagine if even a drop of liquid CBM specifically engineered to create a star was accidentally applied to the outline of what was intended for a house cat?"

Brigsby considered his question. "You'd need one helluva litter box. Okay. Understood. Jar swapping bad. Lawrence, get a team down there. And give Donald and Danielle an extra vacation voucher. They deserve it."

Donald wiped his head. "Thanks. But what should I do until then?"

"Sit tight," Lawrence said. "I'll need you for consultation, since this is your sector. I'm contacting the maintenance crew now. It will take a while, but we'll put the misplaced jars back where they belong."

Donald shook his head. "It won't work."

Lawrence's look projected a mix of annoyance—and fear. "Why not?"

"It's easier if I show you. Here. Watch." Donald leaned over the console, on the safe side of the protective glass. He pressed several buttons, and then, with a small red lever, operated a long mechanical arm on the warehouse side of the glass, to grip one of the jars. The arm rose and then shifted to a designated slot on the immense wall of shelves that stretched almost infinitely into each direction. "Okay. Here goes."

The arm positioned the dislodged jar in front of an empty shelf slot without incident. But as the mechanical grip extended, to place the jar *on* the shelf, the jar suddenly—and violently—darted through the air like a bee avoiding lethal bug spray, and then forced itself into an occupied shelf slot, which then dislodged and catapulted the resting jar into a similar spastic flight path.

What ensued was the equivalent of a swarm of those very bees bouncing off one another in a mad frenzy until thousands of jars occupied shelf slots for which they were not designated.

"Happens every time," Donald said. "They hop around and rearrange themselves, and never in the same sequence."

Brigsby wasn't having it. "But it's our system. Why can't we fix it?"

"Larry. We need to tell him."

Lawrence lowered his voice. "No. It can wait."

"What?" Brigsby said. "Tell me what?"

After a long pause, Lawrence nodded.

"We've tried rebooting the system," Donald said. "But every time we do . . . it makes the problem worse."

"Worse? How could it be worse?"

"The percentage of misfiled jars seems to increase exponentially with each reboot. I've had the engineers down here for days. They're stuck. If the problem keeps up, we'll have to shut down the whole quadrant."

Brigsby didn't like this. Not one bit. "Sounds expensive."

"Very," Lawrence said. "But we may have no choice."

CBM was the most potent—and valuable—substance in Existence. Putting even a single drop, much less millions of jars worth, in quarantine, was far more than waste. It was a galactic sin and a failure that would haunt Brigsby for all time. The *uncreated* was a burden—and guilt—that chiseled away at his deepest resolve.

Donald's shoulders drew tight. He looked away. "There might be another way."

Lawrence zeroed in on him. "What is it?"

"I, uh . . . it's . . ."

Brigsby knew Donald's tells as well as anyone, and better

than most. Plus, he was the Minder of the Universe. "Donnie . . .
Don . . . Are you talking about . . . ?"

"The jar," Donald admitted. "Yes."

Lawrence interrupted. "Which jar? There's so many of . . .
Ohhh. You mean . . . ?"

Eyes still looking toward the floor, Donald nodded.

"The Medley jar," Brigsby said. "Theo Barnes. The one you
and your bride knocked into the Earth while it was still forming. You think *that's* the source of the problem?"

Donald offered a long, deep sigh. He finally looked up. "Yes.
I think so. If we can get that one jar back on the shelf, where
it belongs, I think the system will reset, and the other jars will
fall back in line."

Brigsby didn't need to hear more. He knew instantly that
Donald was right. "Okay, then."

"Okay?" Lawrence said. "That's it?"

"Jamie's already down there. It's up to her."

"But, Brigsby. Sir. I mean . . . should we send reinforce-
ments? Someone to help?"

"No, Lawrence. Jamie has what she needs. It'll be up to her
to get Medley and Barnes on board."

Lawrence then asked the only question that mattered.
"What if she can't?"

"Then I've miscalculated in such a way that will impact the
entire Universe." Fed up with bad news, Brigsby signaled to
Chioma for another pilsner of beer. Upon its delivery, he sipped
the sudsy head off the top. "You know, I used to think Milo
might have actually served a purpose. But now . . . he's turning
out to be more trouble than he's worth."

Chapter 19
Poker Night

Milo
Somewhere in the Universe

Poker night. Milo never missed it.

They usually met in the back room of Hardwicke's office, but this was a special occasion.

So he invited the gang up to the spine of Philbrick's Comet, Milo's favorite perch from which to view the Universe. By human calculus that incendiary slab of rock was tearing across the solar system at more than 35,000 miles per hour, but to Milo and the gang, it was more like a luxury train cruising along the countryside. He tipped back in his chair, chewing on a cherry licorice stick.

Milo had a pair of jacks and not much else.

Randal, a big galoot of a water delivery guy, was giving him the business, as usual. "You gonna chew your fingers off or what? Twenty to you, Milo. In or out?"

"Worry about your own cards," said Esteban, who was nursing a beer. "Lose one more hand to me and you'll be driving my cab for a month. While I take a niiiice loooong nap."

A baggage handler for Galaxy Cruise Ships, Doris chewed her cigar. The fumes drifted off the comet, then whisked into the cosmos. "So you're actually awake when you're on duty? The way you drive . . . it's hard to tell!"

The gang broke into loud, guttural laughs, exchanged high fives at Esteban's expense.

Milo was perpetually and simultaneously everywhere and nowhere in all corners of the Universe, but still he liked to have extra eyes and ears throughout Eternity—his blue collar spies.

Like Brigsby, even Milo couldn't focus on every detail simultaneously, in perpetuity. And even though Milo had been going up against Brigsby since their inceptions, this time was different. He needed to talk it through. Plus, he liked the company.

These were his kind of people.

Milo held up his licorice stick then, just enough to melt the tip on the bottom of a passing nebula. He liked it a little bit gooey. "Okay," he said, tossing his chips into the pot. "Call."

Which brought things around to Hardwicke, a female private investigator who specialized in the galaxy design racket. No shortage of crimes and corruption there.

"So you and the Big M.O.U.," Hardwicke began, her slight frame concealing a capable and, when needed, sly and dangerous operator, "you've always had this part/counterpart relationship. He oversees the Universe . . . and you—"

"Bust a lotta balls!" Esteban interjected, inciting more laughter.

"I was going to say, *do your thing*, but, yes, I think we're making the same point."

Milo nodded. "Yep. That's the deal-ee-o."

They were all his pals, but Hardwicke and Milo had a special relationship. They had been through a lot together. There would be more to come.

"I know he's been the bane of your existence, or maybe the very reason for it, but in any case . . . don't you feel the least bit of sympathy for him? That's a lot of responsibility. Heavy lies the crown . . ."

Randy downed a shot. "Sympathy? He's the Big Fucking M.O.U.! The Minder of the Universe. He's got the *power* to do whatever he wants. . . . Do I have sympathy for his stress? Uh . . . no. Not so much."

"Actually," Milo corrected, "it's a troika, a triumvirate . . . a threesome, as Brigsby would say. He's not personally *the* Minder of the Universe, but one of three. He's got Ira and Howard to help keep the balance, to share the division of labor."

"Yeah," Randy said, grabbing his crotch. "Division of this. How long's it been since they were actual partners?"

". . . It's been a while," Milo admitted.

"Right," Esteban said. "So the way it is now, it's just Brigsby making all of the decisions. That's just a bit too much power . . . no?"

Milo smirked, shook his head, then dug a licorice wedge

from his back tooth. Philbrick's Comet was coming up on his favorite star system—The Vitoff Six. There were only, as the moniker suggested, six planets, although each sported multiple moons. Milo had a special bond with the Vitoff Six. They were all a bit off kilter, and difficult to quantify.

Kind of like Milo himself.

As they shot past the first planet—a fluorescent blue dwarf planet known as Parkedroia—golden particles from the comet's tail lit up the three smallest moons. Matching Brigsby, Milo was an entity without a true shape, definition, or features. But he liked to assume a recognizable state, to feel more connected, depending on the specific point and dimension of Existence upon which he happened to be directing his focus.

Hardwicke flattened and then fanned her cards, keeping them close. She rolled a chip along the outside of her fingers.

When the struggles were beyond him, Milo came to Hardwicke. She had a knack for listening, interpreting . . . and discovering dirty truths. Whether she revealed them or not was another matter.

"The Universe is chugging along just fine," she said, "then suddenly, without warning he wipes it out. Everything. A big, fat, empty nothing. Utterly blank. The ultimate void. And later, finally, after a time, he repopulates the Universe for eight, or was it nine billion years? I forget. In any case, things seem to be back on track. We're all good. And then, yet again, like before, he wipes it all clean a *second* time. And then a third and a fourth. It's been this way ever since."

Randal scratched his chin. "I know it's his job to oversee the Universe . . . his *role* . . . in all of this cosmic lunacy. But that's intense, bro."

Doris poured herself another drink. "Intense, my ass. Fucker's a stone cold gangster."

Hardwicke eyed the table. "Yeah. . . . I don't know about that. The Big M.O.U. is a lot of things, but he doesn't strike me as being sadistic. I think it's something else. He's searching."

The fourth planet—Sansonite—was fast approaching. Milo gazed over the edge. Just as Philbrick's Comet passed over the purple planet's gaseous epicenter, he dropped his licorice stick.

Milo knew it would disintegrate long before it could hit the surface, but it was fun to watch the licorice tumble. No Earth-shattering decisions. Just a simple pleasure.

He reached for a new licorice stick. "I'm not sure what he's looking for, but this is how it is. How it's always going to be."

Doris spit the tip of her cigar over the side of the comet. "Like I said. A real fucker."

Esteban restacked his chips. "What do they call it on Earth? The Big . . . Blam? The Big Bunk?"

"The Big Bang," Hardwicke said. "Brigsby takes all the dimensions of Existence and everything within them, and with force and velocity inconceivable by any other standard, slaps them against each other in one, well . . . Big Bang. An endless cycle of them."

"*Pfft*," Doris said. "He's got no right to do *that*."

"But that's just it!" Milo said. "He *does* have the right! It's who he is. I'm not saying he *should* do it, or that it's a good idea, but right or wrong, for better or worse, it *is* his choice." He sat back in his chair, squeezed his eyes shut. He breathed in the Universe—hot and sultry, like an unventilated locker room, yet semi-sweet, a concoction of lilac, apple pie, and melting chocolate chips.

"But when I finally realized it would never change, *that's* when I knew. I had to *do* something." Milo allowed the *whoosh* of the Universe to roll over him. "I remember the first time I knocked on his door. Wow, what a doofus I was. Yelling . . . pontificating . . . about how he was out of control, where did he get the nerve? Because before I could get another word out—*zap*—he redistributed me. Turned me into a ladybug's ass crack. You wouldn't think it would smell that bad. Especially on Ersi, with all those sharp emerald flowers. But, wow. Let me tell you. That's some real stank."

Milo laughed at himself. The others laughed too, although uncomfortably so.

The fifth planet—Caridi—was almost behind him now, six times the size of Jupiter, and twice as bright. The Ordilacks were terrific folk. Oddly small for a planet so large, but they were as warm and hospitable as you could ever ask for. Milo was going to miss them.

Hardwicke shifted her eyes between her cards, the players, and the messy pile in the center of the table. "Call." She tossed her chips. "And raise fifty."

Esteban, Doris, and Randal all folded.

"But then," said Milo, alone now in the hand with Hardwicke, "I reconstituted myself."

Randal got up from the table, and leaned on the railing, to overlook the Universe. "Took you a while, if I recall. You were gone a long time."

"I was. But after I came back, it was clear to me that the only thing I ever really *knew*, I mean, what I could feel deep down, was that I just sort of . . . *knew him*. Brigsby and me, we were both there from the beginning, if you can call what and where we were a *beginning*."

Milo picked up his cards, set them down again, and then reached upward, above his head. He interlocked his fingers, turned his palms out, and stretched. Time to limber up.

"I was convinced that if Brigsby was going to create *everything in Existence*, then my job was to do the opposite. To destroy. Only . . . that didn't work too well?"

Randal took another drink. "You couldn't keep up. The Universe is just too damn big."

Milo did a left side stretch, held it, then a right side stretch. "Not just. I like my fun . . . I think we all know that . . . but the thing is . . . I don't want to destroy *anything*. Not my style. But I did it anyway, wrecking things all over, because that was my purpose. Or so I thought. So, yeah . . . I kept him busy, but I'm not sure it made a real difference. If I knocked one planet out of its orbit, he created three more. If I diffused one star another took its place."

"That's what I don't get," Doris said. "No offense . . . you know I love you . . . like the brother-in-law of my former mailman's yoga instructor . . . but if you were such a pain in the ass, why didn't he just wipe you out? Why put up with your nonsense? . . . Why waste the time?"

The table offered subtle nods as a passing nebula drifted over them.

"Now *that* is the mother of all questions?" Milo tossed his chips into the center of the table. He wasn't sure if Hardwicke had a strong hand. He could never tell with her. She was that good. "Call." He then offered his cards, jacks up.

"Because he can't," Hardwicke said.

Milo chuckled again. She always knew. "Brigsby. The Minder of the Universe. The Big M.O.U. He can do *anything* he wants. *An-y-thing.* But the one thing . . . the *one thing* he cannot do . . . is control *me*." A crooked smile overtook him. "Now *that's* a heckuva thing to figure out, let me tell you. It messed with my head."

"I remember," Hardwicke said. "I was really scared for you."

Doris gave a look of surprise, rejection, and even a touch of fear. "Milo? Nah. He always bounces back. He's one of the good ones."

"Thanks," Milo said. "But it also meant that in all of Existence . . . I was truly alone. I had no partner."

"Don't say that," Esteban protested. "You always have us."

"Oh, no-no-no. Of course. No, I know I do. I *love* you guys. You know that. It's just—"

Hardwicke interrupted. "You had no *other you.*"

"Yes. That's right. And that's when I *really* went bonkers. Remember my booze-a-thon? The really bad one? I still couldn't appreciate what I was supposed to do with this power. It was overwhelming." Milo stretched his jaw, took a breath. "Until, of course . . . I finally figured it out. . . . And *that's* when I started being Milo. The real Milo. Being the wonder . . . that is me."

Esteban, Doris, and Randal all smiled at him.

"Well good for you, wonder boy." Hardwicke overturned her cards. A pair of twos. And a pair of threes. "But you might want to work on your bluffing. You really suck at it."

Chapter 20
Sketching a Dream

Emma
San Francisco

Emma's latest boy toy wasn't the best she'd ever had, but was more than up for the task.

He'd brought her to orgasm twice already, and had Emma allowed herself to fully submit, it likely would have been thrice.

From the outset of Project *Remake Emma*, she regulated herself by way of an unspoken directive. That she wouldn't engage sexually to her utmost desire until or unless she reached her ideal weight and recaptured the body form she once wore so proudly and to great effect.

But shedding many of her unwanted pounds wielded an unanticipated, counterintuitive side effect. The thinner and svelter she became, the more inhibited she felt in bed. No longer being able to manipulate others with her sexual wiles forced her to slow down, to reconsider how she might better navigate society's byzantine layers, and ultimately reclaim her rightful standing.

Emma had resented the flesh-and-blood prison that had been imposed upon her by the Minder of the Universe as a condition of her banishment from Eternity. Yet the enormous body she had been encased within gave her real physical power.

At more than three hundred pounds she had been slow and lumbering and suffered from heart palpitations if she moved too quickly. But with a massive core, and limbs like tree trunks, she eventually became accustomed to—and even grew to secretly appreciate—that despite her limited mobility, she could wield brute force. An effective complement to her creativity and determination.

Her dissatisfaction with the still oversized body that was now her own remained—the depression she felt over it lasted for years—but strangely to her, as time went by she grew to think of it not so much as a prison and a punishment, but rather as a shield. Her girth was oddly empowering.

Had her own body institutionalized her? Perhaps. But now that she was stepping out from behind those protective layers, she was feeling vulnerable and uncertain. And now that she also had those feelings—and as her body was at least halfway closer to her idealized shape and size—she desired the physical comfort and tenderness of the one individual that she simply could not have.

Lex was a dog now. A canine. Talk about incompatibility issues.

And while Emma had broken her own sexual protocol by experimenting in ways she had previously rejected outright, she wasn't about to redefine *doggie style*.

Face up on her bed, with one of her boobs exposed, she felt a gentle poke in the ribs. Boy Toy's muscled arm stretched across her, offered a toke off the joint he was smoking.

"No, thanks," she said. "I never touch it."

"Um. Hello. You own a weed shop."

"It's just a business. It's inventory."

"Damn," said Boy Toy, who, with a half-thickened noodle, rolled out of bed and craned his neck side to side, preparing for another go. "You're hardcore."

"Yeah, well . . ."

Boy Toy again toked on the joint, and then wandered over to Emma's desk. He picked up her sketch pad, which displayed an intricate configuration of hand-sketched planets, moons, and stars. "Hey . . . what's this?"

Emma instinctively bunched the burgundy silk sheets to her chest. She was getting more comfortable with her body, but not that comfortable. "It's nothing. Give it here."

"Hang on, babe." Boy Toy studied it closer. "Oh. I get it. Is this for your café? Another mural for the wall?"

"Yeah. It's uh, sure, okay, it's for the . . ." But Emma didn't want to hide. She wanted to reveal. At least, she wanted to try. "Actually," she said, allowing the sheets to fall away from her naked, still plus-sized body. "Let me get a hit off that."

Boy Toy brought the sketch pad and weed over to the bed.

Emma accepted both, and then laid back down. She sipped the joint. Once, twice, then again.

"Sometimes," she said, letting the government-grade marijuana course through her body, rendering her warm, loose, and relaxed, "sometimes . . . I imagine I'm from somewhere else. Someplace faaaaar away."

"Totally," Boy Toy said. "Me, too."

"You do?"

"Who doesn't? Every now and then I imagine myself a lot like I am now, only with more money, or a better job, or the awesome girlfriend. It's like shopping in a store full of things I can't possibly afford. I know I'm not walking out with the leather jacket, but sometimes . . . I just need to try it on. Everyday I'm faced with things I'll never have. If I don't at least enjoy the fantasy now and then, there's nothing to shoot for."

Emma unveiled a half-smile, surprised and even just a little bit impressed with Boy Toy's ability to listen, comprehend, and communicate. "Yes. Exactly. To try it on. Only in my world, in my *dream* world," she quickly clarified, "it's Eternity. It's a realm far beyond Earth." Emma checked to see if she still had his attention. He'd already had his way with her and then some, and was now toking on her weed, so she wasn't sure if he'd stick around for pillow talk. "Far beyond the solar system. Beyond the stars."

"Coooool." Boy Toy's eyes glazed over. "Trippy. What's it like?"

Emma closed her eyes, and along the canvas of her mind recalled Eternity, and her place in it, if not exactly how it had been, but the way she wanted it to be. "It's special. Elegant. It doesn't appear on any star map. It's a realm far beyond all others. And in this realm, in Eternity, there's a room. And in this room . . . I sit. And dream. And draw. And when I open my eyes, I look down at the canvas, to see what I've created." Emma handed Boy Toy the sketch pad. "In Eternity, I design galaxies. I envision the Universe. I give it a voice. Texture." She offered a half shrug. "A soul. And when I've finished my dream, when I've laid out my design . . . we build it. A galaxy is born. I am the mother of life. They are my children. I love them all."

"Whoa," Boy Toy said.

"Yeah," she said. "Whoa. And this one, on my sketch pad here . . . this is what I've been dreaming of lately. A new star system. Only six planets, but each one with two moons, and three suns at the core. They're smaller suns, in perfect symmetry. And here"—Emma pointed to the mid-section—"are two comets, one chasing the other. The one in front perpetually out of reach. They're always in pursuit . . . so close, yet somehow alone. They encircle the star system, passing each planet twice each year. And as they pass, they scorch across the sky for all to see."

"What's it called? The star system?"

"I don't know. It's why I can't finish. I guess a child can't really have an identity—a life of its own—until its mother gives it a name."

Boy Toy shifted on his side, propped up his head. Emma had his full attention. "What's holding you back?"

Emma began to shake. She'd divulged more of herself in five minutes than she had in all her time on Earth. It was an important step. But one step only. She immediately slid out of bed, pulled on her silk robe, then tied the sash around her waist.

"Okay, there, chief. That's enough for you. Time to go. Emma needs her rest."

"Go? Now? . . . *Why?*"

Emma patted him on the back. "You're a good kid, but we're done here. It's been fun."

Boy Toy shimmied inside his jeans and t-shirt. "Wait. Don't you want to know my name? Exchange numbers? . . . *Something?*"

Emma nudged him to the door, then into the hallway. "No. Not really."

"But—"

Emma closed the door in his face.

Without further consideration she took the sketch pad to her desk, sat down, then flipped up her laptop. She opened a new email, entered the appropriate address in the *To* field, and then moved the cursor to the body. She started to type:

Lilly-

And then Emma sat, back straight, fingers arched on the keys. But no message came. She wasn't sure what to say. Slowly, she began typing *I'm sorry*, then quickly deleted it. She next went with *Yo, what up girl?* then rolled her eyes at herself, and deleted that, too. Emma started and stopped as such several more times, until finally she decided that only one message would do. She moved the cursor to the *Subject* field and entered *Invitation*. And then from her desktop she uploaded a scanned image of the galaxy sketch into the body of the email.

Beneath it she typed:

E-

And then the *Starlight* address.

That was all she could bring herself to write. It would have to be enough.

Just then the bathroom door opened. Out came her Chinese food-buying neighbor, Nina, with a towel wrapped around her torso, and drying her wet hair with another. Nina stood behind Emma, and kissed her on the back of the neck.

Feeling more nervous than she anticipated, Emma's first threesome hadn't quite been the kinky escapade she expected, but then, it hadn't been half bad either. Although in no hurry to try it again, she was willing to keep an open mind. Nina had a rockin' body and aroused Emma's nether region to surprising effect, but when it came to activity between the sheets, Emma was far more interested in getting up close and personal with a nicely formed dong than a shaved bush bordered by a Stewie Griffin tattoo.

"Whatcha' doing? Checking your email?"

Emma bristled at Nina's sheer stupidity, never more aware that a tight butt and a big rack can only get a girl so far. "Yes," she said, and with her heart mildly aflutter, pressed *Send*. The message disappeared into cyberspace.

No turning back now, she thought. *Here we go.*

"Who are you writing to—?"

Emma raised a finger, stood up, and removed Nina's towel. Exposed were a pair of clean, firm breasts. "I think maybe a little less talk," said Emma, who slid her hand between Nina's smooth, warm legs, "and a little more action."

Chapter 21
The Pirate's Wheel

Lilly
Sausalito, California

Typical for the Bay Area, a cool, damp breeze put a chill in the morning air.

The park at Jackson Corner was only lightly attended, but already at the highest point of the toddler's jungle gym was DJ Tanner, claiming his place as the alpha male. Lilly didn't like DJ, didn't want Benny hanging around him. Only three years old, DJ was already a thug in the making, but Benny insisted on playing with him anyway.

The jungle gym was designed much like a pirate's ship, with portholes, and boardwalks with metal chain link railings, short ladders, and slides, and, at the top platform's midsection, a large, metal steering wheel. Big for his age, DJ was navigating, almost daring the other kids to approach him. An excuse to knock them down.

Lilly knelt down by the benches. She tucked Benny's scarf into the front of his jacket, to keep his chest warm. He probably didn't need it, but she couldn't help herself.

"Mommy?"

"What's up Buh-buh-buh-Benny-and-the—"

"I know, Mom. Jeffssssss."

"Well, look at mister-I-know-my-music-today. My future rock star."

Benny ignored her attempts at humor. "Who's Emmer?"

Lilly immediately untucked then retucked Benny's scarf, to conceal her shaking hands. "How, uh . . . how do you know about Emma?"

Three children ran by, to the swings. Two others were slumped in their strollers.

"I was in my bed twying to sweep, but you said it a-*lotta* times." Benny counted on his little fingers. "One two free four elennen ten times. That's a lotta times."

"You heard that, huh?"

"You were very loud. Seeve didn't know what it was." Steve was his stuffed elephant.

"Yeah," Lilly said. "I guess I was."

"Did Emmer come over?"

"No. She's . . . someone I used to know. She emailed me last night. I wasn't expecting it."

"She sent you a email? On your capooter?"

"Yes. She wants me to visit. But I'm not sure if I want to."

"Why?"

"Because I get upset when I think about it."

Benny lifted his chin as Lilly fiddled with his collar. "Why?"

Because she was a total bitch to me. Because she lied to me and yelled at me. Because she made me feel like a useless tramp, like a used-up nothing. Because . . .

"It's hard to explain."

Benny nodded. "Why?"

Lilly took a deep breath, exhaled, then looked up into the morning sky. A bluebird flew by. "Because . . . I . . . didn't make such great choices back then."

"Why?"

"Because . . . hey. Buddy. Give your mom a break here."

Benny looked up at her as only a three-year-old could, devoid of pretense and ambiguity.

"Oh BennyBennyBenny. You're killing me. Why did I do stupid things? Because . . . I . . . forgot how much I needed good people."

"Why?"

"*Grrr* . . . because I was afraid."

"Why?"

"You're really going to make me say it, huh . . . ? Because I thought Grandpa Marcus was mad at me."

"Why?"

"Because I thought I did something bad."

"You did somefing bad?"

"No, buddy. I just thought I did."

"Papa Marcus isn't mad anymore?" Benny said *anymore* in sing-song. *Ehhhh-nee-more?*

"No, honey." Lilly smiled at Benny, relieved that all was well with his grandpa. "He's not mad. He's loves me. And he loves *you*." She stood up on her tip toes, and reached for the sky. She could feel the cool air on her stomach as her shirt shimmied up from her waist, exposing her navel. "Like this much. Way-up-high much. Super much. High-high-in-the-sky."

Benny smiled.

Lilly knelt down again, straightened his collar, and then kissed his cheek. She ran her fingers through his fine, brown hair. "Go play, honey. Mommy needs to think."

Benny scampered off for the monkey bars. With her mother's eye she watched his every move, joyful at her son's excitement and developing dexterity and coordination, yet filled with dread, knowing that at any moment Benny could miss a foothold by just a few millimeters and then tumble off the apparatus and split open his skull.

She followed close behind, just in case, but needed to give him enough space to feel that he had the freedom to explore.

It's the one thing they never tell you, Lilly thought. *That as a parent you live in constant fear, on emergency room alert. That in every nanosecond the worst possible outcome for your child could be just another nanosecond away. I could be inches from Benny and still it might not be close enough to catch him. I can handle his bumps and bruises, but what about when it's worse? When there's real danger? When the damage could be permanent?*

But if I never let go, if I never let him roam, will he just run away from me, anyway?

Lilly climbed the short stairs, onto the first platform, but backed off a few feet. And then in her mind's eye, as if her hulking physique was actually standing before her, she saw Emma.

But I owe you, don't I, Emma? You pushed me too far. You drove me to face myself. Not on purpose. You didn't care about me . . . but you didn't force me off to Europe, did you? You didn't make me chase Theo Barnes across the globe? You didn't make me find Jason. I did that on my own. I chose to run away. I chose to avoid my fear. Until I couldn't any longer.

And because you scared me into running—showing just how pathetic

I'd become—I decided to come home. To start my life over again. To be a person for real. And even though I shared one last night with a guy I'll never see again I'm good with my dad now and I've got my little Benny and I finally have a life I can actually feel okay about.

So why do I still want to rip your face off? Why do I still hate you? And I mean . . . hate you.

Benny made his way across the jungle gym to a metal mesh wall, and one by one jangled a series of loose metal switches, setting off the five heavy, copper bells.

Clank . . . clank . . . clank . . . clank . . . . CLANK!

But do I, though? I just know the idea of seeing you again brings up all this muck in me and I'm afraid it'll all come spilling out in front of you and the thought of looking so weak and small and pathetic in your eyes feels so unbearable to me that I want to vomit up my soul.

With each step, Benny closed in on DJ, who was lording over the other toddlers. She wanted Benny to avoid him this time, to stay away.

I shouldn't give you this power, though, should I? That's always been my problem. Leave before they can confront me, run from the fear. But I thought I was putting that behind me. I thought I was getting more honest with myself, more solid.

Benny approached DJ, the bully, and let out a terrific, excited smile. DJ was Benny's friend. Lilly didn't understand, but there it was. DJ's mother, Melinda, was on the other side of the monkey bars, scrolling through her phone, not paying the least attention to her little tyrant.

I'm not perfect. God knows, I'm not. But I am kind of okay, though . . . aren't I? I'm doing okay. I'm not ashamed of myself anymore. I'm not the girl I was.

Benny reached then for the captain's steering wheel. A head taller than Benny, DJ grabbed his hand away. "No!" he demanded. "Mine."

Lilly started for her son, to intervene, but Benny engaged on his own behalf. Against her instincts, Lilly restrained herself, waited.

"No, no, no!" Benny scolded DJ. "You can't do that. I get a turn."

DJ pushed Benny. Benny pushed back.

"No, DJ! No." And then, with a contented air, Benny took his place at the steering wheel.

Lilly watched DJ's face turn red with rage and humiliation. He raised his fist, in attack position. But rather than strike, he stood aside, acknowledging Benny's place at the front. The two boys then shared toddler smiles—a negotiation fully transacted.

Lilly's heart raced, filled with anxiety and pride.

So that's it, Emma. I kinda have to see you, don't I? I need to do this. And maybe I'll fall apart in front of you and maybe I won't, but either way I'll know that I did it. I'll know that I stood before someone who scares me, and that I still matter. I don't know what'll come after that, but whatever it is . . . however it goes . . . it'll be better than feeling sick in my belly because it's filled with shame at hiding from you.

Benny put both hands on the steering wheel, turned it. DJ joined him.

Okay, Emma. You win. You sent me an invitation.

The two boys stared straight ahead, and giggled, the way only little boys can.

I accept.

I'm coming.

Chapter 22
Snow Daze

Outwardly calm despite his inner anxiety, Theo checked his phone again for messages as they waited in the hangar at BWI.

A thirteen-seat executive jet landed, rolled into its approach, then stopped on the runway in the near distance. The pilot was visible through the cabin windows. Toward the cockpit, the main white door unfurled, unveiling a short staircase. From within, stepping into the daylight was a tall, lanky figure with short-cropped hair, and wearing a classic brown aviator flight jacket and silver-plated sunglasses.

They hadn't seen Jackie Pellington since Amsterdam.

"Look at that, yeh? Maybe he's changed."

Jackie took the stairs in regal strides. But as soon as his feet touched the runway he ran forth, arms open, with awkward, giraffe-like strides. "Well howdy howdy howdy howdy howdy howdy hay." He wrapped his long arms around Jason, and pulled him close. "My goodness, my goodness. You're as scrumptious as ever. Mm!"

Jason went limp, his face smushed into Jackie's side.

"Okay," Theo said. "Maybe not."

Jackie released Jason. "Thee-ohhhh Barnes. Hoo hoooo. I'm so glad you called. It's been so *long* since I've seen you two. Oh . . . and who's this vision of loveliness?"

"I'm Jamie."

Jackie took her hand, kissed it. "Well, of course you are. How nice." He took Jamie's arm, looped it through his, then led her back to the plane. "Why don't you come with me, dear. There's so much I want to ask you. Although I must apologize for the accommodations. It's the best I could do on short notice. Tim's refueling. We'll be off in no time."

Jason whispered to Theo. "Do we really have to?"

Theo instinctively ran a finger over the face of his phone. Making tactile contact with the device—the portal helping to connect him with his father—gave him an illusory sense of control. Consistent with much of his life, where Theo was and where he needed to be were very different indeed. "Heh. Yeh. Besides . . . he's okay. He's just, you know . . . Jackie."

"I know, I know. But he's already hugging me. It's *weird*."

"Because," Jackie yelled back, from several feet ahead, "you're scrumptious!"

Jason's eyes popped open. "Dude! He heard that?"

Theo laughed, and then headed for the plane. "Come on, mate. Let's go."

Jason

The Starburst 8000 was fully pimped out.

The state-of-the-art private jet came equipped with a flat screen TV, DVD player, stocked bar, kitchen, 13 leather seats (beige), including five sleepers, and three distinct cabin zones.

Jason was a little shaky during takeoff—he clutched the armrests for the first sixty-eight seconds—but once they reached cruising altitude, above the clouds, he settled in nicely. They were headed to Yuma International Airport, first flying over the northern ridge of West Virginia and then crossing over airspace above southern Ohio, to be followed by Indiana, Illinois, Missouri, Kansas, Colorado, and the northern tip of New Mexico, before crossing into Arizona. Estimated flight time was four hours thirty-six minutes, covering 2,461 miles.

Relaxing on leather couches, they all enjoyed cold drinks and a hot towel to freshen up—it really opened up the pores—but Jason couldn't stop staring at Jackie. Unlike the Goth debutante he remembered from Amsterdam, Jackie's long, curly locks were gone, replaced with a short-trimmed haircut. Also gone were his silver skull rings, black nail polish and makeup, purple suede jacket, and ruffled blouse. Instead Jackie was dressed in standard conservative airline pilot attire—blue slacks, white collared shirt, and black shoes, polished to a shine.

Jason was about to inquire—this simply wasn't the Jackie he

knew—when for just a few seconds he was distracted by Theo, who for the third time since they took off from BWI, snuck a peek at his phone. Something was up.

Jackie brushed a strand of lint from his otherwise immaculately pressed shirt.

"Hold on," Jason said. "I thought you guys were a helicopter company?"

"Oooh. Yes, we are," Jackie replied. "But Dad thought it was time to expand. We started with just one private jet, then two, and now we have nine. No . . . ten. Sorry. This gorgeous creature is brand *spanking* new." Jackie winked at Jason. "We were actually on our way from Boston to Denver when you called. Easy peasy. You put a slight dent in my flight time—you have to log in forty hours to get your pilot's certificate—but you guys are worth it."

Jamie seemed amused. "They didn't tell me you were a pilot. That must be exciting."

Jackie pawed his hand, wrinkled his nose. "It has its moments."

"So," Jason surmised, ". . . your dad made you do it."

"Well . . . you *are* a reporter now, aren't you? . . . Did he *make* me do it? Technically . . . no. But I like it. It's fun. The flying is actually the easy part, although . . . it was daunting at first."

"I would think," Jamie said. "It's a beautiful plane."

"Oh, you sweet thing. No, no. Not the plane. I've had my helicopter's license for years. My airplane license was inevitable. It's that my father . . . like so many of them do . . . he wants me to follow in his footsteps. Or wingspan, however you prefer. That's what I was doing in Europe when I met these two." He pointed to Jason, and then to Theo, who seemed to shrink into his leather cushion. "I needed to figure out if I really wanted to learn the business, or try something else. My father told me I could work with him and own a part of the company. The perks are obvious. And so is the responsibility. But if I were to forego the skies and pursue other endeavors—about which, I must confess, I had some excitement—I would also have to *pay* my own way—which, I also must confess, I was decidedly less excited about. He gave me a year and an allowance to think it over. But when the year was up, he said I had to choose, or he was choosing for me. If I didn't have a job by the time I was twenty-five, he was closing out my bank account and boxing up my things. Dad is serious, fair, and never goes back on his word. He gave me options. I picked the best one. Or maybe the easiest. I'm not really sure."

Jackie gestured to the luxury aircraft. "In any case I con-cluded that this life is as reasonable as any other, and more sat-isfying than most. But what I also know is that if I am ever to hold a prominent position within this company I'll need to learn how our ladies operate. I need my . . . hands on the equipment." With his long, bony finger he boinked Jason on the tip of his nose. "Besides . . . I get to do favors. Like this. In fact. . ."—Jamie reached into one of the cabinets and handed them single-serve plastic bottles of pink lotion, which he opened for them—"you should rub this into your hands . . . nice . . . and . . . slow . . . It's pomegranate. So soft. So soothing . . ."

"Um, yeah. So . . . Jackie," Jason said. "Maybe you can give Jamie a tour of the cockpit."

"Ooh. Good idea. Shall we?" He took Jamie's hand, and then winked at Jason. "Sit tight, my scrumptious muffin. I'll be back for you in a jiff."

Left to their own devices, Jason sat opposite Theo, who seemed to nearly vanish, like an apparition drifting through the walls. It was the first opportunity they'd had to sit and think. And talk. Theo then looked to his hands in mild surprise, rolled them together with the pomegranate lotion. It tingled. "Huh. This is pretty good." Jason then turned to Theo. "Hey, man. Can I ask . . . ?" Are your kids okay? What's going on? You keep checking your phone."

Theo smiled, then sank deeper into the leather seat. Soda sloshed in his glass. His lotion bottle was open next to him.

Jason wasn't sure what Theo was going through—he'd been quiet, even for him—but soaring high above the clouds, through unfettered sunlight, Theo's words eked out in shallow, shaky breaths. "I, uh . . . I dunno. It's . . ."

Jason nudged him gently on the arm. "No. It's okay. Really. You can tell me."

Theo leaned forward. He clutched his phone. Jason could almost feel the air seize up in Theo's lungs.

"Last few years, yeh? I've never seen my dad this happy. He loves being a granddad. You should see him with Hope and Tess. And he's a big bloke . . . you've seen him . . . but he's been light as a feather. Moving around really well. And he's been getting on great with my mum. They even took tango lessons." Theo's smile held for a moment, then drifted away. "But lately . . . I dunno. I know I haven't said, but . . . he's really slowed down. He's out of breath, his hands are swollen. His feet, too. They hurt. And now he's having these chest pains. He's in for tests now. Roger's supposed to text me."

"Oh, man. I'm sorry. I didn't realize. He gonna be all right?"

"I dunno." Theo shook his head. "I dunno."

"Ohhhhh. Theo? Why didn't you tell me? Why didn't you say?"

Theo shrugged, let out a sad smile. "I didn't realize how important it was to *have* a dad until I *became* a dad. When Jackie started talking about his father, yeh? It really hit me."

Jason put his hand on Theo's back, held his water in the other. "Yeah," he said. "I—"

Turbulence hit the plane. It violently shook, tossing Jason to the ground. With Jamie in tow, Jackie burst into the cabin, fell into the seat. The *Fasten Seatbelt* sign was met with a *bing*.

"Some bad weather's come in. A big storm. *Huge* storm. A blizzard. It wasn't on the radar. I don't know why. It came out of nowhere, like it's eating up on the sky. Strap yourselves in. I'll help you."

Jason shuddered. His stomach was tight. "Blizzard? But it's September."

For a pilot, even a pilot-in-training, Jackie was nervous and impatient. "That's true. It's also a Sunday. And I'm a Libra. My favorite color is purple, I've only had two boyfriends that mattered, and I've never seen *Casablanca, Citizen Kane,* and, if you can believe it, *Gone with the Wind.* And if you really must know, my favorite snack is barbeque chicken wings, extra crispy, with blue cheese dressing smeared across my face. It still doesn't change the fact that there's a massive blizzard bearing down on us like THE WRATH OF MOTHER FUCKING KHAN! and we need to land this plane . . . *right* now."

Jamie grabbed Theo's arm.

"Okay, okay. Sorry." Jason stumbled to the leather couch, then clasped his seatbelt. The others did the same. "But where are we landing?"

Jackie exhaled long and slow, then offered a smile that struggled to exude reassurance. "I have no idea. But wherever it is . . . just pray that we make it."

Chapter 23
Walking on the Moon

Jamie
Somewhere in Terre Haute, Indiana

As far as near-death experiences go, Jamie was pretty okay with the compromising position this one put her in.

Theo had two young girls and an almost wife, so she wasn't going to be the one to break the forbidden barrier—she never had, and told herself that she never would. But if she was ever going to plant a kiss on a man spoken for by another woman, she had plenty of justifications to do it now.

What happens on Earth, she figured, would stay on Earth. And in her case, it really just might. Permanently.

"You know," she whispered to Theo, who was lying on top of her, nose to nose, in push-up position. Jamie breathed heavy, arms wrapped around his back. The harmonic key dangled from her neck. "That was my first crash landing."

Theo held her in place, gulped. He licked his lips. His tongue almost grazed hers. But not quite. She could feel his thundering heart.

"Yeh-yeh," he said. "Same."

Jamie smiled, stared into his eyes. She craned her neck upwards, to meet him.

I want you. I know I shouldn't and I know it's wrong. But I want you. I want you now.

Until an interrupting Jason ruined the moment. Tangled in a cluster of couch cushions, he picked himself up off the floor. "Me, too. I think I'm shock."

"Tell me about it," said Jackie, who took Jason by the arm. "But just look at those two. So naughty. So cute." He squinted, crinkled his nose. "I love it."

Jamie curled out from underneath Theo, and backed away, trying to distance herself from the awkwardness. It didn't work.

"Whoa-ho-ho," Jackie said and pointed at their naughty bits.

"Looks like you two got a little more excited than we thought. I know it was a scare, but . . . your pants. Look."

Jason and Theo had massive pink stains along their legs, sides, and crotches.

"N-n-no," Jason said. "It was my drink, and the lotion. They smeared! They spilled! They . . ."

"Sure they did," Jamie said. "Sure."

Jamie and Jackie shared a smile.

"Oh, come on! We almost died!"

"*Tt-tt-tt*," Jamie said. "One little plane crash and you wet your pants."

"Yeah, but . . . Theo did, too!"

"Nah," said Jamie, who saw Theo blush, and cover his junk. "He just spilled his drink."

Jackie put his arm around Jason's shoulder. "Don't you worry. We've got spare pants for you two. Come now. We'll get you changed."

And then Tim, the pilot, burst into the cabin. "You folks okay? *Sorry* about that. Don't know *what* the hell happened out there. But whatever it was we're alive fucking yes we're alive! Which means that today's the BEST DAY EVER!" He looked through the windows. Giant snowflakes pelted the plane. "Jackie. Come on. Let's get these guys some jackets and gloves. We're gonna need them."

"One step ahead of you, Tim. One step ahead. . . . I knew that sooner or later I'd get Jason out of his clothes. I just didn't think it would take a plane crash to make it happen."

The Terre Haute Motel Nine wasn't exactly the *Rubicon*, Jamie thought, but it was clean, warm, dry, and most important, on the ground.

Jackie booked them consecutive rooms, connected by a conjoining door. Jamie wasn't sure who was expected to sleep in which room.

Theo hadn't said much since the plane. She didn't know what to make of that, either.

There's so little time, she thought. *Don't hold back now.*

Jason, meanwhile, was bundled up in the desk chair, in a jacket, hat, and gloves, his feet on the bed. "Good thing you had the gear. You get this a lot?"

Jackie was wrapped in full winter attire, including a wool scarf. "Nuh-ho, not really. But we fly year 'round, so we keep gear for every season. Besides . . . when you have as many private customers as we do . . . you never know where you'll be off to next . . . or what you'll need."

Who cares? Just take Jason out of here.

Named by the French for being on *highland,* Terre Haute was a small Midwestern city near Indiana's western border with Illinois, and had become known for its corn fields, meth labs, prostitutes and, thanks to a funky smell that at one time emanated from a local factory in the southern part of the city, as possibly being the tuna fish capital of the world. But a resurgent downtown, an emergence of several nonprofit groups, and the expansion of the Indiana State University campus had ushered in a new energy.

"Good thinking either way. And I have to say," Jason said, "you seem to be taking this pretty well. That was scary as hell."

"Yes, well . . . I like to think that I'm fairly well adjusted, generally speaking, and that it takes quite a bit for me to lose my proverbial poo-poo." Jackie rolled his hand in a stately fashion. "As they say. But the storm that just hit us? Wowser. I was *not* prepared for that." He checked his watch. A *Rolex.* "I don't know about you guys, but after that flight I need to get a little freaky. And I'm talking freaky . . . deaky. I know you big city boys wouldn't think it, but the locals here really know how to par-tay, and the storm's basically passed. Wanna come?"

Oh, yes. Please. Go with him. Leave me with Theo. Then maybe he'll . . .

"No, thanks," Jason said. "Gonna sit this one out. I need to chill. That was a rough ride."

Oh, come on!

"Besides, I need a hot shower and a soft bed. I ache all over."

Jackie raised an eyebrow. "Is that an invitation?"

Sure. Yes! Whatever. Just give me time alone with—

"Ah . . . no. Solo mission. But thanks for the offer. We're gonna go eat."

"Jamie? Theo? . . . No?" Jackie shrugged, unscrewed the top of a tiny bottle, and with an eye dropper, squeezed a liquid dot on his tongue. He reached into his pocket, pulled out a roll of cash, and placed a $100 bill on the TV. "Suit yourself. But dinner's on me. Least I can do. I'll see ya'll later."

Thwarted again, Jamie followed Jason and Theo through a moderate snowfall as Jackie disappeared into the night. They made their way next door to *Sylvia's*, bordered by a 24/7 gas station, *Big Tico's* chicken and pizza joint, a check-cashing operation, *Diamond Lou's Pawn Shop*, and another motel.

Settled into a corner booth, they put down a massive plate each—Theo, a bacon cheeseburger; Jamie, the mac and cheese; and Jason, the spaghetti with meatballs and garlic bread—watching the snow fall on the parking lot. They barely spoke.

Bellies full, they bundled back up into their donated winter gear and wandered through the courtyard, toward the motel. Jamie stood beneath a street lamp glowing in the darkness. She packed a snowball. Her first on Earth. It was colder and had more heft than she was used to. She chucked it at Theo. "So what do you think? This weather? The storm? . . . Is that a Milo thing? The jar? It has to be . . . right?"

Theo ducked, then packed his own snowball. "Maybe. I dunno."

"Gotta be," Jason said. "Storms don't just appear like that. Maybe up in *Eternity*, in the center of the *Universe*, but not around here. . . . But, hey. What do I know?"

Jamie didn't like his tone. "Believe me. We get plenty of storms. Just not like that."

"I'm guessing you don't have planes like that, either."

"We don't have planes at all."

"Yeah. You probably fly spaceships or rockets or have turbo boosters wherever you go. Up, up, and away! Although . . . that's Superman, now that I think about it."

Get out of my face, Jason. You're pissing me off.

"We don't have planes *or* spaceships, and I don't know what a rocket is, but I'm pretty sure we don't have those, either. If you can deal with that. Although we do have CCSs, if that's what you mean. . . . Celestial Cruise Ships. But no planes or anything like that."

Theo lobbed a snowball her way, grazing her shoulder. "How's it work, then? How do you get around, yeh?"

Okay. Finally. I've got his attention.

"It's a lot like here, actually. Cars, buses, trains. The usual. But we don't have—what did you call the big regions—states? Countries? We've just got the Nine Spheres of Eternity. That's it. And they don't really connect. They just sort of . . . drift . . . into each other. To Infinity."

"Um," Theo said.

Jason shrugged. "And beyond?"

"It's like a . . . cloud bank, I guess you'd call it. And it doesn't have any dimensions. There's no obvious top or bottom. No beginning or end. It's just . . . there. If you want to travel from one Sphere of Eternity to another, you just enter Infinity—"

"The giant cloud bank." Theo smiled when he spoke.

Jamie liked that. She was drawn to the way the street lamp illuminated the snowflakes as they drifted all around Theo, like he was floating within a full-size snow globe. "Right. The giant cloud bank. And then once you're in there, you just . . . *think* yourself to your destination. You can walk, or ride a bicycle, or drive your car into it, and then you just . . . *feel* where you want to go. And then Infinity takes you there. And when you exit, you're right where you need to be. It doesn't take more than a second or two."

"So Infinity is a lot like New York then?" Jason offered with sarcasm. "If you could make it there you could make it anywhere?"

Without speaking, the three of them gently lobbed snowballs at each other. Jamie studied the guys, could see their minds at work. Since her arrival on Earth she had felt very much like the stranger that she was. The outcast. The imposter. But the more she spoke about Eternity the less they had to say. In her little fear-filled life, in Eternity, she considered her efforts meaningless. Insignificant. But down here, on Earth, she was exotic, magical even, from a realm they could barely comprehend. And that filled her with power. Electricity. Confidence.

Jason finally broke the silence, kicked snow off his boot. "What's it like up there? I mean . . . why do you even *bother* with us?"

"We normally wouldn't," Jamie said, to push back a little, to diminish him, and elevate herself. But as her words hung in the air—she not only reinforced the notion that she was truly from a foreign world, but also from one vastly superior in the hierarchy of Existence—she for the first time began to appreciate Jason's underlying hostility toward her. Jamie was, at least from Jason's perspective, slumming it, and in epic proportions. "I'm sorry. I didn't mean it like that. I really didn't. The truth is . . . Eternity's a lot more like Earth than you'd think."

Jason rolled his eyes, then resumed chucking snowballs. "You guys . . . what? Create the Universe? Plant the stars?"

Jamie bobbed her head back and forth. A snowflake landed on her nose. "Kinda. Yeah."

"So let me get this straight? You're from up there, from Eternity, which you're saying is a realm—for lack of a better term—located in a distant corner of time, space, and dimension that is unreachable and undetectable in any way we could possibly conceive."

"Basically . . . yes."

"Okay. And you're also saying that this unreachable, undetectable realm is, essentially, an industry town whose sole purpose is to design, build, and provide maintenance for the entire Universe and everything in it? And I'm talking everything. The planets, the moons, the stars, the galaxies? All of it. Every dust particle. Every nebula. Every physical element that exists *anywhere* and all the life forms that go with it."

Jamie turned to Theo, whose eyes revealed that he wanted the answer as badly as Jason did. Earth baffled her, but she baffled them.

"Umm," Jamie said, "that pretty much covers it."

Jason continued. The reporter in him was taking over. "And anyone who doesn't have a direct hand in the construction of the Universe has some job that, at least tangentially, supports that industry or exists because of it? You said you work in a hotel, right? And that's just ancillary to the Universe business?"

"Y-yyes. That's right."

"Okay," Jason said. "Okay. So. How did you describe your-selves? Eterni—?"

"Eternitarians."

"Right. So . . . Eternitarians are basically gods, right? We were created *by* you, in *your* image, to . . . what? Entertain you? Give you something to laugh at? Or is there something more transcendental going on? Are we supposed to be finding our way through Existence in the search for meaning that will one day bring us closer to our makers? You know . . . you?"

Jamie took a deep breath. "Well." She exhaled. "Not me *per*sonally. I have no power to speak of. I'm nobody. Seriously. I can barely pay my rent. I just work the check-in desk at the hotel."

"The hotel where they create the Universe. Oh, yeah. That sounds *totally* like us. You just described my life like . . . exactly. Theo usually drives a comet to work. Me? I prefer to ride a hail of meteors through a wormhole. It takes a little longer, but I can always get a seat."

Jason stomped off, muttering to himself as the snow began to fall more intensely, with large white flakes whisking in a swirl. But then he felt a *thwack* in the middle of his back. "Hey. What the . . . ?" He turned then, only to find Theo armed with another snowball. "Oh-ho-ho."

Jason grinned, and in quick succession hurled snowballs in Theo's direction, landing with one, missing with the other two. And before they knew it, all three of them were engaged in a full-on snowball fight. On Earth. In Terre Haute, Indiana. In September.

"You know," Jamie said, hiding behind a park bench. "One thing I will say . . . the views? They're spectacular. My life in Eternity isn't the least bit glamorous. I know you don't believe me. But trust me. It really isn't. . . . But look there." She pointed to the night sky. "Look at the moon. It's full and round and gives off a milky white glow. It's soothing. Luminous."

Jason and Theo nodded in agreement.

"But it's so *small*. In Eternity, where I'm from, every night . . . I mean *every night* . . . they rotate in a debuting planet, a moon, a comet shower. Sometimes a galaxy. Or a cluster of galaxies. And it's like *thisclose*." Jamie held her hand up to her face. "The moon would be right here. It would take up the entire sky, flush against the horizon. Just an endless sea of glowing white you could practically touch it. Like you could walk to the end of the road and then just disappear, swallowed by the enormity of it all." Jamie paused, smiled oddly. "But . . . I . . . guess it's not like that here, is it?"

Jason and Theo shook their heads.

Jamie twisted the front of her foot into the snow, like stamping out a cigarette. "You just live in a daze up there. One day into the next. The clothes you wear, the food you eat. Your friends, your family, your job, your apartment. And somehow you think that whatever's right in front of you, that whatever you can see, is all that matters. That's all there is." Whether she realized it or not, Jamie drifted to face Theo until their eyes met. Her frosty breath merged with his, white mists sprinkled against the black of night. "And you forget sometimes that you might be staring at something truly special. You're sedated by routine. You just don't notice."

The snowfall picked up both in speed and intensity. Jamie, Jason, and Theo reached their hands up to the sky. The street lamps threw light upon them, catching immense snowflakes in the beams.

Jason removed his finger guns, cocked his thumb triggers, and made the *chk-chk* sound. "Okay, boys and girls. Big J is on the scene. And he's calling for indoor heat. Race ya'!" A challenge Theo accepted.

Jamie dashed off after them, through the driving snow, when there was a blast of white light. There were streaks of screaming fluorescent color. There was the sensation of being sucked through a tornado. And then there were ruins. Lots and lots of ruins.

No longer dressed in winter garb, they were now in shorts, t-shirts, and sandals, staring up at a massive stone temple. Golden beams of light shone down on them.

Jamie turned all the way around, determined that they were alone in the ancient city, and then looked at Jason's hands. She set him straight.

"Do me a favor . . . ? Put those finger guns away. They're loaded, they work, and they're nothing but trouble."

Chapter 24
Union of the Snake

Jason
Yucatán, Mexico

A river of molten orange oozed from the sky.

Before them, at dawn, along the ancient Mayan ruins of *Chichen Itza*, was the *Temple of Kukulkan*, an enormous stone pyramid with a flat terrace at its top. From behind the temple arose the morning sun, brushing the lower sky with golden yellow. Its gradation blended into succulent apricot above.

Jason scanned the ancient ruins. The silence unnerved him. "Where *is* everyone?"

A pretty young woman appeared next to him. She was short, with brown skin and black hair. Her accent had a distinctly Spanish cadence. "Off pre-*perring* for *the-end-of the world*. You know . . . the Mayan prophecy says it is coming soon."

Jason, Theo, and Jamie turned to face her.

"Oh, I am just kidding. It is too early. The ruins . . . they do not officially open for another . . . two . . . hours." She flicked her wrist to accentuate the words *two* and *hours*.

Jason wasn't buying it. "Then how are you here?"

"How are you?"

With no satisfactory answer to her question, Jason offered a slight nod.

The young woman introduced herself. "I am Maria. I will be your tour guide today."

"But I don't think this is a real tour," Jamie said.

"And I do not think I am a real guide. Yet here we are, all . . . *together.*"

With each step along the dirt path, Jason wondered where they might all end up next, as if the bottom of his sandal making contact with the ground would trigger yet another dreamlike transportation. His first few paces demonstrated that he seemed to be on solid footing, but recent experiences had demonstrated that what appeared to be true and real and tangible in one instant was not unto itself a reliable barometer for what might unfold in the next.

Jason was about to whisper a question when Theo looked up at the passion fruit sky, shielded his eyes, and then checked his phone again.

"Oh," Maria said. "I do not think that will work here today. *No*-phones."

"Yeh," Theo said. "I, uh . . ."

Jason intervened. "He's . . . expecting a call. You know. Family business."

"Ah, yes. Familia is muy importante, sí? The fountain from which flows our strength and hopes and dreams. But here, our phones . . . *no*-work. It is like *la Zona del Silencio*, your . . . how do you say. . . ? Ber-muda *Triangle*. The forces of the Universe. . . ? They are most powerful and mysterious and larger than us all." Maria raised her hand, pointing to *El Castillo*—the *Temple of Kukulkan*. "Some people . . . they think our temple is the grand gateway to another dimension. That is how Kukulkan first came to our planet, and why our ships *disappear. . . at sea*."

"Y-y-yeahhhh," Jamie said. "I'm not so sure about that."

Jason side-stepped, placing himself between the two women. He didn't sense a pending brawl, but a conflict far more worrisome.

You're going to say something I'm not ready to hear. I don't know what, but my heart is beating so fast. It's making me nervous. I don't want to know this. I don't want to know.

"Don't mind her," Jason said finally. "She's not from around here."

Maria took in Jamie up and down. "Sí, yes. I figure as much."

Jamie rolled her eyes, as if she'd witnessed this scene before, and knew what Jason was thinking.

But even as Jason neutered her objections, he wondered if perhaps Maria was giving a form and a voice to the many questions gnawing at him.

Yes, we've had several group hallucinations. And, okay, I might sorta kinda actually believe that Jamie is from Eternity, aaaaand it's possible that I'm slightly jealous. But even if I am . . . is that how she got here in the first place? If Eternity actually exists, did she pay a toll at the Bermuda Triangle? Isn't that how she said it works? You enter Infinity and then think yourself to your destination? And that Milo guy? The gremlin?

Did he just slip through a gateway? Are these crazy pockets on Earth like . . . portals, or doorways, or wormholes? I mean . . . maybe? It's not like they can take the Brooklyn-Queens Expressway to the Midtown Tunnel. Or can they?

Maria led them beyond the much smaller *Temple of the Jaguars* to more directly face the *Temple of Kukulkan*. "As you can see"— she pointed to the temple terrace as it met the rising sun— "the *Temple of Kukulkan* is a prominent and beautiful structure. Kukulkan, which means the *feathered serpent,* is one of the three gods that came to us from the stars, and was thought to have created the Earth. I think that is quite an impressive feat, even for a god." Maria smiled, then winked at Jamie. "If you believe such things, Kukulkan is a serpent in his natural form, but he had a human form as well. He was a white man standing six feet tall with *blue eyes* and long *white hair.* When he first came to us, he taught the ancient Mayans a great many things, such as agriculture, medicine, *and* . . . how to run a *civilization.* But after he passed down his wisdom, he returned to the stars, and told the Mayans that he would one day . . . *return.* Twice a year we pay homage."

Jason could see that Jamie was about to say something.

Please don't start with her again. I'm confused as it is.

But Jamie stopped herself, shook her head. Jason sighed quietly in relief.

And then Theo spoke up. "The equinox. The seasons."

"Ah, yes, sí. Very good. At the spring and fall equinoxes, for a few hours in the late afternoon, the sun projects a pattern of light on the temple's northern stairway. The triangles of light *link up* with the massive stone carvings of snake heads engraved at the base of the stairs—a gargantuan serpent, down the temple's . . . *side.*"

"Yeh-yeh," Theo said. "The *descent of Kukulkan.*"

"Sí, yes. Very good again. You know the Mayan history."

Jamie's tone was suspicious. "Yeah. That *is* pretty good.

How *did* you know that?"

"I dunno. I saw it on *Discovery*, yeh? Last few years my dad's been into all these end-of-the-world theories. My brother just thinks it's funny."

"You Kiwis have a strange . . . sense . . . *of humor*. The end of the world. It sounds serious to me, no?"

"Oh, come on," Jason said. "Seriously. I know we're all a little wonky right now. But you really believe all that crazy dooms-day talk?"

"Ohhhh, no. Most people believe it marks the end of an *era*, not the end of the world. But the ones who foresee the apocalypse, I think they are . . . what is the American expression? Batshit crazy. Sí. Yes. Batshit. That is the one. But," Maria continued, and then raised her finger for emphasis, "maybe they are right. Can we ever really know? Time will tell. Is it any crazier than to believe in a god who condemns to Hell two grown men who make love to one another, but forgives the slaughter of millions in the name of that very god?" She shrugged. "My mind . . . I try to keep it open. It is good . . . *for-the-soul.*"

The group continued along the dried dirt and grass of the ancient ruins until they reached the base of the temple. They approached a massive stone snake, faded to white over centuries, with an even larger, outstretched stone tongue.

"You guys really like your snakes," Jason said.

"Ha, yes. I prefer turtles myself, but our culture closely identifies with the serpent gods."

Jason ran his hand along the snake's head and then looked up, craning his neck to follow the enormous pyramid until it met the sky. The golden apricot glow above slowly gave way to an early morning blue.

As a New Yorker it was ingrained in him to never—never ever—stop along the hectic Manhattan streets and gaze up at a skyscraper like he was some kind of ass-backward tourist. But in the hallucinogenic Yucatán of his mind, he was free to gawk to his heart's delight.

Theo slapped Jason on the arm. "Hey. Look at this."

Carved into the temple was another snake head, this one with a separate human face protruding from within the snake's open mouth. But it was the next carving that had Jason, Theo, and even Jamie looking at each other. Before them was a dolphin, blue whale, and leatherback sea turtle. Above each creature, also carved into the stone, was a galaxy starburst.

"These guys are mad bastards," Theo said. "They're up to something, yeh?"

Jason turned to Maria. Just tell me. "Is the world really ending twelve-twelve-twelve? . . . For real?"

"No-no-no. The Mayan prophecy . . . it is a marketing ploy. It sells many, many trinkets . . . *and books.*"

Jason raised his hands. "Well, that's good. Hear that guys? The world's not gonna end."

"Oh," Maria said. "It is."

"Uh-huh. Okaaaay. Um . . . when?"

"What is it you mean? It is happening *right-now.* Do you not read the news? *The Genius de Milo?* They have been shouting it all week."

Jason's eyes popped open. "Whoa! You said it's just a marketing ploy!"

"No no. You asked if the *Mayan* prophecy was true. The world as we know it now faces a different fate *all . . . together.* You will have to ask Jamie about that. She knows it all. She always has."

"What? No. No. Wait. Not again. It's not like that. I swear. It's—"

There was a blast of white light. There were streaks of screaming fluorescent color. There was the sensation of being sucked through a tornado. And then they were back in bed, Jason and Theo on the ends, Jamie in between them. They were fully clothed.

The TV was tuned to the local Terre Haute weather station, with Jolene Roberts reporting the five-day forecast of mild temperatures and clear skies. A ticker scrolled along the bottom of the screen:

Genius de Milo conspiracy theorists now exceed three million followers as Ohio and West Virginia experience major floods with a tornado ripping through western Pennsylvania. . .

Jackie entered then, sipping a cup of store-bought coffee.

"Well-well-well. The crack of noon and you're up already. Morning."

For reasons Jason couldn't explain, his left hip, right arm, and middle of his back were all sore. "What do you mean?" He then followed Jackie's gesture, and looked through the window. No snow. No ancient ruins. Just the motel parking lot. "What happened?"

"Great question, sleepyhead. You tell me. Last we spoke you turned down a fabulous evening with me in Funky Town. That was two days ago." Jackie removed his sunglasses, huffed on the lenses, then cleaned them with a green microfiber cloth. "The storm was quite the ordeal, now wasn't it? It certainly took its toll. But I'd say you were all *pretty* hung over long before that." He stepped closer to the bed. "Now . . . I don't know what kind of naughty pagan rituals happen at JebbFest, but next time . . . invite me. Please. That's one party I just *have* to check out."

Chapter 25
Succession Plan

Brigsby
Eternity

"You bake just the most delightful pastries, Enrique. What's your secret?"

Seated at his barstool perch during the live recording of *Breakfast with Brigsby,* the talk show host pointed to a wood countertop layered with various culinary treats. The audience, in a small stadium seating formation, wore a collection of lip-smacking smiles. Brigsby's guest chef, Enrique, was adorned in the classic white apron and hat motif, which stood out against Brigsby's brown and purple paisley outfit and oversized tinted glasses.

"You know I mustn't tell, Brigsby. What would be the fun?"

Fun? Brigsby thought. *This hasn't been fun for a long, long time. But it needs to be done. So here we go.*

"Ooooh, do you hear that folks? Enrique's being coy. And what do we say to a coy boy?"

The audience responded with one of Brigsby's classic chants:

"Give-it-up, coy-boy, give-it-up!" *Clap-clap.*

"Give-it-up, coy-boy, give-it-up!" *Clap-clap.*

"Ho-ho-ho," Brigsby said. "You heard them, Enrique. Time to give it up."

The guest chef obliged. "Well, if I must . . ."

Audience cheers and applause.

"It is everyone's three favorite ingredients: T, L, and C, or tender loving care, for those who like to say it all!"

I've got Milo on my brain. I can't deal with this right now. I just don't care.

Yet in another one of his signature moves, Brigsby forced himself to lean forward, raised his eyebrows behind his glasses, and held his stare before responding. *"And what do we think of that answer, folks?"*

The audience roared. *"Booooooooooooooooo!"*

"Sorry, Enrique. Looks like you'll need to do better than that. When my honey bunnies say *give it up*, you need to *really* give it up. Am I right?"

More claps.

"Okay, okay." Enrique smiled. "I knew you were too good for that. I, and all of my chefs and apprentices, personally bake each and every pastry by hand. We roll the dough, and carefully fill them with cream, fruit, or various home-made fillings. But for those I won't share the ingredients. Family secrets! Ha! But there is no factory work at *Enrique's Edibles*. There are no conveyer belts or assembly lines. True, it may limit our production, and the empire seekers may not want to follow my business model. But my mission has always been to create the most delicious and satisfying pastries I can, and share them with anyone who appreciates the effort."

Audience cheers.

"Well how-dee-doo," Brigsby said. "We have ourselves a culinary artiste before us. And as a special treat to you all, if you look beneath your seats, you'll find a gift box of pastries from *Enrique's Edibles!*"

Wild applause.

Brigsby was ready to call it in early, but he was an entertainer, and the show, as it had been said many times before, needed to go on.

"Okay, folks, o-kay! Wow. You *are* excited."

Audience giggles.

"What some of you may not know—in fact, no one knows yet, right Enrique?"

Enrique smiled, nodded. "That is correct."

"It seems that your dear friend and mine, our very own Enrique, will be stepping down as CEO and head chef of *Enrique's Edibles*."

"Noooo," the audience clamored. "Noooo."

"Oh, I know it sounds terrible." Brigsby gave a fake sniff. "But it's one of the reasons I asked Enrique to visit us here today. I have long wanted to do a show about succession planning, and thought, why not have an important business discussion for our entrepreneurs out there, *and* serve up tasty treats while we do it?!"

Audience approval.

You didn't pick now at random, did you Milo? The timing was no accident.

"So, Enrique . . . tell us . . . why *are* you stepping down? Don't you love us anymore?"

"Oh, of course, I love you. You have all been so wonderful to me. But it is time to try something new." Enrique could not contain a massive grin. "Should I? No . . . I think you should tell them. Go ahead, Brigsby. You do the honors."

"Ha. Well . . . if you insist. Actually," Brigsby continued, then cupped his hand around the side of his mouth, "I totally insisted." He returned to full voice. "I have a surprise for you, my honey bunnies, my cutie patooties, my super yum-yums. We've been in discussions for about a year, believe it or not, but just this week we made it ohhhh-ficial. Starting in the fall, Enrique himself will have a regular guest spot . . . right here on our show! Isn't that wonderful?"

The audience erupted once again in hearty cheers and applause.

You have a reason, don't you, Milo? A purpose.

"That's right, folks. Enrique will start off by doing one baking segment a week right here on *Breakfast with Brigsby*, and if all goes well—and I have no reason to think it won't, riiiight Enrique?—we'll have him here every day. What do you think about *that*?"

More adulation.

What are you really after, Milo? What do you want?

"So tell us, Enrique, if you will, how it feels to be joining the Brigsby family. Is it as delectable as I think?"

Brigsby forced his resistant eyes to cooperate, but finally he eked out a wink effective enough to convey the appropriate degree of naughty tease. It elicited more expected giggles.

"Oh, yes, of course. It has been a dream of mine for so long. And now my dream is here. Finally. And all because of you."

The audience let out a collective *aaaawwwwww.*

During any other segment on any other day, Brigsby would have drunk in the praise like the rejuvenating elixir he had long considered it to be. But today he barely noticed, leaving a discernible gap—a dead space—among the banter. The audience waited out the silence.

Earth is just the message. But what are you trying to tell me?

"What are you trying to tell me?" Brigsby stared out at the audience, which remained in confused silence. He realized then that he had spoken his thoughts aloud, and needed to course-correct. Quickly. "What I mean," he began, then sat upright again, and smiled, "is that you are a true delight, Enrique. Just a wonderful presence. We are so happy to have you join the team. Isn't that right, folks?"

One last round of applause.

It's not like you, Milo. You've never been so bold.

"Yes, yes, yes, my lovelies. We're going to take a short break, but when we come back, we're going to talk to Enrique about succession planning in general, and who will be running *Enrique's Edibles!* Like I always say, *you only hand over the keys . . .*"

The audience completed yet another one of his signature catchphrases:

". . . *when there's someone to drive!*"

"Ooh. So good. We'll be back."

Brigsby took to his dressing room.

He looked through the window, although he didn't really have to. As the Minder of the Universe, Brigsby didn't *see* the Universe with his eyes—it wasn't a matter of visual acuity. He didn't really have eyes, as they would be commonly known. He wasn't even an Eternitarian. Far from it.

But he stood by the window out of sheer habit, because he liked to linger. It was one of his true pleasures. He mumbled to himself. "Darn it, Milo? What are you *up* to?"

Beyond the various star systems, Brigsby focused his attention on the Milky Way, which was still fluxing. Not quickly, but fluxing nonetheless. But when he laser-focused on Earth, when he drew his gaze onto the little planet, he noticed a pattern, which resonated to the 20th century Earth pop song *Push It* by Salt n' Peppa:

Flux flux-flux FLUX flux
Flux-flux-flux FLUX flux
Flux flux-flux FLUX flux
Flux-flux-flux FLUX flux

The pattern repeated as such, on a continuous loop.

"What are you saying, Milo? What are you . . . ?"

And then the pattern came into focus. Brigsby closed his eyes, and let out a short sigh—the most appropriate gesture his current form could emulate under the circumstances.

Line by line—individually—the flux pattern came across as gibberish, but when taken as a whole, in its entirety, it divulged a message, one that only the Minder of the Universe himself had the presence, filter, and vocabulary to decipher.

Though Brigsby could at least appreciate the top line sentiment, he was truly at a loss as to the underlying meaning: *Too late, SUCKA! Too late.*

"We're back with Enrique from *Enrique's Edibles* to talk about your favorite topic and mine . . . Succession Planning!

"Think it doesn't apply to you? Think again, my little funky monkeys. For successful pastry shops like Enrique's, nebula fabric suppliers, or just small galaxy design firms, succession planning is a critical endeavor, one that can help ensure your long-term success, or potentially put you out of business. Am I right, Enrique?"

Too late for what, Milo? Too late for what?

"Oh, absolutely, Brigsby. At least that's been true for my little shop. I have been the sole owner and head chef of *Enrique's Edibles* since the very first day, back when it was just me. And while there are many good leaders out there—and there certainly are!—not every leader is the right one for your particular program."

"That's for sure, Enrique." *You seriously have no idea.* "What factors must be considered when choosing a potential successor?"

"Oh, good question, Brigsby. There are many."

On the video screen behind them, one by one appeared

Enrique's list, in bullet points, as he continued. "Does your potential successor:

- *Fit the culture you have cultivated?*
- *Have the vision to carry the organization forward in a manner that will satisfy you?*
- *Have the business savvy to ensure the organization runs efficiently?*
- *Share your passion and goals?*
- *Garner the respect of your people? Of the people you serve?"*

"Wow, this is a great list, Enrique. You've given me a lot to think about, that is . . . I mean, uh . . . given *us* a lot to think about. Anything else?"

Focus, Brigs. Focus.

"Yes, yes, Brigsby. Two more key points. First . . . incredibly important, but you need to decide whether you have identified an individual on your team that you are looking to elevate— which, in my opinion, is the best option—or, if you want to bring in someone from the outside. But whoever it is, you must be satisfied that he—or she—is well equipped to handle the full range of responsibilities that come with true leadership."

You got that right.

"As for me . . . I'm promoting my daughter, Julia!"

Audience cheers.

But what if there is no daughter to promote? Or son?

Increasingly distracted by Milo's message—*Too late, SUCKA! Too late*—Brigsby missed his queue.

"Um . . . ," Enrique said, prompting Brigsby yet again. "My daughter . . . Julia!"

"Oh, yes, right right right! Julia! In fact . . . she's here with us today. Come on out, Julia!"

Julia strutted out to center stage. Father and daughter smiled, embraced, and then bowed before the audience, which responded with enthusiastic applause.

"Well, now," Brigsby said. "Isn't that something, folks? Handing over the reins is a big step. Does that mean you'll be renaming your pastry line *Julia's Edibles?*"

"Ha! Maybe my daughter would like that, but no . . . we will always be *Enrique's Edibles,* right Julia?"

"Oh, yes, for sure. *Enrique's Edibles* is not just a brand name on a box, but a stamp of approval. It guarantees that each individual pastry lives up to the standards my father spent years establishing—light, airy, and delicious. I'm proud and honored to be entrusted with the family business, and of course, my father's name."

Entrusted. It may seem like an honor now. But how will you feel when the pressure mounts? When the expectations rise? When it all wears you down?

"I must say," Brigsby said, "your daughter is polite and radiant. It runs in the family!"

Audience laughter.

Brigsby egged on the crowd. "But let's put a pin in the compliments, shall we? Don't want your egos getting too big. It's not like you have your own talk show."

More laughter.

Enrique joined in. "Not yet!"

Even more laughter.

"So, Enrique . . . before we go. What is the last factor we need to consider when forming a succession plan? Tell my honey bunnies. They want to know."

Enrique smiled, then turned serious. "The most important question any leader must ask before finding a successor is—"

"Ooooh," Brigsby interrupted. "Wait for it, folks. Wait for it . . ."

Enrique looked directly into the camera. "Are you truly ready to step aside?"

Brigsby had long contemplated his tenure as the Minder of the Universe, but until Enrique spoke the words aloud, he hadn't truly considered whether he was prepared for an existence in which the Universe and everything in it wasn't under his purview. When he thought of himself possibly stepping away as the Minder of the Universe, he had envisioned himself in a permanent limbo, perched at his private hotel bar, sipping drinks and chatting with Chioma about events unimportant, with no sense of what he might do, or what he might become, if he ventured beyond those dimly lit walls. A pause without an end date.

What would Brigsby's future existence look like? He didn't have the answer, but knew it was coming, and soon.

But before he could ultimately decide—if the decision was even his to make—he would first have to get Milo under control, once and for all. Until that happened, he couldn't fully think about his succession plan, even though it was already in motion.

"There you have it, folks. Thanks for joining us here today, and like I always say . . ."

Brigsby felt a sense of farewell—a tipping point—as he awaited the audience to finish the thought for him in a loud, unified chant, as they did at the end of every show:

"Dream it now, live it wow. The fun has just begun!"

Chapter 26
One Potato, Two Potatoes, Three Potatoes Four

Milo
Somewhere in the Universe

Even within the vast cosmos, the distance between galaxies was negligible.

Such that Milo, while riding on Philbrick's Comet with his poker buddies, broke off five nubs from the tip of his cherry licorice stick, and then, one by one—*plink . . . plink . . . plink . . . plink . . . plink*—flicked them beyond the edge of the Vitoff Six, and into the Beetham Asteroid belt.

The licorice nubs just seemed to get absorbed into the belt's uncountable fragments. But thanks to gravity, velocity, mass, and licorice, a single rock formation crashed into another, pancaking one of the little cherry-flavored bits. Until the two rock formations drifted apart.

With that separation, the nub began to stretch like putty—just stretched and stretched and stretched—until finally it broke away from the asteroid belt. And in doing so it drifted through space like a gooey, rock-tipped *surujin*—two weights, one each on the ends of a rope, designed to upend or ensnare its target.

As Milo had flicked five licorice nubs, so formed five gooey surujins.

"Okay, guys. You gotta try this." Along came the five surujins, which shrank in size to fit comfortably in Milo's clasp. He handed out the others, then casually swirled his.

And then he revealed a moment he had never mentioned to anyone. It wasn't so much a secret as a turning point he hadn't until then felt compelled to share. But now that he was escalating his game with Brigsby, Milo wasn't entirely sure that he would ever be in a position again to see his friends. It was the Minder of the Universe, after all.

"So I got up one day," he said, "took a hot shower, and then did a little grooming. I killed a chin zit, did a touch-up shave, and then started in on my nose hairs. I'm just standing there, staring into the bathroom mirror, and pulling my left nostril aside. I had this long whisker sticking out of my schnozz—it had a gooey booger on the end of it—that really needed to go. Just flicking it made my eyes water."

Randal recoiled. "Oooh. I hate those."

"Totally. Me, too. So there I am, the scissors pass the opening to my nostril, I open up the little blades, and just before I went *snip*, out of nowhere—one of those classic *a-ha* moments—this little poem pops into my head:

"One potato, two potatoes, three potatoes four,
I love my little Brigsbypo when he falls upon the floor.
He thinks he knows just how it goes but oh no he's such a bore.
Just wait until he sees the sign I tacked upon his door."

Doris took a wide stance. "What the fuck does that mean?"

"No idea. I figured it was just a silly little limerick, to amuse myself. But then I repeated the rhyme. Over and over. Especially the end:

"Just wait until he sees the sign I tacked upon his door."

Milo tapped his foot to get his timing down—the target was on its way—and then gave his surujin one last swirl so that it was propelling under its own power. As the shrunken twirling asteroid formations built up incredible energy, he pulled his arm back, and with a sling-shot motion, heaved the gooey surujin through the Universe.

Hurtling through space it expanded back to its massive size and shape until it ricocheted off the third moon of Gorczycki, knocking the satellite out of its orbit. In doing so Milo completely upended the Gringasa star system, which Brigsby had recently sanctioned as a centerpiece artwork consisting of eleven planets—all frozen. In combination they would have formed one of the most beautiful configurations in the quadrant.

"Nice shot," Esteban said.

"Thanks. And that was it. *Tacked upon his door. That* was

the key. I knew there was no way—just *no way*—I could really beat him. First off, there's three of them and just one of me . . . so forget that. But more important . . . and here's where it all started to come together. . . ."

Milo took Doris by the hips, and shifted her to the side, to instruct her in the next gooey launch. "Here. Like this." He evened out her wrist, and helped with her shoulder angle.

"I realized that I didn't *want* to beat him. I wanted to *annoy* him. To hang *KICK ME* signs on his back. To write *the doctor is in(sane in the membrane)* on his door. And that was my epiphany. Like you said, Randy. *Too. Much. Coverage.* The Universe *is* that big, and he's got *way* too much to focus on, even for him. So instead of trying to *destroy* what he created, I started to—"

"*Uncreate*," Hardwicke said.

"Yeah. To uncreate. A little here, a little there. Why wipe out a galaxy if I can knock a moon out of its orbit? The way the planets bounce around like pool balls . . . him getting all farkl-empt. *So* much fun."

Milo's smile faded then. Quietly, slowly, he repeated his rhyme.

"One potato, two potatoes, three potatoes four.
I love my little Brigsbypo when he falls upon the floor.
He thinks he knows just how it goes but oh no he's such a bore.
Just wait until he sees the sign I tacked upon his door."

"Okay, Doris. Let 'er rip."

She sent the second gooey surujin into the cosmos, only this time it took a more herky-jerky flight path, crashing into a star-forming region, short-circuiting its creation. Another upended project Brigsby had recently sanctioned.

"Nice arm. . . . Randal, you're next." Milo moved the water delivery guy into position. "Look . . . I know the score. I can never go toe-to-toe with Brigsby. But if I can throw him *off bal-ance* . . . so he can't finish what he starts . . . if I can do *that* . . ."

"You don't need to match his power," Hardwicke said. "You've got something better."

"Damn straight. The ability to distract the Minder of the

Universe *just* long enough that he has to think about what he's
doing . . . and if it's really worth it."

Milo knelt down, took one last look at the Vitoff Six, then
tapped the side of the comet. Time to head back.

"We've had a good run, me and Brigsby. But we both know
the curtain's about to drop. He's tired. He's losing his edge. The
more he creates, the more I disrupt. And now? With Earth?
Modeling it after Eternity . . . ?"

"Oh," Esteban said. "I gotta tell you. He really got my goat
with that one."

Doris chomped her cigar. "Yeah. Like Eternitarians are *so*
special just because he created this fake, idiotic him—just so
everybody can sniff the butt crack of Brigsby the TV star. And a
talk show host, too. The worst."

"Yes, well," Milo said. "Now it's my turn. He wants to create? Fine. Let him create."

Milo helped Randal get his surujin swirling, picking up
massive rotation, and thanks to some hip action, banked it off
particle debris within the Seibu Nebula, setting the gaseous red
formation to blink on an alternating pattern. That single shift
caused the entire nebula to overheat, expand, and finally, spiral
into another part of the galaxy altogether. Three for three.

Hardwicke and Esteban sat this one out. They needed to get
back.

Milo extended a hand. "Thanks for hanging with me, guys.
I really needed this."

Randal nodded to the others. "You got it, bud. Any time."

Milo stepped to the comet's edge, and with ease sent his
friends back to their respective places in Eternity. Everyone but
Hardwicke. He wanted to get her take on something.

Arms out, in diver's position, Milo leapt off the comet, into
the expansive Universe. "Be right back. Brigsby's gotta see what
I can *uncreate*. He's got no idea."

"Wait wait wait wait wait wait wait wait wait."

Milo floated back toward Philbrick's Comet. He held out a

cherry licorice stick, pointed it like a wand, and in the near distance of space, projected a replay of Brigsby's recent broadcast.

"Succession planning," Milo mumbled, "succession planning. He's not talking about this baker, now is he?"

"No," Hardwicke said, back at the poker table. "He's talking about himself."

"It's you, Brigsby. You're looking for a successor."

Hardwicke let her chips fall. "He wants to *retire*."

"Of course! *That's* why he's been off his game. *That's* why he's been so sloppy. He hasn't gotten too big for his britches. He wants to go small! He actually wants out. It isn't just Ira and Howard. It's him, too. It's Brigsby."

Milo climbed back on the comet, and let an enormous smile overtake his face. He drew his hands down his cheeks, covered his mouth, and then went still and quiet, for the equivalent of millions of Earth years—just a slight pause in the Universe's life span. Finally, he rolled off the comet and back into space, as if from a floating pool bed into the water.

Spirals, figure eights, and many long *whooshes* later, he re-emerged, and rested his cheek on the side of the comet.

Hardwicke was now sitting on the edge, gently kicking her feet as the Universe whisked below. "Here's what I can't figure out," she said. "Brigsby's arrogant and vain and is clearly out of touch, but he's not irresponsible. So he must have a successor in mind . . . right? He wouldn't just quit on us. Would he . . . ?"

"Nah. Not his style. But . . . does that mean he *already* has a successor in place . . . ?"

"Or is he just *looking* for one?"

By way of his licorice stick, Milo replayed the succession plan broadcast over and over, searching for subtlety. Nuance. A clue.

"Okay, we've got Enrique, in his prime, passing the business onto his daughter. I get that. Keep it in the family." Milo surveyed the Universe, concurrently in fragments, and in its entirety. "But this is the mother of all jobs. And okay, sure, Brigsby will need *three* successors, to shoulder the load. But that also means he first needs to *identify* three successors. And . . . hang on a second? . . . Does he actually *choose* them? Is it even up to him? Or does he just know how to find them, and then pass the torch? He's handing over the reins."

Hardwicke jangled poker chips in her coat pocket. "Throughout his existence Brigsby has probably done close to everything that's doable by a Minder of the Universe, but he's never done *that* before. He's never given up the mantle."

"Hang on. Is *that* why he's been—" Milo looked side to side. "Ohhhhhhh. I get it now. Oh. OHHHHHH! I get it! I GET IT! Oh-ho-ho you sneaky little monkey. *That's* what he's been up to. *That's* what it's all about. Oh. Wow. I did *not* see that coming. I really didn't. Well . . . that's why *he's* the Minder of the Universe and not someone else."

Milo reached up to the top of Philbrick's Comet, grabbed his stash of cherry licorice, and hugged Hardwicke goodbye. "Sorry. But I'm gonna be gone for a while."

With a wink he sent her back to Eternity.

"Because this thing between me and Brigsby . . . ? It is so on."

Chapter 27
Bridge Over Doubled Waters

Lex
San Francisco

Lex loved to graze. A carrot here, a string bean there. An entire banana bread.

The morning congregation of shoppers ambled about the outdoor marketplace, behind the San Francisco Ferry Building. But Lex stood there quietly, on all fours, below the clock tower, staring out at the rippling San Francisco Bay. Except for a jumble of white clouds, the sky was clear and blue.

A series of cool breezes rolled over his snout, then along his fine brown coat. Lex closed his eyes, breathed in, and held it—he let his lungs fill with salty bay air, let his body absorb it—and finally let it go.

Ahhhh, he thought. *Yeah. This is all right. This is A-okay.*

In the near distance was the San Francisco-Oakland Bay Bridge, and just yards away again, crossing the San Francisco Bay between Yerba Buena Island and Emeryville, was a new eastern span. The existing bridge—damaged, including a partial collapse, during the earthquake of 1989—was scheduled to be replaced with the newer, self-anchored suspension bridge. Only the project was significantly over budget and had blown its scheduled completion date by more than a year already, with several more years to go.

Construction jobs of every size and scope, both on Earth and throughout the Universe, were plagued with delays and cost overruns. Such was the business. If anything, Lex took a certain pride in the new construction. They had lived in San Francisco for less than a year, but he felt connected to the old bridge somehow, bonded, as if they were kindred spirits—damaged placeholders with new leases on life. A fresh start for them both.

For too long I let myself believe that you and I were in this together, even when I knew that we weren't. You'll never commit to this life, Emma. Not really. You don't want it, don't live in the moment. But I do. It's all I have. I know I can't rely on you anymore, if I ever could. But it doesn't matter, does it? This is my home now. It's my life. And there's no turning back.

Emma approached with a small bag of tangerines. "Whaddaya say, pal? Wanna go? I need to hit the gym. Big cardio. Gotta sweat. I'm not back to a size three. Not yet."

"Actually . . . I wanna hang for a bit. I like it here. It's relaxing."

"Relaxing? What do you have to be stressed about? You're a dog."

Yeah. Sure. A dog like no other, all because I followed you, because I couldn't say no. Couldn't be on my own. I used to hold you in my arms . . . remember that? I tore your clothes off, made your designs possible. And now look at me. What use am I to you really? I'm not a friend, not a partner. I'm just here to stave off your loneliness, your pangs of isolation. How nice for you. But we don't share this life, do we? We never did.

Emma peeled the skin off the small, orange fruit, pried off a section, and bit down. "But I hear what you're saying." She slurped up a stray piece of tangerine. "The view, the breeze. It's not bad."

And what's worse? I'm lonelier with you. You say we're a team, you and me, that we're making this work for us. But let's face it. You're still you, more or less. But me? I'm mutilated inside, twisted and confused. Inside this body I still think like a man, feel as a man . . . ache as a man, like I always have. Except when the dog in me barks and growls and the canine instincts take over. The sounds, the scents, and impulses . . . they reverberate through me like crackling thunder. And don't get me started on thunder!

I'm a man on all fours, Emma. On a leash. Sometimes my two selves are separate. Distinct. And sometimes they're the same, enmeshed in a duel, in a swirling mess, and I have no fucking idea which part of me is where. Which side of me to believe.

Which Lex I am.

But why do I even bother? You can't possibly understand. How could you? How could anyone? And yet . . . you really don't care, do you? For as much as you've changed—and you have, I'll give you some credit *there—you're still the same old you. You're Emma. This is your world and I'm just drifting through it. You say* **we** *sometimes—I think it's your way of genuinely trying to include me, to be sensitive to my limitations—but we both know that* **we** *means* **you.**

If we stay on Earth, I'm going to die here long before you. You're thinking ahead, Emma. Of a life without me. About what comes next.

Lex had a sudden urge to chew his back. He did.

It's time I did the same.

"I took a walk through Chinatown the other night," Emma said. "Just a stroll. I *never* do that. But I heard the girls talking about it, and I thought . . . what the hell? I even stopped into Golden Gate Fortune Cookie Factory. You know . . . the one down Ross Alley? It was a dorky, tourist thing to do, but it was kinda fun. I know this is probably it for us. San Francisco. Earth. I get it. This is our life now. It's who we are."

Lex looked up at Emma. *Whoa. Was I wrong about you? Do you really get it now?*

"But what if," Emma continued, "I mean . . . what if we could get back there? Just what if? I know it's not gonna happen, and I know it's just crazy talk that'll drive me up the wall. But, I've . . ."

Lex didn't know what she was about to say, but there was vulnerability in her voice. In her eyes. It seeped through her skin. He could smell it. Emma, of all things, was being human.

"I've been drawing again. I mean *really* drawing. Designing. Pretending sometimes like we're back in Eternity, in the *Starlight* offices, and we're the biggest firm around, you and me, and it's one huge project after another . . ." Emma held the half-eaten fruit in her hand. "The desire, the . . . yearning? It's been tugging at me. Prodding me."

You're really torn, aren't you? You're genuinely confused.

"I've been having those dreams again. Where I see the galaxies in my mind. And more and more I've been seeing this same galaxy, and these two comets just chasing each other around it. Forever. It's like Eternity is calling me, Lex. Like it wants me back. I know how it sounds. But don't you just feel it sometimes? . . . Don't you hear the call?"

There was a shuffle of footsteps as the ferry docked. A wave of passengers exited down the plank. Lex's heart thumped. Emma's passion was infectious. It always was. Despite himself he almost began to agree with her, to follow her dreams once again. But he knew better than to get sucked back in, so he forced himself to speak, to hold strong.

The words barely eeked out, but he managed them just the same. "Why are you telling me? Why now? I thought you were okay with this life. You just said."

"I know I did. I know. I'm *trying* to be okay with where we are. I really am. But I HATE this fucking life, Lex. I don't want it. I just don't."

As much as Lex didn't want those words to matter to him, they did. He was still seeking her approval, even when he thought he wasn't.

"I mean . . . I don't *hate it* hate it. It's not *that* bad. It's just . . . I was the queen of galaxy design! I was the best of the best!" Emma squeezed the half-eaten tangerine and tossed it to the ground, its guts splayed out. Exposed. "And I was up there on stage for everyone to see. They were all there for me . . ." Emma stopped herself just then. Her eyes fell.

Lex could sense her fear—and loneliness. Her pain. He could sense the vibrations.

"I let uncertainty creep in, Lex, let myself feel the strain . . . for just one idiotic moment, for just a sliver of time . . . and look where it got me. Here. Banished. Tossed aside." She wiped the tangerine juice from her hands with disdainful intensity, as if the mess on her hands reflected her more grandiose failures. "Do I deserve this, Lex? Do I? Was my crime *really* that bad?"

Your life. *Your* fate. *Always about you, Emma. You had me for a minute. You really did. But I should have known better. You don't care what happens to me. It's always about you.*

"Well," he said finally, answering her question. "Yes. It was that bad. It's why you did it. It's what you always do. You *love* to push limits, to invite the dare. . . . Emma . . . you challenged the Minder of the Universe! You violated his edict—on purpose! You taunted him to come after you, to make an example."

Emma scowled, but it quickly faded. "I just thought—"

"You'd get away with it."

"Actually. No. I didn't. I knew I'd get shit for it. . . . Just not this bad."

"Emma. Come on. You were messing with the Big M.O.U. What did you *think* would happen?"

"Honestly? I have no idea. I got so lost in the moment, the spectacle . . . I sort of forgot where I was. Don't you get sick of having to play by the rules? To have to ask permission?"

"I can't crap unless you open the door for me. So, yeah. I know the feeling."

Emma let out a sad smirk. "Yeah. I guess maybe you do. Here."

Purely on his canine instinct, Lex accepted the fresh baby carrot she fished out of the bag. He chomped it right down as the foot traffic bustled on through.

"But you know what, Lex? There's something going on. I'm telling you. There is. Those crackpots? The *Genius de Milo . . . ?* They're onto something."

"Yeah. Some of our lollipops, maybe."

"Don't be such a dope, Lex. Think about it. *Genius de Milo? de Milo?*"

"Yeah. de Milo. So what?"

"Milo, Lex. It's Milo. *Genius de Milo . . . is* Milo. Eternity Milo. Our Milo."

Lex chuckled. "Wait a second. You mean Milo Milo? Got banished Milo? Milo's Smear Milo? Why-the-Big-M.O.U.-updated-all-the-security-protocols-and-banished-us-to-Earth Milo? . . . That Milo?"

"Yes. I think it is. I think he's here. And if he's not . . . he's coming." She knelt down, and whispered. "And I think I know why."

Lex looked up at Emma. Eye to eye. But he already knew. "The jar?"

"Yep. I betcha. I bet it is. He found it, or he wants it, or he knows where to look. But in any case . . . he's coming. I *know* it. I can *feel* it. From my tits down to my feet. Milo's coming, Lex. He's on his way."

"What are you . . . ? I mean, are you . . . ?"

"We need to get ready, Lex. We have to prepare. I don't know when he's coming, and I don't know where. But it's real and it's soon and we'll know it when we see it. I know I sound insane or I'm the biggest dope on Earth. And who knows? Maybe I am. But you know what? I really don't think so. I really don't."

Lex didn't totally believe her. He didn't want to. "Okay," he said. "Let's say you're right. What do we do now?"

Emma let out an odd smile. "I have to do something. Before we leave, before we find our way back. I have to make it right with her. I'm not sure why and I don't know how, but they're connected. They just are."

Lex seized up, overcome by a sad, terrifying jolt of possibility. *Can we actually make it back? Would I really be me again?* But as he envisioned himself in Eternity, he couldn't see himself as the old Lex. In his mind's eye he was still a dog on a leash, a man on all fours. And when he asked himself just then if he really wanted to go back, even if he could . . . he paused.

I know what would happen, Emma. You have a feeling? Me, too. Even if I go back there, and even if I really could be the same old me . . . a man, standing on two feet . . . sooner or later . . . I'd just end up following your lead again. And hating myself for it. I may be a dog on Earth, Emma, but I'd rather be a dog in a dog's body than in the shell of a man. If it's my fate to remain here . . . so be it. I chose to come down here with you. And now . . . I choose to stay. I don't want you anymore. I don't want to think about your dreams. I want to move on. I want you gone.

"Lilly," Emma said. "I have to apologize. To make it right with her. I invited her to visit. She's on her way now."

Just the sound of her name set Lex back on his hind legs. *Lilly. That's it!* His doggie tail wagged to and fro. His doggie tongue dangled with delighted doggie glee. It dripped with doggie saliva. Doggie Lex was never so doggie happy to be his doggie self.

Emma leaned on the rail overlooking the water. "I have a plan. I know just what to do."

Lex chopped, smiled, and then looked toward the Bay Bridge. "You know," he said, while shaking out his fur. "I think I do, too."

Chapter 28
Get Your Motor Runnin'
(Head Out on the Highway)

Theo
Terre Haute, Indiana

With four missed messages from Roger, all Theo could think about was his dad.

So he really needed to ring back, even at 7:18 a.m. Monday, Eastern Standard Time. Given the eighteen hours difference, that made it 1:18 a.m. Tuesday in Auckland—not exactly prime calling hours—but Roger was a night owl, so chances were good that he was still up.

To get a clear signal Theo ambled into the parking lot, which played witness to the early-morning changeover of motel loneliness—prostitutes, johns, the homeless, and other lost souls.

He scrolled through his phone, and clicked on Roger's number. His forefinger grazed the *Send* button, but he wasn't ready to engage—in equal measures desperate to hear his father's voice and fearful of what it might convey.

Make the call, mate. Just make the call.

Theo looked up at the morning sun, took a deep breath, and fighting through his anxiety, pressed the button. The phone rang:

Ruhr-ruhr. Ruhr-ruhr. Ruhr-ruhr. Ruhr-ruhr. Ruhr click—

Roger answered. "What's up, donkey dick? Where you been? I've been calling for days."

"Sorry, mate. Sorry. It's, uh . . . long story."

Roger sighed through the phone. *"Oh, not this again. Well . . . while you're out there sniffing the galaxy's ball sack I've been sitting up with mum and dad. He's going in for tests. He's getting worse."*

The words *tests* and *worse* dangled above Theo's head like an anvil from fraying twine. He choked on his breath. "H-how's he doing?"

"He's kinda fucked up, yeh? He thinks it's over. It's like the old him

came back. Mopey dad. Sour dad. It sucks, Theo. It really does. And he misses you. He's scared."

Fear spares no one, but Theo, like most children, rarely considered his parents' plight in its fullest form. He had long been a Copernican study—Theo-centric—with him positioned as the center sun of his own Universe. But having a family—being a parent himself—meant his desires often came last, and with increasing regularity, dead last.

Parenthood had forced Theo to accept that his problems were indeed *his* problems. Sure, he wanted his girls to learn the important lessons, to become confident and self-sufficient and not take any shit from all the tossers out there. But of the many struggles his daughters would surely endure, worrying for him wasn't a burden he ever wanted them to carry. It was *his* responsibility to protect *them*, not the other way around.

Yet Theo was also a grown son now with an aging father. And his father—a once strong, burly man—had been reduced to a weak and bloated, almost-crippled old sod. And while Oskar Barnes cowered beneath the shadow of Death's scythe, his oldest son—his Theo—was on the other side of the world, nowhere to be found.

There are moments when even a father just needs his boy to hold his hand, and tell him it will be all right. Even if it won't.

Theo wished just then that he could harness the Razzle Dazzle—his daughters' ability to teleport—to where he most wanted to be, in this case, by his father's side. Instead he was drawn to the middle-of-nowhere parking lot view of a harried man with a young boy in tow, a newspaper tucked under his arm, and a store-bought coffee cup in the other hand, fumbling with his keys in the car door. Neither father nor son looked the least bit pleased.

Roger broke the silence. *"Fucknut? You still there?"*

"Yeh. Still here. How's mum?"

"Heh. She's doing okay. The twins keep her distracted, thank god. I don't know how you do it, mate. You've been gone a week and we're exhausted. Lea's a champ, though, as usual."

Lea. Hearing her name made Theo realize that he hadn't actually spoken to her since he left, hadn't heard her voice. The hemispheres were a true, logistical issue, but how, of all times, could he pick now to rely on text messages only? "I gotta call her."

"Yeh, ya' do. Seriously. She's the one with your kiddies, and Dad's in the hospital. It's time to man up. And I'm the one saying it. So what does that tell you? I'm flippin' out here, mate. I'm not built to be the guy. You know that. I'm barely holding it together."

Clearly agitated, Jason interrupted their phone call. "Dude. Sorry. Slight problem."

"What?" Theo said. "Roger . . . hang on . . ."

"I walked down the road, to rent us a car. I filled out the paperwork, then reached for my wallet. Only . . . it's gone."

Theo's eyes went wide. "Gone? What do you mean gone?"

"Gone," Jason said. "Like . . . I can't find it. Like . . . I have no I.D., credit cards, or cash. Nothing. Just the change from dinner. About forty bucks. I paid with Jackie's hundred last night, so I didn't need my wallet. I just didn't think about it. Theo . . . *please* tell me you have yours."

Theo reached into his front pocket. Nothing. Then the other. Same again.

"Roger, yeh? Hold on, mate. I gotta call you back. Don't go. I'll call you right back."

"No, dickhead. Don't hang up on me. Don't hang up. Don't hang—"

Click.

Theo and Jason dashed back to the motel room, and rummaged through their gear, startling Jamie.

"What's going on?" she said. "What happened?"

Theo ripped the sheets and blankets off the bed. Jason opened every drawer.

"Our wallets," Jason said. "We can't find them. They're not here, they're gone, they're . . . ."

"*Both* of them? How could you both lose your . . . ?"

And then Jason's phone rang. Jackie. He put the phone on speaker.

"What's up? Not a good time."

"Now, now my scrumptious little buttercup. Is that any way to talk to a friend like—"

"Kinda freaking out, Jackie. We can't find our—"

"Wallets?"

Jason stopped. "Yeah. How'd you know?"

"Well my grumpy bumpkin . . . I have them right here."

"You have them?! How?! Why?!"

"You left them in your pants. You changed after the plane went down . . . remember? You smeared the lotion. My bad, though. Mother always told me, 'check the pockets, dear Jackie, check the pockets.' Smart lady. I should have listened."

Theo let out a massive sigh of relief. His smile was large and wide.

"Jackie," Jason said. "That's *fantastic*. Can you drop them off? We're in a jam."

"Ohhhhh . . . no. Sorry, darling. No can do. We took off twenty minutes ago. We're out of your airspace. But I can send them to you, if you know where you'll be."

Theo dropped his head, sinking into his abject failure. *I'm a shit son, Dad. I fucked us up again. I'm sorry, Dad. I'm so sorry . . .*

"No," Jason said. "That's all right. It'll be too late. Just . . . hang on to them for now."

"You sure? I can wire you boys some money, if you need. I can't do it until tomorrow, but if it helps . . ."

"Thanks, Jackie. It might, actually. I'll let you know. I gotta go."

Theo escaped back out into the morning sun. A diehard believer in the traveler's motto—there's always a way to make the next stop; just gotta find it—he was pinned down by the call of the *Genius de Milo*. Theo knew time was running out, and with the remaining moments he had left, he was in truth stranded on the other side of the world when all he wanted now was to be in the one place he had spent most of life leaving—home.

And then, like a flare sent down from the Cosmos, he heard a loud, sputtering roar along the main road, between a drive-thru *Burger Buddy* and a canopied *Gas n' Snack*. A biker pulled up to a vacant pump.

Theo's eyes went wide. He dialed his phone. "Hey, Roger. Me again. Look . . . I need a favor, yeh?"

"Another one? For chri'sakes, mate." There was a pause, some muttering, then a sigh. *"All right. What is it?"*

"I need you to make a call for me."

Another pause. *"Fine. Just give me the number."*

"Cool, Raj. Thanks," Theo said while texting the info.

"Yeh yeh yeh. Anything else while I'm here? Mow your lawn? Pay your rent? Scrub the turd stains out of your shorts?"

"Nah. Nothing like that. Just . . . kiss my kids for me, will ya'? I miss them, Roger. I really do. So much it hurts." The digital wallpaper on Theo's phone was a photo of Lea with Tess and Hope at the beach. His twin girls were standing together, smiling, with a twinkle in their eyes, but looking toward the sky, as if there was something in the heavens drawing their attention.

"Kiss the kiddies? Now that I can do."

"Thanks, mate. Seriously. I owe you."

Roger cleared his throat. *"You better watch yourself, Theo. One of these days I'm gonna call in these I.O.U.s. And when I do . . . it's gonna be awesome."*

The picnic area of DeCandido Park, in the heart of a sun-soaked Terre Haute, was unattended except for an elderly couple beneath a row of shade-granting trees. They nibbled on white bread sandwiches and, despite the signs directing otherwise, fed the squirrels.

Theo expected the questions, but now that Jamie was asking, he struggled to answer.

"So *who's* picking us up? And how exactly do you know them?"

We're running out of options, mate. It's our last shot.

"My, um . . . my brother, Roger, yeh? He's got this mate, Davey."

Jason interrupted. "Wait-wait-wait. Davey? You mean the guy who jumped in last time? At your mom's place? With Rufus? The one who tackled what'shisface? Pookie?"

"Yeh-yeh. That's him."

Jamie was already confused. "Rufus? Pookie? Who *are* these people? . . . What the heck is up with you two? I don't even know who *Davey* is."

"Davey, yeh? He's part of this, um . . . motorcycle club in

New Zealand . . . and they're actually here, in the States, on a . . . cross . . . country . . . trip. That's it. Yeh-yeh."

"Yeah," Jason said. "Sure. But when he says *motorcycle club* he means *gang*."

Jamie flared her eyes, conveying a twinge of fear . . . and excitement. "Seriously?"

Theo nodded. "Yeh. Kinda."

"And when he says *cross-country trip*, he means *drug run*."

Jamie shook her head. "Don't even tell me . . ." She knelt down and then reached for the grass, pulled up several blades, threaded them through her fingers. She pulled them taut, snapped each one. "That. Is. It. I've had it. I swear. When I find my brother, we're outta here. And I hope I never come back."

There was an awkward silence then. Jason's eyes pulled serious. Theo hated witnessing confrontation, but there was no stopping it now.

I think I'm crushing on her, mate. She's linked to that jar, which means she's linked to me. I'm trembling here. I'm lost.

Jason squared his shoulders. "Yeah, well who *needs* you? This life might seem small and stupid and inconsequential to you . . . but it's the only one we've got."

"I know, I . . . I didn't mean it. I'm sorry. It's just . . . I have no idea who I'm supposed to be. Up there? In Eternity? Lex was the real success. He built himself up from nothing. A man on the rise. But me? I'm *nobody*. I'm invisible. At least I thought I was. And then Emma gets banished on TV, in front of everyone, Lex goes missing, and next thing I know I'm talking to THE MINDER OF THE FREAKIN' UNIVERSE! Do you understand what that actually means?"

"I . . . think so," Jason said. "He's—"

"The guy who decides what planets get made and which ones die. Which stars appear and how bright they burn. Him. Brigsby. The Minder of the Universe. He tells me that me . . . Jamie . . . . an assistant desk clerk at the *Rubicon* hotel . . . that I'm like *the* most important person ever. I mean . . . ever. That I need to just, you know, pop on down to Earth and prevent Milo—the Universe's ultimate troublemaker—from completing its disintegration. Yeah. Like . . . no pressure! Until I met you guys my biggest responsibility was making sure the new welcome packets were properly stocked . . . and now the fate of this planet is up to me!"

It's not just on you, Theo thought. *It's me, too. The jar's got its hooks in me. When I'm asleep, when I'm awake. I can't tell the difference anymore. I can hear it call. I can feel it. It's not just on you. It really isn't.*

"Can you for just one second think about what this is like for me? My brother is missing. He's the only family I've got. And we're probably going to be wiped out of Existence, in like . . . an hour . . . and now we're off to Yuma, Arizona. Yuma! I don't even know what Yuma is! I'm not even from this PLANET? And I've had to listen to you guys whine about the beautiful children who drive you crazy and the women who love you?! What the bunk?! I mean what? The? Bunk? I've been sent across the UNIVERSE to fix a problem that has NOTHING TO DO WITH ME! AND I HAVE NO IDEA WHAT I'M SUPPOSED TO DO ABOUT IT! You guys have stress? Yeah. Okay. Great. The two of you deserve each other. I swear you really—"

Jason interrupted, staring at his phone. "Whoa! Hang on a minute."

"Hey," Jamie said. "I wasn't finished—"

"Forget Yuma. We're not going to Yuma."

Had Theo not known better, he would have sworn Jamie was about to rip Jason's heart out with her bare hand, show it to him, and then set it on fire.

"Forget Yuma?! Forget Yuma? I can't take this any—"

"We're going to California. To San Francisco."

Theo liked that one. "Oh, yeh? Choice."

Jamie curled her lip, knocked on Jason's head. Hard. "Uh, helloooo. Doofus number one. What the heck is California?"

"Hey. Watch it. But if you must know, it's an enormous, banana-shaped state on the west coast with a cyborg as its governor. But that's not important right now."

"Holy crow, you guys are just the most annoying dweebs alive. What the—?"

Jason gripped his phone. "It's Lilly. I found her."

Jamie let her arms slump to their sides. "I'm just gonna cry,

I swear, I really am. WHO IS THIS LILLY GIRL TO YOU AND WHY DOES SHE REALLY MATTER SO MUCH?!"

Theo laughed. "We met her a while back. She's a crazy bird."

"Yeah, he told me," Jamie recalled. "They met in Venice, had a moment, and then she ditched him without saying goodbye. Sob story sob story boo hoo hoo. But so what? He's about to get ENGAGED!"

"Heh. Because . . ."

Because it's fun. Because it's exciting. Because if you obsess over a problem you can never solve then the chase never ends. Because in some mad way the torture of the unobtainable feels easier than the complexity of routine. Because if you're always on the run, you never have to deal with questions that have no easy answers.

". . . he's still in love with her."

Jason's face turned beet red. "Dude! I am not! It's just that, I mean, maybe once, but . . ."

Theo glimpsed the little bluebird icon on Jason's phone. Even he knew what that meant. Roger practically lived on it. "Oh, piss off, yeh? You've been following her on Twitter? You've been checking her out this whole time, haven't you?"

Jason dropped his head, sighed, and handed his phone to Theo. "Here."

Jamie cracked her knuckles. "Do I even need to know what Twitter means? I'm seriously gonna hurt the both of you." But then she leaned over Theo's shoulder, laser-focused on the tiny phone screen. Jason's Twitter feed was scrolled up to @LillyPainter8. The Tweet read:

Headed to San Fran on Friday 2 c Emma and my boy Lex. Nervous! Excited! Been a long time. Starlight Connect. Here I come. :)

Jamie grabbed the phone. "Lex. It says Lex! And Emma. It's him! It's my brother. How does Lilly know him?!"

Jason shrugged.

"I dunno. But she's bad news."

Jamie moved in close. "You know her, too? You know Emma? How do you know her?"

Theo shook his head. "No, not really. But Lilly was mixed up with her somehow. It was a scam. I'll explain on the way."

Jamie dropped her hands in exasperation. "Seriously. . . . Who *are* you guys?"

Before Theo could respond the roar of rolling thunder sent birds scattering from trees. The elderly couple nearby covered their ears, and scowled. In a long row came a dozen motorcycles. Sunshine beamed off the sea of chrome. The posse all wore blue jeans and black leather chaps.

The lead biker removed his helmet and sunglasses. Davey hugged Theo, shook Jason's hand. "Well . . . all right. How you been, mates? How's this monster motherfucker of a country treating you?" Before they could answer, Davey turned to Jamie. "Well, look at you. *Tsk-tsk-tsk*. Steppin' out on your old ladies with this tasty treat. Didn't think ya' had it in you! But, right on!"

Theo shook his head. "It's not like that, yeh? It's . . . complicated."

"Complicated. Right. You hear that boys? Theo says it's complicated. Give it up!"

The convoy of bikers revved their engines into a mad, frenzied roar.

"So . . . you fuckers gonna leave your thumbs up your arses or are ya' gonna hop right on? Daylight's wastin' and I ain't got time to waste any more." Davey winked at Jamie. "You can ride with me, sweetheart." He winked at her. "Wrap your arms around my waist."

She threw him a snarky smile. "No chance. But feel free to go rev yourself."

The bikers let out a series of laughter and engine revs.

"Oooh, I like her, mates. She's all right. Jason . . . you ride here in my sidecar. Theo . . . think you can still handle one of these bad boys?"

"Yeh-yeh. Definitely."

"Okay, then. We're hung over as the shite on a croc's arse. It was a long week in Chicago. That lake was turning bright orange and hot as molten lava. I don't know what the fuck, yeh? Anyway, some of the boys'll double up so you and your girl here can ride together. If that's acceptable to . . . ?"

"Jamie," she said. "And yes. That's acceptable."

"As long as we're all accepting. So . . . I know you're off to

Yuma, yeh? We can't get you there, but we can take you as far as Albuquerque. Then you're on your own."

"Actually," said Jason, who strapped on a half moon cruiser helmet as he climbed into the sidecar, "it's San Francisco now. We gotta find Jamie's brother. If it's the last thing we do."

On the back of a Harley Davidson dual glide chopper with multi-angle handlebar bends, Jamie gripped Theo's waist, and smiled. "The way we're going . . . it just might be."

Davey and crew let the engines roar. "Frisco?! Same difference to us. Let's go, boys. It's two days to New Mexico and the road ain't gonna eat itself. Time to gas up, get comfortable . . . and enjoy the motherfucking ride."

PART III
GENIUS DE MILO

Chapter 29
The Land of Enchantment

Jason
Somewhere along the Indiana/Illinois border

They roared.

Under the watchful eye of the midday sun a legion of metal and chrome beasts motored southwest on I-70, crossing the Indiana border into southern Illinois. Davey was out front, with crew in tow, including Theo on a chopper with Jamie perched behind him, arms still wrapped around his waist.

And though there was a power, an exhilarating freedom of rolling thunder inherent to the biker's life, Jason figured now probably wasn't the right time to confess his incapacitating fear of motorcycles, that he had never even been on one, and that all things being equal he would much prefer to travel via tank with cross-shoulder seatbelts and airbags, where he was far less likely to end up splattered on the side of the road if they happened to hit a raccoon.

So as far as bike travel went, perched in Davey's sidecar was Jason's ideal option, particularly given the *car* component of sidecar.

But motorcycle time was also a period, ironically, of quiet reflection. Synchronized with the engines' rhythm and roars, Jason felt the noise slowly fade, until finally he was engulfed by a meditative hum. The asphalt slipped beneath them until all Jason could hear was a separate, low-pitched buzz. The tiny grains in the road kept rolling past, with a barely perceptible crackle, like static from an old phonograph.

In the near distance was a smattering of foliage, including black walnut, sycamore, pear, and yellow tulip trees. The caravan then came to a bend in the road, and swerved around a skunk carcass. Jason cringed as they drove through a cloud of its foul spray, but soon thereafter the bitter tinge faded, replaced instead by the scent of manure, truck exhaust, and then, mercifully, American elderberry and bittersweet shrubs.

With that sweet aromatic perfume, the air suddenly—and mysteriously—dropped at least ten degrees, a frigid change, and then warmed again just as quickly. On the move, there was no opportunity to investigate what had happened, or why. Such was life on the road.

Jason looked up to Davey just then, to reconnect with the man controlling his fate, when there was a blast of white light. There was screaming fluorescent color. There was the sensation of being sucked through a tornado.

The pull on the Earth, the force echoed by the *Genius de Milo*, was getting stronger. And then driving the motorcycle . . . was Hank.

"Whaddaya say, Kid? Having fun yet? Feelin' good?"

"H-hank? I . . ."

"Don't look so surprised, Kid. You should be figuring it all out, don't'cha think? Hmm? Well . . . don't say I never gave you a heads up. You always were a slow learner. See ya'."

"Wait! Hank! I can't remember if—"

There was a blast of white light. There was screaming fluorescent color. There was the sensation of being sucked through a tornado. And then driving the motorcycle . . . was H-Bomb, his editor, Glenn Hauman.

"So, Mister Medley. Is your article finished? Did you bother to spell check or confirm your facts this time? By the look on your face . . . I gather not. As expected. Well, then . . ."

There was a blast of white light. There was screaming fluorescent color. There was the sensation of being sucked through a tornado. And then driving the motorcycle . . . was Jason's cousin Brian. Dead more than fifteen years.

"Brian! You're here! But how? I thought you were—"

"Look at you, Jason. How wonderful. There's no need to worry. The future will surprise you. And when you feel trapped by the very choices you'll have to make, just remember . . . at all moments in time and space you are exactly where you are meant to be, doing exactly what you are meant to be doing. If you can accept that, the journey will go a lot smoother, and be a lot more fun. But either way, it will all work out. You'll see. My god, you'll see."

There was a blast of white light. There was screaming fluorescent color. There was the sensation of being sucked through a tornado. And then driving the motorcycle . . . was Anna.

"Hi, Baby! Isn't this fun? I love motorcycles! What a thrill! We should try this someday. Just drive across America. Just you and me. And then maybe we can bring the kids along and we—"

"Kids?!"

"Ha. Don't worry, Baby." Anna offered a wide, loving smile. "We can't think about children. Not yet. You're not ready. Not until you see Lilly."

"W-wait. Lilly? But how . . . ?"

. . . *do you know about her?*

There was a blast of white light. There was screaming fluorescent color. There was the sensation of being sucked through a tornado. And then driving the motorcycle . . . was indeed the one who had gotten away.

Lilly.

Jason's heart thundered as the caravan powered along, through Effingham, and across the Missouri border, transferring to I-55 at the cross-section of I-270. They slowed a bit as they made their way through downtown St. Louis, passing Busch Stadium, the St. Louis Zoo, the bronze statue of Apotheosis of St. Louis outside the Saint Louis Art Museum, and the massive arch.

Time and again Jason and Lilly were on the verge of speech, but no words came. All that Jason could focus on was the slow, deep thuds in his chest. And finally, as they drove beyond the 630-foot arch—a steel rainbow crossing the city center, along the west bank of the Mississippi River—Jason spoke. "Hi," he said from the sidecar.

Lilly smiled uneasily, barely above a whisper. "Hi."

Jason's mouth dried up. He tried to moisten his lips. It wouldn't take. "I . . ."

"You're coming, right? To see me?"

Tears rolled down Jason's face. He nodded.

Lilly nodded, too. She cried a little. "Okay."

Jason reached out, to take Lilly's hand. Just as their fingertips were about to touch, he felt that spark, that palpable electricity between them. They were again as they once were, coursing with a mystical current far beyond passion, desire, or love. Theirs was a connection beyond the confines of the tangible world, an unspoken promise, when suddenly there was a blast of white light. There was screaming fluorescent color. There was the sensation of being sucked through a tornado.

And once again, driving the motorcycle . . . was Davey.

"What the fuck are you looking at, mate? You wanna bang me or what?! Ha! I know I'm a jolly hot bloke who shags like a beast, but I just don't run that way. Eyes on the road, Jason. The future's dead ahead. And it's coming our way."

Theo

Years back, before fatherhood, when it was still all Theo all the time, he would burn up the racetracks on his 2007 Yamaha motocross motorcycle.

Theo didn't care about winning or losing. He wasn't competing against the other riders, didn't care about trophies. He was pushing himself, adrenaline coursing through his veins. Power in his hands. Toying with danger.

And when the race was over he would motor home, sometimes with a girlfriend in tow, arms wrapped around his waist. Often, a good night followed.

But now that he was cruising across America, he settled into the hum of the motor and the warmth of the body behind him. Only it wasn't a body he was supposed to enjoy. The wrong set of arms. Theo was committed to Lea, even if he hadn't realized it at first. They were a family—his family—as much as he could have ever imagined for himself.

Which is why a battle erupted within him, eight back in a caravan.

-Don't go there, mate. She's not your girl. She's not Lea.-

I know, yeh. I know. But she's like no one else. She's . . .

-Like no one on Earth, you mean.-

Yeh. Heh. Like no one on Earth. Like no one on . . .

There was a blast of white light. There was screaming

fluorescent color. There was the sensation of being sucked through a tornado.

And then Theo was sitting on a stool, in a hotel bar. Behind the bar was a black woman in black pants, white collared shirt, and black bow tie. Her long black hair was fastened in a thick braid. She smiled, filled a pilsner with beer, and placed it before him, on a coaster.

Without thinking, Theo drank. Cold. Delicious. Next to him sat a graying waif of a man in orange pleated pants, orange and brown paisley top, and an orange scarf. He wore tinted glasses. His hands and face were wrinkled. A martini glass with blue liqueur.

"Theodore. Well, now. At last we meet."

"What is this place, yeh?"

"This? Oh. Just a quiet little spot, to sit . . . to think. And have a drink. Usually alone. But sometimes . . . with a friend."

"I don't know you."

"Ah, yes. But I know *you*. I'm Brigsby, of course. You may have heard my name before. Or not. . . . But you will. Oh, my darling. You will."

"Brigsby. Yeh. Maybe. . . . Maybe."

"You and I will have much to chat about . . . in due course. But my oh my you're a busy little beaver, aren't you? You and your friend Mister Medley have been having quite the time. Playing with jars. Causing a commotion. But you're a father now, Theodore. A man with children. With daughters. And your daughters. Hooo-boy. Quite a pair, those two."

"Wait," Theo said. "How do you—"

"Don't worry about your girls, right now. My guess is that your father should be top of mind, should he not? After all, his life's about to change."

"Change? Change how? Change h—!"

There was a blast of white light. There was screaming fluorescent color. There was the sensation of being sucked through a tornado.

And then Theo was standing in his father's workshop. Oskar Barnes was working a rag of high-grade natural beeswax leather polish into the bucket seat of a vintage automobile—a

1951 Jaguar XK120 OTS, an open two-seater—he had spent more than a decade restoring, but never put on the road.

Theo attempted to reach out, to speak, but tears overwhelmed him.

"What are you on about, son? It's all right. Your pop's gonna be fine. Bad heart, they say. But whadda they know, yeh? Life's for the living, Theo. You of all people should know that. Don't live the way I did, boy. Don't close yourself off. Don't keep your words inside. My own father barely spoke to me, but that's what battle can do to a man. World War II for him, and then Vietnam for me. Best thing I did was to keep you and your brother outta the military. Away from the guns. From the violence. Deep in my heart I told myself it was enough, that one day you'd understand. But you know what, Theo? It was all bullshit. I needed to tell you just how much I loved you. I needed to tell you each and every day. The feelings were always in me, son. Truly they were. I just couldn't bring myself to pucker my lips and say so. And now look at me? Like this old gal . . . I'm old and busted up inside. I just can't be restored. My time's up, Theo. I have to go."

Theo wiped his tears, reached for his father. "No, Dad. There's still time for us. There's still—"

There was a blast of white light. There was screaming fluorescent color. There was the sensation of being sucked through a tornado.

And Theo was in his wetsuit, with hardhat and miner's light in front, sitting in an inner tube, floating once again deep in the Waitomo Caves, on New Zealand's North Island, hundreds of feet beneath the Earth's surface.

The cave ceiling was only five feet above his head, with jagged rock formations jutting down. The cold, damp air held a mossy tinge. The tiny glow worms, as they had done time and again, illuminated his subterranean path, staving off the darkness.

Laying atop Theo . . . was Lea. They pressed their lips together, floating deeper into the caves. Theo held her; she sank into him. Theo needed Lea then. Truly, deeply needed her in a way he never had before. His miner's light shone on her, disclosing her vibrant presence. He put his hand upon her cheek.

Theo's heart pounded. Because he wasn't holding Lea anymore.

It was Jamie.

"You don't have to worry," she said. "You needed to see me. You needed to know."

"Know what, yeh? I'm not . . . what do you—?"

Jamie kissed him again. Their lips joined as one. They held it.

"It's okay to admit who you are," she said. "There's always three." Jamie's breath was warm on his lips. She kissed him once more. "Always three."

"Three what, yeh? Three of—?"

There was a blast of white light. There was screaming fluorescent color. There was the sensation of being sucked through a tornado.

Theo was back driving the motorcycle, Jamie behind him. The caravan held its formation, cutting through the wind. They came upon a roadside billboard. It read:

Come on, now. Admit it. You're hungry, ain'tcha? Then eat at Donna's. Dinner special. Steak and a beer, $16.99. Desserts plentiful. Choose one of three. Enjoy!

Jamie

Jamie's was an inverse experience.

With each mile they ticked off, getting closer to their destination, she somehow felt farther away. Maybe it was fear of the unknown. Maybe it was the scope of expectation. But mostly it was her pending arrival.

Whether she was destined to find Lex or not, to help reclaim the Earth, she was going to face . . . *something*. And whatever it was, she worried—she assumed—that Brigsby had only shared with her an infinitesimal piece of a grander, more elaborate puzzle she was somehow a part of, but didn't have the perspective or capacity to visualize, much less comprehend.

So she adjusted her arms around Theo's waist. And as she grabbed tighter—to feel more secure—there was a blast of white light. There was screaming fluorescent color. There was the sensation of being sucked through a tornado.

Still in motion but far removed from America, Earth, and even the Milky Way galaxy, Jamie came upon the Four Moons of Dahlerna. A framed print of the planet and its satellites hung above her bed, in Eternity.

Known for its milky white oceans, purple sand beaches, and fresh waffle aroma, Dahlerna symbolized to Jamie tranquility, peace, and eternal calm. But her dream sanctuary was guarded by four mid-sized moons—blue, yellow, gray, and red—each one ineffectual on its own, but in tandem creating a magnetized field that consumed the entire planet, rendering Dahlerna gorgeous, but unapproachable.

Mesmerized by her proximity to the galactic quintet, it took a moment for Jamie to finally appreciate that she had traded in a motorized vehicle for a comet, and that she appeared to be unaffected by the various elements of space. And, as she adjusted her hands, it became evident that she was grasping an unfamiliar midriff, no longer holding onto Theo, but to someone else entirely. Someone she'd met before. And hoped to never see again.

"Pretty freakin' sweet, huh, dollface?"

A panic flutter rendered her arms useless. Jamie fell to the side, practically dangling from the comet. About to fall out, she grabbed onto the back collar of the driver's shirt, choking him. Eyes bulging, he reached behind, and pulled Jamie back atop the comet.

"Whoa. *Kaff-kaff*. Didn't nobody . . . *kaff* . . . ever tell ya' to keep yer arms and legs inside the comet at all times? Sheesh. It's a friggin' *comet* ride. So, you know, like, uh . . . safety first. Know what I'm sayin'? But . . . you gotta admit, the view is beeee-yootiful. Like all romantic. Classy. Like I promised. And it's better'n clams and vino. Eh? Eh?"

"Ch-Chuck? What are you . . . how'd I get here? How did *you*?"

Chuck spun around to face her. "Ohhh . . . I think you know the answer to that one, right, dollface? You know it ain't really me. Chuck . . . ya' see, he's a . . . whatchamacallit? A alias, a gnome de friggin' ploom. A fake name. Like a secret identity. Yeah. That's it. Secret identity. Like a superhero or somethin'.

But however you wanna slice it . . . I ain't Chuck. Well, I am to you, 'cuz . . . that's how you need to see me, to, uh . . . make the introductions. But now we did all that . . . most people know me by anuddah name."

There was a time not long before that extraordinary moment within the crevices of Existence when Jamie would have become immobile, then started to shake, and ultimately ramble on at an escalating rate until she passed out from exceeding the words-to-breaths ratio necessary to remain conscious. Yet now, riding a comet past the Four Moons of Dahlerna, she merely shrugged as Chuck the doorman, Chuck the comet jockey, instantly transmogrified into a short, stocky man-child with a thick brown beard, and dressed in overalls, a red flannel shirt, and tennis sneakers—a pint-sized lumberjack who'd misplaced his work boots.

Jamie squinted. "Milo?"

Milo offered a bow. The red glow of Dahlerna's setting sun radiated around the edges of his silhouette, such that his beard was like a lion's mane. "At your service."

"Wow," she half-whispered. "You're really real."

"Yep. I'm the real deal. The genuine article. I'm as real as Brigsby."

"Thaaaaaat's not as comforting as you might think."

"Fair enough, Jamie. Fair enough."

"Jamie? What about *Dollface*?"

"Oh, that's only when I'm Chuck. He's loads of fun, don't get me wrong. But Chuck requires a certain degree of concentration that I save for special occasions."

The breeze from the zooming comet blew hair in front of Jamie's eyes. She pulled it back into a ponytail. "What am I doing here, Milo? What does Brigsby want from me? I mean, what does he *really* want? And don't tell me it's about reclaiming that stupid jar of his. He doesn't need me for that."

Milo ran his stubby, sausage-like fingers through his beard. "No," he said. "He does not. But let me ask you something. What do you think of my boy, Philbrick, here?"

"I don't follow."

Milo patted the comet's side, and then scratched its top, as if stroking a dog behind the ears. "Woof-woof, Jamie. Woof-woof."

"Woof? I don't . . ." She trailed off then, remembering that Theo's girls, Tess and Hope, said the same thing to her on the beach in New Zealand, when she first appeared on Earth. "What is woof, Milo? I don't understand. I'm not—"

"Come on, Jamie. You know."

"But I really don't, Milo. I . . ."

"Woof-woof," Milo said as he evaporated into the ether, Jamie still on the comet. "Woof-woof."

"No! Wait! How can I—?"

There was a blast of white light. There was screaming fluorescent color. There was the sensation of being sucked through a tornado.

With the blink of her eyes, Jamie found herself back on the motorcycle with Theo. The caravan sped along the highway when each of the bikers raised a fist and revved their engines. There was a sign ahead. It read:

Welcome to New Mexico. The Land of Enchantment.

Imbued with a comet's vapor trail, Jamie clung to Theo, for her physical safety. But she didn't want to hold on anymore. If anything, she wanted to let go. And that's exactly what she would have done had she been just a little more confident in her ability to survive the fall.

Chapter 30
Albuquerque Blues

Theo
Albuquerque, New Mexico

Tumbleweeds tipped along the dusty plain.

Split by Route 66, Albuquerque was a desert city in the northern tip of the Chihuahuan Desert, near the edge of the Colorado Plateau, with one of the highest elevations of any American city. A desert climate with mild winters and warm summers, Albuquerque had mild rainfall and humidity, and copious amounts of brilliant sunshine.

And through it all was the Rio Grande. One of the longest rivers in the U.S., it originates as a clear spring and snow-fed mountain stream more than 12,000 feet above sea level in Colorado, cuts south through the middle of New Mexico, through the desert and mountains, and splits again southeast, into El Paso, Texas, and finally southwest, into Mexico itself.

I could stay here forever, Theo thought, now back on foot. *A thousand kilometers, to watch and wander.*

But the buzzing in his pocket disrupted his moment of tranquility, his meditation. For deserts were inherently vast and strange places, filled with scorching heat during the day, frostbite at night, and creatures crafty and sometimes lethal enough to sustain both extreme environments. And yet Theo knew the inevitable would find him, even half a world away.

So that when he saw the name come up on the caller ID—*Roger*—his heart pounded. The moment he had been dreading most was finally here. "H-hello?"

"It's a rush job. Dad needs it now, yeh? Quadruple bypass. They gotta unclog his whole heart. It's like a Vegemite logjam."

Try as he might, Theo couldn't get the words out. His lip quivered. "What, uh . . . what'd they say? Is he gonna . . . y-you know?"

"Die?"

Die. Theo had never once allowed himself to utter that specific word before in context to his father, and now that it had been said for him, he could barely speak another. ". . . Y-yeh."

"I dunno, mate. But we're all here, yeh? Me, Mum, Sarah, Lea, and the twins. Dad was askin' for you before he went it. Docs say it's gonna be four hours at least. Maybe more. Then we'll see. But it isn't looking good, Theo. You need to come home. You gotta come now."

Eyes filled with water, Theo nodded. "Y-yeh. I know. I'm working on it."

"Well, work faster, dickhead. There's not much time." Roger went silent, just holding the space between them, before speaking again. *"I know it's a fucker, yeh? I'll kiss everyone for ya'. We miss you."*

"Yeh-yeh. Thanks. Call me when it's done." Theo held a hand to his eye, then threw his phone into the desert dust. "AAAAHHHH!"

Jason strode up next to him. "Hey. Was that your dad? . . . How's he doing?"

"In surgery. Lookin' bad. Probably gonna kick it."

"Oh, *man.* Theo." Jason put a hand on his shoulder. "I'm sorry. What'd they say?"

Theo explained.

"We gotta get you home, Theo. They need you."

Almost worse than *die,* those three words—*they need you*—burned for Theo with the ferocity of a thousand suns. *They need you.* He could hear nothing else.

THEY need you.
They NEED you.
They need YOU.
THEY. NEED. YOU.

Never with such intensity had Theo's fear, anxiety, guilt, and self-doubt collided with his inability to reconcile just how ineffectual he considered himself to be when it mattered most.

"I know they do! But you *know* it's not that simple, yeh? Look where we are! I can't go home. Not yet. If we don't set this right . . . there's not gonna be a home to get back to."

Jason expelled a restrained sigh, trying to be the voice of reason at a point when rational options had long since expired. "I know, man. I know. But maybe you should head back anyway.

Go be with them. I know we're all wonked up again . . . but it's different this time. You've got a family now. And this is when it counts. Me and Jamie . . . we'll figure it out."

"Thanks, but . . . you know it won't work. It has to be us both." Jason was a real mate, maybe Theo's best mate, but try as he might, Jason wasn't up to it on his own. Theo didn't want to say as much, because it didn't need to be said, but he had to say something. "We're in too deep, yeh? Gotta see it through."

"I know. It's just . . . I can't be the reason you stay. I can't fail you like that."

Theo pointed. "Look at the road, mate. Look behind us." Facing east along Interstate 40, pavement and sky alike were nothing more than a massive, dark smudge, growing darker and less distinct as it drew to a distant point. Slowly becoming a permanent nothing. "Those nutters, yeh? The *Genius de Milo*? They had it right. The Earth really is disintegrating. The jar? Milo? It's all happening. For real. If we don't finish what we started, none of this will matter. *That's* how I can help my family, yeh? I have to do what no one else can. . . . I have to try."

Jason nodded once more. "I know that, too. I'm just . . . afraid you'll be pissed at me if I let you down."

Theo went down on one knee. He ran his fingers in the dirt. It was dry, coarse. It hurt. He looked up at Jason. "I'm not pissed at you, mate. I'm pissed at him! At my dad. I was. For my whole life."

There was a pause between them before Jason finally spoke. ". . . Why?"

It was a question which didn't require an answer, but one Theo needed to expel from his soul, lest he carry it with him forever. He stood up again, with conviction.

"Because he was too fat, too bald, too old." Blood rushed to his face, his body tense, his throat dry. "Because I didn't know how to be around him without feeling angry or sad or jealous or weak or bitter or condescending or just wanting to bash his face in. Because he couldn't read my mind. Because, fuck . . . I don't know! Because . . . because . . . I didn't know how to be around him and have that be okay. Because I didn't really know him, either. He was young and had a kid and knew fuck all about it. But the thing is . . . when you're a dad . . . you gotta be in it, mate. You gotta be in it every second of every minute of every hour of every day of every week of every month of every year. Forever. Whether your kids are in the room with you or not. And I think . . . I dunno! Fuck! Shit! I dunno! I dunno! I don't . . . I think he resented me, yeh? And I resented him back. I was pissed because he didn't protect me."

"From what?"

"FROM MYSELF! It was easier for him with Roger. I think he's just . . . simpler, more obvious. But me? I think maybe my dad really did try harder when I was a tyke. Or maybe not. I dunno. But whatever it was he didn't figure out how to be happy with the life he had until he started to get old, and now that we finally found a way to be cool with each other, where he really feels like my dad, and I feel like his son . . . he's dead. He's gone."

Jason offered a soft smile. "Is he?"

Theo almost wanted it to be true, because, if nothing else, finality eradicates the torturous strain of uncertainty.

"He's in surgery," Jason said. "And it's serious, I know. I've been there. I know what it's like. You're filled with fear and rage and anxiety and confusion and you just feel so powerless to do anything about it because you can't actually *do* anything to make it better or go away. And that makes you hate yourself, hate your dad. Makes you hate the gods, if they even exist. . . . But I think we both know that they do."

Theo let slip an uncomfortable laugh.

"But doctors . . . ," Jason continued, ". . . some of them . . . they can do amazing things. I saw it up close almost fifteen years ago . . . and they're *so* much better today. You're scared for your dad. I know you are. But have faith, Theo. Trust that the gods are watching. Trust that he'll be okay."

"I want to believe you, mate. But . . . what if he's not?"

Jason exhaled through his nose. "Then it'll be horrible. It will. And it could really happen. He could really die. But you know what? He's still alive today. And knowing your dad . . . he'll probably survive this surgery. You know." Jason offered a wink and a smile. "Just to spite you."

Theo let out a reluctant laugh. "Yeh-yeh. Probably will."

"See? And no matter what happens, you've got your mom and your brother and Lea and your kids. That's more than a lot of people have. A lot more. And for whatever it's worth . . . ," Jason put an arm around his shoulder, and pointed toward the distant mountains, ". . . you got me, Theo. I'm here, man. Whatever you need."

In the desert dust, the two mates hugged it out.

"You know . . . I think you spoke more words in the past two minutes than in all the years combined since I've known you. You ever say that much about anything?"

Theo smiled. "I dunno. Maybe once, yeh? Fucker Arnie Bryant stole my Superman action figure when I was nine. I went mad for about an hour then nicked the front wheel off the little tosser's bicycle. He cried like a wanker. Got my Superman back the next day."

"Good to know, Theo. Good to know. And while we're at it . . . you wanna deal with this whacked-out jar?"

Theo cupped a hand over his eyes, stared up at the sky, facing west. He took a breath, held it, and then let it go. "Yeh," he said, "yeh. Just give me a minute. There's something I gotta do first."

Jason

That day. He thought of it often.

The specifics were hazy, because memories fade and recall becomes less reliable as the flow of life propels us forward. But details remained. Standing on a street corner, in Amsterdam. A sky not gray, but copper. Drizzle. Passing cars. A wet newspaper. A lamp post. Jason had just left the Anne Frank House, confused by his inner dichotomy. Inspired by the courage of others, yet sad and lost and thousands of miles from home with no distinct path to follow.

And then Theo appeared, as if he had been transported to a specific set of coordinates in the Universe because that was where those two young men were meant to intersect.

Yet positioned now in the center of I-40, facing due west,

that reconnection released within Jason a warmth, a comfort. It helped strip away an imbedded layer of fear—a sometimes debilitating mistrust of the unknown—replacing it with possibility. A burgeoning curiosity. And allowed him to embrace the idea that while the future was indeed uncertain and, if mishandled, perilous, it offered the possibility for as many rewards as pitfalls.

The optical illusion of perspective was such that the road ahead of him diminished with distance, the asphalt all but disappearing into a point on the horizon. Dusty landscape on both sides with a smattering of shrubs and tumbleweeds, and a rolling layer of low-lying mountains so far off they appeared more like sacks of potatoes lined end to end.

Standing out in the road, there was an intense pull on him, a resonance, a magnetism throughout his very being. Was it an encroaching storm? Gravity? Space-time? The hum of the Universe? Or were there even more substantial forces at work?

Jason held out his hands, bonded with the energy. It consumed him, penetrated him, reverberating from his eye sockets, down his arms, and stretching to his fingertips. And then he laughed, because even though Hank wasn't there with him— Jason was standing alone on that empty stretch of New Mexico highway—he could almost hear Hank's voice, the wisdom that always seemed to be there when Jason needed it most.

"Come on, Kid. It's the big one. The one who got away."

Jason responded to the empty highway, facing the horizon. "Maybe not, Hank. I don't know. I'm standing in the middle of the road. The center line. I haven't chosen a side yet. And I'm feeling this pull on me, this . . . force."

"Don't go all Star Wars nerdnik on me, Kid. There's nothing galactic going on here. . . . Well, okay . . . that's not exactly true. But for you, it's not. It never was. It's Lilly. You know that. It's because you're close. It's getting real."

"You know what, Hank? I thought it was, but it's not. It isn't Lilly. . . . It's Anna. And it's not that I'm getting close, it's that I'm so far away. Lilly's this enigma, this ghost, and she haunts me because she thinks I love her. And maybe I do. I don't know anymore. But Anna's the one I want, Hank. She's going to be my wife, and I'm going to be her husband. We're gonna have a house and kids and play monster tag in the yard because *that's the life I want. The life I was meant for.*" Jason gazed off into the distance, smiled. "Lilly? She's who I was. But Anna's who I *am.* And the thing is . . . now that Lilly's coming up . . . I'm pissed. I actually hate her."

"Whoa. That's a bit harsh, Kid. . . . Why?"

"Because she ditched me, Hank. Because I spent so much time thinking about where she was and who she might be and if she still loved me, too. And it's easier to blame her for *making* me feel that way instead of dealing with the fact that my problems run deeper than her. She was the catalyst, but not the cause. And now the entire world is literally disintegrating behind me and all I want is to hold Anna in my arms . . ."

"And you're getting Lilly instead."

"Yeah. I'm getting Lilly instead."

"Ha."

"Ha? Even now you say *ha*? Thanks. You're a real mate."

"You have two beautiful women who might truly, deeply love you because of who you are, what you strive to be, and how they feel about themselves when they're around you. That's a world-class problem, Kid. We should all be so unlucky."

Jason nodded sheepishly. "Huh. Jamie said the same thing."

"I knew I liked that girl."

"Not helping, Hank. Not helping."

"That's the funny thing about help, Kid. It doesn't always show up when you want it, but when you need it most. . . . Somebody should write a song about that."

In the distance, to the north, a detonation of thunder and lightning jolted across the sky. Due east, from whence they came, the horizon faded to black. "Yeah, well . . . I'll tell you what, Hank. If this is the kind of help I actually need, I'm in more trouble than I thought."

Jamie

A domino chain of leather and chrome, the motorcycle crew was revved up and ready to go.

But Jamie couldn't leave. Not yet. Jason and Theo weren't ready. Which meant more alone time with Davey. She leaned against the motorcycle, shook her head in frustration. "Is this what they do? I don't get them."

Davey drew on a hand-rolled cigarette. Held the smoke. Exhaled. As he craned his neck toward the sky, sunlight caught the silver of his skull-engraved ring. "How do you mean, yeh?"

"Theo's upset. It's easy to tell. So he wanders off, to be alone. He doesn't want to talk. He's quiet. But Jason . . . ? He withdraws, only . . . so you can see. Look at him out there. Does he want to be noticed? Is he waiting for someone to reach out? He's surrounded, but alone . . . on purpose."

"Uh, I dunno. It's just how they deal with being in the shit, yeh? God knows it's better 'n how I do it!" Davey took another drag, nodded. "I love 'em cuz they're my mates an' all, and they get your back when it counts. I'll tell you that much. But you know what it is about them? And *don't* fuckin' repeat it." Davey shifted, to make sure his crew couldn't hear. "They kinda . . . scare me a little, yeh? The shit they get into? It's a *whole* other thing. And I should know. I ain't exactly a choirboy. But Theo? Jason? Especially when they get together? I don't even like to ask. It's like . . . they knock the whole planet off its axis or some shit. Like the whole goddamn Universe starts freakin' out! Christ on a cracker. Listen ta' me. I'm a fuckin' nutter, yeh? Ah . . . fucked if I know."

"I know, I know. You helped them out before with Rufus and the jar and all that mess you had with Aputa a few years back. At Theo's house."

Before Davey could interject—and he most surely would— Jamie became lightheaded, nauseated, and dizzy. She began to sweat . . . profusely . . . then fell back a step.

"Whoa-whoa-whoa." Davey grabbed her arm. Hard. "How the fuck you know about that, yeh? 'Ats private family business. They'd *never* tell you that." He leaned in close, his breath hot with tobacco and tacos. "Seriously. How do you know?"

"I, uh . . . I don't know. It's just that . . ."

About to pass out, Jamie clutched Davey, to steady herself. And then there was a blast of white light. There was screaming fluorescent color. There was the sensation of being sucked through a tornado.

Suddenly Jamie was a galactic giant, the Earth below her as small as a soccer ball. Clouds drifted past her forehead. Stunned at her own proportions, she held out her hands, palms up, to feel the force of the wind.

From within the cloud she saw Tess and Hope. Theo's Razzle Dazzle. They smiled, held out their bubble jars, and blew through the circled wands. Out came a stream of bubbles. Sunlight refracted off the soapy edges, producing a series of rainbows.

But when ginormous Jamie inspected the first bubble, she noticed something within the fragile shell. Or more precisely . . . some*one*. Jason tapped on the inner edge.

And within a succession of bubbles:

Theo.

Eternity Lex. Emma.

The CBM jar.

The Earth.

The Milky Way galaxy.

The Universe.

Brigsby, then Milo, and the *Rubicon* lobby.

Razzle and Dazzle kept blowing bubbles, a seemingly infinite stream that danced on the wind, until Jamie was surrounded. As the bubbles shimmied around her, like the very molecules of Existence, she could see within each bubble a unique jar of CBM.

And much as the bubbles themselves began to vibrate, the CBM jars started to glow, like white-hot phosphor. They grew brighter and more incendiary around the edges, expanding until the casings split apart. They were all about to explode—to burst—when there was one great POP!

A POP! so intense as to silence the Universe.

And then Jamie herself was encased within a bubble. Trapped.

She floated into space, through the solar system, past the galaxy, transported beyond the borders of the physical Universe yet still outside the confines of Eternity—a nether region for which there is no name.

Jamie pounded on the inside of the bubble. It wobbled like rubber-coated glass. "NO! Let me out! It can't be like this. I can't *be* this. No! No! No! No! No! No! I can't be what you want! I can't I CANNNNNNNN'T!"

She kept on as such until ultimately, in her nothing state, she stopped. Floating in an infinite nowhere, she leaned with her back against the inner edge of the bubble, and slumped down, knees to her chest. She wiped her eyes.

Alone in the timeless planes of Existence, Jamie asked herself why she was being subjected to such clandestine manifestations.

Is this my punishment? My test? Is this what banishment is like? Or redistribution? Or is the joke still on me?

"Go ahead, Brigsby! What else can you do? You've sent me to the void of Existence. I am literally nowhere! So do it, will you?! Burst this bubble. Pop me! I'm through, you got that! I've had it! I'm done with you. I'm so done. I. Am. Done. I'm . . ."

She looked through the edge of the bubble just then, that transparent boundary, and with ease and clarity, the answer to her most worrisome question suddenly presented itself. She pawed at the bubble's edge. Her heart sank. "Lex. Oh, no."

And before she could speak another word, to finish her thought, Hope and Tess appeared before her once again. They spoke with conjoined voices.

"Sszzeeeee? Yyyou juuuust have to trrrruuuusszzt the bubblezzzzzzzzzzzzzz."

"Trust? Trust what?! What do you mean? Trust what?"

"Iiitttzz commminnnnnggg, Jamie. You'lllll sszzeeeeeeeeeeeee."

"No! Wait! Tell me—"

"Bye byyyyyyyyye."

POP!

Jamie plummeted, dropping back through Existence, into the mouth of the Universe, the spiral nexus of the Milky Way, and finally, to her temporal resting place. To Earth.

There was a blast of white light. There were screams of fluorescent color. There was the sensation of being sucked through a tornado.

Jamie couldn't stop shaking. Davey held her hand, helped her up the steps. She saw then that she was entering an old beat-up beast of a vehicle. The word *Winnebago*—whatever that meant—was stenciled on the side in faded letters. By the looks of it—and the wet dog stench—neither the interior or exterior had made the acquaintance of a quality disinfectant.

Jason turned from the passenger's seat, offered a wide-eyed grin. Theo was behind the wheel. He looked at her through the rearview mirror. "You ready, yeh? I got us a ride."

Theo and Jason shared a laugh. And Jamie, for all she thought she understood about who and what she was, sat on a plaid bench cushion, behind a mounted table. Shivering, she wrapped herself in a blanket that stank of moldy Gouda cheese. She nodded at Davey. "You were right about one thing."

Davey's hand was on the outer door handle, roadside. "Oh, yeh? What's that?"

Theo started the engine. It choked a few times before catching.

Jamie looked up front, and then slumped into the cushion. "Whatever those two are up to . . . I don't even want to know."

Chapter 31
Man of the People

Brigsby
Eternity

It had been too long.

Brigsby promised himself when he bought the *Rubicon* that he wouldn't just be an owner in name only, that he would in actuality oversee the operations. He liked the idea of it, and he sure liked living there, but being a hands-on hotelier? Who was he kidding?

And now that he was trying to make peace with the notion that his tenure as the Minder of the Universe—and everything that came with it—was likely coming to a close, he figured it was the right time to do a little management by wandering around. Something he also needed to do more of throughout the cosmos. But for now, he was primarily focused on the *Rubicon*.

It seemed an urgent and important endeavor, although he suspected it probably wasn't.

"Oh, my goodness," said Melissa, the desk clerk filling in for Jamie. "Brigsby . . . I mean, sir . . . I mean Mr. Brigsby. I . . . ."

The lobby was buzzing with activity, including the multitude of birds perched on various statues, fountains, and trees, as well as the cave stream running along the south entrance that filtered into a cave. Dressed in a turquoise paisley pantsuit and scarf, Brigsby took Melissa's hand.

"It's all right, dear," said Brigsby, who smiled from behind his oversized tinted glasses. He rarely made public appearances, engaged with the staff even less frequently. "How are we doing? There certainly seem to be quite a few guests today."

"O-h-h-h. We're at . . . about . . . I'm sorry I can't remember just how . . . ." Melissa took a breath, held it, and let it go. "I'm sorry. I'll check that for you." She clacked a few keys at her computer terminal. "We're at 94 percent occupancy today. There's a Galaxy Cruise Director's convention coming in tonight, which will put us at full capacity through the weekend."

"Well . . . it sounds like you are doing a fine job, Melissa. And I must say . . . I love your earrings." Spirals, each with a diamond stud in the center.

Melissa blushed. "That's so nice of you to say. My husband just got them for—"

"Ow!"

Across the lobby, by the elevator banks, a mustached delivery man went down on his back. Boxes went flying this way and that. Beneath him was a puddle of soapy water, thanks to an overturned mop bucket.

"Sorry sorry sorry sorry sorry sorry," the custodial worker said. "My bad. Let me help you up." He reached down for the fallen delivery man, but in doing so, slipped, knocking down four couples in evening wear, who also flopped in the puddle like fish out of their tank.

Melissa was overcome with embarrassment. "I'll take care of this! Right away."

"It's all right," Brigsby said. "These things happ—"

Down from the marble stairway leading to the foyer came Jacques Abladeujé. Jacques was accompanied by Ileana, a statuesque, rail-thin blonde who had gained celebrity as the latest hot galaxy designer. She had made headlines with her limited-edition designs, wherein five different galaxies rotated in and out of their galactic space. Ileana was scheduled to appear on tomorrow's *Breakfast with Brigsby,* and thus was being treated to first-class accommodations at the *Rubicon.*

Jacques led her through the lobby when a high-pitched wail came from outside. It set the birds off into a shrieking symphony. Patrons and staff alike ducked, and covered their ears. The concierge bell was getting worked overtime.

Klink! Klink! Klink! Klink!

"Hey, buddy . . . can I get a little service here or what?"

The finely dressed concierge, with a nametag labeled *Arthur,* responded to the request. He spoke above the clatter to a short, stocky, pug-nosed gentleman in a bellman's coat and brim cap. "Yes, sir. We're a little bit busy at the moment. How can I—?"

"Hey, yeah. I see. A friggin' mess over there. But that's the hotel biz for ya'. Am I right? Eh? Eh?" Pug nose shot his cuffs. "But enough with the . . . whatchamacallit? . . . the pleasantries. Yeah. That's it. I'm here about the ad. The job. You know. For a new doorman. Name's Chuck. I work over at *The Dooly*. Down by the marina. I figgered . . . you know . . . could maybe work here now. Help ya' snazz up the joint. Real classy, like. Respectable. I'm a man a' the people."

"Yes . . . thank you, but . . . we're fully staffed."

"Ha! You don't look too friggin' staffed to me, pal. Look at this place!"

Brigsby intervened. "That's quite all right, Arthur. I'll speak with him."

"Don't be silly, sir. This won't take but a moment."

Chuck leaned against the desk. "You hear that Brigsby? Artie here's gonna speak with me. Gonna get this all straightened out. How ya' feel about that?"

Since before the beginning of their time in Existence, Brigsby and Milo had faced off on a multitude of occasions, but never before had Milo—as Chuck or any of the other personalities he wore throughout the Cosmos—been so assertive. Overt. They communicated without having to speak.

-Go ahead . . . Brigsby. Mister Minder of the Universe. Put everyone back. Do whatever you want.-

-You don't know what you're doing, Milo. You're making a mistake.-
-Am I? Am I really?-

-You're not ready for this, Milo. It's too soon.-

"The thing is," Chuck said, "this hotel's got all them bells n' whistles. You gotch'er health spa, and chi-chi restaurants, and this friggin' rainforest theme here." He gestured to the multitude of greenery, waterfalls, and shrieking birds. "But you ain't got no *rhythm*. No feelin'. No rhyme."

"I assure you," Arthur said. "We have an exquisite décor. It is perfectly symmetrical."

"Pipe down, Artie. I ain't talkin' to you." Chuck removed his cap, tossed it like a Frisbee. The cap ricocheted off four different marble pillars, and then landed back in his hand. "See? It's too friggin' perfect. People don't like perfect. They only think they do. This place . . . it needs a few dings and dents.

Dose a' reality. A little charm."

-You don't understand what you're doing, Milo. This isn't going to work.-

-Oh, yeah? Why not?-

-That you even need to ask should answer your question. You are out of your depth. This is beyond you.-

"Well . . . I will say this." Chuck looked up, toward the refracted glass ceiling. "I love this friggin' view. It's spec-friggin'-tacular. I mean . . . just *look* at that." The magenta spirals of the Andromeda galaxy were swirling. Swirling. Swirling. "I know it ain't on the schedule or nothin' like that, but tonight . . . let's give 'em all somethin' special. Somethin' to remember."

-Don't, Milo. Don't do it.-

-What's the matter, Brigsby? I thought you liked spectacle.-

In one motion Chuck pulled his hand down, like yanking on a chord. With it came the Andromeda galaxy, which smashed into the *Rubicon*'s facade. Broken glass started to fall, to the chorus of terrified yelps. But the crystal shards hovered in the air.

-I warned you, Milo. I told you not to do it.-

-You've told me lots of things, Brigsby. Lots of things. And some of them have even been true. But I know what you're doing. I figured it out.-

The concierge desk separated Brigsby and Milo, but it might as well have been the very Universe itself. Each on the opposite side.

"Oh, so you ain't lookin' to retire? That's what you're sayin'?"

Brigsby was legitimately caught off guard. "What . . . do you mean? I never said I . . ."

"Succession planning? Passin' the baton? All that blabber on yer show."

"But I wasn't talking about . . ."

-Oh, yes you were, Brigsby. Oh, yes you were. Now go ahead. Deny it. Tell me I'm wrong. . . . Tell yourself.-

The shards of glass held above the lobby, the Andromeda galaxy flush against the hotel. Its stupendous pull drew on the *Rubicon*.

"Ya' see. Difference between you an' me? We want different things."

"And what," Brigsby asked, "if I were to inquire, *do* you want?"

"Oh . . . it ain't what *I* want that matters. . . . It's you."

-You think I don't know what's going on here, Brigs? You're surrounded by all the light in the Universe . . . yet you're totally in the dark.-

-Enlighten me.-

-You think you can control all this. You think it's all about you. How much responsibility you have, the weight you carry. The burden of being the Minder of the Universe.-

"Yeah," Chuck continued, "bein' in charge is a hard job. But nobody's makin' you do all this. This big fancy hotel a' yours. You made all this 'cuz you love it. Which ain't nothin' to be ashamed of. Ain't nothin' wrong with wantin' things. And ain't nothin' wrong with enjoyin' the spoils of bein' the big dog. Woof! But at least *admit* that you love it. Own it. Otherwise . . . you're just another blowhole with too much power. Another phony baloney."

-You have a little bit of knowledge, Milo. But that's not wisdom. Your place in Eternity is not what you think.-

-But that's the thing about Eternity. It's just the place we happen to be. It was here long before you showed up and it'll be here long after you leave. Same with me. You've been at this Minder of the Universe business so long you forgot what you're all about. As for me? I'm just getting warmed up.-

Disrupted by Milo, Brigsby lost his concentration. The shards of glass dropped toward the floor. The Andromeda galaxy encroached within the hotel's inner boundary. Mixed in with various screams, the hotel guests and staff all dove to the floor. They were accustomed to galactic delights of almost every kind—their nightly showcase—but they were not prepared for the forces of the Universe being used against them. Regardless of how else they viewed themselves, Eternitarians were servants of the Universe. And for as much as the Big M.O.U. did his best to oversee it all, the Cosmos was still indeed a mystery to them.

There was the very beginning of a blast of white light.

In a reflexive move Brigsby gave a half squint, then returned the *Rubicon* to its proper working order. The Andromeda galaxy was back within its intended orbit, gently swirling.

"So, like I said, Artie," who was on the floor, ducking behind the desk. "You guys need another doorman . . . gimme a call. You got my number." Chuck tapped a business card he left on the desk. "I'll help you get this place tip-top. If you're inn'erested."

"Yes, thank you," said Arthur, who pawed his way back up. "I'll . . . pass this along to human resources. As soon as I get a moment."

"Yeah. You do that." Chuck placed his cap back upon his head, offered a close-mouthed smirk, and walked toward the lobby doors. But then he stopped, and though he spoke without turning back to face them, his voice was clear. "An' one more thing. . . . Next time you do a special, on that show a' yours . . . maybe you invite a guy like me to stop by. Talk about things the people really need to hear. A little truth, maybe. Assuming you can handle it."

"Oh," Arthur said. "I'm sure Mr. Brigsby's show will do just fine without you."

"Maybe," Chuck said. "Maybe. But the funny thing about a show like his . . . it's only worth watchin' if he's got somethin' worth sayin'. 'An I get the impression your boss is runnin' outta topics. Take it easy, Artie. Have a good one."

Chuck the doorman left the *Rubicon*.

"Pay him no attention, sir. Your show is wonderf . . ." Arthur scanned the tropical-themed lobby. Brigsby was nowhere to be found. The concierge desk phone rang just then. "Concierge. This is Arthur. How may I . . . ? Oh, hello, sir. I wondered what happened to you. . . . Oh, yes. I see. Of course. I tossed it in the waste bin. I'll get it." Arthur retrieved Chuck's card. "No, actually. That *is* odd, sir. There's no number here. Just a message. A rhyme, I believe. And not a very good one." Arthur nodded. "All right, sir. If you wish." And he recited:

"One potato, two potatoes, three potatoes four,
I love my little Brigsbypo when he falls upon the floor.
He thinks he knows just how it goes but oh no he's such a bore.
Just wait until he sees the sign I tacked upon his door."

"No, sir. I have no idea. But whatever it means, I'm sure it's nothing to worry about."

Chapter 32
My One and Only

Lilly
San Francisco

The familiar held a foreboding. A strangeness.

Because when Lilly had parked her car at the Larkspur Ferry Terminal some seven miles from Sausalito, and then looked back over her shoulder, at the hillside community, she thought in some indefinable way that she might not ever return.

As a teenager, but less so as she reached her twenties, she would cut school or ditch work and just ride the ferry back and forth all day. Partly because she wanted to *say* that she did it—to brag that it was one of her *experiences*—upholding the bohemian persona she had so arduously cultivated. But mostly she did it because it calmed her down. The rippling of the bay, the salty mist, the breeze through her hair. And of course the Golden Gate Bridge, Alcatraz Island, and San Francisco proper.

How meditative it was, to let her fears, dreams, and laughter rise and fall without having to speak a word. Between mainlands, adrift, she could think. And wonder. But as with all things her sojourn from the day would come to an end, the cool San Francisco evening carrying a chill, a setting of the sun, and an acknowledgment that she would have to re-engage, whether she wanted to or not.

Yet this particular journey across the bay was determined. Specific. She was a mom now and wanted her little Benny to believe—to internalize—that fears are important. That they serve a purpose. That they're the spirit's way of motivating us to pause, to help ensure that we don't jump ahead foolishly— perhaps dangerously—and make decisions we might regret. But if she wanted little Benny to *overcome* his fears—to become a thoughtful, confident, well-adjusted dreamer who saw his life as an adventure, rather than a burden—she needed to show him how. To set the example.

Oh, who am I kidding? she thought, reliving her son's playground negotiation, where he stood firm against a bully. *You're braver than I ever was. My little Benny. I learn from you. Yes, I do, my sweet. I learn from you.*

So that when Lilly stepped off the Golden Gate Ferry in San Francisco, when the bottom of her shoe touched the off-ramp, it wasn't just a first step. It was *the* step.

Because rather than wanting to turn around and dash back on the returning ferry as fast as she got there, she hailed the first cab she saw, and did so with pride.

Mommy's doing it, Benny. Mommy's not afraid.

The ride through San Francisco took her past the Embarcadero, through Chinatown, North Beach, the Financial District, and Russian Hill, until finally they crossed the southern border by way of Mission Street, and came upon the address, 320 Sherman Drive, just east of Giglio Avenue. Lilly paid the cabbie and stepped out into the sunlight. The signage out front was easy to spot—a crescent moon, with a smiley face wink. The moon sported a wireless headset.

Lilly smiled. She liked that.

Yet now that she had arrived at *Starlight*, she realized that her step off the ferry had been a declaration of intent. But placing her hand on the glass door—about to cross into Emma's domain, choosing to enter the belly of the beast—actualized the fantasy, for better or worse. Lilly leaned against the glass, stopped.

Lilly had been so determined to call out Emma that she hadn't considered—specifically exactly, nanosecond by nanosecond—how that might play out once she got there. What emotions would funnel through her? What words would be spoken? Or unspoken? Would they have privacy? Would there be an audience? Would Emma's inner sanctum reflect the blackness of her soul?

For all Lilly knew, she would walk inside only to find Emma standing there, to again use her immense size and stature as a means of intimidation, to upend Lilly's mission before it ever truly commenced.

Okay, maybe I'm a little afraid. Lilly breathed in, breathed out.

And again. *Enough Lil. You gotta do it. Just go. Just . . . go.*

With one firm push on the door Lilly closed her eyes and forced herself inside. When she peeked again the Internet café was not, in fact, a dark, dragon-stenched cave that reeked of sulfur and doom, but rather—surprise, surprise—an actual Internet café. And a snazzy one, too. An artist herself, Lilly admired the galaxy-themed décor, with planets, stars, comets, and even entire galaxies streaked across the walls.

Behind the counter a cute blonde with a pixie haircut and nose ring was texting, while more than a dozen customers sat behind terminals clacking away on keyboards. A few wore wireless headsets, involved in some sort of swords and sandals online game.

One of the gamers approached, a short, stocky dude with a beard, sausage nose, and dorky buzz cut. He wore a red *Greatest American Hero* t-shirt, with a black trident-style emblem centered on his chest. The emblem was encased in a white circle with a thick, black outline.

"Hey, dollface. You look lost."

Lilly knew the type. *Play it cool, don't engage.* "Yeah. I'm looking for someone."

"Ha. Yeah. Ain't we all? Who in pahticular? Maybe I can help."

"I doubt it."

"Ohhhh, don't be like that. I'm'a reg'aler. I *know* people. Who you need? What are you looking for? I'll hook you up."

"A woman."

Sausage nose cracked a glinty smile. "Ahhhhh. Okay. I gotcha. Girl on girl. Nice."

Gamer Sara redhead intervened as she decapitated a troll with a *control/shift/F5* combo slice. "Don't worry about Charlie. He can't even get laid in *Conquest of Alandra's Fire*. Ignore him. That's what we do. Or dump him in a river of donkey whizz."

"Totally donkey whizz," Sara brunette said.

"Totally," Sara redhead said.

"Butt out, skanks. I'm talkin' here."

Sara brunette gave it back. "Whatever you say, Charlie. Whatever you say."

"CHUCK, you fairy slut bag! Chuck! How many times I gotta tell ya'?"

"Ooooooh, sorry . . . Charles."

Gamer Jeff spoke up. "Settle down, Romeo. She seems like a nice girl. Just let her get on with it. Besides, we're about to drop some *knowledge* on the Fular Dreen. Get back in the game. We need your axe."

"You're busy," Lilly said. "So I'm just going to—"

"Ohhhh," Chuck said. "Don't mind me. It's just my uh . . . whatchamacallit? Insecurities. Yeah. You know? Guy like me . . . I got my heart broke real bad, so now I, uh . . . overcompensate . . . yeah, that's what I do. Overcompensate when I see a pretty girl. It ain't nothin' personal. I get nervous, so I talk big. Sorry. I didn't mean it."

Lilly nodded, smiled. "It's okay. I've met worse."

Chuck raised a single eyebrow. "I ain't sure if there's a compliment in there . . . but I'll take it! So! Who ya' lookin' for? Frisco's a great town. Lot'sa babes."

"Emma. She invited me."

"Emma?! Shit. Why didn'tcha say so? Come on. I'll take ya'."

"You know her?"

"Know 'er? Ha!" Chuck turned to his fellow Pegs. "You listenin' to this chick or what? Of course, I do! I only hang out with the dweebs between shifts. I do the deliveries. On the other side. Where the action's at."

Gamer Jeff craned his neck while his avatar rolled down a hill and then sliced a goblin in half. "Who you calling a dweeb . . . Charles?"

"It's CHUCK, you troll fucker! Chuck!"

"Charles? Chuck? Tomato? Tomahto?"

"Yeahhhh," Chuck said, and grabbed his junk. "Tomato this."

Needing to break through the dweeb trash talk, Lilly took Chuck by the arm, and looped her elbow around his. "So. Chuck. What's on the other side?"

As the gamers chuckled and did battle, Chuck gestured to the entire facility. "You really don't know what this is?"

"Uh . . . I guess not."

"Well, it's *high* time you did. Ha. Get it? High time?"

"N-no. Not really."

"You will, dollface. You will. Come with me. Only . . . just one thing."

"What's that?"

Chuck stopped short, jolting Lilly still. He leaned in close, and, with tuna fish sandwich and gherkin breath, spoke in a soft voice. "Be nice to Emma's partner. He's not too happy here. Heckuva nice guy, but kinda sad. Needs a change. Maybe even meet a nice girl. Like you, maybe."

Lilly removed her arm from his. "Let's just say . . . I'm spoken for."

"Well, suitcha'self. But I gotta feeling," Chuck said as he led them through the beaded doorway and into the dispensary, "you just might change yer mind."

Two glasses of wine after dinner was her max.

On a rare occasion three, and only twice since Benny was born, four, including one especially bad night when she had an ovarian cancer scare and really needed to get to that place in a hurry. But Lilly had been drug-free—no pot, acid, ecstasy, or mushrooms—for three years.

So when she entered Emma's marijuana dispensary, with Pink's *So What* pouncing through the speakers, her gut tightened, to guard herself, as she found herself back in a world she thought she'd left far behind.

In the corner by the front door was a bullet-proof security cage, also guarded by two large sentries—one bald, with several hoop earrings, the other with a long ZZ Top beard, and wearing black sunglasses. Behind the counter was an assortment of THC-baked goods, and toward the side was the entrance to the private counseling rooms. Annabelle was working the counter.

"Not what'cha were expecting, huh, dollface?"

Lilly shook her head. "I had no idea what . . ."

Her chest gripped with heart-thundering anxiety. Her

tongue went rough. Tight, skittish flutters shot through her belly. And though her eyes were open, they couldn't identify what—or who—was standing before them. Lilly's mind seized like the overloaded computers on the other side of the café, her internal central processing unit about to shut down. To crash.

And then a familiar voice crystallized her experience. "Lilly. You got my invitation. You made it."

What Lilly's body language conveyed then Emma couldn't be sure, but what she actually experienced was *holy fuck you're really here and I'm gonna cry and scream and have a full-on stroke and heart attack and probably pee down my leg and just totally freak out.*

There was an adjustment period Lilly couldn't accurately gauge. Because standing before her was Emma, although not the Emma she remembered. Gone was the walking cane, Tweety Bird house frock, and greasy, blonde locks.

No longer an immense, angry mountain of bitterness and contempt, Emma—the Emma before her, this new Emma—was a healthy, well-groomed woman, immaculately dressed in an Ashley Stewart sleeveless blouse with a white and green swirled print, and Capri pants, standing tall and easy, more glamorous than had ever seemed possible. Emma was still plus-sized, but nevertheless seemed to be an entirely different woman.

"Uh . . . wow. You l-l-look great. Emma. You're . . . *beautiful.*"

"Thanks. Yes. I'm a work in progress." Emma winked. "I'm still about halfway to go. But enough about that. What do you think of my place? It's new."

Lilly opened her mouth, to say something polite and deferential to Emma—an instinctive regression to the dynamic of their previous relationship. But as the artificially cooled air rolled over her tongue, years of repressed anger and resentment awakened, came roaring from her belly and up through her esophagus. Her mouth puckered—to unleash accusations, corrosive as viper venom—when the noise around her went silent.

And then a light, metallic jangle altered the room's energy, followed by two sets of faint *chcking* noises on the hardwood floor. As if a baby stroller had entered the room. Or a dog.

"Lex!"

The Labrador, who appeared more anesthetized than

conscious, immediately raised his head. His ears shot up. His tail *thwapped*. And as Lilly knelt down to greet him, the re-energized canine bounded to her in great strides and lapped her face. His big brown paws pressed up on her shoulders.

"Oh, my god, Lex. I missed you missed you missed you missed you."

Lex responded in kind, as much as a dog could. "*A-woo-woo-woo-wooooo.*" He then rolled his head under her chin, leaning his entire body against hers, pushing himself into her torso. His hind leg *thwapped* against the floor. His tail *thwapped* again. The licks, like Lilly's tears, were fast and furious.

"He missed you, too," said Emma, who remained on her side of the room. "We both did."

Lilly heard Emma speaking, but she didn't care. Like a fever that finally breaks, Lilly's inner turmoil—the anxiety she had felt, the dreadful anticipation of seeing Emma again—was gone. Sapped of some energy, she was lighter nonetheless. Unburdened.

"I've . . . been . . . thinking," Emma continued, "and I wanted to . . . you know . . . I didn't want this lurking in the background, so . . ."

"Forget it," Lilly said, cutting off Emma's apology before it could ever really get started. "It's all right. It's funny . . . I spent *so* many nights thinking about you—obsessed with you—worried about whether I might see you again. Or if I wouldn't," Lilly sniffed, then wiped her eyes. "I knew I needed to stand before you—but . . . *sniff* . . . I was terrified, afraid that if I did I'd end up falling to my knees once I got here, tears down my face. Just a blubbering mess." She blew her nose into a tissue. "And now here I am. On the floor . . . crying. A plan well executed."

Rarely off her game, Emma floundered for the words. "I-I . . . don't have the . . ."

"I don't care, Emma. And you know why? Because it was never really about you, even when I thought it was. You used me, Emma. You did. But you know what . . . ? I used you, too. I did. God, I was such a mess. Ha. Kinda like now." Lilly rubbed her runny nose with her sleeve. "I kept coming back because I needed you. Can you believe that? I needed you to mess me up, to push me so far I just couldn't take it anymore. And that's totally on me. But what I was really holding out for . . . and I only see it now . . . is this handsome devil." Lilly took the pooch's face in her hands, squeezed, and kissed him again on the ridge of his snout. "It was you, Lex." She kissed him again and again. "It was always you."

"See? What'd I tell ya', dollface? I knew you'd connect."

Lilly looked up at Chuck. *"This* is her partner?"

"You kiddin' me? He's the brains of the operation. *Hmph.* Sure ain't her."

Emma tensed up. "Watch yourself . . . Charles."

"It's Chuck, for fuck's sake! How many times I gotta tell you people? It's . . . CHUCK!"

KLAM-KA-BLAM!

Like two shotguns going off, the thunderous blasts sent everyone to the floor, with Aaron and Mack unholstering their sidearms, about to return fire. But before they did, a beat-up Winnebago pulled up to the curb out front. A cloud of black smoke funneled from the tail pipe. The engine pinged and rattled before settling down. And then came another *KLAM-KA-BLAM!,* followed by another poof of black smoke.

With Lex by her side already protecting her, Lilly went to the window. And when she saw the Winnebago's side door open, shielding their eyes from the sun stumbled two young men she knew from a time long gone.

But back in her life now, there was no point in trying to hide. Lilly was done with that path. She had betrayed them both, in different fashions, despite their having done nothing to her to deserve it. All she could do now, to honor the Lilly she was trying to be—to demonstrate for little Benny that actions have consequences—was stand in the center of the room, with Lex by her side, and take whatever she had coming.

Although her new friend Chuck needed to sit this one out. "Oookay," he said. "This is too much for my teeny weeny bladder. I gotta pee."

Chapter 33
The Long Kiss Goodbye

Jason
San Francisco

The stench of bacon grease, wet dog, and exhaust fumes suffocated the Winnebago.

So that when the tailpipe backfired, Jason choked out a breath and forced open the door, then stumbled into the San Francisco sunshine. Theo was right behind him. Squinting, Jason checked his phone again, confirming the address through Lilly's Twitter feed, then glanced up at the storefront. *The Starlight Connect.* "Yep," he said. "This is it."

Theo patted his shoulder. "You nervous?"

Jason inhaled through his nose, held it, surveyed the other boutique shops on the block. He thought a moment, then exhaled, shoving his emotions down deep so that he wouldn't get rattled, so that he could remain in control. "Nah. I'm good."

"Okay, then, yeh? Let's go."

The first thing Jason noticed when they stepped inside were the two enormous bouncers and a brown Labrador. The second was the streaking comet painted on the wall. The third was the long glass counter, lined with dozens of marijuana strands, bagged, bottled, and laid out.

Theo was one step ahead. "Are you seeing this? You know what this is?"

Jason eyed a plate, filled with thick green buds, labeled *Yoda's Cane.* "Oh, yeah. This is a weed dispens—"

The farce of his buried emotions was already over. Lilly stood opposite him, and before either one of them could speak, they came together in easy, determined strides, as if the colliding molecules conspired to clear a space in the center of the room that only they could occupy.

Jason closed his eyes, held her face, and gently, with the tip of his tongue, stroked her bottom lip. She reciprocated. As they continued to kiss, entranced, Jason held her like the long lost love that she was. His fingertips grazed her cheek, caressed her skin. And finally, their lips exploring each other, Lilly released an audible sigh, letting him know that in a very real way, she gave herself to him. After all those years, she was finally his.

Pulling back from their first and only kiss, touching nose-to-nose, Jason looked into her golden green irises, and smiled, a shared encounter that could only be ruined with words. Which is why Jason knew that very moment indeed, for all its delight and satisfaction, had to end. That *they* had to end.

Their reunion, if that's what it actually was, was over almost as soon as it began. He sighed, slow and nervous, and released Lilly. Time to let her go. "I'm getting engaged," he said. "As soon as I get home."

Lilly offered a pursed smile. "That's nice. What's her name?"

"Anna."

"She . . . she sounds great."

Jason nodded. "Yeah. She really is."

Lilly flipped open her phone, displayed her wallpaper photo. "Here's my son. Benny."

As Jason looked upon that smiling little boy, he was filled with a blistering pang of regret and loss. That the child—Lilly's child—wasn't *his* child, too. Their child. Yet Jason was also overcome with gratitude toward the gods, for presenting Lilly with such kind fortune. He realized then and there that he and Lilly had never really been meant for one another, but in actuality were destined to meet under incredible circumstances, separate, and then one day reunite, so that they could finally embrace the magic within their own lives, rather than chase the mystery in each other.

And then Lilly surveyed the room. "Wait. How did you even find me?"

Jason turned red. "Oh, ha. That. Yeah. I, uh . . . okay. So, I've been . . . you know . . . kinda . . . checking your Twitter feed for the last few . . . weeks. Months." He gritted his teeth. "Years. But I didn't follow your feed . . . you know, officially, because, I didn't . . . really . . ."

Lilly shook her head. "I don't have a Twitter feed. I've never used Twitter. I'm not even on Facebook."

"What are you talking about?" Jason pulled up her Twitter page on his phone. "Here. Look. @LillyPainter86." The post read: *At Emma's now. With my new pal Chuck.*

"Let me see that." Lilly examined the posts, shook her head. "I'm telling you. I've never seen this before. It's not me."

Jamie

Jamie checked her reflection in the Winnebago's side-view mirror. She wiped the gunge from her eye. The sun reflected back at her.

Come on, James. Just a little bit longer. Those two dumbasses have gotten you this far. And who knows? Maybe they even know what they're doing. . . . Ha! Good one. Come on. Let's get this over with.

"Sorry, guys," she said, entering the dispensary. "I just had to wash the Winnebago smell off my hand—"

Centered in the room were said dumbasses, and a pretty blonde, whom she surmised was Lilly, Jason's forbidden fruit. And next to Lilly, with droopy eyes, was a brown Labrador. The canine immediately unleashed a series of high-pitched whelps, whines, and whimpers, shuffled in place, and *thwapped* his tail hard enough to knock four glass bongs off the shelf. One broke.

Drawn to the dog, Jamie wore a raised eyebrow look of shock and confusion.

Woof-woof, Chuck had said to her.

Gone to the dogs, Ira told her.

Ruff-ruff-ruff, the twins said.

If the journey of a thousand galaxies indeed began with a single flux, then it was clear to Jamie now that the impossible . . . the unthinkable, even . . . was not just plausible, but probable, if not suddenly clear and obvious. The TV switched to a breaking news report:

Panic has stretched across America as conspiracy group the **Genius de Milo** *amplifies its insistence that the end of days is upon us. In just the last hour alone, Minneapolis has been covered in a sheet of ice despite 62-degree temperatures, while cows, cats, and herds of moose—some* *reports say in the tens of thousands—migrate across North and South Dakota.*

"L-L-Lex . . . ? Is that . . . is that you?"

The canine *whoomphed.*

In her mind's eye Jamie saw her brother's face then on the dog's body. She inched closer, knelt down, and whispered. ". . . Lex?"

With the swirling of the dog's tail Jamie spoke louder, more confidently. Her eyes perked up. "*Lex?*"

The dog was practically hopping in place now. And finally knowing it herself, Jamie's smile stretched deep and wide. Her heart opened up. "LEX!"

Labrabrother ran to Jamie, put his paws up on her shoulders, licked her face, and howled. "*AH-WOO-WOO-WOO-WOOOOOOOO! HOMMMMMMMM . . .*"

"Ohhhhh," Jamie said. "Is *this* where you've been? Oh. Buddy. What *happened?*"

But an explanation wasn't required. Because as Jamie turned, there, behind the counter, was a large, well-assembled woman, clearly in charge. And though her physical representation didn't quite resemble the one she wore in Eternity, her energy was unmistakable.

"Emma. I should've known." Jamie shook her head. "You always treated him like a dog. I guess this makes sense."

"Jamie. I . . . it's not what you think. It wasn't me."

"Oh, I know. You didn't choose this for Lex. But it *is* your fault. You did this."

Emma sighed. "I know."

"You know." Jamie offered a head bob. "Right. Okay. Good. Well . . . here's the thing, Emma. I know a few things, too." She encroached, closing in. As she did, the security guards raised their guns. But Emma nodded them off. "Good call, Emma. I think we both know they can't help you. Not really. Because deep in my heart . . . I'm not even mad at you. I'm mean, sure . . . you're a thoughtless wench with a galactic-sized ego . . . but so what? It's really not you I'm pissed at. Hell, it's not even me, although I sure thought it was." Jamie laughed at herself. "You know who it is . . . ? It's Brigsby. He did this. He put us here."

For all her physical might, Emma suddenly held the stature of a wide-eyed wallflower. "B-Brigsby?"

"Oh. That's right! You didn't know, did you? Ha. Well . . . your little doggie friend, here? My brother? Lex? Your ex-partner, your ex, well . . . whatever." Jamie shuddered. "But, yeah. He's known *the whole time*," she said, taking a perverse delight in twisting each word into Emma's dank soul. "Since your first moment on Earth." Jamie took a pause, allowing that reality check to sink in. "So what do you think, Emma? Who's the dog now?"

Though otherwise motionless, Emma shifted her eyes to Lex.

"And now you know, too." Jamie was really enjoying herself—probably more than she should have. "Brigsby? The Big M.O.U.? Yep. One and the same. That scrawny talk show dingbat *is* the Minder of the Universe. Not bad, huh? I didn't know either. Had no idea. Gotta hand it to him. That's a good cover."

The commercial break concluded, returning to the news. The TV anchor spoke:

And with total darkness converging on the Eastern Seaboard and making its way west, the **Genius de Milo** *conspiracy theorists are no longer being scoffed at with laughter and derision. In fact, their theories about the end of the world are taking on a new level of consideration throughout both the secular and religious establishments . . ."*

And then a loud *whooooosh*—a flush—came from the back, followed by the opening of the bathroom door.

Lilly tugged Jason's arm. "That's him!" she said. "That's Chuck! He's the one who brought me here."

Although not surprised, Jamie was shocked nonetheless, as much a she knew that she shouldn't be. "Ch-Chuck?! What are you . . . ?"

Emma turned up toward the TV—the latest update on the *Genius de Milo*—and with a defiant smirk, broke her silence. "That's not Chuck, you nitwits. Don't you get it? The eroding Earth? The sky blacking out? There's no phenomenon. It's just one guy. And he's standing right here. It's him. It's Milo."

The entire room turned to Chuck, who shrugged, and raised his hands. "Oookaay. Well . . ." He unwrapped one of Emma's pot lollipops—vanilla butterscotch swirl—and popped it in his mouth. "Snack? . . . No? It's good." Met with stunned silence, Milo rolled the marijuana treat along his teeth. "Remember, dollface? On the comet? You asked me what Brigsby really wanted from you."

Like the formation of a supernova, Jamie's soul was overcome then with the illustrious unveiling of her truest identity, which she'd harbored all along, gestating within the cocoon of her outer Jamie personality. "Holy crap on a cracker," she said, the room glowing around her. "I know—"

Before she could finish her thought, everyone took a half step back, but also closer to each other, huddled for safety. They inadvertently created a physical link—Lilly's arm touching Jason's, Jason's arm touching Jamie's, and then Jamie to Lex, Lex to Theo, and Theo to Emma—like a series electrical circuit, with each node in physical contact, one after the other, in succession.

"—who I am," Jamie continued, then brushed against Emma, powering the circuit. "Lex! I'm sorry!" She unfastened then reclasped his collar. "I didn't know what happened to you. I swear. But I'll come back. I'll—"

There was a blast of white light. There was screaming fluorescent color. There was the sensation of being sucked through a tornado.

Gone from Emma's dispensary, Jamie leaned forward on a cushioned stool, in a private hotel bar. Brigsby slid her a martini.

It was blue.

Jamie
Eternity

Jamie viewed Brigsby through a more empowered lens.

"You're a real dick, you know that?"

"Now, now, Jamie. I knew you'd figure it out . . ." Dressed in a yellow and white striped blouse and pleated pants ensemble, Brigsby sipped his drink, rotated the *Rubicon*-stamped coaster counterclockwise, and repositioned his glass. ". . . Sooner or later."

"I'M THE MINDER OF THE FUCKING UNIVERSE?! Why didn't you tell me?!"

"And miss all the fun? Nah. It's better this way."

"Better?! For whom?"

"For you, my dear. For you."

Jamie gulped her drink in one throw. She exhaled. "Yeah? Better how?"

Brigsby turned so that his back was now leaning against the bar, crossed one leg over the other knee, and lit a cigarette he smoked through a long, black filter.

"Ask yourself, Jamie. If I had invited you here, after your shift, and without preparation or context said, 'forget the life you think you've lived. Forget everything you think you know about Eternity, the Universe, and the meaning and purpose of Existence. You are not a hotel desk clerk, you are not a sister. You are not Jamie. You are not even an Eternitarian. You are, in truth, my successor. You are the Minder of the Universe.'" Brigsby took another sip. "Now that you are actually here . . . knowing everything you know now . . . how do you imagine that meeting would have played out?"

"You know," Jamie said, "I'm having a sudden urge to crack your head between a couple of really big moons. Maybe a few times, just to get it right. And then rip your face off and shove it through a black hole. Now that I can do that sort of thing."

"I know the feeling."

"All right. Fair enough." Jamie nodded to Chioma. "Two times. Fill 'er up." Then to Brigsby, "But still. . . ."

"I know. I'm a . . . what did you call me. A d—"

"A dick. Yep. A total dick."

"Perks of the job," Brigsby said. "Perks of the job."

Jamie raised her glass. They toasted. "So," she said, looking around the bar. "This all mine, now? These my new digs?"

"Hmm. Already redecorating, I see. Yes. You can move in once I finish up a little more business. You and Chioma will become fast friends."

Jamie craned her neck. "That was a pretty big mind fuck. You'll have to forgive me if I don't just take your word for it."

"*That's* why I didn't tell you. You had to figure it out, on your own, as it was meant to unfold. You needed to be *of* Eternity before you could *oversee* it. It's an adjustment, as it was for me, and as it will be for your successor, when the time comes. And on and on."

"Right. I haven't even started yet and we're talking about my replacement." Jamie gave a closed-mouth nod, then spun on her barstool, soaking it all in. But mostly she needed a private moment, such that it was.

Minder of the Universe? Yeah. Okay. I could get used to this.

"So . . . ?" she said finally. "How does it feel?"

"I don't follow."

"To retire? To hang it all up?"

"Oh. Ha. No, I'm not quite ready to do that yet."

"Okay, so . . . how *does* it work? Is there a training manual? Cheat sheet? Prep course . . . ? Please tell me there's a transition period of some kind."

"A succession plan? Oh, yes. Of course. We'll review the basics, and then get into some of the nuance you'll encounter. But to begin . . . we have a quandary to deal with."

"Milo?"

"He's part of it."

"Okaaaay. Are you gonna share, or are we just gonna get hammered?"

Brigsby nodded. "Both."

"Well, then. I better catch up."

"Indeed, you should. Because you'll need to work things out with your partners . . . roles and logistics and such. It takes a while."

Jamie chortled on her drink. "P-partners? What partners?"

Brigsby looked upon her then, and smiled. "First things first, dear. First things first." He signaled to Chioma. Another round. "Might as well get comfortable. We have lots to talk about."

Chapter 34
Gone to the Dogs

Emma
San Francisco

"Oh, no. Not this shit again. No no no no no."

If Emma had been anyone other than who she was, from whence she came and how, even the most renowned neurosurgeon would have diagnosed her with head trauma as the result of a car accident. She had all the symptoms: confusion; disorientation; dizziness; sensitivity to light and sound; drowsiness; headache; short-term memory loss; nausea; lack of muscle coordination; numbness; slurred speech; and she was having trouble walking and balancing.

And she had a wedgie.

But Emma wasn't just anyone. She wasn't even of the planet, but, rather, an Eternitarian, displaced on Earth. Banished. So that when Jamie—literally the last person in all of Existence Emma ever expected to see—walked into her shop, and, almost as inexplicably, vanished before her eyes, with nothing but a vapor trail of piercing light left in her wake, it evoked in Emma a traumatic reflex memory.

Gorgeous darling of the galaxy design community one moment and earthly white trash the next, Emma was truly and utterly terrified that all she had done these past three Earth years to remake herself—maximizing on her exile—would disappear just as quickly as Jamie had, tossing Emma into an even more humiliating corner of the Universe.

Emma leaned on the glass countertop with one hand, pinched the corners of her eyes with the other. Her vision was coming back into focus. Jason, Theo, and Lilly were still linked up like a chain. Annabelle was on the floor, rocking back and forth behind the counter. Emma's bouncers—Aaron and Mack—clung to each other in a bear hug. Their eyes were peeled back.

And through it all, Milo was slurping his lollipop, grooving a wicked high, and smiling at the mosaic of mayhem he had created. The galactic gremlin at work.

Lex shifted over to Lilly, taking his place at her side.

Emma smacked her lips, breathed in, breathed out, and again, until finally, she regained her balance. "Okay." She pointed, softly, matching the cadence of her words, searching for clarity of thought. "Jamie was here, and then *zappo* But Milo's still here. I'm here. And," she continued, nodded at Jason and Theo, "you two numb-nuts are here. So . . . that means," her eyes jolted open, "you're after the jar. You're after the *jar!* And that means . . ."

She gesticulated forcefully with her hands, advancing toward Lilly. But in doing so she inadvertently triggered Lex's canine threat response—a dog protecting his new master. Such that before Emma could finish her thought, a deep rumble broke her rhythm. Or as she realized, a growl.

Lex's tail was now firm and still, pointed, marking his place. His eyes were pulled taut, fangs showing. For the first time on Earth—for the first time anywhere—Emma actually feared him.

"Ooohkay." She held her hands out forward—with the intention of calming Lex down—but instead her movements once again served to escalate his canine perception that Lilly was in imminent danger. "Take it easy, Lex. Take it easy. I was only trying to say that—"

"*Grrrrrrrrrrrrrrrrrrrrrrrrrrrrrrrrr . . .*"

"Ha-hah!" Milo rubbed his hands together, taunting Emma in sing-song. "Your dog-gie hates you. Nanny nanny poo poo."

"Stick it, you little turd. This is between me and him."

Milo pointed to Jason, Theo, and Lilly. "And them."

Ignore him, Emma. Ignore him. That's his game. To stir up trouble, to pull you in deeper, to confuse you. Don't let him win. Just ignore him. Focus, Emma. Stay focused.

Far lighter and more agile than she had been for most of her time on Earth, Emma was still a large and physically powerful woman. But she knelt down, to even herself with Lex. He growled again, which she respected. Despite the warning, she continued her approach. No matter what they'd been through, it was still Lex.

"Don't you see, pal? They came all this way, just to be here. Right now, in this room. That means it's close. The jar. It's *gotta* be. I knew if we waited long enough, if we were patient, if we just hung in there . . . our time would come. And now it's here. If they actually find the jar . . . we can go home. Back to Eternity. Off this dump. Don't you want that? Aren't you ready? Don't you see?"

Though offering Lex what she knew was the most stupendous news of all, his body remained rigid, giving her nothing to hold onto. Just the distant memory of a relationship that had never truly existed. Because for all of her attempts to make the best of their time on Earth, her only real role involving him had been as his lord and master. And while Emma had been able to modify her own physique, Lex continued to fade from his identity, trapped inside a canine's body. A pet. A man on a dog's leash.

Emma was only able to whisper now, her voice choked with tears. "I-I'm sorry, Lex. I'm truly, deeply sorry. I-I never meant this for you. P-please don't leave me." She wiped her eyes. "You're the only one who knows me. You're all I've got left."

With Emma's please hanging in the air, Lex's eyes—offering a window into the soul of a man—began to soften. He retracted his teeth, let out a low, grumbling sigh. He looked up at Emma, at Lilly, and Emma once more.

Sparked by a glimmer of hope, Emma smiled, eased her hand forward again, to let Lex come to her, in his way, and rub his head against her side. Which he did.

"Ohhhh, Lex." Tears rolled down Emma's face. "It'll always be you. We'll make it right. You'll see."

But Lex turned away from Emma, circling back with Lilly. He took his place, perched by her side. Lex made his choice.

Never one to take insults lightly, Emma's breaths were now as heavy and labored as her footsteps had been. Even though she built the *Starlight* franchise from nothing, through sheer force of will, Emma had a delusional fantasy just then, of burning the building to the ground just to spite everyone around her.

But ever the pragmatic schemer—the survivor—Emma wiped her face, took a breath, and composed herself. "Okay, then. Fine. Go, you mangy fleabag. Just go. And since you're going anyway . . . go screw yourself. Screw you, Lex. Screw you, Lilly. Screw you, Jason and Theo and *definitely* screw you, Milo. You want to play gremlin? Go ahead. Play gremlin. Just make sure you tell that asshole Brigsby that I'm ready. I'm coming for him. And you're gonna help me, whether you like it not."

"Brigsby," Jason said, and rolled his fingers, as if searching his memory banks. "Why do I *know* that name? Brigsby, Brigsby . . . BRIGSBY! Oh. Crap! It was Jean. Hank's wife! . . . Theo?! When I was at your place, that very first time. . . . Remember? I called home, and Hank and Jean had just gotten married. She said it was her *new name*. Mrs. Hank B. Monroe. She said that *B* stood for *Brigsby*. . . . *Ohhh . . . shiiiit*. Does that mean Hank . . . is *Brigs*—?"

"Well, then," Milo said. "That's my cue. But hang on. I just wanna send a quick Tweet." He typed a few characters into his phone, and then winked at Lilly. "Don't ya' just love social media? Okay, boys. Off we go." Milo grabbed Jason and Theo, the three of them bundled together.

There was a blast of white light.

Witnessing her last and only chance to escape banishment vanishing before her eyes, Emma dove into the light, leaving Lilly and Lex behind. Leaving it all.

Then there was screaming fluorescent color.

There was the feeling of being sucked through a tornado.

And as had happened once before, Emma disappeared, abandoning an environment she had worked so diligently to create, all because she couldn't find contentment with all that she actually had, instead chasing a dream she could never be certain would ever come true.

Lilly and Lex

Lilly blinked, slow and deliberate. Lex nestled against her.

Aaron and Mack, Emma's loyal and sober bodyguards, viewed the disheveled dispensary, at Annabelle, Lilly, and Lex, back at each other, then the counter. And with the butts of their guns they smashed the glass, downed as many weed brownies as they could shove into their mouths.

Lilly looked down at Lex, scratched his head. "Guess it's just the two of us, huh?"

Lex whapped his tail.

She expelled a chortle conveying equal parts befuddlement, resignation, and acceptance. "Look . . . I *seriously* have no idea what just happened here . . . although . . . I suspect you do. But I'm gonna need a very large glass of wine, regardless. So . . . what do you think, Lex? Do you want to maybe . . . come back home with me? Meet Benny? Our lives aren't too exciting . . . nobody vanishes in a flash of light or anything like that . . . but we really do love each other. So if you'd like to come live with us, we'd love to have you."

"*Whoomph!*"

Lilly smiled again. "Sounds good, Lex. Sounds good. Now, let's go home."

Chapter 35
Genius de Milo

A sharp edge dug into Jason's rib.

He opened his eyes, only to find himself face down on solid rock, arms trapped beneath him. There was a nip at his pointer finger. A small shelled creature was working his digit as if it were a baby carrot. "Huh," he said. "Turtle." Jason then picked himself up, and with his foot, nudged the turtle along.

Only then did he realize he was on a long stretch of black rock, sloped up in the distance toward a volcano. In the other direction was a rippling blue ocean and a white, rocky shoreline. The warm, dry air held a mixture of flora and reptiles baking beneath the midday sun.

Theo sat cross-legged on a rock mount. He clutched his phone.

A pack of gila monsters trundled across the sand. Nearby were blue-footed boobies—white-bellied seabirds, with black wings and aqua blue feet.

Jason wiped pebbles off his arm. "What's going on? What is it?"

Cloud cover rolled in from the south. The sky was growing darker. Wherever they were, the great erosion had followed them once again. "It's my dad, yeh?"

Jason stood in place. One of the blue-footed boobies faced the other, then bowed, spread its wings, and with its neck, head, and bill stretched upward, pointed to the ever darkening sky. Some sort of island mating ritual. A strong breeze brushed through.

"Is he . . . ?" Jason said. "I mean . . . ?"

Theo's eyes exploded with water. "He's good, yeh? He's okay. Roger says he'll be in the hospital about a week, then he's coming home. Should make a full recovery. He did it. He really did it."

"Dude! That's incredible! That's great news!"

Theo picked up the turtle that had tried to graze on Jason's finger. "Yeh," he said, and choked out a tear. "Yeh."

Theo held the little guy, stroked its shell, then placed it back down on the rock. "My kids kept telling me about the turtles, yeh? I thought they were just takin' the piss, 'cuz that's what they do. Some TV show they saw. But they knew." It took some effort—Theo went weak in the knees—but he got up on his feet. He wore a smile of mild astonishment. "Somehow they knew. If I found the turtle, it would mean my dad's okay."

Two quick *whooshes* suddenly led to a double entrance that confused him again.

"G'day, Dad," Hope said.

"G'day, Dad," Tess said.

"G'day, Jason," they both said.

It took Theo a moment to react—he'd been given a lot to process in a short time—but he scooped up his girls, smothered them with hugs and kisses. A father and his children, reunited.

"What are you two doing here, yeh? W-what is this?"

"We tol' you," Hope said.

"Yeh-yeh," Tess said. "The turtles."

"Yeh. I saw. He's right over . . ."—Theo scanned for the little finger muncher—". . . there. Heading over that ridge."

"Not *that* turtle," Hope said.

"Yeh-yeh," Tess said. "The other ones."

Jason and Theo asked together. "What other ones?"

The twins then led Theo and Jason by the hands. "Come wiff us," Tess said. "Fowow the turtle."

Still uncertain as to where in the world—or the solar system—they actually were, the winsome travelers did as instructed. But Theo stopped to survey the island.

Offshore was a school of Byrde's whales, whose blue-grey backs and pointed, crescent-shaped dorsal fins jutted from the sea. Water shot from their narrow spouts. The distant sky grew darker still. Blackening. Dissolving. Eating away the atmosphere like a saltine in a vat of acid.

"Wait a second. When you do your Razzle Dazzle thing, yeh? When you teleport—"

"They *teleport*? Wait . . . is that what you meant before? The Razzle Dazzle?"

"Well . . . kinda. Yeh. I dunno what else you call it." Theo continued with his twins as they approached the rock's high ridge. Dozens of Sally Lightfoot crabs crawled by. They were bright red on top and blue underneath. "So when you do your Razzle Dazzle thing . . . is *this* where you go? Have you been coming here all along?"

Tess and Hope looked at each other. They shook their heads in exasperation.

"We tol' you," Hope said.

"Yeh-yeh," Tess said. "Turtles."

Jason took a breath, held it, let it go. "Yeah, okay. Fair enough. I guess I can . . ."

The four of them stopped at the uppermost point, before the terrain sloped down again, overlooking a white-sand cove. The ocean water brushed up on shore, breaking into white foam. And populating the cove like a trove of fallen acorns, were turtles. Lots and lots of turtles.

"*Ohhhhh*," Theo said. "*Tuuuurtles.* Yeh-yeh. But . . . where the heck *are* we?"

"The Galápagos," Jason said. "Where else?"

Theo looked at him with a raised eyebrow. "Galápagos? How do *you* know?"

"Common sense, dude. The slope of the terrain, the moisture in the air, the heat of the rocks. We've got to be on a volcano of some sort. And the angle of the sun only hits the land at certain points on the Cartesian plane. So . . . yeah. The Galápagos."

Theo looked at him again. He blinked.

Jason glanced at the twins, who both shrugged, and then pointed behind Theo. There was a sign. It read:

Welcome to the Galápagos. Nature Preserve. Do not touch or feed the animals.

"Okay," Jason conceded. "Maybe that."

"Don't worry," Hope said.

"Yeh-yeh," Tess said.

Theo looked to Jason. "Worry about what?"

Hope and Tess produced their little bubble jars, removed the plastic wands, and then each blew through the circled openings. Two individual bubbles emerged, small at first, which then grew larger, larger, and larger still until Theo's children were cocooned within them.

"Gotta go," Hope said.

"Yeh-yeh," Tess said. "Mom's wooking for us. In your greenhouse."

"Bye!" they said. "Say hi to Mi—"

"No! Wait!" Theo reached for them again. "I just want to—"

And his children were gone, leaving behind croaks, bird whistles, and the *whoosh* of the ocean.

"Okay," Jason said. "Teleport. You never said. Now I see why."

Following the twins' instructions, Theo and Jason wandered down by the cove—toward the ocean and the bale of turtles—when an incredible energy radiated over them. An intensity, as if approaching the sun. The wind picked up.

"Wow," Jason said. "You feel that?"

"Yeh-yeh. Where's it coming from?"

"I don't know, dude. But the turtles. Look at 'em. They're rolling over like cats. On their backs. I didn't know they could do that."

Theo shook his head. "They can't."

With the island's energy growing in intensity, they tiptoed around the squirming turtles, along the shoreline, then made their way around a bend, shimmying beyond a cave just feet from the ocean, and into the mouth of another alcove.

Theo made it first. But shards of sunlight peeking through the blackening sky reflected off a beveled rock edge, blinding Jason, who was close behind. He pivoted, to avoid the light, but in doing so lost his balance, and tumbled off the rocks.

Face down on the beach, once again Jason lifted his head, and spit sand from his mouth. Another small turtle was staring at him. "I'm telling ya', dude. These turtles are really starting to annoy m—"

As his eyes focused, before him, half-buried in the sand, was an item Jason had only seen once before, but one that had taken him around the world, through the galaxy's dream space and then back again, and that was now threatening to unravel the fabric of life as he knew it.

At long last, they found their missing jar. And it was projecting brilliant light.

Up on his feet, Jason shielded his eyes. "Oh, man. Theo. Is . . . is this it? Is this the jar? It's humming, it's glowing, it's . . ."

Theo tapped him on the arm.

"I know, I know. It's glowing. It's incredible. I've never seen—"

Theo tapped him again, only with more force and conviction.

"Dude. I know. I see it. I'm staring right at it. I'm—"

Theo slapped him on the back of the head this time. Hard.

"Ow! Dude. What the hell, man? What are you . . . ?"

Their long-lost jar notwithstanding, it was suddenly apparent that the one item they had long pursued was now pretty low down on their list of worries. Filling the cove was not one, two, or even three such jars. There were thousands of them. All swarmed by turtles. And every jar was glowing. Pulsing. The source of the incredible heat and power.

"That's a lot of jars," Jason said.

"Yeh-yeh," Theo said.

"So . . . ? Whaddaya say, boys?" Milo slurped on watermelon-flavored ices, scooping the treat from a yellow paper cup, using a small wooden spoon. "Damn, I love this stuff. Nothing beats it on a day like this. Although it looks like the storm's finally here. The big one."

After years of feeling confounded, curious, and occasionally pee-their-pants terrified with the unpredictability of the Cosmos, Jason and Theo were never more so. In the near distance, beneath that nasty, threatening sky, a pod of bottlenose dolphins jumped from the sea, and splashed down.

Milo worked his ices. "Oh. Shitburgers!" He whacked at his forehead, stomping in place. "Brain freeze brain freeze brain freeze! *Ow ow ow ow ow*! Man! You never see that coming, and when it does . . . but . . . I'm . . . guessing you have other things on your mind."

Theo and Jason nodded.

"After all this. . . you guys really don't know why you're here . . . do you?"

They shrugged.

"Well . . . Brigsby does have a flair for the dramatic. Ha. Then again, so do I."

Theo eyed Milo. "What does that mean, yeh? About why we're here?"

Milo sniffed, shot his cuffs, then thumbed his nose, slipping back into Chuck mode. "Ayy ohhhh . . . look who's finally askin' some questions here. I love it! See those over there? The jars. Glowin'? Pulsin'?"

"Yeh . . . ?"

"And the one you got there, by your feet? The one you should'a left where it was, back in them caves?"

". . . Yeh?"

"Well . . . under normal circumstances . . . that one jar is what I guess you'd call 'bout average, as far as these things go. If you ain't figured it out by now, these jars . . . they got some juice in 'em, ya' know? Called . . . whatchamcallit? CBM. Yeah. That's it. Short for Cosmic Building Material. Kinda like the Universe's liquid DNA, if ya' will. Cosmic jizz. . . . With me so far?"

They nodded, squinting as the wind whipped through.

"Good. Now . . . the good news is that, unless you got the right harmonic key, which, like, hardly nobody's got, there just ain't no way to open these things. And I'm talkin' im-friggin'-possible. So they're safe . . . more or less. However . . . just a drop—and I mean just one teeny tiny drop a' the cosmic jizz—is potent enough to wipe out the planet and half the galaxy. An' when I say *wipe out*, I mean rejigger. Reformulate. Like . . . shakin' up a margarita, swirlin' the ingredients all around in the tumbler and then seein' what new kinda drink comes out. And *trust* me when I say it just ain't never the same. Ever. And all that happens from just one friggin' drop! So whaddaya think happens if ya' spill the whole damn thing?"

Jason blinked repeatedly. "It's not good . . . ?"

"No. It ain't good. But that's exactly what you two dipshits've been messin' with. It's *that* powerful."

Theo and Jason both took a step back from the jar.

"Now . . . those jars over there? With all the turtles on 'em? Although, technically, they're tortoises. You know . . . tortoises only live on land. But I, uh . . . whatchamacallit? I digress. Yeah. That's it. Digress. But the turtles, the tortoises, that is . . . ? You see 'em, right?"

Jason gulped. "Yeah . . . ?"

"Each jar, by itself, is like *ten* times more powerful than this one. Ten? Ha. What am I tallkin' about? Gotta be hun'reds? Thousands? Millions? Hell . . . I don't even know . . . but they got way way *way* more potent jizz than yers. So I'm talkin' big-time jizz here. Mega jizz. Ultra galactic jizz. And there's so friggin' many jars I lost count."

Theo put it back on Milo. "Then what's the point, yeh? What are we even doing here?"

"Now that's the mother of all questions, ain't it?" Milo pulled their jar out of the sand, and spun it on his finger like a basketball. "Thing is boys . . . this jar here? Your jar? It's like a . . . whatchamacallit? A trigger switch. Yeah. A detonator for the other ones. So if this one goes boom . . ."

Theo finished for him. "They all go boom."

"Ayyyyy ohh! We got a genius here! I love it! A real genius friggin' de Milo, like yours truly. Problem is . . . this jar of yours? It leaked. And it's countin' down. Nothin' you can do about it."

"Whoa!" Jason said. "Hold on. You said they can't be opened!"

"No," Milo corrected. "I said they *more or less* can't be opened, unless you got the specific harmonic key assigned to that jar. Which Jamie actually had on her the whole time. But she disappeared, so . . . bummer, bro. Thing is . . . last time, when you dumped the jar in the ocean . . . you plowed yourselves good n' hard. Like . . . gang-bang style. You dropped it right where you abso-friggin-lutely shouldn't have . . . with those burnouts Ira and Howard. Now those two . . . ? *They* can open it, key or no key. And guess what . . . ?"

"They did," Theo said, confirming what Ira and Howard had already told them.

"Betcher' ass, they did."

Jason threw up his hands. "WHY?!"

"Wow. You guys *really* don't know why you're here? You seriously don't know?" Milo gave a head twitch. "Well . . . okay then. The Minder of the Universe? Teams of three. Brigsby. Ira. Howard. One. Two. Three. . . . You follow? And just like Brigsby up there in Eternity, callin' the shots for the whole friggin Universe . . . Ira and Howard . . . ? They're ready to move on. And opening this jar of yours—this very specific jar—was a way to make it happen."

Ducking into the wind, Theo struggled to keep up. "Move on? From what?"

"What else? From here, from there. From *every*where. They're gettin' outta the Universe business. They are d-u-n done. They're gonna *retire*."

"Done? How can they be done, yeh? How can you walk away from overseeing the Universe? That would leave us totally fu . . ."

The raven-black sky, thick with dark purple patches, surrounded the island. Wind-blown sand tore at their faces. Lightning crackled. The ground began to shake, as if the volcanic embers beneath their feet were now coming alive.

R U M B L E R U M B L E R U M B L E R U M B L E -RUMBLERUMBLERUMBLERUMBLE . . .

Theo and Jason were throttled to the side. Milo floated above ground. "Sorry, boys. Time to wrap it up. Your jar's about to go." He tossed it back to the sand. "And I think you know what that means."

Their jar was growing brighter, with numerous specs—minute DNA helixes—swirling within it. And like popcorn kernels in a microwave bag, the legion of turtles were flipping up and down on the alcove of jars.

There was a blast of white light. There was screaming fluorescent color.

Jason called for Milo. "What do we do now?! How do we stop it?!"

Milo shouted back from within his swirl. "You don't!"

"Screw that! Theo! Let's chuck it back in the ocean. Just get it out of here!"

Milo's swirl was more intense. "And how'd that work out for

you last time?! Nope. Sorry. Ain't one a' the choices. Only one thing you *can* do!"

Theo looked at Jason. Jason looked at Theo. They both looked at the jar, and then back at Milo. A massive lightning bolt scorched the heavens.

"We gotta dive on it," Jason said. "We gotta absorb the blast."

Milo nodded. "Yep. You gotta take one for the team. 'Cuz if you don't, this game called life you've been playing? It's all over. And everything you've been through? It'll all've been for nothin'."

RUMBLERUMBLERUMBLERUMBLERUMBLE-RUMBLERUMBLERUMBLE. . .

"So, good luck! I'll catch you boneheads later! *Peace!*"

There was another blizzard of white light and the sense of being sucked through a tornado. And Milo was no more.

Left in his wake, a circus of turtles flipped through the air.

"Well," Jason said. "I'll give him one thing. Dude really knows how to make an exit."

Their jar glowed brilliant white light against a sky as black as ink. The winds were brutal.

Theo played out various scenarios in his head, with instantaneous leaps of logic. They all ended badly. There was only one real choice. "Go!" he said. "Get in the cave, yeh? I'll do it!"

"No way, dude! You've got kids! A family! . . . It's my fault anyway! I dropped it in the ocean!"

"But I'm the one who found it! It's on me, yeh? I started this crapstorm. I gotta finish it!"

The rumbling island chucked Jason. He grabbed Theo, to hold on. "I was a whiny little putz before I met you! And now look at me! . . . I think!"

Scorched by another lightning bolt, two large chunks of rock broke off a cave entrance and fell into the sand. A few inches to the left and they both would have been decapitated. Which sent Theo and Jason into raucous laughter.

Theo wiped his yes. "Go get married! It's my wedding present yeh?!"

"The hell with it! We need to . . ." Jason stopped mid-protest, because just then a huge figure came barreling down on them through the storm-imposed darkness.

With her considerable heft Emma built up enough momentum so that between her kinetic energy—and the rumbling island—she dove from the top of an embankment, bashing them over. "Gimme that."

Like from a rugby scrum, Emma emerged disheveled, bruised, and covered in sand. She dusted off the jar. Her eyes were wide with maniacal delight.

"Don't do it, yeh?! You don't—"

"Fuck off, chirpy! It's mine! You hear me! It's mine it's mine it's MINE!"

RUMBLERUMBLERUMBLERUMBLERUMBLE-RUMBLERUMBLERUMBLE. . .

Jason recoiled from the inevitable eruption. "Watch it! It's gonna blow!"

"Blow yourself, jerkwad!"

RUMBLERUMBLERUMBLERUMBLERUMBLE-RUMBLERUMBLERUMBLE. . .

The jar grew even brighter, more volcanic. Emma held it up toward the heavens, now as black as night. Thunder roared. Lighting detonated. The rains came with a vengeance. "Now, you fucker! You banished me here, now send me back! To Eternity! I did my time! I paid my dues! Come on, Brigsby! Do it now! Send! Me! BACK!"

As the jar reached its critical mass the very first turtle they encountered inched its way, through the rain, toward Emma.

RUMBLERUMBLERUMBLERUMBLERUMBLE-RUMBLERUMBLERUMBLE. . .

The island jostled her. And as her foot came down, it caught the top of the turtle's slick shell, causing Emma to lose her balance. She toppled into the wet, mushy sand.

The jar sprang loose. It rolled before Jason and Theo, like a grenade with the pin already pulled.

All the jars were rumbling now, percolating, the entire

island about to break apart.

RUMBLERUMBLERUMBLERUMBLERUMBLE-
RUMBLERUMBLERUMBLE...

Drenched in downpour, Theo and Jason grabbed hold of each other, shared a smile, and without having to speak, made a unified decision. To dive on the jar. Together.

"Been a good ride," Jason said.

"Yeh-yeh," Theo said.

RUMBLERUMBLERUMBLERUMBLERUMBLE-
RUMBLERUMBLERUMBLE...

They leaned forward in the driving rain, anticipating the blast, prepared to leave this life for whatever awaited them next. Then suddenly and inexplicably, the ground went still. The jars stopped shaking. The rain stopped. There was no movement of any kind. No wind. Not a leaf out of place. The turtles were gone. Emma, too. It was just Theo and Jason and the easy *whoosh* of the ocean rolling up on shore.

And the sky—just moments ago blackened almost into oblivion—was now clear, steady, and blue.

Clutching one another so they didn't drop into the ocean, Theo was the first to let one eye open slowly, then the other. Seeing the island calm, he exhaled, which inspired Jason to also take a peek.

A breeze wafted through. Leaves shimmied. A single nut fell from a tamanu tree.

Jason and Theo held in place, bracing themselves, as if even the slightest movement—just a single grain of sand, blown in the breeze—would disrupt the island's fragile integrity, triggering its final destruction.

A glance toward the alcove; the jars were still. A glance at the sand before them; their jar was still; motionless rocks; hazy blue sky. There were no vibrations or tremors, no detectable warning signs. Like the rest of the island, they were dry.

Theo once again looked at Jason. Jason looked at Theo, still suspicious that even an upturn of his mouth would reignite the cacophony of jar disturbances. But as he allowed his pursed lips to eke out a smile, Jason did the same, until finally they accepted that the earthquake, the Milo quake—the cosmic quake—had passed.

Jason sighed, chortled, then reached for the sky. "He didn't need us to take the blast. It was a test, a joke. He just wanted to see if we'd do it. Milo! Ha! You fucker!"

"Heh-Heh! Yeh!"

Jason and Theo threw themselves together in a jump hug, like bouncing on a trampoline. "I knew it," Jason said. "I knew it couldn't end like that. There's just no way it could . . ."

Theo went still.

At their feet, their jar shimmied just then. And the lid, with a slight *pop*, came off.

They froze again, their hug no longer of joy, but of quiet, curious terror.

The island was silent. Motionless. Like animals sensing imminent danger, there wasn't so much as a single sound. Theo and Jason didn't dare move.

And then with force great enough to rip a portal through the Universe—knocking them halfway across the beach—brilliant white light shot out of the jar. An endless stream of cosmic energy channeled into the newly cleared heavens.

Their jar was—as Milo said—the great detonator.

In the alcove, another jar popped open, releasing its own beam of light. Then another jar and another jar and another jar still until finally lids popped off every jar on the island. Cosmic energy streams filled the sky.

Just then Jason recalled the dreamscape advice from his cousin Brian:

Just remember . . . at all moments in time and space you are exactly where you are meant to be, doing exactly what you are meant to be doing.

And then there was a blast of white light. There was screaming fluorescent color. There was the sensation of being sucked through a tornado.

Subjected to their own Big Bang, Theo and Jason were decimated by the primal force of the Cosmos, disintegrated from their souls to their toes—tendons ripped from cartilage, muscles ripped from bones, bones burst to dust—and then reintegrated.

Their very essence—both the texture of who they were as

individual creatures and their connective tissue to Existence—was eviscerated, then reconstituted. Uncreated, then recreated.

And then there was another blast of white light. There was more screaming fluorescent color. Again sucked through an unseen tornado.

Disintegrated, reintegrated.

Uncreated, recreated.

Eviscerated, reconstituted.

The pattern continued. Faster and faster, repeatedly fluxed in and out of their existence in synchronicity with the Earth continuing to flux in and out of its own cosmic skin.

Disintegrated, reintegrated.

Uncreated, recreated.

Decimated, reconstituted.

Yet each pulverizing flux seemed to cleanse Theo and Jason much as it cleansed the Earth—cleansed Existence—sifting out the pollutants, each flux bringing them all closer to their truest identities, the purest, most genuine version of themselves.

Beyond their individual cosmic purifications, Theo and Jason merged with the creation, destruction, and re-creation of the Universe, bonding them to the very nucleus of Existence.

From the farthest reaches of the Universe, from Eternity itself, their cycle registered as a neon sign the equivalent to *Eat at Joe's: Open All Night.*

But close enough to hear the magnum opus of creation, destruction, and re-creation, as there was actual screaming.

Because it hurt like a muthafucker.

Theo and Jason articulated those sentiments.

"AAAHHHHH!!! OW-OW-OW-OW-OW-OW!! FUUUUCK MMEEEEEE!!! FUCK-FUCK-FUCK-FUCK-FUCK!! OW-OW-OW-OW-OW-OW!! AAAHHHHH!!!

The cycle repeated. Again and again.

And then, inexplicably and without warning, it stopped.

Face up, on the beach, Theo and Jason were huffing, puffing, panting, gasping, groaning, and squirming. Their very selves radiated with agonizing pain. Like pouring water on a sizzling skillet, steam billowed off their skin as the calm ocean breeze washed over them.

A herd of sea lions was laying quietly by the shore. They barked.

Jason spoke first. "Are we . . . *kaff-kaff* . . . dead? Are we gone? Are we . . . ?"

"I . . . I dunno." Theo heaved. *Hrrrraamphfff.* He wiped spittle from his mouth. "I'm not sure. I'm . . ."

They continued as such for a time, until finally their breathing returned to normal. Their skin no longer tingled, their essence no longer subjected to pulverization.

They were simply Theo and Jason, whatever, and whoever, that meant.

On their feet now, they eased toward the surf, let the ocean waters wash over their ankles. The sky above took on a deeper, richer blue. They squinted at the horizon. The alcove was now only a trove of sand. The jars were gone.

The great storm—the dissolving Earth—had passed.

Jason was woozy and still in pain, but upright nonetheless. "I think . . . I think we did it."

"Yeh-yeh. Same."

"Hey . . . where's Emma?"

Theo shrugged. "Up there, I guess."

"Ya' think?"

"Dunno. Don't care."

Jason chuckled. "Me either. I need to get home and kiss my girl. I've got a ring to deliver. You're my best man . . . right?"

"Yeh-yeh. Of course. I'm gonna call my dad. Can't wait to see him." Theo reached into his pocket, to look at his phone, and even though his eyes were directed toward the digital clock, he couldn't focus. Because in their cosmic re-creation, what was time, after all? "Remember that first day. In Venice, yeh? You offered me a pistachio? One bite would've closed my throat. My allergies."

"Ha. Of course. I felt like such a dork. . . . What made you think of that?"

"I dunno. Just . . . you ever think what would have happened? If you hadn't come up to me that day? If we never spoke? I wouldn't have approached you, yeh? I just wouldn't have."

Jason thought on it. "You know . . . ? I really don't know."

"I think about it sometimes, yeh? And you know what?" Not prone to making physical gestures—Theo wasn't a comfortable hugger—he patted his friend on the back. "I think we would've have met anyway, one way or another . . . sooner or later. We would have. I just know it."

Jason smiled again, nodded. "Yeah. I think you might be right."

As they turned from the ocean, back toward the black rock, Theo and Jason took a step forward, to head back home. And then they stopped. Because before them were giant tortoises.

The huge reptiles were four feet long and almost 600 pounds each, with massive, domed shells, long limbs and necks, and small, sunken faces. They milled around, in their lumbering way, encircling an item. Protecting it.

With their tiny black eyes the island creatures looked at Jason and Theo, out to sea, and then back again. The largest tortoise let out a grunt. There was a silence then, an anticipation, until the next tortoise made the same noise, and the rest of them in succession, until finally there was a steady drumbeat of Galopagean grunts:

Huhn . . . huhn . . . huuuuhhhhn
Huhn . . . huhn . . . huuuuhhhhn
Huhn . . . huhn . . . huuuuhhhhn

Then the largest tortoise of them all let out a final *HUUHHHN HUUHHHN* that silenced the rest, which, like a royal guard making way for the king, all moved aside. And there, sticking out of the sand, was the very last jar. Their jar. As if it had never been disturbed.

"Huh," Jason said. "Look at that." He breathed hard. His head suddenly throbbed, doused in fog. He heard Hank's advice funnel through his mind.

Keep it together, Kid. This is where the magic happens.

Which motivated him to ask Theo: "Um . . . are we in trouble?"

Theo paused before answering. "Yeh. I think maybe we—"

There was a blast of white light. There was screaming fluorescent color. There was the sensation of being sucked through a tornado. There was a single flux of the Universe.

More intense than a shift of realities.
More significant than a Big Bang.
Before them was a singular object.
A jar.
Their jar.
And it just.
Went.
. . .

. . .
BOOM.

Chapter 36
End of the Line

Lilly
Sausalito, California

The kitchen billowed with the aroma of sizzling enchiladas. Lilly turned the burner down, sipped a glass of red wine.

Benny was in the living room, engaged in a game of rope-toy, tugging on one end, Lex on the other. Benny egged him on. "Who's a good waggie?" Lex's tail *thwapped* back and forth. "Who's a good waggie? Who's a good waggie?"

"Okay, you two. Enough waggie-waggie. Dinner's ready."

"Not yet, Mommy. We're not done."

"You can play later. It's enchilada time."

"Yay! Encheraders! Lex! Come on! Encheraders! Encheraders!"

Lilly fastened a Batman bib around Benny's neck. He slurped milk from his Spider-Man toddler cup, completing the superhero ensemble, and then plunked a cut-up piece of chicken enchilada in his mouth. He snuck a piece to Lex, under the table.

"Mmmmmmmm." Benny grinned, rubbing his tummy. "So good."

"*Whoomph!*" Lex agreed, his tail now swirling like a propeller. "*Whoomph!*"

"I'm glad you like it, boys. There's plenty more. Eat up."

After dinner, Lilly and Benny retired to the couch, to read a book. Benny picked it out, third day in a row.

"What do you think, Lex? . . . *Horton Hears a Who!*"

Without further consideration Lex leapt up on the couch, and covered them like a canine blanket. "*Whoomph*," he said, licking Lilly's face. "*Whoomph.*"

"Okay, okay!" Lilly guffawed, inspiring giggles from Benny. "We'll read *Horton*, we'll read it. Okay."

Though not the life she planned—she had never really planned at all—Lilly was grateful for her two boys, hard pressed to think of a life that would have suited her better. And while she would never understand the bizarre machinations that brought them all together, she was thankful to the great unknown for setting it all in motion. Had it been within her power to do all over again, she wasn't so sure she would have changed a thing.

"Seffie, Mom! Seffie! Take a seffie!"

"Another selfie? Okay. Let's do it?"

Playing a game of keep-away with her phone, Benny tried unsuccessfully to conceal a smile. Lilly smiled back, then slowly wiggled her fingers, alerting him to the onslaught of tickles headed his way. Benny dove into the cushions. In the silliness, Lex clutched Lilly's phone from Benny, and with his mouth, dropped it in her lap.

"He got it! Ha! Good boy, Lex." Lilly scratched under Lex's chin. "Who's a good boy? Who's a good boy?"

Lex wriggled against her, inspiring another set of giggles.

"Okay, guys. Okay. Picture time. Selfie!"

They gathered, to inspect the results. Lilly cut her head off in one photo, captured a close-up of Lex's snout in another, and managed three blurry ones in a row. But the last one was perfect. Lilly was in the corner, with Benny in her lap, head underneath her chin, and Lex curled across them both. His tags jangled.

"Oh, look at that. I'll have a print made. We'll hang it right above the . . ."

Before Lilly could even finish her thought there was an unmistakable tremor in the air, a disruption, like an ethereal warning before a thunderstorm. She turned to Lex then, her heart already beginning to sink. Sometimes you *know* without being aware that there's anything to even know about.

There was a blast of white light. There were streaks of screaming fluorescent color. There was the sensation of being sucked through a tornado.

And on the camera screen, on her phone, the three of them were pulled together. Lilly in the corner, with Benny in her lap, head underneath her chin. But rather than the Lex they knew—the lovable brown Labrador they had adopted into their little family—in his place was a guy she had never seen before, curled across them both.

"Who's that man, Mommy?" Benny looked around the room. "Where's Wex?"

As all parents do, Lilly had come to understand that throughout their days, her son would pose many questions to which she would have no reasonable or satisfying answers. But to this one precise query, all Lilly could think to do was hold her boy close, kiss his forehead, and rock back and forth.

Perched on the couch with Benny in her arms, Lilly shifted, to pull away a throw pillow caught beneath her leg. As she removed it, Lex's dog collar fell to the floor. Secured to his collar, along with his new I.D. and rabies tags, was a metallic item, flat like a key card. Lilly hadn't noticed it before.

She picked it up, stared at it. Smooth like polished marble there was a vibration almost. A hum. It reverberated throughout her body, as if she was connected somehow to the molecules in the air—a part of it all.

But what did it matter? It was just one more item, a reminder, that her wisest path was to keep her life with Benny as small and uncomplicated as possible. And hope that the bad dream they were sharing—of true heartbreak—would lose its potency in time, until, finally, it just faded away.

Emma

Emma opened her eyes.

She turned her head slowly, to the side, and then the other way, to make sure that she was actually seeing what she thought she was seeing.

Desk lamp. Mounted print of the Milky Way galaxy. And on her office door, on frosted glass, the crescent moon logo of *Starlight Designs*.

I'm back? Am I back? I'm . . .

Emma was, in fact, back. Back in Eternity. And back finally-can-I-have-a-hallelujah back in her own body. She was once again the svelte, raven-haired vixen who could undo most any man she wanted, and, if it so met her mood, most any woman.

But she still needed convincing. In her form-hugging skirt

and blouse, Emma went for the door, reached for the handle. She paused, took a breath. *Come on, Emma. Don't worry. It's real, it's real, it has to be, real. Right?* She nodded, to assure herself, and then breathed out.

"Okay," she said. "Fuck it. Let's go."

Eyes clenched she darted into the hallway, pulled the door shut behind her, to outrun the possibility she was being toyed with. Yet another of Brigsby's games. But when Emma heard it *click* she finally peeked, slow at first, and only then did she take in *Starlight Designs'* common area.

Just as she left them, there were a dozen desks, the conference table, and various galaxy designs on display boards, awaiting her approval. It was as if she had never left. Which, of course, she had.

Because Lex, her former lover, companion, and partner across the vast and mysterious Cosmos—the backbone of *Starlight Designs*—was no longer with her. Which almost rendered her return from banishment . . . from Earth . . . a disappointment.

Almost.

She had really made it back, so it was difficult for her to get too worked up that Lex, yet again, showed the weakness he'd always had, letting sentiment stand in the way of success.

Yet from across the dark foyer, illuminated only by strands of moonlight creeping in through the windows, she stared at Lex's door, wondering if somehow, someway, he might just emerge from within his office, and join her again, by her side.

Emma smirked at herself for wishful thinking, but her time with Lex had ended much as it began: with one of them face down on the floor, unclear as to how they got there, rejected by forces greater than themselves.

And then a noise startled Emma—*click*—as if the mere thinking of his name somehow reconstituted the man. His office door opened from the inside.

Standing before her . . . was Lex. Her Lex. The right Lex. On two legs. Tall and lithe with his dark hair and chin whiskers, dressed in his classic getup—blue jeans and a black t-shirt. He spoke, the emotion all but drained from his voice.

"Why did you bring me back, Emma? Why didn't you just leave me there?"

So happy to see him, Emma almost exploded with tears. But she forced herself to hold them back, lest she admit to being just like Lex—an emotional fool. "It wasn't me. I don't know what happened."

"It doesn't matter. I'm stuck here now."

Emma wiped her eyes. "Stuck here? Are you insane? Lex. We made it. We're back!" She started toward him then, but he patted the air ever-so-slightly, like a master instructing his dog to stay. To heel.

"Yeah," he said. "I see."

"You see? Lex. . . . You're . . . you're a man again. . . . You're you!"

He shrugged.

"You're shrugging? You shrugged? . . . Lex. You were a dog!"

"Yes," he said, and offered a steely-eyed chuckle. "I was. But it's where I wanted to be. I had a family. I was happy."

"But . . ."

"There's nothing left to say, Emma. You broke my sister's heart, and Lilly and Benny and you broke mine, too. You should've stayed away. You should've let me be."

Despite her return to the place she thought she knew best, Emma couldn't remember ever feeling more lost. "Isn't there anything I can do for you? . . . Do I matter at all?"

Lex looked around the office, took a long breath, and let it out. He reached into his front pocket, removed his keys, and gripped them tight. "No," he said. "You have your ideas about what's really important . . . and I have mine."

Emma's pose and tone were far less defiant than she was trying to conjure. "So that's it? You're leaving? . . . Are we done?"

Without so much as a nod, goodbye, or further acknowledgment, Lex went to the door, stepped into the hallway, and left Emma—a woman ever desperate to be the brightest star in her galaxy—sad, rejected, and alone in the dark.

Theo and Jason

Theo's greenhouse was just as he left it. With one exception.
Jason was there with him.

"Dude. Are we . . . are we back? Is this real? I mean . . . are we really, really back? Is it done? Is it okay? Is it . . . ?"

The soft New Zealand sunshine shone down on them with gentle confidence, nary a dark horizon in sight. The eroding skyline, that expansive nothing—the languishing call of the *Genius de Milo*—was no more.

The tinge of delphinium purple passion flowers inspired Theo to smile, and finally, to laugh. "Yeh-yeh," he said. "I think we're good."

The back door of his house burst open then, followed by the scamper of his Razzle Dazzle. Of Hope and Tess. They jumped into his arms.

"Daddy-Daddy-Daddy!"

"My goodness, yeh?" Theo held them tight. "Were you good for your mum? Did you behave?"

His twins nodded. "Mm-hmm. Look who's here."

Lea came out to greet him. The family together at last. "Good trip, yeh? Got it all done?"

"Yeh-yeh." Theo kissed her flush on the mouth. He let it linger. His love for Lea was cemented then and there, for all time. "We're set. We're all . . ."

Theo didn't remember the steps he took to get there, but the distance he crossed from the center of his yard into his father's arms was the best journey he had ever taken. Because after all the time and space he had traversed already, where else did he really need to go?

"Hey, Dad," he said, buried in his father's burly hug. "Love you."

"You, too, son. You, too. You gonna stick around awhile? Thought maybe we could get to your greenhouse, yeh? Needs a little work. Maybe I could help."

Theo's mother, Lydia Barnes, standing behind, never looked so happy, even as tears rolled down her face.

Misty-eyed himself, Theo nodded. "Yeh-yeh, Dad. Sounds

good. Not going anywhere. I'm staying home."

"That's good, son. I'm glad."

Roger opened the kitchen window. He was gnawing on a drumstick. "Get your arse in here, fart knocker. We've been waiting to eat, yeh? Come on."

Theo laughed. "Yeh-yeh. Sounds good."

"Wait," Hope said.

"Yeh-yeh," Tess said. "One more thing."

Theo smiled again. "Oh, yeh? What's that?"

Hope and Tess took Jason by the hand. "Your turn," the twins said.

Jason stood beneath the New Zealand sunshine, looked over to the house. He was stunned at what he saw, yet not the least bit surprised. He ran over to Anna—his pal, his partner, his love—and held her close.

"W-what . . . what are you doing here?"

"I fly nine thousand miles and *that's* your question?"

"I-I-I . . ."

Anna offered him a twinkle-eyed smile. "Don't worry. Just playing. Lea told me about Oskar. I wanted to be here. And it's *possible* that I missed you. . . . A little."

Jason smiled back, and kissed his girl in the only way he knew how—a kiss meant only for her. "But how'd you get a flight so fast? The erosion? The black sky? *The Genius de* . . . ?" He saw Theo subtly but quickly shaking his head *no*. "I mean . . . the-the . . . storm looked . . . kinda bad and I figured . . ."

"I don't know. Weather's crazy. Things cleared up. Besides . . . your friend Jackie got me on a flight. First-class, too. It was nice!"

"Jackie's here?!"

"No. He couldn't make it. But he also said you two lost your wallets. Here." She handed over a sealed, padded envelope. "This is for you."

Inside Jason found, indeed, their wallets, as well as a small box, and a note. It read:

Didn't want to take any chances, Kid.
Ask her already!
And don't fuck it up.
-Hank

Within the box was the engagement ring.

Jason didn't need convincing. He got down on one knee.

"Wait-wait-wait." Anna's hand shook. "*Th-this* is what you were up to? You wanted to do this *here?*"

"In a long, crazy kinda way . . . ? Yes. It really was." He put the ring on Anna's finger. "Whaddaya say? Wanna get married?"

Anna exploded with happy tears. "I'll think about it." She admired the ring, her smile beaming brighter than the New Zealand sunshine. "But things are looking good."

Jason nodded to Theo. "Thank, God. 'Cuz I don't think I can take another trip like this. I just don't have it in me."

Most everyone had gone inside to eat, to celebrate good health, the future, and just being home—being together—when Theo turned to his girls. They were running in circles, giddy with laughter.

And then he saw that in their hands were bottles of bubbles. With each toddler step a single bubble grew from each of the circled wands, small at first, and then larger, larger, larger.

Immediately Theo accelerated his gait, to intercept them. He couldn't let it happen. Not again.

He reached out one hand. Hope's bubble engulfed her.

He reached out the other. Tess's bubble engulfed her, too.

Theo went to grab them up, to hold them closer and tighter than ever before so that they would know just how much he loved them, how much joy they sent surging through his heart.

His children were only an arm's length away.

And then there was a blast of white light. There was screaming fluorescent color. There was the sensation of being sucked through a tornado. The bubbles burst. And Theo's children, his Razzle Dazzle, were nowhere to be found.

Milo

Milo was back atop Philbrick, his loyal comet.

"Whaddaya say, pal? You miss me?"

The comet arched beyond a blue-tinted nebula.

"Yeah," Milo said. "Me, too. Sorry to leave you like that, but I had some business to take care of. You know. Something important. Went pretty well, though. . . . All things considered."

Milo sat cross-legged on the comet. He held the jar in his lap.

The Theo Barnes jar.

The Jason Medley jar.

"It's amazing to think this one stupid jar can reset all the headaches Brigsby is having in the CBM Warehouse. Heck . . . in the Universe. I told him this would happen someday, if he wasn't careful. I tried to tell him. I warned him." Milo smiled at the thought. "Well, maybe not *warned* him, but . . . I certainly pointed him in the right direction. I gave him Milo's Smear. What more did he want?"

Milo peeked over the edge of the comet. The Universe felt different somehow. Smaller, and yet also bigger. Both at the same time.

"So, Jamie, huh? She's really the one? She's good. I like her. I think she'll take to this whole Big M.O.U. thing pretty well. Better than you, that's for sure." Milo turned away just then, Hardwicke's reality check sinking in. "Actually . . . I shouldn't say that. I never give you enough credit. The Minder of the Universe . . . ? That's no easy job. I know I don't want it! Ha! . . . Thing is, though . . . you? Me? And I guess Jamie now, too? Nobody's going to feel sorry for us, for the responsibility we carry, for the pressure that comes with it. So for right here, for right now . . . I'll give it up to you, Brigs. I'm not going to miss you all that much . . . well, maybe a little. For so long I've been defining myself as *your foil*. But now that you're leaving, it's a chance to redefine myself. To rethink my place in Existence. For the first time . . . maybe ever . . . I'll have the space to figure out who and how to be, without comparing myself to *you*."

Milo stood up then, rolled the jar in his hands. "But you have Jamie by your side, ready to replace you, and now Theo's kids. The twins. I was a little distracted at first, trying to piece it all together. I'm not totally sure what you're up to, but . . . I have a few ideas."

Constellations twinkled in the distance.

"Take a little time, Brigsby. Settle your family business. Because one way or another . . . you and I are going mano-y-mano. Toe-to-toe. The brawl to end it all. And I'm pretty damn sure that when there's just one of us left standing . . . it's gonna be me."

Brigsby

The Minder of the Universe set out two bowls of ice cream, chocolate for Hope, pistachio for Tess. With little spoons they went to work on their treat.

"Is it good, my little ones? Did Uncle Brigsby pick the right flavors?"

The children smiled.

"Good," he said. "Good. Enjoy it while you can. There's much to be done."

"We know," Hope said.

"Yeh-yeh," Tess said.

"Ha. Of course. Indeed, you do. And do you remember my friend, from the beach?"

"G'day," Hope said.

"G'day," Tess said.

Jamie sat beside them, smiled, ran her hand through their hair. "Such clever little girls. More than I was."

"It's okay," Hope said.

"Yeh-yeh," Tess said. "Lex didn't know who you weally were. But we have each uver."

Jamie nodded, impressed. "That's true. I didn't think of it like that."

"You'll get used to it," Hope said.

"Yeh-yeh," Tess said.

Brigsby helped them down from the chairs. "Okay, children. Why don't you go with Mister Lawrence. He'll take you into the playroom. There's a lot of toys."

"What about Mywo?" Hope said.

"Yeh-yeh," Tess said. "He wants to pway, too."

Brigsby smiled again. "Don't worry about Milo just yet. We'll talk about him later. For now . . . I need Jamie. A word, please."

The Razzle Dazzle twins followed Lawrence into the next room, Hope was arranging a wall of dolls into a tea party, while Tess went to work on a tower of blocks, far less interested in the design than she was in the forthcoming satisfaction of knocking it all down.

"They're coming, aren't they? Theo and Jason? To get them back?"

"Yes," Brigsby said. "I would hope so."

Jamie nodded, and then through pure reflex—she wasn't yet accustomed to the powers of being a Minder of the Universe—used her eyes to look through the window, at the swirling magenta pinwheel of the Andromeda galaxy, and finally to the Milky Way. To Earth. "Seems hard to be a dad. The responsibility. The way it affects you. Especially with them."

"Hmm. Yes. But Jason and Theo have a lot more to do."

"What do you mean. I . . . ?"

Brigsby reached for a tumbler, poured himself a blue martini. He took a sip, then offered a glass to Jamie. "One of them's going to be your partner."

Even with the incredible power, knowledge, and comprehension inherent to any Minder of the Universe, Jamie, for the moment at least, was bewildered and a little bit mortified.

"Say what now? Those two? . . . *Them?*"

"Yes."

"You mean me and one of those two numbskulls? Jason or Theo? We're going to be . . . ?"

Brigsby nodded. "Yep."

"*Forever* . . . ?"

Brigsby took another sip, wiped his mouth. "Pretty much."

Jamie blinked several times, looked toward the other room, toward Hope and Tess, then back at Brigsby. "Do they know? The twins?"

Brigsby shook his head. "Nah. They have other things on their mind."

Jamie nodded, followed by a moment of clarity. "Wait. How do they even get here? Jason and Theo. The jar's gone, right? They've got no way to make it."

"Don't worry." Brigsby laughed, took another sip. "They'll figure it out."

Jason and Theo

Though Hope and Tess were not his children, Jason felt their loss just the same. Their fate was tied to his, as much as his was tied to Theo.

Like being back on the *Cyclone*, he seized up, in a panic. But then he let it go. With the ride ahead of them both treacherous and unavoidable, the most he could do was exhale, accept his plight, and find some way to make peace with whatever he would be faced with next.

He stood by Theo's side, in silence, next to the greenhouse. They didn't need to ask what happened, or where Hope and Tess had gone. Jason looked to the heavens. Theo did the same.

Because they already knew.

As he had come to expect at the end of his many travels, Theo once again found himself outside his home, exhausted, unsure if he was the cause of his latest predicament, or somehow part of the solution. Or both. He looked at Jason. Jason looked at Theo.

A breeze came along just then. With it floated a small, rectangular paper. A postcard. It settled at their feet.

Jason picked up the card. On it was the logo for a local nightclub: *GenderBender*. An Asian drag queen was in the foreground, a galaxy in the background, and a sprinkling of stars.

Theo reached for the postcard, so that they were both holding it, together.

The galaxy on the card began to swirl. The stars twinkled.

"You ready?" said Jason, who had only been engaged for five minutes. He wondered if there would be even five minutes more. "One last trip?"

There was a blast of white light.

"Yeh-yeh," Theo said.

There was screaming fluorescent color.

"Let's get my kids."

There was the sensation of being sucked through a tornado.

Connected now to the microfibers of the Universe—able to hear its siren call—Jason and Theo understood that their impending arrival at the farthest reaches of Eternity would be unlike any journey they had experienced before.

Such that the two young men, best friends and traveling companions in a manner neither of them could have envisioned when they first met outside a youth hostel in Venice, Italy, would never set foot on Earth together again.

About the Author

Russ Colchamiro is the author of the rollicking space adventure *Crossline*, the hilarious scifi backpacking comedy *Finders Keepers*, and the outrageous sequel, *Genius de Milo*, all with Crazy 8 Press.

Russ lives in West Orange, NJ, with his wife, two children, and crazy dog, Simon, who may in fact be an alien himself. Russ is now at work on the final book in the *Finders Keepers* trilogy.

As a matter of full disclosure, readers should not be surprised if Russ spontaneously teleports in a blast of white light followed by screaming fluorescent color and the feeling of being sucked through a tornado. It's just how he gets around — windier than the bus, for sure, but much quicker.

For more on *Genius de Milo* and Russ' other wacky tales, you can visit www.russcolchamiro.com, follow him on Twitter @AuthorDudeRuss, and 'like' his Facebook author page at www.facebook.com/RussColchamiroAuthor. Russ encourages you to email him at authorduderuss@gmail.com

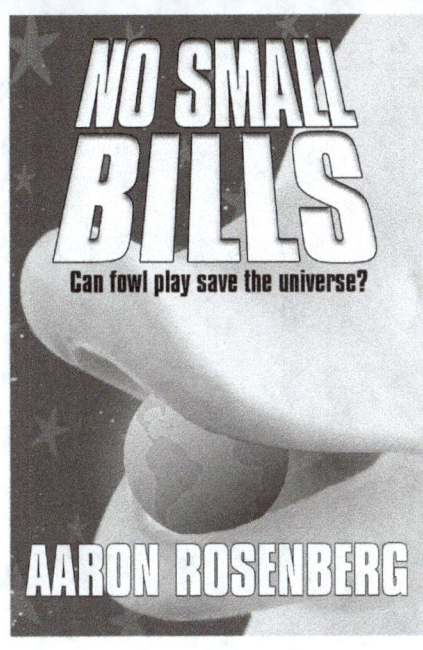